We do not want riches. We want peace and love.
REDCLOUD

As I look to the east I see dark ominous skies. So seeing my whole family together for Christmas was the perfect gift for me. Mitchell Strongbow 1962

# Thanks & Acknowledgments

Confidence is either your best friend, or worst enemy. When I first started to write or tell the story about my character. By the way I really consider myself more of a story teller then a writer. I really lacked confidence. Especially education wise, or at least on paper, I have none to speak of. I started off as just a 40 page short story. I was so nervous to show friends and co-workers what I was working on. It was just silly thoughts about a magical night that takes place New years Eve 1966. On the cusp of the Summer of Love in San Francisco.

But so many of you boosted my lacking confidence. Encouraged me to continue this story, tale of Mitchell Strongbow and his warriors journey through life.

So Thom Barth, Andrea Pitts, and so many other family members, friends and co-workers, thank you.

# About this book

Santa Dies Once Again is the first book in the series that follows the warrior Mitchell Strongbow.

A young Mitchell learns of his Sioux family roots through his father Iggy a career soldier and his grandfather who is a Shaman on the Pine Ridge Reservation.

His mother Katharina is a proud German war bride and school teacher. She is also the stepmother to Mitch's half brother Jake and sister Pam. Jake is starting to become that fuck you attitude towards his government and life in general, while his sister Pam is all about being a hippie – flower child.

Mitch also has a full blood sister Rachel. Like there mom, Rachel is extremely smart, but also that bratty annoying little sister.

This book deals with a lot of the hot issues of the sixties. The Vietnam war. Mitch as a teen whose dad is not always in the picture.

Every first happens to Mitch in this book, first love, first heart break. First time he is allowed to attend the family hunt on the reservation. The first time he sensed fear and the reality of life and death. The discipline of living on a military base to the freedom of San Francisco in the 60s.

About The Series: Strongbow, A Warriors Journey To Hell And Back.

Come join along the journey of a young and innocent bright eyed Mitchell in the 60s. To him becoming one of the most feared and heartless criminals in North America in the 90s.

# About the Author

I was born 1961 in Hamilton Ontario. Dad was a steel worker and my mom also worked in a factory. I am the oldest of three sons.

I too am a steelworker, a good honest job if I do say so myself

Happily married to Catherine and have two wonderful daughters Sarah and Meghan. I also have two wonderful grandchildren, Victoria and Nathan. They truly keep me young at heart.

All characters, organizations and events in this novel are either products of the authors imagination or are used fictionally.

# June 18th, 1991

In life you are given several choices, and some of those decisions are harder to make than others. Some people will need time to reflect upon these choices so they require some quiet time to ponder the options in front of them. Thanks to the State of California, who has so generously granted me this six by eight foot room in which to ponder these decisions, I have plenty of time to consider the choices recently presented to me by some of their finest civil servants.

Choice number one right off the bat is for me to be attending a wedding, for someone who is very special and dear to me in New York City. I must first talk to a special Grand Jury for this to happen, and there ain't much chance of that happening. There is a second captivating choice, a long walk to a special, but very unique room in San Quentin. Behind door #2 is where I also get the privilege to decide; lethal injection or gas chamber?

I never thought in a million lifetimes I would ever have to ponder these decisions. I have always had an invincible Superman, fuck you attitude towards the legal system. But the cops are now using Kryptonite to cripple me. They've brought me to my knees, weak knowing all along who and what, makes me the most vulnerable.

All of a sudden my cell, which is supposed to keep me from the freedom of an outside world, has allowed the ghosts from that outside world to enter with haunting voices and visions of the past.

My dad, the career soldier, always drilling into my young and impressionable mind, "You are a Strongbow, you are a warrior." I can hear and see my mom telling me, with a tear in her eye, that one day I would be the death of her. My oldest sister Pam telling me that I am just like our older brother Jake, a PIG, and one day I will get what I deserve. Jake instilling the hardcore, no-nonsense, criminal code values into me. "The only good rat is a dead rat." My younger sister Rachel jokingly saying, "Sisterly advice is always free; legal advice, however, is one hundred and twenty-five dollars an hour." Maybe she wasn't joking after all!

Right now I would sell everything I own not to be in this situation. I must, however, make these difficult and life-altering decisions. The one voice that is deafening and causing the internal struggle brewing inside me is Natasha's. She's warning me, "Don't let her down. Don't make her HURT!"

And in case you were wondering how did I get myself into this cluster-fuck of a mess. Let me tell you the whole story.

# December 6th, 1957

I was around eight years old at the time I found out Santa Claus wasn't real. One of the loudmouth bullies in my class told me on the playground during recess that he was a fraud, not the least bit real. He claimed the real Santa died a long time ago, and that our parents were the ones putting gifts under the tree.

He also went on to say that with me being half Sioux, or as he called me, a wagon burner, that all I really needed was some booze and a bow and arrow set.

This kid really enjoyed telling me this. I'm not sure whether it was to belittle me or to make his miserable life a little better.

The feeling I had at first was a lump in my throat, then a knot down deep in my stomach. I wasn't sure if I was going to cry or throw up. The once colorful world that I lived in was now suddenly gray and gloomy.

I can still recall that Kentucky December. I remember the cold winter air numbing my bones and muscles.

This kid got off on hurting anyone and everyone with his big mouth. He enjoyed seeing others miserable. What he didn't enjoy quite so much was being on the receiving end of my first ever blackout rage. The details are hazy to me but witnesses later claimed I went wild on him, slinging punches right and left in a crazed assault that finally drove him cowering to the ground.

I didn't stop there. Once down he turtled on me, begging for me to stop, begging for mercy. I remember thinking, fuck that and fuck you! In my world mercy was for the weak. Without hesitation I started to stomp on him like a worthless grape, the frightened screams of students and frantic commands of teachers nothing more than white noise as I felt his body squish and crack beneath my boots. Even when the teachers drug me away from him I continued to stomp, too lost in my own rage to realize he was no longer beneath my feet.

It wasn't until much later, sitting in the principal's office staring at the blood smeared across my hands and clothes that I fully returned to my senses. The beating I dished out to him felt like something I might have watched on TV, or experienced in a dream I couldn't even remember half of what had gone down, not the punching, not the stomping. They told me I was grinning the whole time. I don't remember that either.

Unfortunately for me, my mom was also a teacher at my school. There wasn't a chance in hell of me trying to bullshit my way out of this one. I was stone cold busted in my bloody temper tantrum tracks.

The principal just eyed me up and down. Mom sat beside me as he asked me one very simple question. "Mitchell, in my school our goal is to always educate the young mind. Know that communication will always be the one and only logical choice to resolve disputes. What gives you the right to settle your differences with fists?"

I stuck out my boney, scrawny chest and said proudly. "I am a Strongbow! I am a warrior!" My mom closed her eyes and sighed. The principal pulled out the strap and asked my mom to leave his office.

I didn't cry as the principal rained down the strap. I didn't even flinch. When the stinging leather ripped into the flesh of my palms, it made a bloody mess all over the floor. I did not, would not cry! Dad always said, "That pain is a temporary sign of weakness. You are a Strongbow! You are a Sioux Warrior!"

I just looked at the principal and thought, what a fucking hypocrite. You just said that communication was the logical choice to settle any resolutions, and yet I see this smirk on your face with every lash I received.

Yeah. I know hypocrite is a big word for an eight-year-old, but my mom made sure, we all knew Webster's dictionary inside and out! Mom was the educator, dad was the career soldier. What a perfect combination of brains and brawn.

My family, the Strongbow family to be exact, is a direct descendant of the Red Cloud bloodline. Red Cloud was a Sioux Indian Chief and warrior of the Oglala Teton Sioux of Pine Ridge, South Dakota.

My father, Iggy Strongbow, was born in Shannon County South Dakota on the Pine Ridge Reservation. My dad was also previously married. He lived and worked on the reservation, until 1942, when his country called. Dad, the proud Strongbow Sioux warrior, was just like his older brother Jack, and together they joined the 101st Airborne.

My older brother Jake was already two years old, and my dad's first wife was three months pregnant when he was shipped over to England with the 101st Airborne in 1943. Six months later, my oldest sister Pam was born on the reservation. Pam's healthy birth sadly came with tragic consequences as her mom died while giving birth.

My father came home for the funeral, but within a week headed back to England. During the war, dad proved to his superiors what a great soldier he was. Iggy also showed the Nazis what a determined Sioux warrior is all about.

Dad received several medals for valor and his legend grew at the battle of Bastogne. He was shot several times but he never left the line. He continued to fight until he passed out from blood loss. The medics said most men would have died, but my dad was not most men.

His body count was twelve Germans confirmed dead. Four of them he killed when he had no ammo left. Hand to hand; Mano a Mano! The man was just as deadly with a knife as he was with a rifle.

At the end of the war when most men dreamed of going home to their families, my father re-enlisted. The military was going to be his career. The idea of living on the reservation in poverty was not for him, or his children. After all, it had already cost him the life of his wife.

In everyone's life certain stories or core values will always stand out. I take with me this conversation I had with my dad, about him making a career in the army. Dad told me he was a warrior. His destiny was to fight and die in battle if need be. A Sioux warrior, just like his ancestors before him; fearless was the only word to describe him.

Dad met my mom Katharina Kohler, at the end of World War Two. He was stationed in Germany, and just like his first wife, she too was a grade school teacher. She was also much younger than my dad; ten years younger to be exact.

At first they were discreet when dating. Post-war Germany was in turmoil and as the daughter of a decorated soldier killed in combat; my mom would have been ridiculed and ostracized for dating the enemy. The last thing my dad ever wanted to do was cause her grief, especially from fellow Germans who lost loved ones in the war. So they kept their relationship under wraps, and it didn't take long before they fell in love.

Dad chose the military as a career and he was soon to be redeployed to another base. Dad saw the madness and despair of a post-war Germany and he offered my mom his hand in marriage; and also a better life for her.

Mom knew she would have an instant family with Jake and Pam back in the United Sates if she chose to marry my dad. Mom also knew dad having a military career, it meant not having secure roots, as the family would often move from base to base. Grandpa Kohler was also a career military officer, SS to be exact, so my mom already knew what to expect.

Mom agreed to marry dad, on one condition. Karl, her younger brother and only surviving family member, would also move to the United Sates. At the time my Uncle Karl was just starting law school. Dad taught all his children to bank as many favors as you can in life. He called in a few of those favors he had accumulated and Uncle Karl would continue his law schooling in the good old USA.

I was born Friday, May 13, 1949. I was told by mom that I came into the world just kicking and screaming. That perfect Strongbow Sioux blood line was now crossed with a Nazi -Kohler bloodline. I'm sure this also had the reverse effect on the pure Kohler bloodline.

Mom said the first time my dad saw me, he proudly held me up to the sky and told Wakan Tanka that the great Sioux nation now had a new warrior. Then my dad's face changed, and he had this horrific look come over his face.

Mom picked up on this right away and was concerned. She asked my dad, what was wrong with Mitchell? *"His eyes are blue! How can this be? He is a Strongbow, he's Sioux."*

She went from being a concerned new mother to a mamma bear really quick. She asked my dad, "What color are my eyes?" Dad was confused as he stared at my mom's eyes, deep as the ocean blue. "I am Sioux. Mitchell is a male and he's Sioux."

"Iggy my dear, Mitchell is only half Sioux. He is also half German. I think we can both agree he is male." Christ I'm not even an hour old and I have caused tension between my parents. If only they knew what was still to come.

The year 1950 was one of the most trying years for the Strongbow family. In January I was just eight months old when dad decided he wanted to see if that Kohler blood running through my body corrupted me as a Sioux warrior. I am not even able to walk, yet here I am being tested.

Dad placed two objects fifteen feet away from me to crawl to. The object on the left was a bright red ball; the second object on the right was dad's M-1 carbine assault rifle. Jake had already passed this test.

It was now my turn. Without hesitation I eagerly crawled straight to the assault rifle. My father was smiling from ear to ear as he knew I was a warrior. My mother was happy for him, but she knows the horrors of war all too well.

On October 9th that same year, my youngest sister Rachel was born. Like me she also had blue eyes, and also came out kicking and screaming. Dad shipped out to Korea on December 17, 1950, with the famous 8th Ranger infantry battalion. They were known as the "Devils!"

My poor mom was left at home with four kids to raise. Jake and Pam were nine and seven respectively, while I was nineteen months old and Rachel was just a little over two months old.

Four kids under ten and two of us in diapers. I am surprised my mom didn't enlist.

# OCTOBER, 1962

The second warrior test that dad put me through came when I was thirteen years old. A male Strongbow rite of passage, it spanned from generation to generation. Every year in the second week of October, no matter where my dad was stationed, he would take leave and go deer hunting for a week. He headed back home to the reserve in South Dakota as long as there weren't any wars going on.

The first time dad went with his father, he was thirteen. The first time dad took Jake, he too was thirteen. Now it was my turn. I turned thirteen this past May. For my thirteenth birthday my dad bought me a 22 caliber rifle. I was excited for my chance to prove to my family that I was a hunter and warrior.

Dad had already taught me how to catch fish, and the proper way to fillet and clean them. He also taught me how to survive in the woods if lost. I was already shooting a pellet gun with deadly accuracy. I was an orange belt in both Judo and Wado Ryu karate. I was ready. Or so I thought!

Mom, being a teacher, wasn't so sure about this. She was more interested in me working on my math and reading skills. But she also knew this was a part of my Sioux heritage, and would never stop me from going. I guess Rachel would be her scholar and I would be the warrior.

During the 'Cold War' dad's unit was part of the Strategic Army Corps, which meant they were always on full readiness alert. He was a Staff Sergeant and in charge of survival skills. This was for all personnel, including both non-com and officers.

Dad made many contacts and banked many a favor from cooks to pilots. He taught me at a very early age, never to say no to anyone. His response was always, "I will see what I can do" and get a favor logged in the bank. When we were to go hunting, dad would call in a couple of favors. Jake and I would fly with him in a C-117 from Fort Campbell to Ellsworth Air Force Base in South Dakota. We then took a chopper to our hunt camp right on the reserve.

If we had to drive this it would've taken us over fourteen hours. Perhaps another reason my dad felt safe in the air was the fact that he always brought 2 M1 rifles, 1000 rounds of ammo, 4 cases of beer and 3 bottles of bourbon along for the ride. Even the thought of the police pulling us over was something I didn't want to contemplate. I'm pretty sure that dad had no favors banked with the cops.

The US Air Force was the way to go and only four hours by air. This would've also been my first time in a Sikorsky UH-34D helicopter. When we were in the C-117, dad was real quiet as he sharpened his knives.

He may have been on leave but once inside the plane you could tell he had on his game face. I wondered if perhaps this C-117 had taken him into battle at some time or another. When dad got quiet and looked like this, I could tell no matter how tough he seemed on the outside, he had his demons to battle, just like the rest of us.

About a half hour into the flight we hit an air pocket. I was thrown from my seat and landed on the deck of the plane. I guess my eyes grew to the size of saucers! Dad and Jake couldn't stop laughing. It was always good to see my dad and Jake laugh. Their relationship had been growing apart.

Jake was always getting in trouble with the law and getting suspended for fighting at school. This really pissed my mom off! When Jake and mom would get into it, he would do the usual. He would say, "You're not my mom." Dad would jump all over Jake and sometimes it would get physical.

Dad made sure all his kids knew how to defend themselves. He made it mandatory for all of us to earn at least one black belt in a martial art. He had a firm belief that a strong, disciplined body meant a strong, disciplined mind. Even though Jake thought he was a good fighter in his mind, my dad would have him on the ground within two seconds. He would be grimacing in pain without dad ever even throwing a punch.

I guess Jake became more rebellious as we would move from base to base. Just as you made new friends, dad would be redeployed to another base.

I was born while my dad was stationed at Fort Benning, Georgia. We then moved to Fort Jackson, South Carolina, and in 1956, we moved to Fort Campbell, Kentucky. I was feeling the same rage that Jake felt, moving from base to base. Being an army brat wasn't fun and games.

I was teased about being half native and my mom being German. Fortunately like dad and Jake, I never backed down from a fight. Always proving myself with the new kids at school, or the base bullies. That is just who we are. We are Strongbow.

During the flight my dad would point out certain landmarks on the ground and tell me stories about the flatlands. He spoke of the Sioux history, how they were great warriors. He really wanted me to be proud of our heritage. He often said, "Hopefully one day you will take your sons to hunt on the reserve, just as I am doing now." "Keep the spirit alive," he would say. It was drilled into my head that we don't kill just for just the sport. We would eat whatever we killed and the skins would be used as blankets at the hunt camp.

The hunt camp consisted only of a long house. It had one large room, enough to sleep sixteen adults.

There was no running water, no bathroom, and no electricity. I was there to learn about my roots, and this was indeed my roots.

As the C-117 landed, I was starting to get butterflies about being in the helicopter for the next leg of the journey. This would be my first time. Even though I have seen them many times on base, I was still nervous. I know dad would never put me in harm's way. Yet here I am, nervous! There were no doors to stop us from falling out! I had to somehow show courage. After all what this weekend was all about.

Once the plane stopped, dad thanked the pilots and promised them some deer sausage once he was back on base. Dad then told Jake and me to grab our gear, and off we went to the helicopter pad. Even though I was only about 5'8" tall, I still thought the blades were going to take my head off. I was getting goosebumps, but the good kind. The butterflies were gone from my stomach and replaced by utter excitement.

Dad gave the pilots the coordinates to the hunt camp and off we went. The engine revved and we were lifted up. It was like the elevator from hell at first. Taking off, it felt like my balls and stomach were still on the ground. I had this lump in my throat and wasn't sure which body part was in there. Dad just looked at me and smiled and told me to enjoy the ride.

Our flight was about forty-five minutes long. On the way, we passed over my grandfather's house. Normally an army helicopter flying over an Indian reservation wasn't a good or welcome sight. The locals knew who was in the helicopter, however, and knew this was Strongbow hunting season.

Dad taught me to respect the elders of the tribe and they would respect me. We always shared our meat with the locals and it was always appreciated. "Do not take them for granted because they are old. Their wisdom is a time-honored tradition, and another aspect of your heritage."

We landed in a clearing about 500 yards from the Longhouse. Once again dad thanked these pilots and promised them some deer sausage. Dad told them to be back in a week, at 17:00, and if his unit was called for duty, just come back here. And even though he was in the bush he would hear the blades and head back to camp. The helicopter flew off into the sunset.

I could see several of my relatives coming from the long house to greet us; some I have never met before. The first person I recognized was my dad's older brother Uncle Jack, and his son Jerry. They lived in Oakland California but came every year for the hunt. They were both longshoreman, and judging by the size of their arms and shoulders, they worked hard for their money.

A couple of my younger cousins were also there to greet us. I'd never seen them before, although they were around my age. I could tell they thought I was different from them; even natives could be racist! Whether you were from the same tribe or not, with me being a half breed it was there.

Dad taught me to always make eye contact when challenged. Let them know you aren't scared or intimidated. That is what I did, even if I was standing maybe a little closer to Jake and dad.

We were the last of the hunting party to arrive, and in the best Strongbow tradition, we had a great feast that night. We sat around the camp fire and told stories of great Sioux warriors of the past. It seemed to awaken an ancient memory. I was so inspired! I felt proud of my native heritage.

As I watched the breeze stir the flames and the smoke disappear into the heavens, the elders started their fire dance. I felt alive! The blood flowing in my veins was pure Sioux. My German ancestry was pushed into the shadows. Visions of ancient warriors from a time long ago danced in my mind. The flames, stirred by another gust of wind, transformed me into a warrior from the past on his annual hunt for deer and bison. The ancient ones, my ancestors, were once again patrolling the landscape as they followed the venison. The shaman was awakening!

It came to me why my people fought to the death; for their land and traditions against the white man. This was truly worth fighting and dying for. A hundred years ago, I too would've gone after Custer and killed the bastard.

As the booze was flowing, dad offered me a beer. This was the first time I have ever seen my dad drunk; he had a funny side to him after all. He showed he could actually be a nice, down to earth person, not this twenty four hour, by the clock, military regimental person.

Jake was really catching a glow. He and Jerry always seemed to have to piss at the same time. They would both go into the woods and come back with glossy eyes and a really goofy looking smile. Returning from their third piss together, my dad stood up, stopped the both of them and said, "Have you two turned queer on me? Do you need to hold each other's hand when you piss? Perhaps it's a little too dark, in the woods?"

"Now, are you going to share what the fuck you are smoking out there with the rest of us?" Jake looked confused, and I saw military dad once again. All of a sudden the joyous celebrations turned to animosity; they were insulting my dad's intelligence. "Boys, I have smoked some of the best weed from all over the world. Final time! Are you going to share the weed with the rest of us or do I confiscate it from you two?"

They passed my dad a joint that he lit it up, took a couple tokes, exhaled looked at me and said, "Too young, Mitchell." But he did let me drink quite a few beers that night.

It was different but in a good way, seeing him let his guard down and being almost like a normal human being. It was one of the fondest memories of my dad. I don't really remember going to sleep that night. Between the beer, fire and dad being normal, it all just overloaded my brain.

I felt kind of sore the next day, but it was a good sore. My dad was making breakfast and asked how I slept. I told him, "I do not really remember." He laughed and told me, "This night can never be repeated to your mom." Mean and lethal as dad was, mom put the fear into him. If she knew that I was drinking under age with my dad, well, my dad would be like Custer and he too would have had his last stand.

We broke camp into several hunting parties. Unlike the white man, we don't sit in a tree and wait for the deer to come to us. We tracked them by horse and used our bows. Dad, Jack, Jerry, Jake and I all went together, which I liked. My two cousins, however were still giving me dirty looks. During breakfast, the one named Patrick bumped into me purposely and caused me to fall. Dad noticed it but told me to let it go, as we are family.

I learned so much from the hunt that day; how to track, how to watch the vegetation. It will show if deer have been there lately to feed. Find out where the water is, as the deer will need to drink. Watch for hoof prints and deer droppings. I felt like a little brave, and I took in and absorbed all that my father told me.

Eventually we broke for lunch. After eating, my dad took me aside and instructed me on the proper use of my new rifle. I had gone down to the rifle range on the base and used military weapons, but this was my rifle. Dad drilled it into my head, "This is a weapon for killing. You must and will respect it! You must keep it clean to function properly. Not once in a while, but every day. Know how to dismantle it and put it back together blindfolded. You will know what every working piece's function is. Never point this at another human unless you are going to kill them. This is not a toy!"

After a thirty minute lecture for my own good, I assumed this was the same lecture that dad gave to his men in the army. Dad and I stayed behind to work on my shooting skills. He left out some meat, knowing the ever populous Black-tailed Prairie Dog would be along soon to eat it. That would be my first beast to kill!

While waiting for the prairie dog to show, dad and I had some great quality talks. He was so different away from the base and out of his army fatigues. I guess he was giving me the tools to develop my character. He also told me something that would change my whole life, and showed him in a different light.

"Mitchell, as you know, war is hell! There are no winners or losers, only survivors! When that day comes and you are asked to serve your country, I hope you will answer that call. During that time of war you must realize that to survive, you must make certain sacrifices to be a survivor. Sometimes those sacrifices will haunt you once the shooting has stopped."

"The politicians all pat each other on the back, and tell the world what a great job they did. Fuck them! Their hands were never bloodied. They slept in their cozy beds every night, while I slept in a foxhole 30 below zero, and prayed the dead body next to me stayed warm until the morning. That was my only source of heat, as a fire would give away my position. War does strange things to the mind and the conscience, Mitchell."

Dad had this look in his eyes that I had never seen before. He was almost humble. He was cleansing his soul through me; but why? "Mitchell, what I am about to tell you only one other person knows, and that is your brother Jake. This being your first hunt camp, you are now considered a man. I feel that you are now old enough to hear this."

Dad then went on to say, "During the Battle of Bastogne, my unit was under very heavy fire. We were getting pounded, not only from the German artillery but also by their snipers. We were taking a real shit kicking! We're told we had to hold the line at all costs, until Patton arrived."

Dad stopped a moment to recall the details, then he began again. "Being the 101$^{st}$ Airborne, there's no way would you run away from a fight. No matter what the cost was. You fought till the end. I'm not sure whether or not the Germans knew it, but had they known how bad off we were, they would've killed us all within the next couple of days. Fortunately for us, on Christmas day they asked for a truce."

They wanted to have a drink with us, share a little good will. Merry Christmas and all the crap that went along with it. Our Captain agreed, thank God! I had been stuck in that damn foxhole with Brad Millbury. He had been dead for almost two days by then and when the sun would shine on him, he really stank. But if I popped up out of my foxhole, to take his body out, I would've been picked off by one of their snipers."

"The Germans had this one sniper that was really picking us off at every opportunity he could. The man was one of the best shots I had ever witnessed. When both sides agreed to have a Christmas drink together, I met this German sniper and we talked for a bit. Actually, Smitty, a Krout from New York City translated for us. It turned out that the sniper was actually a decent sort of a gentleman for a Nazi officer. Like me, he had two kids at home, a boy and girl. Too bad we were busy shooting at each other, as he would have been a great guy to go grizzly hunting with."

"Anyways, when both sides went back to their own battle lines, I watched exactly where this sniper went back to. I had made sure I knew his position. I also knew he too, was watching where I was going."

"Fast forward a couple hours, and the damn Germans started shelling us again. It was pure hell Mitchell, each time our medics would move, I would see the rifle flash coming from the sniper's position. He was picking off the boys, and this continued for a couple more days. I was totally fixated with taking this sniper out. Just killing him was more important than winning the damn war. Patton's tanks eventually arrived, and when the Germans started to retreat, I saw my target."

"The German sniper tried his best to find cover

behind one of their tanks, then it looked like he might have dropped something. When he bent down to pick it up he exposed himself wide open. I knew my weapon was clean, and my mind was focused. I took the head shot and saw his lifeless body drop to the ground. In my shell-shocked brain, my war had now been won."

"As we advanced on the retreating Germans, I purposely looked for my dead German sniper. What was worth exposing himself for? In his hand was the answer; a small wallet. It contained no cash, just his German identification, home address and pictures of his wife, daughter and son. They were his reason to live and to fight."

"I kept his wallet. I knew he would want the wallet returned to his family. As much as we were adversaries; I respected the soldier and the family man in him. I checked the name in the wallet and the address. His name was Erich Kohler, his wife Eva, and his children's names were Karl and Katharina."

My heart stopped beating for a minute once I realized I knew all these names. My dad had actually killed my grandfather during the war! "Mitchell, after the war, I kept that promise I made to myself. I delivered the wallet to the surviving members of the Kohler family. That was the first time I saw your mother and I fell in love with her. That picture didn't even begin to show the beauty that she was."

I had so many questions, but my mind and my mouth wouldn't co-operate with each other. Dad said, "Just take slow breaths through your stomach, concentrate on your breathing, and think what you're going to say first. Nice and slow Mitchell."

"Why didn't you tell mom this story? Don't you think she would've forgiven you? It was the war, dad!"

"I couldn't take that chance. I didn't ever want your mom to think I only married her out of pity or regret for killing her father. I didn't feel guilt about killing him. He would've killed me if he had the opportunity. I didn't give him that chance. Had your mom forced the issue, I would have given her that exact response. I know your mom would never look at, or treat me the same way again."

Wow talk about a holiday of knowledge and growth. I thought it would just be learning how to kill a deer. "Do you understand, Mitchell?"

"Yes sir, I do. Does Uncle Karl know this? Why just Jake and me? Why don't Pam and Rachel know?"

"Mitchell, just you, Jake and my father knows this. The women do not need to know this. We men are the warriors of the family, not them. They would never understand. Your Uncle Karl doesn't need to know this while I'm still alive." Dad smiled and winked at me. Was this a hint that once he is dead, for me to tell Karl? If so why me; and not Jake?

After lunch my dad taught me some proper sniper shooting skills. He taught me how to "Box Breathe." This technique slowed down your breathing, and curtailed the production of adrenaline, so you control your excitement. That way, you can stay focused for the whole shot.

You would breathe in through your stomach, hold it for a count of three and then exhale for a count of three. The whole process would then start all over again. As I was practicing this, I could feel myself relax. "Mitchell, a good soldier is calm, cool and collected for whatever comes his way."

My next assignment was to focus on the target, whether it was moving or stationary. "Son, you must feel the energy of the target. Know and feel what his next move will be. Anticipate this, being in sync with them!"

Next up was squeezing the trigger. "You do not pull the trigger, but squeeze it ever so gently. Just like your breathing, stay in control." This was probably the closest dad and I have ever been. I was a nuisance when I was younger, and stayed firmly classified in that category until I turned twelve.

My gut told me this hunting trip was for my coming of age into manhood. I'm not sure what would've happened if Pam or Rachel wanted to come along. I do know that Pam had gone to the firing range on the base with my dad. I guess in the mind of my dad and his father, and his father's father, hunting was a tradition for the men only.

Eventually a prairie dog went for the bait we left him. Dad reminded me of all he explained to me earlier. I just wanted to shoot the damn thing. Dad had trained thousands of people the exact rules he taught me. I did my breathing, took aim and fired a shot. I heard the "yipe," and knew I had made contact. The feeling was unbelievable! It was like coming downstairs on Christmas morning!

We approached the prairie dog to find my shot had only wounded him, not killed him. I hit him in the lower spine and the dog was in severe pain. Dad looked at the dog, then at me and said, "We can't leave this dog to die like this." I nodded to my dad and went to put a bullet in the dog's head. Dad stopped me and handed me his hunting knife. He told me to slice the dog's throat and make it quick. I just stared at the dog and then stared at my dad. Was he serious? "NOW BOY, Slice its throat and be done with it; or should I have left you back home with the women?"

I was now mad, real mad at my dad; and I sliced the dog's throat. Dad smiled and said, "That's my warrior, good job Mitchell." He put his hand into the severed throat of the dog. He then used those two fingers covered in the dog's blood to mark the sides of my cheek. He then did the same thing on my forehead, and let out a Sioux warrior battle cry. I didn't feel sickened by this. I felt proud! This was my initiation, into being a Sioux warrior.

Dad spent the rest of the afternoon teaching me to track. We didn't find any deer so we headed back to camp. The sun was just starting to set as we approached the hunt camp, and I thought the fading light was playing tricks with my eyes.

I could see some large objects hanging from the tree, but couldn't figure out what they were until we were almost on top of them. We dismounted our horses and gazed upon three dead deer hanging upside down, their throats slit to bleed them out.

The eyes were the first thing that intrigued me. They had a horrified look in them, as if they knew they were going to die. That sound that they heard would be the last thing they would ever hear. It mesmerized me to no end, just trying to figure out what their last thought was. Did they worry about their fawns? I could read things from their eyes. The eyes were talking to me and telling me a story. Just then my jerk cousin Patrick pushed me right into the dead deer, and laughed at me.

Without warning I turned around and started to throw punches and kicks his way. I had enough of him, and like the deer with blood running from its neck Patrick now had blood from running from his nose. This caused dad and Jerry to get in between and break us up. I looked at his brother Billy and said he was next if he wanted some.

The fact that these two were both older didn't bother me. Patrick was a year older, and Billy almost two. It didn't matter. When we were separated, dad looked at me and smiled. The same smile he had when I sliced the dog's throat. He was proud that I didn't put up with Patrick's bullshit, proud that I not only fought him but kicked his ass.

My grandfather said, "No more fighting, we are family, we are all Strongbow." Patrick started complaining that I started it. I knew exactly what to say, "You are right grandfather. I am sorry! We are all family, all of us are Strongbow." I tried to respect my elders, while Patrick still continued to beak off. My grandfather told him to shut up and listen, or he would be sent home to his mother.

That night I went to sleep knowing I was now a true Sioux warrior. I could feel it. I showed courage on the battlefield killing the dog, and kicking Patrick's ass. More importantly I had shown respect for my elders.

Over the next couple of days, I learned more and more tracking skills. I learned how to gut a deer and fire my rifle. My cousins Bill and Patrick now stayed away from me. Maybe it was out of respect for what my grandfather had said. Perhaps my fighting skills, along with his broken nose, had put some fear into Patrick.

On the last day and night of hunt camp, dad, Jake and I spent all day hunting. We decided to camp on our own. It was good quality father-sons time, even though Jake and my dad had been at odds with each other more than normal. Being out here in the wild, you could feel the respect they had for each other. It seems the tension between them was left at home on the base.

Dad said whenever he was stressed, he would head to the wilderness and get back to nature. She never lies, and her beauty will erase any demons playing with your mind, heart or soul. At night, when we watched the stars, it was better than any show on television. There was never a commercial or repeat. Dad showed me all the different constellations and what each one meant to the Sioux people.

He told us there was war brewing in the Far East and he expected to be posted there soon as an adviser. That was the first time I ever heard the word Vietnam. As much as I was a warrior that weekend, when my dad talked about this upcoming war in Vietnam I felt scared like a little boy again.

Dad said if anything happened to him, Jake would be the man of the house. "Mitch if you ever want to talk to me, just find the North Star in the sky. Talk to it, as that is where I will be listening to you. I will guide you when you need me."

I just hugged my dad as tears come to my eye. I would not acknowledge that I was frightened. I did not want to lose my warrior status with my dad. I knew that I had made him proud this past week.

The next day, we all headed back to hunt camp. I never did get to kill a deer myself, and had mixed emotions over it. Much as I would've liked to kill one, I wanted to show everyone at camp that I too, was a great warrior and provider. I didn't need to look in the eye of the deer that I just killed. I already knew its last thought. Why did I kill him?

# Tuesday November 6, 1962

Election Day in the United States: The day when all legal aged Americans can vote. They vote to keep the current government, or elect a new one. How ironic that day was also the day dad and several hundred Special Advisers were headed to South Vietnam. They were headed half way around the world to help protect their government and overthrow the communist government of North Vietnam.

Voters in the United States placed an "X" by the politician of their choice. In Vietnam, they voted by killing the politician. Dad told our family that they would just be training the troops and he shouldn't see any battles himself. "This should be a routine assignment." He promised he would be home for Christmas.

We had a big family dinner the night before and dad said goodbye to all of us individually. The girls both cried. Jake and I had to be strong. After all we were the men of the house now. Mom now had to be both mother and father till dad came home.

This would be dad's third assignment in a foreign country. He had been overseas for World War Two, shipped off to Korea, and now back east to Vietnam. We hoped it would be his last assignment. We wanted him home and safe for good.

The press didn't really cover the war in Vietnam at first. Every day we would rush to the mailbox to see if there was a letter from dad. Once a week without failure he would write us. We just wanted to read dad's letters to know he was safe.

Somehow it seemed that the base personnel and their families were the only people in the United States who actually knew a war was going on. Did anybody else in the United States know or even care? I wasn't really sure.

Periodically a letter wouldn't make it home, or some kids were out of school for a couple days. We knew their dad wasn't coming home alive. Another soldier killed in Vietnam. This caused emotions to run high in the schoolyard. Kids were scared. It seemed there were more fights than normal. Yours truly was in at least one fight a week.

Dad's letter would arrive and I was good for a couple of days. Then the tension would begin to rise again as I waited for the next letter to arrive. A fight was never far away! This escalated the tension at home as well.

Mom would lecture me about fighting while Jake would give me a dollar for every fight I won. He was now twenty and on the verge of getting kicked out of college for cutting classes.

The collage claimed he wasn't only doing drugs but

selling them too, although they couldn't prove it.

Pam was ready to go to college next September, and Rachel was now only one grade behind me. Her brains advanced her through school, and she skipped from grade four straight into five.

# December 21, 1962

It had now been two weeks since we received a letter from dad and we were all starting to really worry. The base commander said he hadn't heard anything bad about my dad, so we should just assume he was safe. He could be far in the jungle and not able to write or get the letter out.

All I thought about was dad promising us he would be home for Christmas. He had never broken a promise to us, ever. I could tell that my mom was worried. Even Jake was getting worried. Perhaps that's why Jake and mom had been fighting so much lately.

Later that night, my mom found out that Jake had been kicked out of college. She went off on him. She said, "People in Germany after the war had nothing, but still continued their schooling. You have everything at your disposal."

His comeback was, "Yeah, and the Germans lost the war. What did all that schooling get them, other than getting their Nazi asses kicked?" This was the worst fight ever between the two of them. My sisters were both crying and I wasn't sure what to do. However if Jake hit her, I would crack him with my baseball bat.

All of a sudden, who comes in walking through the front door? My dad! Everyone just stopped what they were doing. No crying, no yelling and no choking up on my bat for me. It was like a cold breeze on a hot humid summer day. Much needed relief!

We all raced over to hug my dad. That is everyone but Jake. He just stood there defiantly with his arms folded. After dad hugged us all he told Jake that he could hear his loud mouth all the way to Saigon and they would talk after dinner. Dad said, he hasn't had a normal American meal in seven weeks; "Let's all go out for some burger and fries, and a chocolate milkshake."

It was so good seeing dad. I think we all agreed this was the best Christmas present we ever could receive. After dinner, Jake and dad had a long talk on the front porch. Like the little shits Rachel and I could be, we crawled under the porch to listen. "Kat tells me you were kicked out of college, boy. You want to tell me why?"

"College is for squares man. They don't want any Indian to succeed in this country. They just want to keep every native, down and dumb."

"Boy I hate when someone bullshits me. Right now you are on the top of the hate list. I know you were kicked out for dealing drugs, skipping classes, and fighting."

"The drug dealing was never proven."

"Yeah, only because everyone is too damn scared of you. Well boy, I'm not putting any more money into your future. You are twenty and old enough to do your own thing. Isn't that what you kids call it now?"

"Something like that, aren't you pissed?"

"What is the point? I have seen kids your age over the decades come home in body bags by the hundreds, make that thousands. So what are you going to do now boy?"

"I'm moving to Oakland. Jerry has a place for me to crash. He can get me a job with the longshoremen."

"I see you have thought this out. When are you leaving boy?"

"When would you like me to leave? What about Kat, and how long are you home for?"

"Don't worry about Kat. She loves you like you were her own. If she didn't, she wouldn't give a shit. She fought with you about schooling because she loves you. Remember, she's a teacher. I'm not sure how long I am home. I think it will be short visit. That whole damn stink dink country Vietnam is a goddamn mess. I've never seen so much corruption and lawlessness in my life. It's truly insane over there. I hear Kennedy wants to up the troop force. Leave when you want Jake, although I hope you'll at least stay for Christmas."

"I will old man. I will leave on the 27$^{th}$. Sound good?"

"Sounds good. Now get us a couple of beers and a couple cigars."

Things were now good again with dad home. I didn't like the fact that he figured he wouldn't be home for long.

# February 12, 1963

Lincoln's birthday. Call me superstitious but sending hundreds of Special Forces off to war on a president's birthday who himself was shot in the head isn't such a good idea. Either way, dad was deployed back to Vietnam, still not for combat, but as an adviser.

He took me aside and told me that with Jake being in California, I was now the man of the house while he is gone. He is counting on me to live up to his expectations. Was I man enough for this assignment? "Of course I am sir!" Did he really expect me to answer any other way? I was ready.

As usual, the only send off was by the local base. There were no politicians or dignitaries, just the "Brothers in Arms" themselves. Dad promised he would be home in time for my birthday and hunt camp.

I promised him I would take a deer down myself this year. I assured dad my shooting skills would astound him. I would prove it once he returned. This made dad smile. He even gave me a salute, and called me "sniper!"

I really liked the sound of that; "sniper!" Perhaps one day, dad and I could go to war together and shoot the bad guys; just like they did in "Have Gun Will

Travel." That will be me and my dad.

# Things are changing. Spring, 1963

With dad over in Vietnam and Jake in California, I enjoyed being the man of the house. However, I needed someone to talk to about guy stuff. I noticed several changes starting in and on my body. I was now starting to grow hair on my balls! I watched the Beverly Hillbillies and I felt warm and fuzzy every time I saw Elly Mae. I couldn't control my penis from getting hard, no matter what I did. Every show, I had to put a pillow over my groin area. Pam called me "a little perv!" I didn't know what that even meant till later in life.

Then there were the girls from school who were starting to develop breasts. I would get that same fuzzy feeling, like I was watching Elly May by the cement pond all over again. This was also the first time in my life where the music actually had some meaning. I sort of dug how it made me feel.

Whenever I saw Rhonda Ryan, this girl in my school, walk down the hall with her blondish red hair, the song "Be my Baby" was playing in my head. When the Beach Boys sang any of their songs, I pictured Jake and me in California surfing. Waiting for me on the beach was none other than Rhonda Ryan. I guess she was my first crush. Eventually, I would walk her home from school, and at one point I even held hands with her.

I really put a lot of effort into my martial arts, as I knew that is what dad wanted. I was hoping to be a blue belt in Wado Ryu karate, and maybe judo, by the time he came back home. Mom stayed on top of my school work, but with her being a teacher that was normal.

Dad would try and write every week, but sometimes he had to go deep in the bush and couldn't promise the weekly letter. Dad's letters were now becoming monthly instead of weekly.

# SUMMER, 1963

By now, the only thing that came once a week from Vietnam was a dead soldier returning home. Whether they were your schoolmate's dad, or the father of a close friend, it was sad. Knowing that your dad was still stuck over in Vietnam made things tense on the base and in our house.

From time to time, when I knew no one was watching, I would go outside and look for the North Star. I would talk to dad and he would come to me in spirit. I always knew where to find him.

With Pam, Rachel and me now out of school for the summer, mom did her best to keep us busy. She tried to keep our brains from focusing on the amount of death we were now exposed to.

Uncle Karl helped mom out by taking us to Sacramento, California for a couple weeks. He even took us to Disneyland. Growing up during the Second World War, he knew what it was like to have a father fighting in the war. Sometimes I wished dad had never told me what happened to my grandfather, Karl's dad.

Jake and my cousin Jerry came to Sacramento to see us. We were so happy! He was now wearing leathers and belonged to a motorcycle gang called the Hell Hounds. Jake came by and took me for a couple of motorcycle rides. I really enjoyed bombing around on his bike.

I never saw any of the Beach Boys when we were there, but something else weird happened. While sleeping one night at Uncle Karl's, I had a dream about Rhonda Ryan. I woke up with this thick liquid all over my leg. Man, I was so embarrassed! Thank goodness I could sneak into the washroom to clean up the mess before anyone noticed. I did have to throw out my underwear though.

Uncle Karl was now an established and respected lawyer and I knew when Jake and Jerry came around he wasn't too happy. He had a talk with both of them about their lifestyle choices. It was in one ear and out the other with them. The only downside of the trip was when Jake took me to see "The Longest Day." I found the killing scenes too close to home.

We were only gone two weeks, but when we returned home, several more men on the base had been killed. This included Rhonda Ryan's dad. I got on my bicycle and rushed over to her house right away. The smile she always had on her face was gone. We went for a walk and I tried to cheer her up.

I told her all about my trip to California but no matter what I tried, I couldn't cheer her up. I even brought her home a pair of Mickey Mouse ears. Then the magic happened! My first kiss! Rhonda kissed me and told me to hug her close. She broke down and cried about her dad. This even choked me up. What could I say to ease her pain? Nothing!

# SEPTEMBER, 1963. Another School Year, Another Loss.

In grade eight you are almost royalty; the kings and queens of the school. However the teachers always still let you know that they were in charge of the playground. Rhonda was now my first, true, steady girlfriend, and she was really hurting over the loss of her dad.

Rhonda showed up at school one day all upset and crying. When I asked her what was wrong, Rhonda told me that the army had told her mom they had to move off the base. New families needed their housing unit. Her dad officially was no longer a member of the United States Army so they had to move!

Rhonda said they would move to Kansas. Her mom was from there and still has family that will help them out. I felt like throwing up! My breathing became shallow and I felt this lump in my throat. It was the same feeling I got when I was eight and found out that Santa wasn't real.

Harry Swanson came over and said, "Look at the two babies ready to cry." Harry was the loudmouth bully of grade eight. I tried to let it go, but when Harry pushed Rhonda to the ground I just lost it on him. Another blackout, another kid with a bloody face! He was shaking on the ground and pleading with me not to kill him.

Once I came around, I knew I was in real trouble. I grabbed Rhonda by the hand and told her, "Let's run away! We can go to California. My brother will have a place for us to stay."

Rhonda said she couldn't go. She was all her mom has left now that her dad is gone, and she needed her mom too. I couldn't understand this. "Rhonda I will protect you. No one will ever hurt you or make you cry again. I promise!" Rhonda just stood there, watching as the teachers took me away to the principal's office.

Mom was called once again. However, because this was a military base school, the beating wasn't reported to the police. I was suspended for a week and Rhonda's mom didn't allow her to see me anymore. Why would she do that, when I was just protecting her? I was just doing what her dad would've wanted. That is what dad would have wanted me to do, being that I was the man of our house. With her dad dead, I sort of felt like I was the man of her house also. Rhonda's mom didn't see it that way though.

My mom wasn't impressed with my actions either. I think deep down inside she knew why I did what I did. I was grounded for two weeks and had to see the base psychologist. He told my mom that I had serious anger issues. While the whole warrior ideology was great for the soldiers going into battle, the same can't be said for a fourteen year old. When my dad came home, the psychologist told mom, he should have a long talk with him.

Mom just laughed at that notion. She asked the psychologist if his G.I insurance was paid up. She made it clear that Mr. Strongbow would've been upset if Mitchell hadn't fought the bully for pushing around his girlfriend.

"My husband is a full blooded Sioux warrior. This is his third war and he's still alive. Iggy drilled this into his family, daughters included. There's so much death consuming the base, and the army has done nothing to help the families cope. They also have their breaking points. My kids are all involved in extra school sports, and their marks are all decent. What else should I be doing, tell me?" Mom was pissed! I would've dropped the psychologist, but that's what got me here in the first place.

When we got home, my mom, who had also taken on the role of my dad, said, "Mitchell, what Harry did was wrong. You sticking up for your friend was right. However, hurting him that bad was wrong. Just knock him down and embarrass him, or for once, try and talk your way out of a fight. Do you understand?"

"Mom, first, Rhonda is my girlfriend, and second, a Strongbow never fights to lose. Talking is for cowards who either can't or are afraid to fight. That is what dad always says, 'Hurt your opponent and show no mercy'."

"Mitchell, there will come a time when you must use your brains and not your fists. Doesn't your dad also say, 'Your brain is your greatest weapon in battle'?" Damn, she was right!

I didn't see Rhonda until the day she was moving back to Kansas. I told her I was so sorry that I screwed up. I made it so we couldn't see each other, until this day.

Rhonda kissed me and said, ""Harry was being a jerk and he deserved it." She admitted it made her feel real good inside, and she liked how I fought for her honor.

I told Rhonda when I got old enough I would go to Kansas to see her again. We could then move to California together, if she wanted. We just hugged each other until her mom said it was time to go. All the while she just kept giving me dirty looks.

I told Rhonda the same thing my dad had told me. "Look to the North Star when you want to talk to me. I will be listening, and will come to you." Hell, if my dad had that power, and being a Sioux warrior myself, perhaps I too possessed the same powers.

As soon as we kissed her mom grabbed her by the

shirt and said "Let's go, Rhonda." For weeks I dreamt about Rhonda and me together. It would wake me from my sleep, thinking I might not ever see her again. Two weeks to the day, I received a letter from Rhonda with her new address. I wrote back but my letters were never answered.

# HUNT CAMP, 1963
# MONDAY OCTOBER 3, 1963

After my schoolyard beating of Harry Swanson, none of the other students wanted to give me a go. Whether they were in grade eight or not, it didn't matter now. They knew I was a bit whacked in the head and could really throw 'em. No one pissed me off or dared to challenge me. But all this new power and respect couldn't take away the emptiness in my heart. I was still moping around the house and school about Rhonda moving away.

I received no more letters from either Rhonda or my dad. It was almost six weeks now. In his last letter home, he assured me he would be home in time for us to go away to hunt camp. I had to promise him that I would kill a deer myself this time. There was still no sign of dad, either by letter or in person. Hunt camp was now only a day away.

Jake drove up to Fort Campbell from Oakland in his V.W. microbus. He sensed that I was worried about our dad. Jake said, "If dad can't leave with us, it would be brother and brother bonding time; a chance for us to get caught up." He also assured me that he had a couple treats for the journey.

The original game plan was for dad, Jake and me to drive to hunt camp together, with everyone's weapons including Jerry's and Uncle Jack's in Jake's van. Uncle Jack and his son Jerry would fly to Lincoln, Nebraska, where we would pick them up. All of us would then head to my grandfather's house and hunt camp.

I was up early the morning we were to leave for hunt camp. I never slept that night. I didn't want to miss dad opening the door to our home safe and sound. He wouldn't forget this was hunt camp week, or his promise he made to me.

I had this knot in my stomach worrying about dad. I knew right then, if I was to look in the mirror, I would have the same look that Rhonda Ryan had on her face after learning her dad had been killed in Vietnam. Why hadn't dad written us? Where the fuck was he? He promised he wouldn't miss hunt camp!

Mom had made breakfast for us that morning. I was anything but hungry, if anything I felt like puking. Hunt camp had lost all appeal. I just wanted to go back to my room and sleep, and not wake up until dad got home.

Mom, the proud German, sensing I was feeling sorry for myself told me, "You have to eat something so straighten up and act like a Strongbow warrior! Mitchell, if your father saw the way you are acting right now he would be ashamed of you. He might even give you a good licking!"

"I wouldn't be surprised, with your father knowing

how much hunt camp means to the Strongbow men, that he will surprise you. He might already be at your grandfather's, or at least on his way. Your dad is all about the element of surprise, correct Mitchell? Has he ever let you down in the past? No! Now eat up and get on the road. You don't want to make your dad upset by being late, do you?"

I truly believed everything mom said. It did make sense after all. Even though the knot in my stomach was still there, I ate breakfast, just not as much as food as I normally eat. Mom had also made us up a cooler full of food, pop and treats for the road. At 06:35, we left Fort Campbell, Kentucky. Next stop, Lincoln, Nebraska to pick up Uncle Jack and Jerry.

We were maybe on the road five minutes, and I got curious as to what surprises Jake had for me. He said to go in the gunnysack bag that was on the back bench. Eagerly I went back there. I moved Jake's leather jacket out of the way, and found a couple Hell Hounds Oakland Chapter T-shirts. Now those put a smile on my face! When I asked if both shirts were for me, Jake answered that they were as was the leather jacket.

Wow! Talk about Christmas coming twice in a year. I was ecstatic! I had always wanted a leather jacket. The surprises weren't all done. Jake told me to look inside the leather jacket's right pocket. Goddamn! I pulled out a baggie with these joints already rolled up just waiting to be smoked. I asked Jake if we should light up a joint now. To quote Jake, "Get your ass up here, and light up that fucking joint."

By the time we were done with the joint the anxiety I had built up for the past couple weeks was gone. Driving across country with Jake is all a little brother could ask for even though he tried to embarrass me about girls. I was still a virgin, but no way would I ever admit that to him.

Jake was the kind of guy who bragged he had slept with over a hundred women. He said, I have to come to California alone this summer. He was going to get me high and also laid at least twice a day, by different girls that hang around his gang. He called them "Splashers," and said they do whatever a club member asks, or tells them to do. That alone gave me a boner that lasted for the next twenty five miles or so.

Perhaps all this talk about pussy and being high made Jake pull over and pick up this hitchhiker just outside Paducah. She was a heavy set girl, black curly hair, maybe twenty or so, nice lips and kind of a pretty face. But still a big girl! Her name was Rosie, and she was thumbing her way to back home to Saint Louis. Jake was truly a snake around females. Soon as Rosie got in the vehicle, I was kicked to the seat in the back, while she sat in the front with him.

Jake asked her if she wanted to get high. Rosie liked that idea. Jake then had me go the back and get them a beer. Hell next thing you know, they can't keep their hands off each other. They almost caused us to have a head on crash with an 18 wheeler. They may have laughed, but I didn't find it funny and voiced my displeasure. Jake pulled over the vehicle and told me to take the wheel!

Now being only fourteen I didn't have a valid driver's license. Dad had taught all his children to drive everything from dirt bikes to military jeeps to even five ton trucks. Well, I would rather die with me at the wheel, than Jake killing us all getting a blowjob.

I assumed the position in the driver's seat, as Jake and Rosie went into the rear of the microbus. They pulled a set of curtains across. Once the giggling started between the two of them, I turned up the volume, kept my eye on the road, and my hands on the wheel.

The song that was playing on the radio had not even ended when I heard Rosie moaning away like a humpback whale looking for her calf. Damn she was loud! It seemed the louder she would get, the harder it was for me to drive. I wasn't thinking dirty thoughts but I did have a boner. I was thinking about Rhonda Ryan.

It was hard to drive because the whole damn

vehicle was now starting to rock from side to side. At one point I swear I felt air beneath the tires and not pavement. Jesus H. Christ, Jake. Hurry up before we flip over. I would say Jake was done, or at least the rocking and moaning stopped after about four, maybe five songs. Jake pulled the curtains open and jumped in the passenger seat with this big smile on his face.

Jake asked if I wanted a piece of Rosie. She was back there waiting for me. I looked in the rear view mirror and there was Rosie, naked, lying on her side with her legs wide open. Her whole genital region looked like the forests we hunt in, dark! If you get lost in there, you will die. Ugh! I told Jake, "Thanks, but no thanks." Jake laughed as he told Rosie to get dressed.

We pulled into Saint Louis and dropped Rosie off at her apartment. It was just after 11 A.M. and she invited us both up for some lunch. It would give Jake a chance to have sex in a bed instead of just the backbench of a vehicle. Jake said, "Thanks for the offer but we are on a tight deadline. We have to pick up two relatives in Lincoln, Nebraska in just over seven hours and it would be too close."

Rosie gave Jake this really long, wet kiss goodbye before thanking him for the ride and picking her up while she was hitchhiking. She was laughing as she said goodbye.

As soon as we got back on Highway US40-W Jake taught me a life lesson. Well, at least a lesson according to Jake's life. "I got the vibe that Rosie repulsed you and that's why you chose not to have sex with her, correct?"

"Pretty face but fuck Jake, she weighed about as much as you and I combined. Fact is that I' m not into sloppy seconds."

"I respect the sloppy second's issue. However Mitch, a heavy girl like Rosie doesn't get laid that often, unless they can find guys who actually like the large ladies. When she has a chance for a stiff cock to slam the inside of her walls Mitch, she will fuck you senseless. Rosie doesn't know when the next piece of cock will come her way. If I asked her to lick my asshole, she would have."

Well, that comment just grossed me out.

"So what I am saying my little brother is this. Don't be so picky. Some of the best sex I ever had was with plus size ladies."

Now Jake was a total racist. Even though I'm half Sioux and half German, Jake is all Sioux. Yet he's more of an Arian Nazi than I ever could be. To test this theory and to also make him think, I said to him. "I get it now; so Aunt Jemima would be someone you would fuck."

Jake didn't even give me any warning. He just drilled me in the arm, full force. Damn, it fucking hurt! "There, there little brother. Maybe you better find yourself a big girl to fuck you. I don't think you'll be able to jerk off now. Hurt?"

It hurt alright, but it was worth it!

With Jake now living in Oakland, he wanted to know everything going on in Pam and Rachel's life; the dating scene, school marks, partying lifestyle, sports, everything. Rachel will turn thirteen this week, so she doesn't have much of a life. Just schooling, which she loves, along with karate and gymnastics."

Pam was now in grade twelve and looking forward to going to College next year. "I guess she will be leaving the house too?" I said, "She has been seeing this guy Leon." Jake asked me if he was a good guy or not. I told him he was and that mom likes him although he was scared of dad. That made Jake laugh and he asked about my mom, his step-mom.

Jake actually opened up quite honestly to me about her. "You have a really good mom there, Mitch. I know I was a bit of a dick to her when I lived at home. For her to raise two other children that weren't hers and to take the shit she took. Hell, just coming to post-war America, and being a German, she took a lot of shit from a lot of people. I never ever saw her back down from anyone. She would stand up and fight for

Pam and me as much as you and Rachel. She's a smart woman who will win every debate she gets into whether she started it or not. She's a proud German woman, Mitch. Dad did very good marrying her."

I felt so warm and fuzzy inside. This was a side of Jake that I had never seen before. Yeah, this trip was going excellently so far; a great bonding time between the two of us. If dad were here right now, he would be sporting an ear-to-ear smile.

We pulled into the Lincoln Airport at 18:30, just thirty minutes behind schedule. Considering we had been on the road for over eleven hours by then, that's not too bad. Uncle Jack and Jerry were outside with their luggage. They were having a smoke when we pulled up.

After they put their luggage in the rear of the truck, Jake and I near died laughing. Jerry sat in the bench that Jake nailed Rosie on and asked, "Did something spill here?"

As we pulled away from the airport, Jake said he needed a hot meal before he could carry on. Since I wanted the same, we pulled up to a drive-in restaurant. With all these firearms in the vehicle, it seemed like a safe place.

The girls working there made it seem like it was one of those old 50s diners. They were on roller blades and brought your food right to your car. Very nostalgic! Uncle Jack said in his day, these styles of drive-ins were on every major intersection. I can't say that I've ever seen one on the base. Very cool indeed!

For the rest of the trip Jerry drove for four hours, and then Uncle Jack would drive the final three hours or so. We would soon be at my grandfather's house. That damn tray of tacos I ate kept repeating on me the whole time.

As soon as we crossed the border and headed into South Dakota, I really felt dad's presence. My shoulders dropped, and I started to relax. These were the lands that I grew up on. I wasn't just a visitor here. I really don't think I could ever live in a big city. The countryside is so amazing; actually breathtaking this time of year, with the leaves on the trees changing color. Fall has always been, and will always be, my favorite time of year.

We pulled in just before midnight. Grandfather met us all with hugs, and told me just how much I looked like my dad, when he was fourteen years old. He had a pot of stew on the stove for us; deer stew to be exact. Even though it is one of my favorite meals, the tacos were still sitting pretty damn heavy in my guts. My grandfather said he had some good news for all of us. That seemed to settle my guts down a little.

It seemed mom had called to say she received three letters that morning, all from dad. At first I thought maybe it was just to ease my pain of dad not being there. However my grandfather assured me that my mom would keep the letters for me to read once I got back at home. Grandfather said that in the one letter, my dad apologized for not being back stateside, but duty called. Dad also wrote he wanted photos taken of me bagging my first deer.

Hearing the news about dad and his letters, I seemed to get a little of my appetite back. I was more determined than ever to kill my first deer. Uncle Jack asked if I would like to be his hunting partner during this trip. I could think of no one else that I would rather hunt with. They look and sound so much alike.

That night before I closed my eyes, I looked out the window and just stared at the North Star. I said a little prayer, and had a chat with my dad. I told him I wouldn't let him down.

The next morning I was up at the crack of dawn, spraying out the remnants of the tacos. Grandfather and Uncle Jack were both awake; Jerry and Jake were both still sleeping. After I ate a couple pieces of toast, my uncle said, "Saddle up the horses and let's get at it."

Deer tracking! A true Sioux hunting tradition. I can hear my dad now, "Any idiot can sit in a tree for hours or days on end, and shoot a deer. What kind of challenge is that? A hunter tracks his prey!" That is what Uncle Jack and I were now going to do. I would be using my dad's old .306. My uncle was going to bring a couple bows as well, for me to hone my skills.

As much as dad and my uncle firmly believed in the traditions of the Sioux, the Strongbow traditions were more important. This included a saying little prayer with my grandfather before we left; a prayer to the Great Spirit. "Wakan Tanka, Great Mystery, teach me how to trust my heart, my mind, my intuition, my inner knowing. Teach me to trust the senses of my body, the blessings of my spirit, so that I may enter my "sacred space," and love beyond my fear. May I continue to walk in "Balance", with the passing of each glorious sun."

Uncle Jack told my grandfather we would be back in a couple of days, and to tell Jake and Jerry when they dragged their lazy asses out of bed, to meet us at the Longhouse. We would be hunting in the north east acreage of the Strongbow land.

It was a brisk morning when we headed out on day one of the deer hunt. You could see your breath. The horses trotted along with the steam venting from their noses. It made you realize just how much power they possessed. They were just like a steam engine locomotive.

Along the trek, my uncle asked me how everyone in the family was doing. He apologized for not seeing much of us; he was really busy these days on the docks; lots of overtime.

Dad and his brother had served together during World War Two. I was always curious and asked him why he didn't make a full time career out of the army. His answer really hit home with me. "Your dad is, and will always be the family hero; the one that nobody could ever take down."

Yet I still worry about him, and my uncle just confirmed my fears. "I saw enough killing during the Great War in Europe, Mitchell. I saw men do stuff to other men that still bother me to this day. I saw firsthand what the German's did to the Jews. It takes a special breed of person to make a career of it. Your dad is one of those people, Mitchell."

"Your dad is as good a tracker and shooter as there is. He is one of those guys that everyone in his unit looks to. Mitchell, your dad is a true fearless leader. I saw us so many times in one kind of jam or other, being pinned down by the Germans. We all thought it was the end for us, but your dad would save the day. During D-Day, our units were strewn all across France. The whole 101$^{st}$ Airborne was in disarray. Iggy took leadership and reorganized our whole platoon; made us the elite fighting unit we were trained to be. Your dad is a hero, Mitchell! He has saved so many lives."

"Anyone can fire a weapon, but your dad is all about survival. Survival for him and the men in his squad! I have even seen Generals ask him for advice on the battlefield. I'm sure, that he's representing our country well in Vietnam. He's there as a Special Advisor, to help the people of the south defeat those Commie bastards! He's there for a reason, Mitchell. President Kennedy wanted the best of our military to help out the South Vietnamese. I'm positive General Westmoreland knew your dad was one of those elite soldiers; he could be counted on to follow the President's orders."

I always remember all these people were willing to help dad out whenever he needed a favor. Like last year, he managed to get us to the hunt, just by asking a couple of air force buddies. He was very well liked in Fort Campbell. Even when I got into trouble, as soon as they found out I was Iggy Strongbow's son, they would relax and cut me some slack. They would then quietly have a talk with my dad.

My uncle asked. "Have you got a special girl in your life?" Why was everyone so worried about me having a steady girlfriend? "I did but her dad was killed in Vietnam. Her family moved back to Kansas. Her name is Rhonda Ryan. She's a redhead with thick lips and boobs." This made my uncle laugh. "So you are a boob man, are you Mitchell?"

"I think I might be. Yeah, I seem to be attracted to girls with big boobs. I really miss Rhonda, even though her mom doesn't like me. I beat up this one kid in our class who was picking on her."

"Well, I know your dad would've been proud of you for that. I'm also sure Rhonda's dad would have liked that you protected his daughter. I remember your dad always hated bullies. Sooner or later they would end up fighting with your dad. He was always knocking the shit out of them. I have never seen your dad lose a fight. I know he never went looking for one. If it happened, pity the poor fool who started it. They would end up with either a bloody nose or black eyes; usually both."

With dad so far away, I wanted to hear as many stories about him as I could. When my uncle spoke, if you just closed your eyes, it was uncanny how much they sounded alike.

After about an hour on horseback, I could tell that my uncle had seen something. He gave me a hand signal to be quiet, as he stopped his horse. I did the same. I started to scour the direction he was concentrating on, as my uncle pulled out his rifle. Both horses seemed to be agitated or spooked!

My uncle told me to hold tight to the horse's reins. I could tell it wasn't a deer that drew my uncle's attention. Like a good army brat, I did exactly what he said. He raised his rifle and took aim at a gold colored object about two hundred yards away. He fired his shot! My horse jolted but because of being forewarned, I managed to stay on board. The object he fired at now took off like a bolt of lightning.

"Fucking mountain lions. They're starting to make their way back to the Black Hills from Canada. They are dangerous creatures Mitchell. Don't ever take one lightly! You see one, you shoot it! I want you to carry your rifle with you at all times."

Just mentioning the name mountain lion would put a bit of fear into anyone. Hell, my uncle was a seasoned hunter and he viewed them as dangerous. I knew I better heed his warning! I will view them as the dangerous killers they are.

Speaking of killers, from time to time I would have to dismount. I needed to find a bush to squat and spray. The remnants of last night's tacos blasted free. I was now starting to sweat and was feeling weak.

My uncle commented that I didn't look so good and asked if I wanted to go back to my grandfather's house.

"No" I said, "I have waited for this all year. I promised dad that I would kill a deer on my own this year. It will pass. It's got to be the hot sauce!"

"I think you might have food poisoning, Mitchell. You were the only one to have tacos, and the only one stinking out the forest. Hell, even the skunks are getting out of your way."

We did as we normally did during hunt camp. We headed right to our Longhouse to drop off our supplies before heading out looking for deer. I was starting to burn up, and the cool weather was refreshing to say the least. Fuck, right about then I couldn't track a deer if my life depended on it. My stomach was having all kinds of explosions, and the gurgling noises even spooked my horse.

It seemed I couldn't go more than a half mile without spraying liquid shit and toxins out of my asshole. I was so pissed at the drive-in restaurant I wanted to go back and shoot them. Fuck the deer, I wanted revenge. Just when I thought it couldn't get any worse, without any warning, it did.

My uncle said if we weren't so close to the Longhouse, maybe a ¼ mile away, he would take me back to my grandfather's house. The Strongbow Longhouse goes back to the days of my great-grandfather Red Cloud. It was built maybe eighty plus years ago. The Longhouse has no power, no washroom, or running water. It really makes you respect the elders. They needed none of the necessities that we take for granted.

I was so happy to finally dismount, as my asshole was a burning ring of fire. The saddle offered no relief. I could really use an ice cube between my butt cheeks. The one item I did bring along was a couple rolls of toilet paper. I'm sure my ancestors would also have appreciated the toilet paper.

After we unpacked everything, I really seemed to take a turn for the worse. I ran outside and started to hurl my guts out. My uncle told me that I wasn't going into the bush until I get back to normal. He said I would be dangerous to the other hunters as well as to myself. To be honest I would scare the deer all the way to Manitoba.

I was done! I just wanted to curl up in a ball and sleep. I had no energy at all, so I rolled out my sleeping bag. My uncle built a fire inside the Longhouse and within two minutes, I passed right out. Now, I have never taken a hallucinogenic drug in my life; weed, hash and some decent oils, but nothing to cause me to trip out and hallucinate. I had the most bizarre intense and damn realistic dreams once I passed out. The dreams were a little too close for comfort, and way too close to home.

I had this nightmarish dream that I was hunting along beside not only my dad, but Rhonda Ryan's deceased dad, Steve. All three of us were wearing military combats and carrying M-1 rifles. We weren't in a forest but in an old abandoned town, like a ghost town in the old west.

We heard all these blood curdling screams. We couldn't figure where they were coming from, or who was making the shrill sounds. We all walked towards the center of the town; a thin layer of fog had crept its way in. A raven came out of nowhere and dove at our heads, all the while cawing. *"You're gonna die! You're gonna die!"*

Dad looked at me and barked out, "Kill that messenger, private Strongbow!" I pointed my rifle at the bird and pulled the trigger. The weapon didn't fire. It just made a clicking noise. I pulled back the bolt, to reload the chamber. The bullet magazine fell out from my weapon.

This seemed to infuriate dad even more. *"I gave you a direct order, soldier. Shoot that messenger before he gives away our position!"* Once again, I pointed towards the bird, squeezed the trigger with everything I had. Click!

Dad now got into my face and started to scream at me, all the while spraying my face with spittle. *"Are you a killer or a pussy, soldier? Kill that messenger now! I didn't raise you to fail soldier. Look at Ryan! He failed and he's dead. Do you want to die, just like him?"*

Once again, I raised my weapon but it had now somehow turned into a broom. The same broom I just used to sweep out the Longhouse. I instinctively raised the broom to whack the bird out of the sky. Dad said. *"It's too late soldier, drop your weapon! They are among us."*

I looked at dad in disbelief. He was now fixated on several humanoids that were approaching us. Their faces obscured, all that was visible were the clothes they were wearing. There was a Japanese WW2 soldier, a WW2 Storm Trooper, and a Mexican bandit. The strangest one of all though, was the girl from that 50s drive-in diner. She roller skated around doing figure of eight patterns. The tray she carried was full of weapons instead of food. Just like the raven, she cawed out, "*You're gonna die!*"

I looked at dad and asked, "Now what?"

Dad had this smirk on his face and answered, *"You know how this ends, Mitchell. You have always known."*

Like hell I know how it ends! I watched in horror as the Mexican bandit now raised his knife. It was still dripping in fresh blood! His sights pointed right at me, he went into his throwing motion. I couldn't move! The only thing I could do was plead to my dad for help. He did not, or could not, answer me.

I followed the flight of the knife as it left the Mexican's hand. I watched it fly through the air towards me. Like a magnet, I seemed to attract that blade. With every single revolution of the knife, it got closer to me. I was fixated on it! The knife drove hard into my stomach. I felt every single organ burst open!

The pain was unbelievable, as I let out a death scream. It was loud enough to wake myself from the nightmare. It might have been only a dream, but the pain in my stomach was real. I raced outside and found a convenient spot to once again spray the toxins I had left in my body. Uncontrollable contractions of liquid shit were spraying all over the ground. It fucking burned! My body, drenched in sweat, was now trembling. God damn, this isn't good.

I was still in the squat position, trying to pull myself together as two riders approached. It was Jake and Jerry. They started to laugh at me, which I have to say wasn't appreciated. I let them know this in no uncertain terms, by telling both to "FUCK OFF!"

Eventually, the shakes and sweats stopped. Lord knows I couldn't possibly have anything left in my bowels. I gingerly walked back into the Longhouse and sat as close to the fire as I could. I was freezing. The smart asses Jake and Jerry now seemed to be more concerned than cynical. Uncle Jack told them he believed I had food poisoning. I was the only one to order tacos, and that would explain why I was the only one sick.

Jake and Jerry now cut me some slack. Jake asked if I wanted to stay at grandpa's house until I felt better. There was hydro and running water there. I said, "No,

I will feel better by the morning. I really need to embrace the strength and powers of the Longhouse." It has served as inspiration, for so many generations of Strongbow family members.

Jake said that our grandfather was still waiting for my cousins Pat and Billy to show up. He would wait until 18:00, and if they were no shows, he would head up here. I guess he wanted to travel while there was still daylight. It was safer, especially during hunting season.

Around 13:00, Jake, Uncle Jack and Jerry wanted to start tracking deer. They told me to stay put at least until tomorrow. I would be fine once my strength was built back up. I was disappointed but respected their wishes. The way my ass was burning, there was no way I could even think of mounting a horse. Before they headed out, they told me to just keep an eye out for grandpa, and if he doesn't get to the Longhouse by 21:00 maybe go for a little ride. I said, "No problems you can count on me."

For the next little bit, I wandered around the Longhouse, while scarfing back a whole whack of crackers. I just tried to really embrace the Longhouse and its history. How could you not feel the spirituality that was being emitted? All the great Sioux leaders had been in the Strongbow Longhouse at one point or another. I looked at several pieces of wood that had carvings on them and wondered if Crazy Horse or Geronimo had left their marks here.

I know that I should be just as proud of my German roots, but fuck; my Grandpa Kohler was a Nazi Officer. What should I do, visit a Holocaust Camp?

There was no medicine at all in the Longhouse to help with me the food poisoning. But Jake had left me a couple joints to help ease my pain and suffering. I sat back in one of the big wooden rocking chairs beside the fireplace, and sparked up the joint.

Why is it that the first toke always burns the lungs but tastes so damn good? Each time I exhale, the pain and suffering seemed not quite as bad. When the joint was finished, I looked around the Longhouse once again, trying to pick up a feel or vibe. I wondered if the elders, when they smoked their "Peace Pipe," used weed in them? I felt really at peace. Man, a high world would be a peaceful world. Fuck, if Kennedy could get the Communist Vietnamese high on weed; my dad would be here with us right now.

Yeah, I was pretty bu**zz**ed after that joint. With the food poisoning draining from my body, and the radiating heat coming from the fireplace, I started to nod off. I quickly found myself once again wanting to lie down and fall asleep. While awake the weed mellowed me right out, but once I fell asleep, I was back in the nightmarish dreams all over again.

This time I was a soldier in World War Two trying to evade capture from the Germans in the French countryside. No matter how fast I ran, I couldn't evade the Germans. I even stole a motorcycle. It didn't matter; eventually I was captured and beaten. They wanted the information on my top secret espionage mission. Even in my dream I knew not to be a "Rat."

The next thing I knew, I was lined up against this brick wall facing a firing squad of blue-eyed Nazi's. Bastards didn't even offer me a last joint or a blindfold. They wanted me to see the faces of my killers. They offered me the chance to say my last words. In true Strongbow fashion I uttered, "FUCK YOU."

The Nazi Officer who commanded the firing squad called me, "A traitor to the Fatherland," looked at his men and yelled "FEUER." Unlike my last dream in which I felt pain, this time I felt nothing. I was awakened from my dream by the sound of the Nazi's rifles being fired. It sounded like they were right in the Longhouse with me.

I was drenched in sweat, shaking and just trying to come to my senses. I heard another rifle being discharged, this time I am awake. My head and gut instinct told me things weren't good. I pulled the hair on my arms to make sure I wasn't dreaming. That was clearly a rifle shot.

I couldn't see any of my relatives firing a rifle so close to the Longhouse. I grabbed my .306 hunting rifle, and went outside to investigate. The hairs on the back of my neck stood up as soon as I stepped outside. My lips went numb as I felt the adrenaline start to flow through my body, readying my muscles for battle as my eyes scoured the land

Even though it was jet black outside, something wasn't right. I could sense my dad's presence, telling me to stay calm. I thought back to what he had taught me over the years, *"If you can't see, Mitchell, use your other senses."*

I stopped and listened for anything unusual, something that could be perceived as a threat. Within seconds, I heard growling, a snarling sound. I took the safety off my rifle and walked at a real slow pace. With my rifle in the firing position at shoulder level I started to sniff the air for anything unusual. I smelled blood, fresh blood.

It sent shivers up my spine and for the first time in my life I tasted fear. However this feeling didn't stop me. I heard some movement in the brush, maybe twenty yards ahead of me. It was so dark my eyes were playing tricks on me. I knew from hunting with dad, the lessons he taught me were the same survival skills he taught the pilots.

You absolutely do not open fire on anything you can't see. It was a waste of ammo for one thing. The fact that I only had one bullet in the chamber and six in my clip so I had to be careful. No way was I going to waste bullets on a phantom object. I let out an "Owl Hoot" and heard nothing back, other than the snarling.

I came right out and asked, "Is anyone out there?" I tried to stop breathing so as to raise my senses even higher. Then I heard a faint voice asking for help. I realized that I was still just a kid, scared of the dark and boogeyman. Could this be just a practical initiation joke? Something dreamed up and played on me by Jake, Jerry and my Uncle Jack; fuck, what to do?

I walked slowly towards where I believed the faint voice was coming from. I'm not sure what the hell I thought I would see. What I ended up seeing was another part of the nightmarish dream. It just had to be! Lying on the ground, with blood coming from the right side of his head, was my grandfather. He seemed to be drifting in and out of consciousness.

That however wasn't the biggest threat or my biggest worry. A mountain lion started to crouch and slowly walk towards my fallen grandfather. Dream or not, I have to save my grandfather's life. I trained my rifle on the mountain lion who had now realized I was present. The lion stopped his walk towards my grandfather, and looked at me. Sticking out his chest to show no fear the lion let out this roar which showed off its menacing fangs.

Dad always taught me to never be afraid of fear. He would say, "Make fear your friend not your enemy." I took a deep breath. The mountain lion now seemed to build up his momentum, from a slow crouch to a faster run. I knew I had to shoot him before he had a full head of steam built up.

I now felt dad's hands on my shoulders. He whispered in my ear, "You are a Strongbow warrior! Take the shot, shoot to kill, son." That is exactly what I did. I aimed for his chest and just kept shooting until I was out of ammo. The mountain lion lay motionless and lifeless on the ground.

My next priority was my grandfather. I threw my rifle on the ground and raced over to him. He was hurt pretty bad. He asked if my dad and I killed the mountain lion. I said, "Yes we did." I just assumed that the head wound was making him delirious. He kept looking to the side of me, and talking to the air. He believed my dad was there. "Iggy my son, you have raised a great warrior. He reminds me of you at his age."

I took my jacket off and covered up my

grandfather so he wouldn't go into shock. I asked if he could get up. Grandfather was too delirious and injured to answer. I picked up his rifle and once again used the SOS message. It had been drilled into my brain for such an occurrence. I fired three shots into the air, all the while hoping my Uncle Jack, Jake or Jerry had heard. I waited the designated Strongbow SOS alarm time of thirty seconds, and fired another three shots in the air. I followed up by yelling HELP!

I took off my shirt and tried to wipe the blood from the head wounds. I then asked my grandfather "Does anything else hurt?" He just rubbed his ribs which bothered me: I wondered if they were broken? Had a broken rib also punctured one of his lungs? The last thing I wanted to do was to try and move him myself. I tried to get him sitting up and as comfortable as possible.

I built a fire as quickly as I could. I needed to keep him warm and also to show the rest of my family exactly where we were. I just kept trying to keep my grandfather talking with me. I had to keep him conscious until help came. More times than not, he would talk right through me. He was carrying on a conversation with my dad, even though I knew he's 10,000 miles away.

For the first bit I couldn't take the conversation seriously between him and the air, a.k.a. my dad. Then just the way the fire flickered and the stars twinkled down on us, I thought I saw a shadow of a male behind me. I once again felt my dad's hands on my shoulders. I knew it wasn't my uncle, brother or cousin. I also knew not to turn around. I didn't want dad to leave. I wanted that shadow to stay with me and to feel his presence.

Just like my grandfather the Shaman, I too started to talk out loud to dad. I knew he couldn't answer us, but I wanted to say some things that I forget to put in his letter. "See dad, I always listened to your hunting tips and I saved grandpa. I may not have shot a deer like I promised, but I think a mountain lion is pretty damn good. Dad, right now I really need you to alert Uncle Jack. They are out here somewhere. I want to talk to you dad and hear everything about Vietnam, but I think grandpa can really use your help right now. Can you go and get them? He is hurt really bad."

Just like a magician throwing a flammable substance into the fire to captivate and thrill his audience; a huge flame shot to the sky. I heard voices yelling. It was Uncle Jack, Jerry and Jake. I yelled back and told them to come to the fire.

As soon as I had a visual of them on horseback, I raced over to them as fast as I could. I told them that grandpa was hurt really bad. All three galloped over to him while their horses jumped over the dead mountain lion. They dismounted. My Uncle Jack headed right to my grandfather.

Jake and Jerry, with rifles in their hands, approached the mountain lion. "Did you shoot this thing or did grandpa?"

"I did!"

"Did the lion attack him, Mitch?"

"I don't believe so. I think the mountain lion spooked his horse and it threw him. You know grandpa, he never wears a saddle, and I haven't seen hide nor hair of his horse. Grandpa hit the ground hard, but he managed to get off a shot that alerted me. I came out and saw grandpa on the ground injured, with the mountain lion getting ready to pounce. I emptied a full clip into him."

They were in total disbelief, but both smiled when they took a closer look at the mountain lion. "You know Mitchell, too bad you blew his head half off. This would've looked great mounted, but you did the right thing. The old man would be proud of you, great shooting little brother!"

I don't think my chest or head could get any bigger. I felt euphoric! I felt like I just truly entered manhood. I felt like Crazy Horse, Red Cloud and all other Sioux leaders would say that I am a WARRIOR! As long as my grandfather was going to be O.K. then today was the most perfect day in my life; food poisoning and all.

My uncle did a thorough check on my grandfather and said he had a concussion for sure, but he wasn't sure about whether his ribs were broken or not. He did say that he hadn't punctured a lung. When I asked, "How did you determine that?" My uncle said he told my grandfather to spit in his hand. It hurt like a bastard for him, to even breathe deep enough to spit. The phlegm was clear, there was no blood. My uncle suggested that he could ride back to grandfather's house and call Doctor Cooper. But grandfather said he was fine: he was more embarrassed than anything else. He just needed to rest up. Tomorrow he would be in the bush with us, tracking and killing deer.

So Uncle Jack and Jerry helped carry him back to the Longhouse. I carried both of our rifles, while Jake walked the horses back. Uncle Jack and I then took a walk back to see the dead mountain lion. He patted me on the shoulder and said my dad would be so proud of me. Uncle Jack said the words I had been dying to hear out loud, *"You are a true Strongbow Warrior, Mitchell."*

My uncle spread the mountain lions legs and said it was a female. She weighed maybe a hundred pounds. He wondered if, maybe she just gave birth and all her cubs died, making her so aggressive towards humans.

My uncle also reiterated what Jake said about too many bullet holes to stuff the lion. He pulled out his hunting knife and cut the tail off for me, which was nice. He then hung the tail still dripping in blood around my neck. He also grabbed a pair of pliers and pulled out the big fang teeth. Yeah, my first hunting trophy!

My uncle then tied a rope around the lion's neck, and the other end of the rope to his horse. He said with all the bears around, this dead lion would attract too many of them. I jumped on my horse, he jumped on his, and we dragged the dead mountain lion deep into the bush, away from the Longhouse.

On the way back from the bush, I truly rode taller in my saddle. The stars looked brighter and the sky looked crystal clear. Even my stomach, that had suffered the effects of bad tacos, felt like a million bucks. As soon as we walked in, my uncle grabbed me a beer while my grandfather looked at me and just smiled. Jake and Jerry toasted my triumph and sure shooting while in serious danger. Life was great! I just wished dad were here to celebrate with us. Something told me he was.

That night we woke up my grandfather every two hours; whether he liked it or not. He didn't! When the sun rose that morning, he was up making us all breakfast. I was the first to rise and a smiling grandfather asked how I would like my eggs. I was pleasantly surprised to see him not just back to his normal self, but acting like nothing major had happened to him.

I asked, "Are you all right?"

"My grandson I am fine. Thanks to your bravery and the Great Spirit Wakan Tanka, I am still alive and able to cook your breakfast."

"I'm glad you're fine grandpa and thank you. I have learned so much from you, dad and the other elders."

"Very good, so how would you like your eggs Mitchell?"

"Whatever is easiest for you grandpa."

That morning my grandfather made me the best scrambled eggs I have ever tasted. I couldn't get enough of them; green peppers, onions, ham, cheese, quite the combo. I believe I had nothing but room in my stomach as lord knows I either puked up or shit out whatever was in there the day before.

With everyone still sleeping, grandfather asked me to go outside with him as he wanted to talk to me about something. Without hesitation, I respectfully honored his wishes.

"Just before your father was deployed, he and I had a long talk about you Mitchell. He worries about you, my grandson. He worries about your soul in the afterlife as you are not pure Lakota Sioux. Did you know I had a vision of your birth the night before you were born? In that vision I went into the real world, the spirit world that is behind this one. All the shadows that you see on this earth are that of the spirit world. In my vision you were on display for the great Sioux warriors of the past. Crazy Horse, Little Wound, Young Man Afraid of Horses, American Horse, Crow Dog, Old Chief Smoke and your great grandfather Red Cloud were all there. We passed around the peace pipe and discussed your future as a Sioux warrior. All agreed that you possess tremendous strength, courage and wisdom and you would be a great Sioux warrior, maybe even a great Chief one day. Well, make that everyone but Crazy Horse."

"Crazy Horse reminded us that you have the blue eyes and blood of a Hessian. You are not pure Sioux and your soul should never see the Spirit World once you die."

"Red Cloud called Crazy Horse a fool. He told him to look deep into his heart, and see that you would die defending the Sioux nation."

"Crazy Horse said, 'The Hessian helped to kill Sioux in the past, and what would stop him from turning on the Sioux?'"

"It became so heated that I summoned the Great Wakan Tanka to intervene. Wakan Tanka looked into your heart Mitchell and agreed with us that you are strong, but he also saw the Hessian in you. He summoned White Buffalo Woman, as it was she that taught the 'First Sacred Rite' to the Lakota people."

"She said that if your soul was pure, then you would be reunited with the Great Spirit and all those Strongbow Sioux family members who have died before you."

"Your great grandfather Red Cloud has agreed to be your 'Soul Keeper'. Once you die on this planet, a piece of your hair will be cut off and then held over burning sweet grass. The hair will be placed into a piece of sacred buckskin which we call the 'Soul Bundle'."

"All the Great Chiefs agreed on her judgment including Crazy Horse. A part of me deep down believes Crazy Horse is jealous of your strength and courage, Mitchell."

Grandpa now pointed to the sun that was just starting to rise. "I see your soul is as bright as the new day's sun. You must keep it that way, Mitchell. Your brother Jake's soul is now starting to set like the sun. It is diminishing with strength and purity each time I see him. But he is pure Lakota soul. He will have others who have passed before him help make his way to the Great Spirit World. Be wary of those throughout your life that try to poison or take your young soul, Mitchell."

I just nodded to my grandfather and said, "I won't let that happen." However deep down I had so many mixed emotions running through my head. I knew my grandfather garnered so much respect, not only from his relatives and tribe elders, but also from the whole Sioux community on the reservation; but fuck, I'm fourteen. What did this all mean to me?

His eyes told me he was telling the truth or at least what he thought was the truth. Maybe falling off his horse had made him more lucid. Reminded me of my parents telling me when I was younger that, I better be good or Santa wouldn't leave me any presents.

Alright, so is this just to keep me on the straight and narrow? Not to be a gang member like Jake? Is everything just a fable?

If I told the gang back home about this conversation, they would say my grandfather is dropping LSD. Yeah, I think this conversation is best not to be discussed with anyone.

Over the next couple days, grandfather was still nursing his injuries, but he still made sure we woke up every morning to a hot meal. When we arrived back at night time, he made sure another hot meal was waiting for us.

The first two days none of us were able to kill any

deer, although we had come close on several occasions. The one thing I was good at was catching fish. Every morning before the sun would rise I would jump into the canoe by myself and fish for our night time meal.

Yeah, unlike most teenagers who sleep their lives away, I really looked forward to just slide off into the lake while the mist was still coming off the water, especially before the sun rises and the moon is my only source of light. The water is clear as glass and the whole forest seems as if it is still in a slumber. The only sound you might hear is a loon or the odd fish jumping out of the water. I would paddle out maybe a half mile from shore, all the time just looking around and being overwhelmed with Mother Nature's beauty. The reservation hasn't yet been ruined by man and his insatiable desire to make a buck off every square inch on the planet.

This was also my time to reflect on my life. All I could think about was how much I missed dad, and yet I have felt his presence the whole time that we have been here. I thought about Rhonda Ryan and how it would be so damn cool for her to be in this canoe with me right now. I swear as soon as get my license, I'm driving to Kansas to pick her up. We could both live here on the reservation.

On day number three, Uncle Jack found a fresh set

of deer tracks, possibly a small herd. We decided to dismount our horses before we got to the top of this valley. Uncle Jack figured that the deer would be on the other side of the valley feeding off the blueberries. He also said, "Let's do this the true Strongbow Sioux way with our bows and arrows, no rifles."

Each day my uncle had me practicing my archery skills. Now we will see just how well I have honed this ancient skill. From this point on, it would be nothing but hand commands. We all crouched low so the wind wouldn't carry our scent downwind to the deer. You just hoped that your horses didn't give you away.

All four of us now looked down from the top of the peak to the valley below. Sure as fuck, my uncle was right! There had to be at least twenty deer chowing down on fresh berries, unaware of the danger. Uncle Jack hand signaled for us to get our bow and arrows ready. He gestured for all of us to get into a kneeling position. We did a countdown until firing our arrows; 3-2-1, fire away.

As soon as we fired our arrows, the deer all looked in our direction. I was fully concentrating on my specific arrow and hoping it would find its designated target. The deer now dispersed as Uncle Jack, Jake and Jerry all jumped up, and started to belt out a Sioux War cry. We ran down the valley firing arrows at the deer. Talk about a fucking rush! I jumped to my feet and started to yell in that familiar voice. I belted out the same cry several lifetimes ago, while running down the same valley and firing off my arrows.

I have never done hallucinogenic drugs, but this whole trip has been nothing short of an LSD experience. I was running down the valley after the deer, when I swear I felt I've done this before. However, it wasn't deer that I was chasing; it was Blue Coat Soldiers.

Every single time I was in pre-flight, with my feet off the ground I had these flashbacks; and every time my feet would touch the ground, I would come out of my flashback. In pre-flight, I saw the yellow bandana the soldiers would wear. I could actually smell the gun powder from their rifles being fired. I could hear the screams of men in pain. The Sioux battle cry, piercing the air wasn't coming from the four of us; but from hundreds of Sioux screaming at the top of their lungs. It was deafening and yet exhilarating all at the same time.

I didn't stop running and chasing the deer until all my arrows were fired. Even then I felt as if I had enough power and strength to run and slice all their throats. Talk about pack mentality. I looked back to see where everyone else was. Damn, all three of them had to be at least fifty yards behind me and all of them were bent over trying to catch their wind. I stopped my pursuit and started to head back to everyone. I counted at least five deer on the ground; a couple dead, others in obvious pain. Once the adrenaline rush ended, it kind of bothered me.

Uncle Jack said seeing as how I was the only one not ready to die of a heart attack, I was to go back and get all the horses. Several deer were wounded and should be tracked down and killed. I said, "Sure" and headed to the top of the valley. As I started to head up the valley, I turned around and saw Uncle Jack, Jake and Jerry slicing the throats of the maimed deer that weren't quite dead.

I jumped on top of my horse and led the other three horses down into the valley of dead deer. Uncle Jack asked if I wanted to start bleeding the dead deer out, or to go with him and track down the wounded deer who had escaped. I looked at Jake and Jerry who were already covered up to their elbows in blood, and decided to help my uncle track the wounded deer. As we trotted off, I thought of dad tracking down enemy combatants. Yeah, this was my search and destroy mission. Sorry Bambi.

Uncle Jack had taught me how to find a blood trail and then how to track it properly. Even though we were going to kill the deer, he was very serious about not leaving an animal to suffer. At first I thought he was joking, but when he said, "We are all creatures under Wakan Tanka. Would you let a human suffer who was dying?" It just made sense to me!

He also said any animals that were injured really badly would always head to the forest to die. Why would we let them suffer in pain? We ended up finding four more deer; one was already dead by the time we found it, the other three were badly hurt.

Uncle Jack put a bullet in two of them. He then told me to put a bullet in the last one we found. The deer looked at me with these big brown eyes that seemed to be full of tears. I really had a hard time taking the deer's life. Killing the mountain lion was easier, a hell of a lot easier as my grandfather's life was in danger!

This deer seemed to be anything but a threat. But, as Uncle Jack said, I have to do the right thing and put the deer down. I raised my rifle and aimed at the deer's head, but that trigger on my rifle seemed to get stiff. Uncle Jack reiterated to me that I am doing the right thing and to just squeeze the trigger. I had this flashback to when dad yelled at me for not killing the Prairie Dog. It was also in severe distress. I squeezed the trigger, heard the shot go off, and the deer was no longer suffering.

That night back at the Longhouse we stayed up until at least 4 A.M. cutting up the deer. We made sure every single piece of meat could be salvaged. Nothing was wasted. The deer were cut into steaks, roasts, sausage, and cubes for stewing. It's the way it has always been with the Sioux.

I barely remember crawling into my sleeping bag, but I do remember the dream I had. It had nothing to do with deer hunting; this was called pussy hunting. I had a dream about Rhonda Ryan. We were here at the Longhouse, just her and me kissing by the fireplace. Soft gentle kissing turned to some heavy petting, with me kissing her pink nipples.

Rhonda gave me the nod and I laid out my sleeping bag. A naked Rhonda took me by the hand and I lay on top of her. We continued our kissing until I slowly and gently guided my hard cock into Rhonda. Her huge eyes seemed to look right through me. I felt myself going into her, one inch at a time. I began to ejaculate before I was in all the way. Hell, not even a single pump. Premature ejaculation at its finest!

It's kind of funny when you realize it is only a dream. You wake up and look around; fuck here I am in an open concept room with cum all over my underwear and leg. You pray that no one else was awake to see you get out of your sleeping bag soiled with go-go juice. Luckily for me, everyone else was still sleeping. Like a cat burglar and… fuck there is no washroom to sneak into.

Hell, the sun is up. How cold can the lake be?

Yeah, I will jump into the lake to hide all the goopy evidence. I walked out to the dock and put a toe in the water. Fuck! I wouldn't have to worry about wet dreams anymore. Sure as hell, I jumped in there, and it felt like my balls and probably my dick are going to fall off. Damn, that was cold!

Fuck it, just jump right in off the end of the dock. With any luck, I'll touch bottom and come right back up. Good enough! I pulled myself back up onto the dock, and then made a mad dash back inside the Longhouse. I took my underwear off outside and hung them up to dry and then headed for the fireplace.

I sat naked in front of the fireplace muttering "Holy Fuck" repeatedly. My chattering teeth soon woke everyone up including my smart ass brother Jake. "Mitchell, why are you naked in front of the fireplace. Are you expecting Santa Claus?"

"No just trying to warm up. I decided to go for a swim and realized as soon as I jumped in that the water was freezing."

"It's October, you are lucky you didn't drown. Fuck, were you into my stash? Maybe smoking a little bit too much weed, Mitch?" As much as I love and trust my brother Jake, I'm way too embarrassed to tell him the truth.

After breakfast all five of us saddled up our horses.

We headed back to grandfather's house to freeze the butchered deer meat. All of us were on a heightened alert as we rode. We knew that every animal in the forest and the surrounding badlands would be able to smell the fresh meat from miles around. Wolves, bears, and mountain lions were abundant in the area. This time there would to be no bow and arrows used, only rifles; definitely, it was shoot to kill!

We arrived at grandpa's house without incident. As we approached the front door, we noticed there was a note attached to the front door itself. My grandfather took a look at the note and said out loud, "This is not good!"

Uncle Jack asked him, "What's not good?"

"The note is from the local Sheriff. He wants me to call him as soon as I get this note."

I could tell that this note had truly shaken up my grandpa. His hands were shaking just trying to open up the door to his house. At one point, he even dropped his keys. Uncle Jack picked up the keys and proceeded to open up the door. He asked my grandfather if he should call the Sheriff.

Grandfather didn't answer him, he just stared out the window deep in thought; he wiped a tear from his eye. With one hand placed right over his heart he said, "Death has once again paid a visit to the Strongbow Clan." He then he sat down and just stared at the phone.

Once again, Uncle Jack offered to call the Sheriff and my grandfather said, "No, I am the elder Strongbow, I will call him." Watching my grandfather's index finger going around and around in circles until he found the exact number in the rotary phone was driving me crazy. Seven numbers to be dialed shouldn't take ten minutes.

I was now totally freaked out, my gut was right, my dad is dead! I knew he wouldn't miss hunt camp unless he was dead. "Jim, its Fred Strongbow. You left a message for me to call you." You could see the color leave my grandfather's face as he clinched his jaws. "I see, and when and where did this take place?"

Grandpa started to jot down some information. His hands were now shaking, trying to write down the information provided to him by the Sheriff. He hung up the phone and just looked ahead deep in thought. Uncle Jack asked if everything was all right.

I knew he was going to mention dad. I fucking knew it! My stomach flipped once again, this time even worse than the food poisoning. I could feel the blood rushing from my head. "There was a bad car accident. Patrick and Billy are dead! Rita is fighting for her life in a hospital in Billings Montana. I have to go and see her."

Uncle Jack said, "I will take you there, dad. Gather

up some clothes and we can be on the road in ten minutes."

Rita was my dad and Uncle Jack's sister. Her sons Patrick and Billy were goofs to me because I was their blue-eyed, half-Strongbow cousin. Still though, I wouldn't want to see them dead. Fuck, they were only a couple years older than me. No wonder they didn't show up.

My grandfather was in shock, Uncle Jack now took control. "Jerry I know that you and Jake have to be back to work on Tuesday, and Mitch you have to be back in school. I guess once we get to Billings, we will figure things out. Christ, did Rita even have life insurance to bury those boys of hers?"

"OK Jerry, you wanna come with us or go back home, son? Either way, I will respect your decision. I will get time off work until everything is taken care of. Mitch, you have to go back to school on Tuesday; I promised your mom. I need you and Jake to close up the Longhouse. You guys can stay here until Sunday before heading back. That is up to you. However Jake, Mitch has to be back in time for school come Tuesday. Understood?"

"Understood, sir! How about Mitch and I stay at the house until we hear how Aunt Rita is doing? There will always be more hunt camps."

Uncle Jack patted Jake on the shoulder, gave him a

nod and said, "Good man."

Jerry decided he was going with his dad and grandpa, family comes first. Within fifteen minutes they were on the road, with Uncle Jack driving grandpa's big old Cadillac.

When you are a kid you remember certain things. I remember Aunt Rita being married and then one day she wasn't. No one ever told me what happened to her husband, Uncle Larry. I asked Jake, who now had a couple belts of rye into him. At first Jake just smiled that evil smile that he normally produces, just before he gets into a fight. "He disappeared somewhere in the woods around here."

I was confused and shocked! "No one went looking for him? Dad, grandpa and Uncle Jack are trackers, they couldn't find him?"

Once again Jake had that evil grin, or should I say smirk on his face. "Mitchell, those three could track down Bigfoot if they really wanted to. They are also really good at making sure, that if someone was to go missing, they would never be found again."

I had a million thoughts and visions going through my head. I was a bit confused and yet too nervous to dig any deeper into what Jake just told me. But I was fourteen and I was curious. "Why would they want him to go missing Jake? I promise I will say nothing to nobody. I swear on dad!"

Jake took another swig of rye, put the now empty glass on the table, and poured himself another shot. He looked at the rye in his glass and said. "It seemed that Larry was slap happy with his fists on Aunt Rita and the boys. I guess she sported one too many back eyes, broken noses and knocked out teeth for it to be accidental. One day the four of them went out to the Longhouse, and only three came back. They told Aunt Rita and the Sheriff that Larry had gotten drunk and wandered off into the woods. He was never seen again."

"How do you know this, Jake?"

Jake gulped back the rye and slammed his glass on the table. "I was there! Dad and Uncle Jack told Jerry and me to stay at grandpas and make sausage. The four of them went back into the woods for one last day of hunting. Yeah, they fucking murdered him! If I was alone, I would have put a bullet in the cocksucker's head too. No one and I mean no one, ever hurts a Strongbow and gets away with it. You remember that little brother, with Rachel and Pam. You take care of them. If you can't, call me and Jerry. I will be on the next plane to skin the bastard alive."

Jake's whole demeanor changed the more rye he drank. He became nasty, real nasty! He was also really loose with secrets about his new lifestyle in Oakland with the Hell Hounds Motorcycle Club. These guys just didn't sound anything like the fun loving Harley riders. These guys sounded like really bad guys and my brother Jake seemed to fit right in with them. My cousin Jerry was the Sergeant at Arms for the club.

Jake said, "If Jerry snapped his fingers, a girl would come over and without hesitation, suck my cock. Suck it bone dry! If Jerry wanted someone beaten up, their bike stolen or house burnt down, guys in the club would do it for him. If anyone gets out of line in the club, Jerry punishes them."

I asked Jake what he does in the club. He just snickered and said that he would be one of the guys to either burn down the house or lay a beating on someone.

The soul talk with grandpa was still running through my head like a runaway freight train. As much as I tried to reroute it or even derail it, I couldn't. And seeing as how Jake was opening up to me, I thought I would run the whole soul talk by him, but in a jokey kind of way. I still wasn't sure if I should take what grandpa told me seriously.

"So I guess Billy and Patrick's soul would have made it to the Spirit World by now, unless they were eaten by wolves along the way."

Jake thought deeply what I just said to him and

snickered a little. Then he looked at me with a real serious look in his eyes. "Grandpa or the old man ever talk to you about souls, Mitchell?"

I just nodded my head.

"And what all did they tell you?"

"It was grandpa. He told me that because I'm not pure Sioux, I may not be joining you guys in the afterlife. He told me to keep my soul pure, whatever the fuck that means. I guess that also means no Easter Bunny, Tooth Fairy or Santa either in the happy hunting grounds." I snickered but Jake didn't find any humor in my last part of my statement.

"Do you want to join us in the afterlife Mitchell?"

"Does that mean you believe him?"

"Yeah, I do Mitchell. He is the real deal man, no P.T Barnum shit with him. The man is a Shaman. He is the holiest and most spiritual being on this reservation. He sees all and knows all. If anyone has a connection with the Spirit World, it is him."

"So how do I keep my soul pure, Jake? This stuff is kind of freaking me out."

"You don't worry about that. I will keep your soul pure!"

"Jake, you're thousands of miles away in Oakland, and dad's in Vietnam. Just tell me what will poison my soul. What will make it impure?"

Jake poured himself another drink which he cranked straight back, then poured himself another drink before saying "I'm kind of fucked up right now from the hooch but I will try and remember the guidelines. Be kind to your fellow man and give assistance when needed. Don't abuse your body or your mind. Do what you know is right. Be truthful and righteous. There are a few others but fucked if I can remember them. Bottom line is this, Mitch, the earth; everything comes back to respecting the earth."

Everything Jake said he went against in his own life. Well, everything except the earth part.

"So Jake, you really don't follow all the rules. You don't worry about your soul not making to the Spirit World?"

Jake started to laugh like a maniac, he was laughing so hard he was even starting to spill some of his drink on himself. "This is the way I look at it Mitchell. I am pure Sioux, nothing personal little brother about you being a half-breed, but my soul will make it there, and you know why? Fucking Crazy Horse is why. Of all the Sioux warriors and Chiefs, Crazy Horse himself would respect my lifestyle. He would want me to ride along his war party; my soul will make it. I want you to also make it in the spirit world. You killed a fucking mountain lion, Mitch. You were fearless; you saved a

Shaman from death. All the great warriors will have seen your bravery, Mitchell. Fuck, I will keep you in line, little brother. I will make sure that soul of yours stays pure. Do you know what else helps getting that soul of yours in the spirit world?"

I just shrugged my shoulders.

"Making your big brother dinner! If I am to keep your soul pure, least you can do is keep my belly full."

I just laughed and told Jake, "That's not a problem." Actually with him being so drunk he would probably burn down the house if he cooked.

I cooked us some dinner. Jake took one bite and passed out face first into his plate of food. Seeing as how I was now all by my lonesome more or less, I called mom to tell her about the tragic car accident. She said to keep her posted and to make sure Jake drives safer than normal.

Jake's talk about horny girls and my wet dream last night got me to thinking. I am only a couple states away from Rhonda Ryan. I called directory assistance for Denise Ryan in Kansas City, Kansas. The operator said there was no one by that name. I then tried it under her deceased dad's name, Sean Ryan. Nothing! Last, but not least, why not try Rhonda Ryan. Fuck me, three for three.

I was antsy and I didn't feel like hearing Jake snore.

I jumped on my horse and went for a dusk ride, with my rifle tucked into my scabbard. I also grabbed a joint from Jake's cigarette package. I sparked it up and just trotted around, watching the sun slowly set on the reservation. *This is truly nature at its finest. It's so breathtakingly beautiful here, being this close to nature. Fresh air, you can go out and get your dinner fresh, no supermarkets here, and none needed. Fish, deer, rabbit and even cattle were available. Damn, no way will I ever live in a big city. I want to live here when I get older.*

I felt my dad's presence but not because of any danger. I could see why he loved it up here, even though the poverty on the reservation is one of the worst in the nation. Fuck the death rate of natives here is at least ten years earlier than in the city. I rode around until I started getting cold, then I headed back to grandpa's place. When I arrived there Jake was now semi-conscious on the couch listening to some Art Blakey. He asked me where I'd been.

I said, "Just for a ride." His response was, "Cool." He said that Uncle Jack phoned and Rita is in a coma. She is expected to live, but it's going to be a long road back for her. Grandpa wants Patrick and Billy buried on the reservation in the Strongbow family graveyard." I still can't believe someone a couple years older than me could die so young. Fuck!

Jake and I crashed at grandpa's house that night.

First thing the next morning we jumped on the horses and headed back to the Longhouse. We wanted to spend one maybe two more nights there. We had to clean it up, but not before Jake and I went fishing to catch our dinner. Sometimes when you're in a canoe you don't need to say anything. You just dig the vibe of solitude off the water and wait for your line to be hit; then you come back to life.

We ended up catching six pickerel before heading back to shore. After filleting and breading them with cornflakes, we cooked them outside and had quite the feast. A few beers and a few joints later, and before we knew it the sun was setting. Jake and I sat outside around the fire pit and just stared at the stars. I even made a wish after seeing a few shooting stars.

I could hear the wolves howling under the full moon as I watched the fire do its own dance and tried to relax. I knew tomorrow we have to clean up the Longhouse. I would be heading back to Fort Campbell and Jake would head to Oakland.

I stayed up all night just shooting the shit with Jake. We talked about life, my mom and our dad, as well as Pam and Rachel. This was the closest that Jake and I had ever been by far. Amazing brother time! As much as I missed our dad, Jake had managed to fill the void. I was so glad I decided to come.

That morning we started to clean up the

Longhouse before crashing out in the afternoon sun. Jake said he couldn't drive eighteen hours without a couple hours sleep under his belt. Since a car accident had just cost two members of the Strongbow family their lives, it was better to be well rested. Between you and me, well, I was hung-over. I knew Jake is used to partying a hell of a lot more than I am but he had to be hurting somewhat too.

That intended couple of hours snoozing turned into almost five hours. It was just before 21:00 when we locked up grandpa's house and headed back home. Jake said he liked night driving a hell of a lot more. Less traffic meant fewer idiot drivers to piss him off.

After maybe three hours or so on road we were really making good time, but we needed gas. Jake stopped for gas in Lincoln, Nebraska, right across the street from the 50s diner that gave me food poisoning a week earlier. Trust me, if there were no witnesses around, I'd empty a full magazine clip right into the gas meter. I would have blown up the fucking place, but I knew better.

Jake told me to go inside the gas station's 24 hour coffee shop to fill up a couple thermoses full of the black juice from hell, as we needed help to stay awake through the night. Jake checked out the engine to make sure all the belts and hoses were still intact.

As I walked in there, I caught the attention of some

guys. They looked like Lumber Jacks and they eyed me the whole time. Even when I rather politely asked the waitress to fill the thermoses, I could feel their glares burning a hole in the back of my head. My ears went into overdrive hearing them tell the waitress not to serve me; that I was nothing but a wagon burner.

These guys had to be in their mid-twenties, all bigger than me, really rough looking but in decent shape. I could tell that whatever their jobs were in life, it kept them fit and trim. I could also tell they were bullies looking for an easy target to pick on. I heard a chair screech across the floor and one of them walked towards me. I knew they were looking for trouble.

The guy that walked towards me had a full fucking beard and said rather sarcastically, "Nice leather jacket. It looks like the one someone stole right out of the front seat of my truck yesterday. In fact, I think that is my jacket. You had better turn it over before I take it off you or have the law arrest you, Indian."

"The jacket is mine. It was a gift and I wasn't even in this state yesterday."

"Are you calling me a liar, Indian?"

His two other friends also got up from their chairs. They also asked if I was calling their friend a liar. The waitress told them to let me be. The one that was coming onto me told her to shut the fuck up and stay out of it. This was not her concern.

"I'm not calling you a liar. I am just telling you this isn't your jacket."

My Uncle Jack and Grandpa may have just taught me how to track and kill deer. But my Dad and Jake taught me street smarts. First thing is to never show fear, so I just stared at these fucking assholes while getting ready to fight if need be. Eye each one up and recognize who is the biggest threat. Which one will make the first move and see what items in the diner I could use against them.

I wish I had my .306 on me. I would have humbled those assholes really quick. Then again, I didn't need a .306 to humble those assholes. After all, I was the brother of Jake Strongbow, and right about then he came rushing in like Jim Brown and swinging a baseball bat like Harmon Killebrew.

Jake nailed all three with his bat with lightning speed and pin point accuracy. You could hear the thud of the bat land against their back ribs.

The one who first came at me turned to get away from my maniac brother, as he'd seen Jake in full flight.

I nailed the bastard right in the nuts and started to throw punches into his face until it was a bloody mess. Jake then whacked him from behind with the bat and knocked him out cold. All in all, I would say it took Jake maybe thirty seconds to lay out all three and render them in a whole world of hurt, with my help of course! Jake put down $10 for the gas and coffee and then we hauled ass out of there.

Dad would be so proud of his two Strongbow sons. We didn't go looking for a fight but when all was said and done, we kicked major league ass and hopefully these three fucking bullies will think twice about picking on any Sioux ever again.

Jake said we had to get into Missouri right away before the Nebraska cops found us. We took as many country side roads as we could, even driving with our lights out. Jake asked if I was all right. I said I was fine. Wow, quite the fucking rush!

Jake was so pissed and told me that in life, I'm going to run into all kinds of assholes. They want to start shit with me because I am Sioux. Even though I'm only half-Sioux, I could pass for a full blooded Sioux if it wasn't for the Kohler blue eyes. Jake, being the typical wise ass, said. "You're double fucked! Bad enough you're half-Sioux that all rednecks hate; but fuck Mitch, you're also half-German. People still haven't forgotten all the shit your family back in Germany were involved in during the war."

As we entered Missouri I asked Jake if maybe it would be safe enough for us to head to Kansas. I wanted to try and track down Rhonda Ryan.

"I really think we should just keep driving. We have

all these weapons in this vehicle. Man, those redneck cops see them, and they will shoot to kill us. That would be their damn excuse. Find out where she lives and one day I will take you there. I promise, Mitchell."

The rest of the drive was pretty uneventful, thank fuck. We pulled up to my house around 16:30. My mom and sisters were just getting home from school. Jake was bagged, and we all decided it would be best for him to stay the night before heading home the next morning. It was nice seeing the house full of so much family once again; just dad was missing. I could feel him back home with us, just like I did on the Strongbow property.

I proudly showed off the mountain lion tail as well as the lion's teeth. I chased Rachel around the house with them of course. As much as mom was happy for me, she said after hearing this story, I just gave her at least fifty more gray hairs. "Mitchell, my son, one day you will be the death of me."

She laughed but no way would I ever purposely hurt her. After hearing from Jake, who before this trip I thought despised my mom as the evil step-mom, I truly realize what a wonderful person she is. Yeah, my dad did well! See, some good things did come out of the war.

Jake decided to stay an extra night before heading

home, which is exactly what Pam and Rachel needed. I had my Strongbow bonding time with him. It was now their turn. With our dad so far away, Jake was truly the man that this house missed.

It took Jake two days to get home and he called us as soon as he arrived safely. I thanked him once again for the greatest time of my life! He was glad I went too and he said he really got to see me turn into a man during the hunt trip. Yeah, the little brat brother who would annoy the hell out of him, finally grew up.

Uncle Jack called to say that they buried Patrick and Billy in the Strongbow family graveyard. Grandpa was still really devastated by the car accident. He also said that if Aunt Rita did fully recover, she would have some serious brain damage. She might never walk again as she went clear through the driver's windshield. Aunt Rita was thrown almost fifty feet onto the asphalt. Fuck, that wasn't good!

I wrote dad a letter and told him about my hunting adventures. Told him when he came home I'd show him the lion's tail and teeth to prove I wasn't bullshitting him. Yeah, he would be proud for sure. I also wrote that grandpa told me the story about my soul and the spirit world. I told dad that I would keep my soul pure so we would all hunt together in the afterlife.

# NOVEMBER 21, 1963

It was a typical boring day at school: reading, writing, and as always, arithmetic sucked. Gym was the only class I truly liked.

I noticed when Rachel and I were walking home from school that there was a US Army Officer's car in our driveway, and another vehicle parked in front of the house. I told Rachel that dad is finally home.

We ran the final two blocks as if we had wings; I don't think our feet touched the ground. We were so excited! We approached the front door at the same time as several army officers were exiting. I recognized Colonel Babalitz, dad's commanding officer in his unit. All of them were looking really serious.

No words were spoken as they passed us. However, all four of them nodded to us, and Colonel Babalitz eyes told me things weren't quite right. He patted me on the shoulder and kept walking towards their car outside. Inside we didn't see our dad, but a chaplain was talking to mom.

She had tears rolling down her cheeks and he was trying his best to console her. Mom saw Rachel and me standing there and she asked us to have a seat at the kitchen table. Every time she tried to talk, she just choked up. Even though we didn't know why she was so upset, Rachel started to cry as well.

I was getting more confused and antsy, "Mom, what is wrong? Why are you so upset? Why was Colonel Babalitz and the other NCO's from dad's unit here?" She couldn't answer! The chaplain then said, "Children, your dad isn't coming home." I guess maybe I knew what the chaplain was saying, but my brain didn't want to process what was going on.

"Dad is coming home, he promised me! My dad never breaks a promise." Mom's tears had now stopped, although her voice was still trembling. I am sure the memory of her own father being killed in battle must still have seemed like yesterday. She lost a husband and the father to her children in this war; but old wounds from 1945 must have been reopened too. "Mitchell and Rachel, your dad was killed in battle. He died protecting us, and our country from communism."

Rachel was now crying hysterically! I went into this cold numbing daze. I felt just like I did when I was eight and found out Santa wasn't real. This time, instead of him not being real, my dad played the role of Santa. There was no one that can replace my dad.

That night my parents' friends and dad's army buddies, kept dropping by the house giving their condolences. Pam was also taking it hard; her biological mom and dad were now both gone. Eventually we tracked Jake down and told him. He was coming home as soon as he could along with Uncle Jack and Jerry.

At first, I didn't cry. I also didn't want to see any of my friends. But I would have moved the heavens and the stars to see Rhonda Ryan. I just wanted to let her know she isn't alone; my dad wasn't coming home either. The longer the night went on, the madder I was at dad for breaking his promise.

I was pissed that he wouldn't ever take me hunting again, or see my lion's tail and teeth. I just stayed out back deep in thought. I looked for the North Star and once I found it, I let dad know I was mad. He lied to me. How could he do this to us? I eventually broke down that night and cried alone in my bed. I couldn't let anybody see this side of me. I was a Sioux warrior and the man of the house now.

# NOVEMBER 22, 1963

I don't remember falling asleep that night. I guess I must have cried myself to sleep just like when I was a little baby. The next morning when I woke up, my eyes were burning and I had this horrid knot in my stomach. At first I thought it was just another Friday, the last day of school. When I opened up my blood shot eyes, that knot in my stomach punched me harder than Rocky Marciano.

I began to realize the knot was a reminder that it isn't just a normal Friday. The weekend won't be normal. Nothing in my life will ever be normal again. This is a nightmare. Dad is fucking dead! He died for this Country. That's the bullshit propaganda that mom and the army are telling us. As for me, fuck I don't know what to think. Right now, it's probably best I don't think.

Mom's brother Karl, and his wife Sandy, live in Sacramento. Uncle Jack, Jerry, and Jake live in Oakland so they were all able to get a flight together. The flight would land in Nashville, where they would rent a car, and make their way to our house. They would stay with us, even though they told my mom they wanted to stay in a motel. Mom felt it best that we kids could really use them for moral support. Mom tried putting on a brave front with that stoic German pride of hers. However, she was hurting too, just as bad as us.

During breakfast no one really had much of an appetite. Mom asked if we could all help with some house work. She needed to get the house ready for our family. Mom asked Pam if she would mind bunking with Rachel. Uncle Karl and Aunt Sandy would be using her room. Jake would be bunking with me, and Uncle Jack and Jerry would be using the spare room. We all agreed.

After the house was shipshape and ready for company, mom asked me if I could go with her to the grocery store to get some food and booze for the family. I said, "Sure I can do that." My friends were all in school and I also truly believe mom shouldn't be left alone right now. Whatever she asks for, I will do my best to be there for her. That is exactly what dad would have wanted.

We drove down Main Street towards the grocery store. All the people seemed to have stopped what they were doing. They were watching televisions in the various store windows. They seemed to be in shock, with blank looks on their faces. Hell, some were even crying. I've never saw anything like this in my life. It was like the whole town was feeling our grief.

We parked the car and went into the grocery store. The life seemed to have been sucked right out of the customers. Mom and I were confused. They were all teary eyed and moving as if they were in a drunken stupor. They all acted like we had last night. A couple of ladies who had kids that my mom had taught, asked, if we had heard. Mom answered, "About what happened to Iggy my husband?" They said, "No, the President has been shot."

My mother pushed the shopping cart and the items she grabbed aside. She told me that we have to leave. Leave right now! Mom was once again starting to tear up and her voice was now trembling. I knew not to ask why but to just do as she asked.

We drove about a block away and mom pulled over. She put the car in park, leaned into me, and broke down. This was the first time in my life that I had seen my mom, the proud and fierce German, break down. I just kept rubbing her back telling her, "It was OK, It's OK"

"They are all fucking hypocrites, Mitchell!" This was also the first time I had heard my mom swear in English. I have heard her swear in German before. I know she would smack me for swearing in any language.

"Who are hypocrites, mom?"

"None of them asked about your father, just about Kennedy. Even when I told them about what happened to Iggy. They were only concerned with Kennedy." Then mom said something in German. I believe roughly translated as, "They can all rot in hell."

That anger brought back my mom's composure and she drove to the Liquor store. We both went in and she picked up bottles of Schnapps, Rye and cases of beer. Then, as if nothing was wrong in our world, the cashier asked if we had heard the horrible news about Kennedy being shot. Mom answered back, "People die every day in this country, and for this country. What makes him so special?"

When we arrived home, Rachel and Pam were both glued to the television. Sitting on the couch together with fresh tear stains on their cheeks, they asked had we heard about Kennedy being shot and killed. "We heard he was shot, but not that he had died."

They said, "Walter Cronkite announced that President John Fitzgerald Kennedy has been declared dead and Lyndon Johnson was just sworn in as the new President." Mom took a deep breath and in all her infinite wisdom said, "Now the whole world will feel our pain! We will show the whole world we are Strongbow's, and we will show the world that life does go on.

Mom then put the beer in the fridge, took out a glass and poured it half full of Schnapps. She sat down and like the rest of the world, watched the news about Kennedy's assassination.

As morbid as this may sound, our family watching

another family and the whole nation suffering took us out of our grieving zone. We were all mesmerized! In between the phone ringing, the flowers and cards of condolences being sent to the house, fuck even the people delivering the flowers were asking for updates. What a diversion for us.

Shortly after 15:00, a group of my friends dropped by the house and asked if I was sick or just playing hooky from school. No one knew that my dad had been killed. My friends, who have dads in the military, some in the same unit, went pale after I told them what happened. They showed fear. The reality that it could be their dad next seemed to hit home. Being without a dad really sucked and they knew it.

Perhaps the Great Wakan Tanka wanted to reward one of his young Sioux warriors. Knew that I needed something to soothe my soul, and comfort me during these troubling times. Susan Harper would whisper in my ear that she would do whatever it took to help me through these sad times.

Before you knew it, the house was filled with teenagers. Rachel and Pam's friends all dropped by once the word had gotten out. There were a few of Pam's friends that I was interested in. I was more than willing to accept their generosity if they want to comfort me. Rachel's friends however were just plain annoying.

Mom's fellow teachers came next. Many of them have taught me over the years, and they also came to give their condolences for our loss. I know I should be thankful that they did, not only to mom, but also to us kids. To be perfectly honest, some of them are absolute fucking assholes. They probably enjoyed seeing me in so much pain.

Mom's advice was to shake their hand, or accept their hugs. She said, "Show the world we are Strongbow's and life will go on." That is exactly what I did, well sort of anyway. Mr. Anderson, I made sure to shake his hand as hard as I could. Mrs. Bishop, hell, I must have masturbated over her, at least a thousand times. Fuck, I just kept hugging her. There's nothing like feeling those large breasts of hers pressing against me every time she breathed. She just kind of looked at me in shock, once I let go of her hug, and my grope. I think she saw a vulnerable side of me, but the fact was that I popped a massive hard-on. I'd let her whisper in my ear how she could help ease my pain, Damn!

Our front door seemed to be like a revolving door with people giving their condolences. Personally, I appreciated all the well wishes, but it seemed that everyone was just as upset over Kennedy being shot and killed. Fact is, it seemed people were crying harder over Kennedy than my dad. The conversation was all about Kennedy and what will the country do now? Fuck Kennedy! My fucking dad, he was ten times the man that Kennedy was.

With the house so busy I was able to sneak the odd beer. Friends would ask me if I wanted to go out and smoke a joint. Well you know what they say, A friend with weed is a friend indeed.

I was just starting to catch a good glow in the garage. My hands were making their way up Susan Harpers blouse, when I saw my family from California pull up. I looked at Susan. I wanted to see if my hands could also make their way down south without being slapped, but I knew right now I needed to see Jake. I said to Susan, "My brother is here, come with me." Susan repositioned her bra to cover her breasts, straightened out her blouse and came out front to meet my family.

Uncle Karl, my mom's brother, was the first to come over. Uncle Karl was a big man, 6'4 weighing maybe close to 260 solid pounds. Blonde hair and blue eyes, yeah, he would have been the perfect Arian male if Hitler would have won the war. Uncle Karl was also a smart man, one of the top criminal defense lawyers in California. Uncle Karl reached out his bear paw of a hand, and with this almost stern look on his face, shook my hand. He said, "Sorry for your loss, I really liked your dad. He was a good man."

Aunt Sandy, his wife, was also blonde with blue eyes, maybe 5'2" and 105 pounds. She, too has brains and works for the State Legislature. Aunt Sandy hugged me, but it was like she didn't know how to hug. She was very rigid and showed almost no emotion. She too said, "Sorry for your loss," and echoed Uncle Karl's statement about my dad being a good man.

Uncle Karl asked where my mom was. "In the house," I told them. He and Aunt Sandy headed towards the house. Uncle Jack, Jerry and Jake approached me wearing just jeans, sweatshirts, leather jackets and motorcycle boots. I know Uncle Karl and Aunt Sandy are good people, but I'm more Strongbow!

Jake approached me first, hugged me and then we just rested our heads on each other. He asked how I was doing. I said, "All right, I guess." Jake looked at Susan Harper, and gave her the once up and down and he said, "Good for you." This must have made her feel uncomfortable. Susan said she had to go home and that she would call me.

Uncle Jack and then Jerry also hugged me. They asked the same question and also asked how everyone else was. I told them, "Mom is as usual keeping everyone positive. Rachel and Pam have cried enough to fill the Mississippi."

Uncle Jack then asked if we had any more

information on how my dad, his brother, died? I said that, "I heard from a couple NCOs that his chopper was shot down outside Nah Tran. Dad died of a broken neck and internal bleeding."

Just telling this made me tear up. Though they are family, I didn't want to cry in front of them. We are all Sioux Warriors. I couldn't show this weak side of me. What would they think of me? Then, much to my surprise, I saw Uncle Jack pull out a hanky to wipe away tears from his eyes. I had forgotten to look at the bigger picture; Uncle Jack had lost his one and only brother.

Jake and Jerry just smiled at me and said nothing. They just nodded which was also nice. All four of us then went into the house. Once inside, my sisters went racing over to them. Once again, they were crying and hugging them; that also teared me up again.

I looked over at the kitchen table that mom had just pulled away from. She was now headed towards us, her shoulders were pressed back, and her chin was high. Mom showed no pain or suffering as she thanked everyone for coming. Mom and Uncle Jack hugged first. They both said sorry to each other for their loss. Jake and finally Jerry were next. Mom didn't shed a tear; that damn German pride of hers once again!

Mom said, "The fridge is full of beer, help

yourselves." She then went over the sleeping arrangements. Mom kept apologizing for not having any meals ready for them. She would order pizza for all of us tonight and then tomorrow, she would get groceries. Uncle Karl said he would pay for the pizza tonight. Uncle Jack said he would go with her and get groceries.

I thought these were really nice gestures by both of them, until I saw mom's face change. She had that look on her face! A look I normally only see when I have really, and I mean really, fucked up. Mom looked at both Uncle Jack and Uncle Karl and said, "I may be a widow now, but I'm not poor, or a charity case. Iggy may be gone, but I can still manage the family finances."

Did I just hear what I thought I just heard? My mom actually lost her composure? Mom's face then went beet red, she covered her mouth and started to shake and cry. Uncle Karl went over gave her a hug, and told her to just let it out; she would feel better.

In between mom's cries, she was trying to apologize to everyone. Rachel and Pam then started to cry, followed by Aunt Sandy. Fuck, I could just picture dad right now. He would be barking out about a bunch of split tails not being able to turn off their water works. Yeah, clear as day I can hear him saying, "Call a plumber for them."

Mom finally agreed to allow Uncle Karl to buy us all pizza tonight. When dinner was finished, we all sat around and talked fondly of dad. Uncle Karl especially, who said dad made sure that after his unit was recalled from post-war Germany, he not only brought home his war bride, my mom, but also her younger brother. He even helped pay for his Law School. Just like for my mom, if anyone who gave Karl a hard time, my dad would straighten them out, even though Uncle Karl had five inches and several pounds on dad.

As Uncle Karl was talking so highly of dad, all I could do was think about the secret dad told me. He shot and killed my grandfather, mom and Uncle Karl's dad, during the war. Man that is one secret I will take to my grave! All of us stayed up late that night. For the adults the booze was flowing and so was the laughter. It was kind of nice, after twenty four hours or so of grieving.

I woke up early the next morning with Jake's snoring sounding like a Miles Davis solo. I went downstairs and heard mom and both uncles having a heated discussion at the kitchen table. I sat down on the last stair where they couldn't see me and listened in.

Both Uncle Karl and Uncle Jack had very different ideas on where dad should be buried. Uncle Jack said dad should, and wanted to, be buried with the rest of the Strongbow relatives. That was in the family graveyard, on the family land on the reservation. He then reminded Uncle Karl that my dad's first wife died giving birth to Pam; it wasn't like they were divorced.

Uncle Karl argued that wasn't fair to his sister to bury dad where his first wife was also buried. Doing so would deny her the right to share his final resting spot.

I have to say it was starting to get heated when my mom finally said, "Iggy will be buried as he always wanted, on the reservation in the Strongbow family Graveyard. Jack is right; it is his family tradition, his Sioux spiritual rite. Iggy hasn't said anything different to me. In fact, I checked his will last night. He stated that he wants to be buried there. So he will be buried there!"

I felt so bad for mom, knowing she would not be buried with dad when she passes. Uncle Jack said that he would see about her being buried on the reservation. He would have to bring it up with the Elders. Mom stopped him in his tracks. "No offense Jack, but I want a Christian burial in a Christian graveyard."

"No offense taken! I respect your rights. When is Iggy due home? Shit, that doesn't sound right, does it?"

"No, it doesn't. His body's on its way home as we speak. Colonel Babalitz has told me he will let me know once the plane carrying Iggy's body enters American airspace. There are two other deceased soldiers accompanying Iggy on his flight home. They all went down in the same helicopter. They will have a ramp ceremony on the tarmac, with a full Honor Guard. We can then view the body if we wish. I wish to view his body and I really hope one of you two will be there beside me."

Both of my uncles agreed to view my dad's body. I too wanted to see him; I hope mom would allow me. Mom then asked my uncles if they would accompany her to see Colonel Babalitz. She wanted to make him aware of the family's wishes for my dad's burial. Colonel Babalitz said he would arrange a service for all three soldiers with the base Chaplin. However it now sounded like perhaps a Chaplin might not be used for all three.

I cleared my throat before coming off the final step. Everyone said "Hi." Mom asked how I slept. I told her I slept well until Jake's snores woke me up. She then told me to have a seat and she would cook us some breakfast. I actually offered to help which shocked my mom, until I said, "We all have to pitch in now, right mom?" Well, she came over and gave me a kiss on the cheek; right answer for sure!

After breakfast mom asked Aunt Sandy if she could take Rachel and me into town. I needed a suit and Rachel could use a new dress. Pam said she was fine, as was Jake.

Mom and both uncles went to see Colonel Babalitz, while Rachel and I went into town to get some new clothes for dad's funeral.

At the suit shop the salesman asked, "Did you need a suit for a graduation or a wedding?" I said, "No, my dad's burial." As whacked as this sounds, just watching their faces change was worth me trying on different suits. They treated you differently, like you were actually special, not just some customer. The exact same thing happened with Rachel at the dress shop.

After we purchased the suit and dress, mom gave me a list of groceries to pick up. This time the grocery store wasn't such a mess of blathering idiots crying over Kennedy, even though every single newspaper in the store either had a picture of Kennedy or Oswald on it.

When we got home, we starting putting away the groceries right away before mom and my uncles arrived. Mom asked Aunt Sandy how we made out. She said, "Good." What wasn't good is that mom said the army is giving her "Red Tape," about dad not being buried in a military graveyard.

Uncle Karl picked up the phone and called his office back in Sacramento. He asked his secretary to put him through to General William Westmoreland at Fort Bragg, North Carolina. This I had to hear! After a couple minutes, Uncle Karl's secretary said she had the General on the line.

"General Westmoreland, it is Karl Kohler, how does today find you sir?"

"Sorry Bill, no today doesn't find me well at all. You see, my brother-in-law, Sergeant Major Iggy Strongbow, who served under you at one point with the 101$^{st}$ Airborne, was recently killed in Vietnam. We are having problems getting him buried on his family property in Shannon County South Dakota."

"Yes Bill that would be him. You're damn right, best deer sausage in the world! His widow is my sister Katharina. I just came from a meeting with Colonel Babalitz, and he said there is nothing more the army can do."

"Yes Iggy was a career soldier. From what we have been told, his helicopter was shot down. No one survived the crash!"

"Well we are to be informed when the plane bringing back the deceased soldiers is in American airspace."

"Very good, Bill. I will be looking forward to your

phone call. The number here is 270-555-1862. I will indeed pass along your condolences, thank-you."

Mom asked him how he ever got to meet, and know General Westmoreland, on a first name basis?

"When Bill was at WestPoint, I gave several lectures there on American Civil Rights. Bill indeed remembered Iggy and he passes along his condolences to each and every one of you."

Within ten minutes, General Westmoreland called back and talked to Uncle Karl. Uncle Karl began to write down all kinds of information and thanked the General for his help. My uncle then said he owed him one.

After he hung up the phone, we all wanted to hear what happened in the conversation. My uncle said he had some good news. General Westmoreland said "Iggy was a hero in World War Two, a hero in Korea and died a war hero in Vietnam. It would be less than honorable for this nation, not to honor his last wishes." So, once the ramp ceremony has taken place at Fort Campbell, we are all going to accompany Iggy's body on a C 117 airplane.

"The general has arranged for a flight to Ellsworth

Air force Base in South Dakota. An Honor Guard will be there to greet us. They will drive the family, along with Iggy's body, to the burial site on the Pine Ridge Reservation. All expenses incurred will be taken care of courtesy of the United States government. Does that work for you Katharina?" Mom teared up, nodded yes, then hugged Uncle Karl and thanked him.

Uncle Jack said, "This changes a few things, and now I need to use the phone." He phoned my grandfather and told him what the new plans were. Uncle Jack then asked grandpa if he could get a couple of the locals to dig the grave for my dad. Grandfather said he would take care of it.`

Now we just had to wait for the phone call from Fort Campbell to tell us that dad was over American airspace. We would then bring all our belongings to Fort Campbell and wait for the plane to arrive. The final journey would then begin to finally bring dad back home. Talk about a hurry up and wait scenario! Every time the phone rang, you stopped what you are doing and wondered if this was the call you had been waiting for. Needless to say mom told all of us to stay off the phone and stay close to home. Really close.

# NOVEMBER 24, 1963

At 01:17, the house phone rang. It was the Officer of the Day from Fort Campbell. He told us the plane carrying my dad and the other two soldiers had just refueled and left Edwards Air Force Base in California. It should be arriving at Fort Campbell at around 08:30.

The phone call woke up the whole household. No one felt like going back to sleep, at least right away. My mom, both uncles and Aunt Sandy poured themselves a drink. Jake, Pam, Jerry and I went into the backyard to smoke a joint. Poor Rachel didn't smoke pot, and in no way would mom give a thirteen year old any booze. I guess maybe she found her comfort in the stuffed animals on her bed. Then again, maybe not. The previous night she had cried herself to sleep.

Jake brought the pot we were smoking up from California. It was called California Gold. Damn good weed is what it was. Absolutely mind numbing weed, exactly what the doctor ordered, and I needed. I had to turn my brain off and dull the pain.

I did end up going back to bed, although I'm not sure if I slept or not. I remember just lying there and then my body went into a comatose state. I guess I did drift off, as I was awakened by mom at 06:30.

Mom as usual had breakfast prepared for all of us. She said we had to eat something as today is going to be a long day. We will need all our strength to get through it. Looking at Jake and Jerry at the breakfast table, I am pretty sure neither one of them went back to bed. They both looked like they had a nice little glow happening. They also had one hell of an appetite, unlike the rest of us.

At 07:40, mom phoned for two taxis to take us to the base. On the ride over no one talked. The only noise you could hear was Rachel and Pam sniffing their nose. From time to time. I could see them wipe away the odd tear. We were all dressed in our new outfits mom had bought for us. Even the taxi driver seemed to pick up on what was going on and offered no small talk at all. I guess in a small town word gets around.

When we arrived on the base the flags were drawn half staffed. We were ushered into the officer's lounge. We had to wait here for the arrival of the flight carrying dad's body. Also in the lounge were the families of the other two soldiers killed alongside dad. The families of the pilot and co-pilot of the downed chopper were also there.

We walked into the officer's lounge. I have never felt such a negative, thick and smothering vibe in the air. People were crying and asking out loud, over and over, "Why?" People pacing; yeah, there's lots of tension in the air.

The base Chaplin was walking around trying to ease everyone's pain along with Colonel Babalitz and several other officers and NONCOMS. In reality, what can they say to take away our grief, or ease our pain? Fuck all! And that is the truth.

You would think with everyone in this room losing someone that meant a lot to them, that they would be supportive of all the men who died. These men were all truly brothers-in-arms, who would die for each other.

However, when the Strongbow clan walked into the room, everyone just looked at us as if we were still barbarians. Could it be because Jake and Jerry had long hair? Is it because Rachel and I are half-breeds, with a blonde-haired, blue-eyed mother? Fuck, the correct answer would be all of the above! There wasn't to be any warm support for us; now there's a fucking surprise.

DISCRIMINATION at its finest! I have endured this all my life. When we first moved onto the base it was the same thing. In reality, for the most part still is. As for yours truly, hell I'm only fourteen. Yet I'm willing to bet you, I've had at least a hundred fistfights. Why?

Well here it is; # 1, you are a half-breed; so they either hate you being half-Sioux, or they hate you being half-German. Remember this is a military base, and World War Two ended only eighteen years ago. # 2, you are an army brat, so the local kids hate you. # 3, you live in a border town called Hopkinsville, Kentucky, about five minutes away is Clarksville, Tennessee. The rivalry is always present and ready to combust between a Kentuckian and a Tennessean; damn rednecks!

Then there was the most important reason. Your mom, who you love, is a teacher at your school. When people slam her, as far as I am concerned, they are also slamming me. I let no one slam my mom. It was part of the Strongbow way, reinforced as always by dad.

Before every fight, you just know deep down it is time to go. Right now, the mood in this room and the racist attitude towards us from the grieving families, well, it's a little hard to take. Yeah it will soon be "go time". I need to vent on someone, and that venting will come by fist and foot.

I watched Jake and Jerry make rather intense eye contact with the other families. They too must have picked up on the same hatred vibe that I did. Jerry even asked the one mourner in a suit, "What the fuck are you looking at?" The mourner looked away. He wanted no part of Jerry. I guess it is easier for him to degrade us like a woman, than to be a man, and actually do something about it.

Colonel Babalitz made his way over to us. He said that he would also fly on the same plane that will carry dad's body. They would have a hearse waiting for us at Ellsworth, along with several other vehicles to take us to my dad's burial spot. Uncle Karl and my mom thanked him.

Colonel Babalitz also reiterated his condolences for my dad's death. He said that he has served with my dad for over twenty years. He went on to say, "Your dad was the best tracker to ever wear the 101$^{st}$ insignia, and one of the greatest career soldiers I have ever served with." I have to say, that statement by the Colonel, for me anyways, helped to ease the tension I felt in the room.

He shook all our hands and looked into our eyes. For me, this was huge, as the eyes tell it all. Dad had always talked highly of him, and dad always told it like it was. I guess Babalitz was a good person as well as a good commander.

Just shortly after 09:00, a soldier came in and informed Colonel Babalitz that the plane was making its final approach. He then asked if we would please follow him. I took a deep breath and said to myself,

"Holy fuck this is real, too real." You feel like you're lost, and you need your dad to tell you, "Things will be all right." But you know those words will never come from his mouth ever again.

I walked over and started to rub Rachel's shoulder, as she was starting to cry. Everyone in my family took a partner to comfort; Uncle Karl with my mom, Jake with Pam, me with Rachel and Uncle Jack with Aunt Sandy. Jerry sat by himself. He was one of those guys who didn't need anyone to hold his hand; tough as nails, inside and out.

We were all ushered into this hangar, where a platoon of the 101$^{st}$ honor guard was all dressed in their parade uniforms. We all stood in the entrance and watched the plane come closer and closer. The plane circled as it came lower and lower to the ground, until it finally touched down on the tarmac.

I was watching the plane approach and I just knew dad was on it. However, there is still a huge part of me that still expected him to walk off that plane. Then, as he has always done, he would run over and hug us all. But not this time.

He would have tales of adventure and of course presents for all of us. I don't just mean crap gifts. These were the kind of gifts that you would never find in a Sears Roebuck catalogue. He would bring us home gifts like a war mask and spears from Rhodesia, or a necklace made up of volcanic rock from the Philippines.

Now I find myself starting to choke up as I'm rubbing Rachel's back and telling her, it's all right. But it's not going to be all right, things will never be the same in our family. Tears were now starting to puddle in my eyes. I was brought out of my sadness by the sergeant of the honor guard. He was calling his men in a loud and firm voice, "ATTENTION, by the left, march!"

Colonel Babalitz then asked all of us to follow the honor guard to the plane. Rachel was a full stream of tears and crying out loud. I wanted to take away her pain but I couldn't, because I didn't even know how to take away my own pain.

My eyes were burning and tears were rolling down my face. I had no energy. Almost in a zombie state of mind, one foot went in front of the other until we were lined up beside the plane.

The side door to the hull of the plane opened up. The honor guard stood to full attention, with their rifles pointed in an upward position. All other armed forces personnel also stood to attention. They had their hands in the salute position, as a steel ramp was now being attached to the hull door. What happened next is something that I will take with me to my grave.

I was perhaps expecting something a lot classier to

be provided by our government. These men gave their lives for their country and they were killed in a foreign land. One by one, flag draped caskets was carried from the plane by four soldiers. They went down the ramp and into an Army Field Ambulance.

At first I couldn't comprehend what exactly they were carrying; malfunctioned weapons, dead animals, meat for the base canteen. It wasn't until both caskets were placed inside the ambulance that the salutes stopped. The Honor Guard said, "About Turn" when I finally realized that inside these caskets were the remains of the deceased soldiers

Colonel Babalitz said, "The plane just has to be refueled, and then the pilots will take us to Ellsworth." He told us to head back to the officer's lounge, where someone would come and get us. He also said to mom and Uncle Karl that once we got back home, if she needs anything, to let him know. He would personally help out in any way that he can. He then shook our hands goodbye and said, "May God be with you, during these troubling times."

When we walked back into the officers' lounge there were several officers and NON-COMS present who had served with dad. They all came over and gave my mom a hug and praised my dad for not only being a great soldier and mentor to all of them, but also a wonderful person in life who would give you the shirt off his back. They said he was the perfect Sergeant Major. He would train them to a higher level of soldiering than they ever thought was possible. Iggy challenged them mentally and physically to the point of exhaustion. He would then be there with an open hand, to help them get up off the ground, when they collapsed.

It took about twenty minutes for our plane to be refueled. We then grabbed our suitcases and personal belongings to take with us. This was the first step in our personal journey, to bring back dad's body to the reservation for his burial.

As we boarded the plane, there was a black cloak draped so you couldn't see the rear area of the plane. We all knew what was back there, and also what was behind it. There was no secret. A huge part of me still wanted to go back there just to make sure it was indeed dad's lifeless body. At 10:43 A.M., the DC3 raced down the runway and within seconds the plane was airborne. Our arrival time at Ellsworth was to be around 17:00, that's a long time to be in a plane; then again dad will be dead forever.

As I looked around the plane, I wondered if this was the same plane dad took me to my first hunt camp in. A year ago, I can still remember dad being very deep in thought. He looked around the plane much as I'm doing right now. Did he know a year ago he would be taking this plane home for the final time? What was he thinking so deeply about, during that flight? Once again it started to choke me up. Fuck, I wish we had parachutes aboard so I could just jump out and leave all these heartaches in the sky. Reality is just really hard to handle right now.

We were in the air for about an hour when, the pilot came back just beaming. He told us he was just informed that Lee Harvey Oswald was shot dead. He then said, "Whoever did it should be given the Medal of Honor."

That was the final straw for Jake, who spouted off exactly what I was thinking. "My dad lying in the back of this plane deserves the Medal of Honor. As far as Kennedy goes, he sent my dad to Vietnam to die, and for what? To stop Communism? The way I see it, Oswald also deserves a medal. Kennedy was going to send many more American soldiers to Vietnam, and many of them would be coming home in black body bags too."

Yeah if looks could kill, Jake would skin him alive before throwing him out of the plane with no chute. Uncle Jack then told the pilot he should stick to what he does best, flying the fucking plane.

The total flight time was just over six hours. It was the longest six hours of my life. We couldn't land quick enough. I often caught myself wanting to go into the rear of the plane to see dad. At one point, I asked mom if I could go back there or have dad's lifeless body brought up here with us. I felt so sorry for him being alone and not part of our family. Everyone who he loved and who loved him was in the front part of the plane.

My mom truly felt my pain. Even though mom would do anything for her kids she said, "That would not be a good idea and we will be landing shortly." Jake pulled out a flask and told me to take a drink. He also backed up what mom said.

So I took that drink and looked out the window of the plane. I recognized one of the landmarks on the ground. Dad had told me about it the last time we flew to Ellsworth. I tried to play back and remember every single landmark dad said would be coming up next. Memories can never be taken away. They brought peace to my aching heart, as well as my mind.

As soon as we entered South Dakota, the rains started. Were the skies also crying for my dad? Did they know this would be the last time that he would ever travel through this state? Was this their own little salute to one of the greatest warriors and leaders ever?

Before we knew it, the co-pilot came back and asked us to put our seatbelts on. We were beginning our descent to Ellsworth. I can't describe with words, the feelings of floating downwards from the skies. As soon as the plane came to a stop, several military jeeps and a hearse pulled up to greet us.

As we walked down the stairs, lined up on both sides were Air Force personnel. They were saluting us with eyes straight ahead. I didn't recognize any of them from landing here before; but what I did recognize was my grandfather and several cousins and elders from the reservation. My grandfather, the proud Sioux Shaman, stood there with wide open arms and a tear in his eye.

We all stood beside the hearse as the six members of the Air Force carried dad's body over. I'm not sure what sent more of a chill up my spine; seeing the Stars and Stripes flag over the casket containing dad, or the cold drizzle from the sky.

Two Air Force personnel did the folding of the flag ceremony and presented it to mom. The officer in charge said that the whole nation owes heartfelt gratitude to my dad, as he gave his life for his country. My mom sobbingly accepted the flag. Then they put the casket containing my dad's lifeless body into a wooden casket inside the hearse.

With us getting in later than first expected, my

grandfather told us that my dad's body would be sent to the funeral home, where he will be embalmed tonight, and the burial will be tomorrow. The same fucking day, they are burying Kennedy. Doesn't that just figure!

Mom mentioned none of us had actually seen him and asked if it would it be possible for us to see him before the embalming process took place. Grandfather asked the men from the funeral home if that would be a problem. They answered, "No problem at all."

We split into three different vehicles with mom, Pam, Rachel and I driving with my grandfather. Uncle Jack, Jake and Jerry would be driving with my cousins, and Uncle Karl and Aunt Sandy would be driving with some of the elders.

Like a caravan of grief and misery, we followed the hearse on rain-soaked roads to the funeral home. It took us about ninety minutes in total. I went deep into myself and just looked at the scenic countryside, but you know I didn't see the scenery. I had visions of dad and I hunting and fishing.

The two guys from the funeral home said they would make my dad presentable before having us come in. We waited in this large viewing room, the smell of fresh flowers from a funeral earlier that day were still present. The smell was so clear and strong, like being in an indoor garden.

After about fifteen minutes, the funeral home Director himself came out, and told my grandfather that Iggy Strongbow was now ready to be viewed. We all stood up but mom told Rachel and I to just have a seat and she will come back and get us. I was shocked by this, as was Rachel.

The one person who wasn't shocked by this was my Aunt Sandy. She said she would stay with us until my mom came back. After everyone else went in, I came right out and asked Aunt Sandy, "Why were Rachel and I left behind?"

"Mitchell, your dad was killed in a helicopter accident. He died a traumatic death! Your mom and both uncles all agreed, they want to make sure he, he...."

"Make sure he what?"

"He may not look like your dad. We know his neck was broken and that he also bled to death. We all agreed we don't want to scar you two. You are both so young and impressionable. Perhaps it will be best for your last memory of your dad to be positive."

Rachel let go the water works once again. Me, I was pissed! "I want to see him regardless. I'm not sure what he looks like in that casket. I can't tell you the vision I already have in my head. I need closure!"

"Mitchell, have you ever seen a dead body before? Never mind the fact it is someone you love?"

"I've shot a mountain lion dead. I've killed and skinned many deer. I'm Sioux, and I need to see my dad."

"That will be up to your mom, sorry honey."

So once again I have to sit and wait. No, I can't just sit. I sat on that fucking plane for six hours, and then another two hours sitting on the drive here. I couldn't sit anymore, so I got up and paced like a caged animal, back and forth and ready for a battle. I'm not quite sure how long I paced for. It was long enough to build up some pretty impressive sweat stains under my arms.

When I saw mom and Uncle Jack come out, I stopped my pacing. I looked at mom and she nodded her head yes. I walked over to Rachel and said, "Hey sis, you wanna walk with me and we will see dad together?"

Rachel stood up, still crying, and held my hand, while resting her head on my shoulder. That knot in my stomach that I have had every morning since learning of dad's death was back full force. I felt like puking my brains out, even my legs felt awkward and heavier than normal. I was taking really quick short breaths just trying to calm myself down.

Rachel and I followed mom and Uncle Jack down this flight of stairs to the basement. The smell of death was in the air, and seemed to just hang there. We walked to the last room on the right. The room was bright, with really bright lights, but had a cold feeling to it.

All my relatives were in a circle looking down at an object on this steel table. Pam was crying and being consoled by Jake, who himself had tears rolling down his cheeks. Uncle Jack asked Rachel if she would like him to take her up. Rachel couldn't answer because she was crying so hard, but nodded yes. Mom then put her arm around my shoulder and said if I didn't want to see my dad, she understood. But I had to see him, needed to see him. Just like Rachel, I couldn't talk; we just walked with mom towards the steel table.

Every single emotion raging inside of me was halted after I made visual contact with dad. He looked peaceful just laying there. The people in the funeral home cleaned him up real nice. They had a white sheet covering up his body right to his chest. Had you not known any better, you would swear he was just sleeping. Every once in a while I swear, you could see his chest move and his nostrils breathe. That legendary Iggy Strongbow smirk was still on his face. My shoulders dropped and the knot in my stomach went away.

I found myself walking around the table. I just wanted to absorb everything about dad from every angle I could. I touched his hair, touched his cheek and squeezed his toes, he looked healthy. How could this warrior die? His body is whole and intact. I then noticed this dark ring around his neck. The makeup artist at the funeral home couldn't hide the black and blue ring. Fuck, why did I probe so hard?

Eventually one by one, members of my family left the room. There was now only Uncle Jack, Jake, Jerry and I left. Much to everyone's shock, I approached the funeral home Director and asked if he would he open my dad's eyes. I have to see them one more time! The funeral director looked at my uncle, who nodded his head yes. The funeral director walked over and peeled open dad's eyes.

If there ever was ever going to be closure for me, this would be it; I have to see my dad's eyes. They have brought me comfort and sometimes pain over the years; those eyes of his never lie. I wanted to see if they could still tell a story even in death. Did he feel his life was worth the sacrifice he made to his country? What about the cost to his family? What was his last thought in life?

I'm not sure how long I stared into dad's eyes for answers. Even in death his eyes didn't lie, they told me everything I wanted to know. I now had my closure. I have my answers. I told the funeral director, "Thank you" and told Uncle Jack, "I have my closure, and I'm now ready to leave."

Just as we arrived at the funeral home in three cars, we left the same way. We headed to my grandfather's house. Strangely enough, I had this semi-smile on my face. My body was relaxed and that knot in my stomach left.

# A WARRIOR'S FUNERAL MONDAY, NOVEMBER 25, 1963

I felt at peace waking up the next morning. Dad's eyes told me everything I needed to know. This would be the last day dad's body would ever be above the grass we now walked on.

The funeral home brought dad's body as far as my grandfather's property. Dad was then met by the Strongbow clan and fellow mourners. His body was wrapped in a Buffalo-robe then put on a sleigh and pulled by horse to the burial site. His face was painted red and he was dressed in his native battle outfit, complete with a bow and several arrows. Once we arrived at the burial site, the 'Ghost Keeper' ceremony began.

After removing a lock of his hair, Uncle Jack then erected a scaffold against a tree. This was done by fastening poles from branch to branch. Dad's body was placed on the scaffold. His friends and relatives started this loud wailing and crying. Food was now left with dad's body. When all the friends and relatives had finished their wails and cries, Uncle Jack shot the horse that pulled dad to his burial spot. The horse's spirit could now take dad's spirit to his hunting grounds in the sky. The whole ceremony was very moving; even the non-natives who had served in battle with dad were moved.

I'm sure with mom, Uncle Karl and Aunt Sandy being Christians, the whole ceremony might have seemed rather barbaric to them. The burial was done in tradition of the Sioux. Strongbow Sioux tradition, more importantly! Mom had known since day one, how important Sioux traditions were to dad and his family.

But dad also respected my mom's Christian beliefs, and part of his will and death wish was that he would also have a Christian burial the next morning. So that night Uncle Jack, Jake, Jerry and my grandpa would take turns guarding my dad's body from the animals and those spirits not of this world.

I asked if I too could also have a shift guarding my dad's body.

Everyone went silent, which means this has been talked about by the elders in my family, just like Rachel and I viewing my dad at the funeral home. I knew my grandfather supported me being there as did Uncle Jack. It was my mom and Uncle Karl who didn't think it was such a good idea.

I looked at my grandfather, who helplessly just smiled at me, and then at my mom who looked worried; you know, worried this may scar me or fuck me up royally sometime down the road.

With no side willing to talk or commit one way or another, I felt I had to say something. "Mom, whenever dad would leave us and go on maneuvers or even before he headed to Vietnam, he told me I am now the man of the house. He taught me how to hunt and fish, how to be a Sioux warrior and, most importantly, to always make sure as the man of the house to protect you, Pam and Rachel from any harm. Dad needs me now to help protect him from evil spirits and animals that will pick at his lifeless body."

A forced, awkward smile came to Mom's face as she looked at my grandfather.

"That is fair, Mitchell. I will let you stand guard but not alone. I will allow you to stand watch with your grandfather and once he has been relieved, you must come back inside and get some sleep." I smiled and gave my mom a hug and thanked her. My watch with my grandfather was from 22:00 to 01:00.

I just stared at the clock in the house and couldn't wait to go outside. Time fucking dragged for me and just as it was a couple minutes before my watch I realized that minutes, hours, days and years would mean nothing more to my dad.

Mom gave me a long hug before we went outside and said, "Your dad would be very proud of you for acting like a Sioux warrior."

It was a cold windy night. The moon was full but

the clouds were doing their best to stop the rays from giving us any light at all. Jake had built a fire for warmth; he also had a bottle of Jack Daniels in his hand. I'm not sure if that was to help with extra warmth or to dull his senses.

Grandfather watched my reaction as Jake passed me the bottle. I said I was good, and my grandfather smiled and nodded. I didn't want any of my senses dulled. I was truly there to watch over my dad and that is what he would have wanted. Subconsciously, I found that I couldn't look up at my dad. That was hard; I'm not going to bullshit you about that. Grandfather also picked up on that so he turned to me and said "Your Father is not up there."

I felt my throat close as a rush of fear and adrenaline went rushing through my body and brain. I instinctively looked up but the cloud cover was blocking the distinctive features of my dad. All I could see was a dark object.

"Your father's spirit is all around us Mitchell, can't you sense his presence?"

I closed my eyes and nothing. I opened my ears and nothing. It was not until a tear rolled down my cheek that I now truly realized how spiritual this holy land was. The clouds seemed to part just for me, the moon with all its power and glory shone a brilliant ray right through my dad's lifeless body and unto me. The warmth coming from the ray embraced me like a warm hug on a cold winter's day.

I closed my eyes and could see my dad having "The Talk" with me. You know the one; "I am not coming back, Mitchell. You are the man of the house. I have done all I can do to help mould you to be a Strongbow; to be a Sioux Warrior. Don't let me or your mom and sisters down." Surprisingly, there was nothing about Jake.

I opened my eyes and saw the clouds had once again eclipsed the moon. The chill and dampness in the air returned to me as if it had never left.

The only place I still felt warmth was in my heart.

Grandfather just smiled at me; he knew what had just taken place. For the rest of our watch my grandpa and I just talked about my future, a future my dad would want for me. I listened to every single word as I knew my grandpa made my dad the man he is and was; a proud and honorable man.

The next morning my dad's body was no longer in the trees. He was now in a casket and placed into the ground his final resting spot.

I guess no matter how much understanding you might have, for mom to be a widow at forty-three years old must be painful. I doubt mom had ever imagined that because of his traditions, her husband

and the father of her two children would be buried beside his first wife.

All of the family and mourners grabbed a handful of dirt, and tossed it on top of dad's casket. Mom made sure to stand on the opposite side of the grave to dad's first wife. She was crying, Pam and Rachel were crying, but I still felt at ease. I once again sensed dad's presence. It told me to go over and hug my sisters as well as mom.

One by one the mourners and relatives left the family graveyard. They were headed back to my grandfather's house for drinks and lunch. As they left, you could clearly see all the headstones that mapped out the deceased Strongbow clan.

Aunt Rita and her two sons, my cousins Pat and Billy, were there. My grandma and other relatives, who died long before I was born, were interred there. Dad's first wife was buried here and now my dad. I felt drained the longer I stayed in the actual graveyard itself. It wasn't so much an emotional but a physical draining, like my shoulders were carrying two hundred pounds of grief and misery.

When it was time to leave the graveyard, mom said we should go inside my grandfather's house as a family to celebrate my dad through stories told by the mourners and family. I was in there only a few minutes when I felt the walls were closing in on me.

People would talk to me but I couldn't answer, my brain wasn't there. I needed fresh, spacious air, more than being told a story about dad. I said to mom, "I have to jump on a horse and go for a ride to clear my head."

Mom said, "No, it would be rude for you to leave."

I could feel my heart start to pound, fuck, the walls moved in even closer, and I felt severely claustrophobic. For the first time since dad's death, I disobeyed mom. I said, "I am going for a ride!" My legs were now shaky and my breathing was really erratic; my eyes were trying to focus on the fresh air, and the freedom the door represented. I was feeling anxiousness with each step I took. I bumped past several people who tried to talk to me, but I wanted no part of them. I needed to be out of this morbid house, now!

As soon as I stepped outside, the fresh cool air was like a slap of reality. I could breathe; I could focus. More than ever, I really needed to go for a ride. I went into the barn, found dad's horse, threw on the saddle, straddled it and then headed west to the Longhouse.

The cool weather and the freedom on the reserve was the only prescription I needed. The spectacle of Mother Nature at her finest! I didn't need any booze or dope, much less hearing stories about dad. That ride is what I needed to feel normal once again, and to be in control.

After about thirty minutes or so of riding, I could tell I was being watched. I could feel it. In my abrupt haste to leave, I didn't pack a rifle, or even my bow and arrow; hell I didn't even have a knife; no defense at all. I knew the dangers on the reserve. Wolves, and bears abounded; and I already had firsthand experience with mountain lions. I halted my horse to have a look. I didn't see any animals and my horse didn't seem to be spooked. From the east, two riders were approaching. They were riders I knew, Jake and Jerry.

I held up and waited for them. I thought I was going to get a lecture. Instead they both asked if I was all right. I said, "Good now, I just needed to get away, get some air and clear the head." Jake and Jerry respected where I was coming from. I was curious who sent them to look for me. Jake told me mom had sent them after me to make sure I was OK.

I asked if I had to head back to grandpa's house. They said no, that my mom wants me to release whatever anger I was feeling. Maybe she thought I was afraid, or embarrassed to cry or show any emotions around the rest of family.

Jake asked where I was heading. I said "The Longhouse." Jake then looked at his watch and said it would be dark by the time I got there, that is way too late; that if I wanted, we could head there at first light. We could maybe do some fishing and head back tomorrow before it gets dark.

Jerry said, he would come along too if I didn't mind. Maybe we should also ask grandpa, Uncle Jack and Uncle Karl, if they would like to come along as well. It would be an outing, for the guys only.

I told them, "I would like that, yeah good idea." Jerry then pulled out a bag of weed and asked if I thought the weed could help me unwind. Surprisingly I said, "No." Shocked the fuck out of both of them! I said, "I just want to ride." Jerry put away the bag of weed and said, "Let's ride then."

I'm not sure how long we rode for. The sun was starting to set and my ass was getting pretty sore, so we headed back. I wasn't sure what to expect as we walked into grandpa's house. A part of me felt like a coward, bolting out on everyone. Mostly however it was not listening to mom's wishes; I should've stayed put.

So just like when I was five years old and got caught with my hand in the cookie jar, I sheepishly went inside. Mom came right over and gave me this big hug. She asked if I was all right. I said, "I am good." I also apologized for not listening to her wishes.

Mom stopped me half way through my apology

and she said, "Sorry for not respecting your feelings or wants." Well, right now I wanted some food. I was starving, and thank goodness there was enough food to feed the whole Lakota Nation.

I didn't have to tell my grandfather where I wanted to go when I stormed out. He knew exactly where I was heading. Jake then suggested what we discussed earlier, that the men head to the Longhouse at first light. Uncle Jack and grandpa were in, Uncle Karl was the only one left to commit. He said he had a busy workload at his office, and was planning on phoning the airlines tonight. He was hoping to catch a flight out of Bismarck tomorrow and head home.

Mom and Aunt Sandy both gave him that look, the one that women do all too well. The "guilt trip look" was out in fine form. Finally Uncle Karl relented and said he would phone the airlines tonight and catch a flight home on the Wednesday. We were now set: an all-male trek to the Longhouse was on.

Everyone was in until Pam and Rachel both said they too wanted to come along. Jake and Jerry both laughed, which pissed off Pam to no end. "Equal rights to women," she declared. My grandfather laughed and said, "They are Strongbow blood the same as us, they are more than welcome to come along."

Rachel now had that smug look on her face until I

said, "Good, if the bears, wolves or mountain lions come sniffing around for human flesh, they will eat a female before a male. In the animal kingdom, they don't discriminate about who's on the menu, they just chow down."

That comment changed the smug look on Rachel's face. She has heard the stories about what the wildlife is like out here. Pam said, "Pay no attention to him; you are just as good a shot as he is." Mom also echoed Pam's statement about equal rights. Uncle Karl snickered and asked if she and Aunt Sandy would also be joining them. They looked at each other and decided to stay there, and have a nice dinner ready and waiting for us upon our return.

That night we sat around my grandfather's fire pit. He told us stories about dad and Uncle Jack as youths. Man, it was nice to hear that at one point in his life, dad wasn't as tough as leather.

I caught myself also being fascinated with the North Star. I found myself having a conversation with dad in my head. Every once in a while, I swear I thought I saw dad for a split second. Whether it was the flames casting their shadows as they danced in the fire pit, I'm still not sure. Dad was close. Yeah, he was near, very near.

The next morning I didn't have to be awakened by anyone. I was up before the first light of dawn, as was my grandfather. He was grilling up some bacon and potatoes so I decided to give him a hand. My family members were surprised to see me helping out with the cooking and serving of the meal. Hell, afterwards I even helped grandpa with the dishes, something I would never do at home. I guess now I'll have to start doing a lot more things around the house. Things that I've never had to do before.

We were all on our horses by 8:00 o'clock. It was going to be about a three hour ride to the Longhouse. The fresh air and sunshine topped off a perfect ride for all the members of the Strongbow clan. Everyone was laughing and joking around with each other on the ride out. You never would have guessed in a million years, we just buried dad. I swear there's a mystical healing power on the reservation; or maybe it's the fact this is where dad grew up and lived as a child.

Dad loved the land here on the reservation, the whole Sioux history, and the pride that goes along with it. No wonder he would always return home for hunt camp. It didn't matter where he was in the world, he always returned. I don't think it was the hunting and killing of the deer, but just getting back to nature, back to his roots.

Once we got there, we all tossed our fishing lines in the water. Low and behold, Pam and Rachel caught more fish than we did and they let us know it every chance they could. We had one hell of a fish fry over an open fire, and then spent the rest of the afternoon just relaxing out in the sunshine.

Uncle Karl told us he hadn't been to hunt camp in four years, and he regretted it. He had forgotten how much he appreciated getting back to nature and the slower pace of life. He said the first thing he was going to do when he got back would be to schedule a week holidays for the first week of October next year.

Uncle Jack suggested they could all fly up together. Yeah, it was nice seeing a Kohler and the Strongbow males getting along. I also found myself closing my eyes when Uncle Jack talked; he sounded so much like dad.

We headed back to grandpas just after 4 pm. By the time we got back, the sun was down and it was getting quite cool. Mom and Aunt Sandy had a kick ass, full course meal of wild turkey all ready for us. At the dinner table that night, there was so much joy and laughter. I dreaded heading back to Fort Campbell; that is where I will really notice that dad has gone.

Just like the previous night, I stayed outside around the fire pit. I looked at the North Star and silently talked to dad. Every once in a while that North Star would just sparkle. It was almost like dad was looking down on us, watching events unfold. He would have been mighty happy, that we were all getting along. I know deep down the pain will never really leave; we will just have to learn to cope.

The next morning we all got up early, as we were all flying out of Bismarck. Flights to California were at 2 pm, ours was scheduled for 3:30. It was a hard morning indeed. The joy and happiness we had shared for the past twenty four hours, seemed to have been destroyed. We had to say goodbye to dad at the graveyard. Somehow you almost felt guilty, knowing that you had so much fun the day before. It was like his death, wasn't taken seriously; whatever healing that had taken place, was now ripped wide open.

Grandpa had just lost his oldest son, someone very special to him; yet he seemed to be more upset seeing his granddaughters cry. God, Uncle Jack is the only child of his still alive. He's buried a wife, a daughter, a couple of grandchildren and now a son. Yet he was more there for us, than we were for him. Had he dealt with death so much, he has desensitized himself?

As for the rest of us, hell, even Uncle Jack went quiet. He now had no siblings left. Jake looked angry with this scowl etched on his face. Jerry, he didn't look much better than my brother. Pam and Rachel were both a mess, and mom was silent.

I now had to be the man of the house, be the strong one for mom and my sisters. That is what dad would've demanded of me. I would make sure to honor him by doing just that; I would be strong for them.

Just like the car ride from Ellsworth to here, driving to Bismarck seemed to take forever. Everyone was quiet, deep in thought, mentally exhausted I guess.

For me personally, it was just as hard saying goodbye to my grandfather at the airport as it was saying goodbye to dad at the graveyard earlier. I guess with me only being fourteen, I will be at the mercy of others to bring me back to see him; actually to see them both I guess. I gave him a hug goodbye. He told me to be a warrior and to make my dad and the Strongbow name proud.

I told him, no make that, I promised him, "I would." Grandpa said he is only a letter or phone call away if I ever need him. I thanked him and he said he would pray to Wakan Tanka to guide us in our new journey without my dad. That hit me in the gut hard! I know dad is dead, but when someone says it out loud, it just hurts; too damn realistic.

It was also hard saying goodbye to my uncles, along with Aunt Sandy, Jerry and even Jake. Yeah Jake and Pam hugged for a longtime before their flight took off. Once again the verbal aspect of what happened is what I found hardest to deal with. I know Jake meant no harm when he said my mom has been the perfect step-mom to Pam. But Jake also said to Pam that they are now both orphans. Hell that did it; cue the waterworks from Pam. I can't say I needed to hear that either.

Jake also gave mom a long hug goodbye. He told her that if she needs anything, to let him know. He then hugged Rachel goodbye and told her that he loved her, and to listen to our mom. Jake then gave me a hug and light slap on the cheek. He said I have to step up more now than ever before and not to piss my mom off, as she has enough on her plate. He then told mom, loud enough for me to hear, that if I get out of line, he will fly up and "kick my ass."

Yeah, it was hard seeing them go down the hallway, to their flight. We had almost ninety minutes till our flight leaves. It was lonely let me tell you, really fucking lonely. There were just the four of us left now, and each one of us seemed to be deep in thought. At the same time we were so close to each other. Just like grandpa said, the pain never really leaves. You just learn to cope.

Our flight to Nashville was good. But just like the car ride, everyone was quiet. Every once in a while I saw tears rolling down my sisters' cheeks, I would just squeeze their hands and smile. Sometimes actions are better than words.

# CALIFORNIA DREAMING DECEMBER 28, 1963

Well, in 1966, the Mama's and Papa's had a # 1 hit with this song *California Dreamin'*. The tune talked about a dream of being warm and safe on a winter's day in California. It was a rather cool December 28. Mom had just accepted a job as a full time teacher in San Francisco. Uncle Karl was good friends with a Mr. Bill Bain. He happened to be the president of the school board for San Francisco.

Mom agreed to the move for a couple of reasons. It was only an hour outside Sacramento, where my aunt and uncle lived. The other factor was that Jake, Uncle Jack and my cousin Jerry lived in Oakland; which was only one bridge away.

Pam was going to be enrolled in University of San Francisco. Rachel and I would have a new start in life after the death of our father; everything in Fort Campbell reminded me of dad.

Just like when Rhonda's dad died, the military gave mom ninety days to vacate our on-base residence. So off we drove, all 1916 miles from Fort Campbell Kentucky to San Francisco. Just like the song, the sky was gray and I went for a walk that winter day. One last time around the base, and then over to the place where Rhonda had once lived. I went to the exact spot where I kissed her for the first time. Too bad I never did get a chance to tell her I was moving away. All the letters I wrote to her were never returned.

I wasn't so much California Dreamin, as dreaming of Shannon County, South Dakota. That's where dad was buried. I thought about all that he taught me on my first and last hunting trip. I wondered if dad knew he was going to die during what would be his final tour.

Thinking back, it now seemed he unloaded so much of life's weight onto me. He told me all about how he had killed my grandfather during World War Two. He made sure I was a full-blooded Sioux warrior, and knew how to communicate with his spirit through the North Star. I now talk to him every night. I know the first thing I'm doing once we spend the night in our new house. It will be to look for the North Star, and let dad know where we are now.

We did pass along many churches along the way, but no one felt like going inside to pray. We finally crossed the Golden Gate Bridge on December 31. It was New Year's Eve. This would be a new beginning for the Strongbow family. I hoped our new future would be as mighty, and sturdy as the bridge itself.

Mom went out to San Francisco a month earlier to go house hunting. Like us, she was sick of moving from base to base. The thought of the family being moved to another county didn't sit well with her. After dad's death, mom really wanted to establish some roots and stability. With dad's G.I insurance money she bought a four bedroom house. We would actually have our own bedroom. Living on the base, it was something we didn't ever have before. We would own it. No one could ever kick us out, or force us to move again. Rachel and I both had our bedrooms upstairs, while mom and Pam had their bedrooms on the main floor.

Mom would be teaching at a different school from the one Rachel and I were to attend.

Her new high school was for the snotty, rich kids. Rachel and I were going to our first school that didn't comprise mostly army brats. At those other schools, us army brats always stuck together and would always end up fighting the local kids. I had no allies here, the fights might become more often and uneven. I was now a warrior and dad had prepared me for this challenge.

Uncle Karl invited us to his house for a New Year's Eve party, but we were all pretty tired from the drive. Mom just ordered some Chinese food and we all stayed up for the midnight countdown to usher in the New Year. We hoped all our bad luck was left in 1963, and that 1964 would bring new found luck in our new found home.

Over the next week, as I waited for school to start back, I would drive my bicycle around the neighborhood just checking out all the sights and sounds. I did get a few smiles from some girls and frowns from some guys. I knew once I was enrolled in my new school, I would have to prove myself once again. I would fight who ever came on to me. There was no choice, you fought or you would be pushed around, and be the "Whipping Boy" for all. I'm a Sioux warrior and I could never let that happen. Anyone decides to pick on Rachel; I will come to her rescue. Dad would expect it from me.

Across the street from us lived this girl named Mary Lee Wilkinson. Her mom was also a teacher at mom's new school. Uncle Karl introduced the two women to each other. Mom forced Rachel and I to come over and meet Mary Lee. She was a cute girl and in eighth grade at my new school. She and Rachel seemed to get along, which meant Mary Lee was also a book worm.

Eventually, Mary Lee took Rachel and me to her friend's house. There were about ten people our age there. They were all book worms and squares, but this one girl did more than catch my eye. Her name was Kerry Dubrowski and she had these huge freaking boobs for a girl in grade eight.

She wore her pants real tight and I'm not sure what turned me on more, the large "D" cup breasts or her "camel toe." I could tell right off that she also liked me. I did the whole smile/flirt routine. I overheard Mary Lee tell Rachel that Kerry was a big slut and her bother Larry was a real bad guy. I continued flirting with my smile and eyes. Slut was all I needed to hear. It was time to move in to see if I could get a peek at those "D" cups or her crotch bulge.

Later on, a record player was brought out and people started dancing. Naturally I asked Kerry if she would care to dance. First real test for a California Girl and Kerry didn't disappoint me. We danced real slowly. Each time she took a breath, I could feel her chest expand, and those breasts get bigger. Hell, I wanted to just bite her breasts. Of course, I had a massive hard on the whole time. Eventually Kerry accidentally on purposely rubbed her hand over my hard on.

She just looked at me to check out my facial expression. When I did a big smile, she gave me a big smile back. We soon found a corner to start necking in. I went to play with her breasts, but she said, "Not here. In time, big guy." So, was she calling me "Big Boy" because of my hard on? Maybe it was because I was taller than anyone else at this get-together.

Rachel was the complete opposite of me. She

wasn't into boys just yet, at least not around me anyways. Rachel would only dance to fast songs. I made sure that any boy that asked her to dance was given the "I will fuck you up" look. I let them know that if they should try to do with Rachel what I was planning to do with Kerry Dubrowski, there would be trouble.

Around 9 pm, Mary Lee said she had to go home. I didn't want to leave. Damn, Kerry and I were having too much of a good time. I wanted to find another place to continue making out, somewhere a little more private. I wanted to play with those breasts!

Rachel then told me, "We should also be going home; mom will worry." Damn, I hate squares. I asked Kerry where she lived and if I could come by tomorrow and see her. She told me it would be better for her to come and see me. I gave her my address and home phone number. As I gave her a final kiss goodbye, she slipped my hand up her top. Damn she was hot!

Needless to say, as soon as we got home Rachel went straight for mom. She told her I have a new girlfriend and I spent the whole night making out with her. It was gross and embarrassing! Later on that night, Kerry was also the first girl I masturbated about in the State of California. I really liked having my own bedroom, I actually had privacy. I just had to remember to throw out the crusty Kleenex the next day.

Mom knew to keep Rachel and me as busy as possible; especially to keep me out of trouble. She asked some of the neighbors where there was a good Karate studio. They suggested Adams Dojo.

I was already a blue belt and Rachel had an orange belt. As luck would have it, the Sensei taught the same style Rachel and I were trained in. I was anxious to start my training in the Wado Ryu style once again. I knew dad wanted me to get my black belt, like Jake had already done. With me starting a new school, I knew the fights would come often and I wanted to be ready.

Mom and the Sensei seemed to be hitting it off well as she signed us up. Once he saw our last name he asked if we were related to Enapay Strongbow. Mom covered her mouth, teared up a bit and asked, "How do you know this name?"

"I served with "Iggy" Strongbow in Korea with the 8th Ranger Devil's Brigade. He's a great soldier and a great man!" Charlie was smart and he could tell that something wasn't right. Mom being this upset, and both Rachel and I looking extremely pale, his instincts kicked in. He knew something had happened. "Iggy's not OK, is he?"

Mom composed herself and told him that Iggy was

killed in November in Vietnam. Charlie made sure he looked at all three of us in the eye. "Iggy was a great soldier and an even better human being. It was a pleasure and honor to serve with him. If I remember correctly, you were just born Mitch when I served with your dad in Korea. I also remember him telling me about his daughter, little Rachel. Your dad was very proud and talked about you two all the time. He would take your baby pictures out before battle, and tell you how much he loved you. Iggy also had other children, correct?"

He then told mom, "Mrs. Strongbow, I can't take money for your children joining my studio." Mom insisted on paying for us to join, she wasn't asking for charity. "Fine then, I will charge you one dollar a month for Mitch, and one dollar for Rachel. It would be an honor to train them in your husband's memory. Mitch, can you fight like your dad?"

"I'm a full-blooded Sioux warrior just like my dad."

Charlie told us classes were every Tuesday and Thursday night and that Saturday is full-contact fighting. I could attend with my mom's permission, once I had proven myself.

Now that is what I wanted. Much as I liked and understood the whole concept behind kata's, nothing was better than putting on your fighting gear; it was great to just fight. I wanted to see if I was stronger, faster and more conditioned than my opponent. Mom thanked Charlie for his kind words and said he would see us all on Tuesday.

Jake also would drop by every day to see how we were doing. He helped out mom with any repairs that needed to be done around the house. Since dad's death, Jake has really stepped up to the plate. Actually everyone's been really great helping us out, on both sides of my family. It made you appreciate your family even more.

What I could also really appreciate right now was Kerry Dubrowski and her "D" cups. I'm not sure why she hasn't called or dropped by. Oh well, I'm sure I will see her at school tomorrow.

Mom had a sit down pow-wow chat with Rachel and me the night before we went to our new school for the first time. I'm still not sure why Rachel was there because I knew the whole conversation was orientated towards me.

"Children, tomorrow's a fresh start at your new school. Your dad would want you both to make him proud by studying hard, paying attention in class and getting excellent grades. Mitchell, I know you're a Sioux warrior like your dad. Try to honor your dad by getting good grades, not spending time in the principal's office for fighting every person who challenges you. You have nothing to prove by fighting. Prove to them you are smarter than they are. This is not a base school where I can always come and bail you out. You're becoming a young man now, Mitchell. Make us proud."

I knew better then to argue with mom, at least not right now. She had enough on her plate, with her starting a new job tomorrow. Mom's school was in the posh part of San Francisco called Nob Hill. All the kids I met called it "Snob Hill."

We lived on Central Sunset and most of the people at least seemed to be down to earth. Although only living on military bases all my life, down to earth here might be anything but that for me. Hell, do I even know what exactly that means? Maybe I'm just so used to hearing that saying. I will have to find out what it means for myself.

# MONDAY, JANUARY 6, 1964

Mom dropped us off at our new school on the way to her new school in Snob Hill. I didn't have the greatest night's sleep the night before. I promised mom I would make an honest effort. I would try not to fight or do anything else that would get me expelled from my new school.

When I did finally fall asleep, my dreams were very restless. The kids were taking their turns beating me up; while mom patted me on the head and saying, "What a good boy you're being." Dad was there dressed in his Sioux tribal outfit asking me, "What type of warrior are you?" Needless to say, I didn't eat very much at breakfast. Rachel was all set for her new school, but that was her, not me.

My new principal, Mr. Diloreto, had me pay him a visit before I started my new classes. He sat in his chair rolling a pen in his hands. He said that he read my transcripts from my last school and that 'Hooliganism' would not be tolerated at his school. He ran a quiet school, where problems were solved through communication, not fist fighting.

I guess he must have read about how many fights I was involved in back at Fort Campbell. Fuck if only he knew, maybe ¼ of my fights were never reported. Diloreto then said, as much as he doesn't like to give the 'Strap,' he must sometimes use this method to keep hooligans in line. I commented, "Mr. Diloreto, we can't solve all our problems in life through communications." Let's just say that statement did not go over well.

"I'm watching you, Mr. Strongbow. You already have a bad reputation from your last grade school. Don't think for a second that I won't fail you, and have you repeat grade eight. If that's what it takes to deter you, I will do it. I have weeded out your kind before, either by the strap or expulsion. You will see that I run this school my way, not your way. One would think with your mother being a school teacher herself, discipline wouldn't be an issue with one of her children. However, lack of regard for school rules appears to be with you. Your father was a career military man, so where does this lack of discipline come from, Mr. Strongbow?"

So, do I just knock out this loudmouth wop right now and face the wrath of my mom; or do I sit here and take his bullshit? "Dad died standing up for what he believed in. Like my dad, I also stand up for what I believe in. Sometimes, you have to spill a little blood for your beliefs."

This made Diloreto slam the pen down on his desk and jump out of his chair. "I see we have a trouble maker on our hands. I won't tolerate any insubordination, Strongbow. You have only five months of schooling left before you leave for high school. Consider yourself on notice! You cause any trouble and you will be expelled. There's a juvenile hall for delinquents. You can finish your schooling there. Make no mistake Strongbow, I'm watching you."

It took everything in me not to laugh at this man. He was a short, fat and bald wop. The only thing about him that scared me was this vein in the middle of his forehead. Man, if that ever burst, he would flood out the whole school. It was neat watching the vein pulsate though.

I left the principal's office and noticed there was this kid Norm Sinker, outside sitting in a chair. He was waiting for his turn to be called in. He gave me the thumbs up and smiled. I guess he heard the whole conversation. Norm looked like a trouble maker. I'm sure he's a regular at the principal's office. My kind of person! He was a big kid, much like I was.

What are the odds that the vice-principal of my school is also my teacher? Mr. Tolich was his name. He eyed me up and down as I walked into my new class. Mr. Tolich introduced me to the class. I already knew one classmate, Kerry Dubrowski. She just smiled at me with the same lustful eyes from the other day.

The so-called tough guys all sat at the back of the class, and that is where I was headed, right beside Kerry. This one kid shot me a big time dirty look when I said, "Hi" to Kerry. Maybe her boyfriend, I'm not sure and I don't care. Fifteen minutes later, Norm Sinker made his way back to his desk. He was rubbing his palms which were beet red. Fuck, I guess Diloreto gave him the strap. Hell, at least Sinker seemed friendly.

At recess I went out and purposely looked for Rachel to see if she was all right. I couldn't tell her about my run in with Diloreto. Sure as hell, she would rat me out to our mom.

Kerry Dubrowski then made her way over to me and whispered in my ears, "Want to continue what we started the other day?" I just nodded my head yes. Several males approached us. The guy who shot me the dirty look in class told me to stay away from Kerry. I asked him if he was her boyfriend. He responded, "No, she is my sister."

Kerry put her arm around my waist. Man, she was pissing her brother off, big time. But if she was willing to put out all the way, I was willing to fight anyone who interfered with me losing my virginity.

I responded "Fuck you, tough guy! Wanna go?" Kerry's brother then said, "After school, we will fight off school property." I responded, "Why wait, let's just go now." I thought I saw some fear in Larry Dubrowski's eyes. He told me, "After school, at the baseball field just down the street." I smiled and said, "Looking forward to kicking your ass."

I know from experience, when you're the new guy and you are challenged, you have to knock the living shit out of them. Send a statement to the rest of the damn school you're not someone to fuck with. Many have tried and many have failed. It's just the way it is.

My only fear was that if I hurt him too bad, I would kill my chances of getting into Kerry's pants.

Kerry and I then walked hand and hand to seek out Rachel. Once we found her, Rachel wasn't amused. "Gee Mitchell, it didn't take you long to find a girlfriend, did it?"

"Do not be jealous my homely sister. Are there no blind boys that find you attractive? That is the norm for you, is it not Rachel?"

"Mom said you have to walk me home after school. Me, not her, Mitchell."

"I have to take care of something first after school."

Rachel could tell by the smile on my face that I was going to fight someone. "Mitchell, you promised mom you wouldn't fight at school."

"Relax little sister I am still keeping my word. I am

fighting him, but not at school, just down the street."

"Mom will not be happy."

"Mom doesn't need to know about this. Does she, Rachel?"

Rachel, the schemer, then smiled and said, "What's in it for me? I'm thinking McDonalds every day this week after school, Mitchell."

"I will buy for today and tomorrow. Mom is not to know anything, right Rachel?" Rachel shook my hand and said, "Deal."

The final school bell rings at 3:30 pm; that to me was also signaling the fight bell. I already figured out Larry Dubrowski is right handed and I have my game plan all set. I will fake a left jab and he will try to protect his head. I will then give him a solid right to the stomach. When he is doubled over, I will come up with a knee to his head. This move works on a regular basis.

On the way over to the baseball field, you could feel the buzz from the students. I can hear them now, "Yeah, let's see what the new guy is all about." The only people walking with me and in my corner are Kerry and Rachel. Damn, it would be nice to have someone guard my back, oh well.

Larry Dubrowski and I are now eyeing each other up, as the crowd's keeping us at least ten feet away from each other. They are now starting to chant "FIGHT, FIGHT, FIGHT." Dubrowski has his crew with him, including Norm Sinker, who I was hoping would have my back. Trying to pump up Larry was Blais MacDonald with his crazy looking hair and Kurt Wilson. Should they want some of me after I knock out Larry, I'm more than willing to oblige. I don't get the hatred vibe from Norm Sinker though.

The crowd is now getting even louder and you can feel the energy. They are hoping blood will be spilled! Larry and I walk closer: eyeing each other up and down. The chanting from the crowd "FIGHT, FIGHT, FIGHT" suddenly stops. Fuck, are the teachers here to break us up? As Larry and I look around perplexed, part of the crowd parts and six Italian looking kids pull up on their bicycles.

The first kid that gets off his bike is huge. I would say he has at least two inches and maybe thirty pounds on me. Hell, this kid already had a freaking full moustache. I could tell by the way that Larry, Norm and Kurt acted; these six weren't fans of theirs. The big "wop" now was circling me and eyeing me up and down.

The rest of his crew was now all off their bikes. Most of the kids that came to see fight had backed right off. The fight circle was now getting bigger. I guess they knew shit was about to hit the fan. The big wop asked Kerry if she was going over to his place later on. She could take care of him in her own special little way.

Larry looked at the wop and told him, "Luch why don't you and your greasy wop fag friends go fuck yourselves."

Luch wasn't amused. He then walked over to Rachel "Hey Pocahontas, how about I poke you?"

I looked at Norm, Blais, Larry and Kurt for backup. I knew they hated the Wops more than me at this point. I sensed they would have my back; sometimes you have to go with your gut instinct. Luch pulled on the back of Rachel's pony tail and did a mock Indian call.

By the time Luch had his hand touching his mouth for the second mock call, I got in one of the hardest overhand rights I have ever thrown. "No one touches my sister, no one!" You could hear Luch's jaw break. As he was on his way to the ground, I followed up with a left uppercut. The blood from his nose sprayed everyone, within ten feet of the action.

The rest of the wop pack now charged towards me, but they were met by Norm, Blais, Larry and Kurt. Let me tell you, those boys could throw punches. Everybody was paired up fighting; so that left one wop for me.

He was such a dumb ass. He tried to intimidate me by doing some sort of Karate moves. I just looked at him, smiled then did a double snap kick. The first part of the kick nailed him right on the inside of his knee. The second part of the kick landed right on the bridge of his nose breaking it. He fell to the ground, right beside Luch. However, unlike Luch he wasn't knocked out cold. He was dazed, confused and bleeding mighty fine though.

Seeing as how my 'crew' was paired up, and starting to lay beatings on the rest of the wops, it was time for me to send a statement for all to see. But this really cute Asian chick is smiling at me, with this unusual look on her face. I can tell she is really enjoying all the madness.

I started to kick out the spokes of all the wop's bikes. I picked up Luch's bike and slammed it on top of him. I was clearly in the 'Psycho Zone.' The only reason I didn't drive the kickstand into Luch's head was the sound of a police siren heading our way. I grabbed Rachel by the hand and Norm told me to run with him.

Run with him we did, jumping backyard to backyard until we ended up at Larry Dubrowski's parents' house. I have never seen my sister Rachel so scared. It actually made me laugh. She was crying saying the police was going to throw us all in jail. I did eventually calm Rachel down.

Within fifteen minutes, Blais and Kurt joined us in the basement. Norm rolled up a joint and asked if I smoked weed. "Absolutely" was my answer. It was my first toke circle in California. Kerry, Larry, Blais, Norm, Kurt and myself; Rachel passed of course and went out back to sit, as the smell bothered her. It was good weed, good buzz, things were good all round. I asked, "What was with the wops?"

"They are from St Martin's and they're our rival school. Normally we seem to hook up and fight at least once every three months or so." No one had ever laid a beating on Luch their leader before. We spent the next couple of hours getting to know each other. This was much to Rachel's chagrin as she had homework to do.

I knew deep down how badly I had beaten Luch. I also knew the cops might be waiting for me at home and I was in no hurry to go there. I didn't want Rachel to walk home alone, so I told her to call mom to pick her up. Rachel passed me the phone and I knew I was in trouble.

The cops were already at my house. I told the guys. "I better go home." I'm pretty sure they don't want the cops crashing the little post-fight weed party. They all wished me luck, and I knew that I was accepted; but at what cost? I guess the cops will inform me of the price. Hell, Larry even let me kiss Kerry goodbye. Of course, Rachel did the gag choke bit. Anyways, Rachel and I proceeded to walk home.

Along the way, Rachel thanked me for protecting her and gave me a huge hug. Whatever trouble I was in, was well worth it. I was the man of the family now. I know deep down dad would have been proud of my actions protecting my sister. Mom, however, would be a different story.

As Rachel and I rounded the final block home, I noticed a marked and an unmarked police car in front of our house. I always remember mom saying to me, "You reap the harvest that you sow" Now it clicked in, what that saying really meant the harvest I had planted though was my knuckles upside Luch and his wop friend's head.

Mom was rather stoned faced as we walked into the house and ordered Rachel up to her room. Two detectives and two uniform cops are waiting for me. The detectives asked me, "Do I know why we are here?" I told them, "I have a pretty good idea."

They told me, to sit down and to tell my side of the events. Despite the good case I presented to the cops, they told me the bottom line is this. "Two boys are in the hospital. One has a broken jaw and needs surgery, the other has a broken nose." They went on to say, "Plain and simple it was assault, no doubts about it; a rather serious assault at that!"

That is when I hear Rachel march down the stairs. She was in a rather pissed off mood! Rachel started to spout off, "An assault is any, unwanted touching, regardless of the nature or injury involved. That one boy assaulted me, and my brother came to my rescue. Has the other boy been charged? I want him charged right now, if he hasn't."

Bravo little sister! Where the hell did she learn this from? Wow, what a combination, my brawn and her brains. Mom now looked at the lead detective. She also asked, "Is the other boy being charged as well?"

The two detectives were caught off guard to say the least. "Right now, your son is the only person going to be charged tonight. Tomorrow, we will meet with the District Attorney, and see if more charges are warranted. You have to understand, those two boys are in a serious world of pain. Your daughter seems to be fine. Put yourself in the other parent's shoes."

Mom now snapped at the cops, "My son may have a mean streak, and sometimes he has difficulty controlling his temper. However, he doesn't pick on, or try and intimidate females. He was not raised that way! Had the other parents raised their boys properly, perhaps they wouldn't be in the hospital. Would they now?"

The detectives assured mom they would talk to the

District Attorney in the morning. They also gave her their business cards, as well as the District Attorney's phone number. The detectives asked me to stand up. They put me against the wall, patted me down, and then handcuffed me. They proceeded to take me down to the police station to be processed and formally charged. Rachel was starting to cry, and mom just hugged her. She gave me the "You reap the harvest you sow look."

Photographed, finger printed, I then gave my statement. The cops wanted my whole life story, and for the most part, it wasn't as bad as I thought it would be. I was then taken down to my cell for the night where I would stay until the bail hearing in the morning. The cop escorting me was an old fat Italian, named Pasquale Ricci.

Ricci loved to play bad cop and had a serious dislike towards me. He had found out who I beat up; turns out it was a cousin, twice removed. Man, he laid a good beating on me. Bastard didn't even give me a chance to fight back. He kept my cuffs on the whole time. I will remember him, and his day will come.

The next morning, I appeared before the judge and was released to mom's custody. Jake, true to form, had the Hell Hound club lawyer, Cole Winters present at my bail hearing. Once I was released, Cole asked to meet with the District Attorney right away. He wasn't impressed with the new bruises on my face and body.

Cole read the police report and said it appeared I was just coming to the defense of my sister, who was being assaulted herself. I had used as much force as I felt was necessary to halt the assault. The District Attorney agreed to meet with my lawyer in a week's time.

Mom said she wasn't sure if she could afford a lawyer. Cole told her not to worry, as Jake would be picking up the tab. Cole then told me to stay out of trouble.

I had a curfew imposed on me as part of my bail conditions. I had to go straight to and from school. Cole would drop by tomorrow when I'm home from school. We would talk about the charges, and figure the best legal defense for my situation.

Mom and I thanked him, then it was time for school. Even though I had missed almost all the morning, mom still insisted I go back to school. With her just bailing me out, I figure school's not so bad. Mom parked the car and followed me into school. I told her I was fine and she could go to her high school teaching job now. Mom now grabbed me by the arm, "Mitchell the principal will not let you back in the school until he has met with BOTH of us."

I haven't seen mom that pissed ever. I knew not to make matters worse, so I said nothing. Dad may have been the warrior in the house, but mom would have scared a thousand Sioux warriors. With those ice-blue eyes and that death stare of hers, it was a lethal combination. On the way to principal Diloreto's office, I told mom, "Be prepared, he doesn't like me." Always plant that seed when possible!

Mom and I sat outside the principal's office. She didn't say a word, she just looked straight ahead. I tried to strike up a conversation, but was met with silence. I realized after a while, it was best not to say anything. I tried the old sympathy trip, but I should have known better.

I was touching the bruises on my face, more specifically my nose, and making the "ouch" sound. Mom then opened up her purse and handed me a handkerchief. She said in this very cold German accent, "Cry Baby, your diaper need changing next?" Man, she was cold when she wanted to be! I never thought I'd be happy to see the inside of a principal's office.

Diloreto was just a dickhead, pure and simple. When Diloreto came out he just eyed me up and down as if I had shot JFK. He shot the same look at mom. She extended her hand for Diloreto to shake, but he just ignored her peaceful gesture and summoned us both inside his office.

Mom just looked at me and I could tell Diloreto

was really winning her over. As we both sat down, Diloreto was reading a report of some sort. He then lowered the report and took his glasses off. "Mrs. Strongbow we have a very serious problem with your son, Mitchell. I can't allow his kind to be near my diligent, hard working students. His kind is a menace! School supervisor Skinner and I feel the normal public school system isn't for your son or his type."

Mom now slammed her fist on Diloreto s' desk, "And just what is my son's type?" Diloreto now cleared his throat and straightened his tie, "Your son is a hoodlum, a juvenile delinquent! He seems to intent on solving his problems with his fists. I can't have my other students exposed to him and his violent ways. As a fellow educator, you must appreciate my dilemma. I must do what is best for my school and my students."

"Principal Diloreto, first and foremost, have you already convicted my son of his charges? The last time I checked the American Constitution, you are innocent until proven guilty. I assume that was the police report you were reading when we entered your office. You will notice that Mitchell was coming to the defense of his sister. I don't suppose Mitchell's being punished because he just happened to beat up two of your fellow Italian thugs? Because if he is [Mom slams down Cole Winters's business card], I'm sure our lawyer would like to hear all about it." Way to go mom!

Diloreto now stood up and his face was a nice color purple, "How dare you suggest that I'm biased, Mrs. Strongbow? Supervisor Skinner and I both feel that Mitchell is not to be allowed back into my school until all legal matters have been settled."

Mom looked at Diloreto. She was actually very calm and had this smile on her face "May I borrow your phone, please?" Diloreto then asked who she was going to call. Mom replied "School board President Bill Bain. We talked for great lengths last night. He instructed me that if Mitchell wasn't allowed back into school, I was to call him right away."

Diloreto's purple face quickly was drained of all color

Without asking for the phone again, she reached across the desk and dialed a number.

Diloreto s' composure changed visibly, especially when it became clear that the phone number went directly to Mr. Bains' personal phone. Mom spoke only spoke three words "They're expelling Mitchell"

She listened and after a short pause, she handed Diloreto the phone.

I loved it, hearing Diloreto stammer and stutter. It was a moment I will never forget. Eventually Diloreto's shoulders started to slump; he was being reprimanded by Mr. Bain. Mom looked over towards me and gave me a wink and a smile. Things were good between us once again.

Diloreto hung up the phone. I know it was killing him to say what he did next, "Mitchell, after much consideration, it has been decided to let you back into school. This is your last chance. Any outbreaks of violence or breaking any of the school rules again and you will be suspended! This is your last chance, young man!"

With that we all got up. Diloreto went to shake mom's hand and she snubbed him, just he had snubbed her earlier. I walked mom out to her car, with a huge grin on my face.

"Mom you were so cool in there. Thank you very much! How did you know that Diloreto didn't want me back in school?"

"Mitchell, being the wife of a Special Forces soldier, your father taught me to always be ready for battle. Expect the unexpected and be ready to adapt to all situations. A little homework on Diloreto did help. Mitchell, I can't always be here for you. You keep saying you're the man of the house now, with your father gone. I really need you to act like a man. Make your father and me proud. Please, no more getting into trouble! I had to call in favors just to keep you in school."

I nodded yes, gave my mom a hug and told her I loved her and thanks. Mom also said she loved me and told me straight home after school; straight home.

I watched mom drive away, before heading back into school. I saw another side of mom today that I've never seen before. She was a cool mom who went the distance for me. I'm really going to try and not let her down.

As I re-entered the school it was now lunch time, so I headed for the cafeteria. I could feel the buzz of all the students, looking at me and whispering to each other. I felt energy coming from them. I was the great warrior! After the beatings inflicted on my enemies yesterday, any doubts of my fighting capabilities had been silenced. They knew I was a force to be reckoned with and not to mess with me. I loved the power that came with being a warrior. It was a very addictive high, knowing that I could put fear into others. Very addictive indeed!

I scoured the cafeteria to see where Rachel was. Larry Dubrowski stood up and yelled at me to come join him and his crew at their table. I spotted where Rachel was and gave her a wave. I then sat down with Larry's crew. Larry, Blais, Kurt and Norm all shook my hand before I sat down. I was clearly their new best friend. Larry didn't even flinch when I sat beside his sister Kerry, after she gave me this big hug.

I talked about yesterday's events with the boys. Kerry had her hand under the table, rubbing my crotch the whole time. She wasn't the only female giving me positive attention. That cute Asian chick at the fight yesterday sat two tables away. She was now looking at me with this serious, yet very seductive look.

I have such hatred towards Asians, as they killed my father. I don't care if they are Japs, Chinks, Korean's or Vietnamese. They are all slant-eyed gooks to me. Damn, she was freaking cute though and kind of innocent looking. But I just knew she possessed a naughty side, and that was intriguing the hell right out of me.

She would put the banana she was eating in her mouth while pretending to perform semi-oral sex on it. She is freaking toying with me. When the girl stood up, she had to be no taller than five feet, with jet black hair almost touching the top of her ass. What a shapely looking ass to boot. Damn, she flashed me almost a half smile when she left the cafeteria. It was just enough to leave it etched in my brain. I hoped I could find out what it would take to get a flash of the whole smile one day.

Yeah, the boys accepted me as one of their own. They told me, "After school come back to Larry and

Kerry's house, for a couple of tokes." Kerry now squeezed my full raging hard on. I felt like crying when I had to turn them all down.

"Sorry guys, but it's one of my bail conditions. I have to go straight to and from school. My mom really went to the wall for me, so I can't fuck this up. But there's no reason why we can't have a toke or two while walking home is there?"

The rest of the afternoon I kept fantasizing about Kerry, yet was mesmerized by this mysterious Asian girl. I also had this knot in my stomach. I wondered when or if retribution would come my way, for me beating up the wops yesterday.

I know if I was put in the hospital, my brother Jake would seek a mighty powerful, violent, bloody revenge. I wondered if any those wops had a brother like Jake? I know I promised mom not to get into any more trouble, but I will be dammed if I take a beating without fighting back. After all, I'm a Sioux warrior!

As the school bell rang and class let out, I walked to Rachel's locker and said, "Let's go, sis." This was followed by Rachel saying, "Right home, correct Mitchell?" "Yeah, right home, sis."

We left the school and stood on the front steps. We were met by Principal Diloreto who also said, "Straight home, Mr. Strongbow." Man, did they think I had a brain cramp? Diloreto wasn't worth even responding to, the way he treated mom earlier in the day. I just looked at him for thirty seconds and then nodded my head.

Rachel and I started to walk towards my new friends for the great toke walk home. Kerry was all over me like a cat in heat. She was purring and I was ready to pounce on her. As soon as we stepped onto the city sidewalk and were off school property, I heard what sounded like loud thunder in the distance.

It was a steady sound and was getting louder. Our crowd now stopped and my gut told me this sound was coming for me. Over the hill, came three Harley Davidson motorcycles and they were approaching us at high speed. These guys were weaving in and out of traffic, with reckless abandon. The lead rider pointed right at our crowd. Yeah, they were here for us or more specifically, me. Kerry was holding my hand and I released it. I asked the boys, were they willing to back me? They all answered "yes."

Rachel said she was going back in the school to get the principal. I didn't stop her. I didn't need Diloreto's help, but I wanted Rachel at a safe distance. The bikers were about one hundred feet from us. The adrenaline junkie in me is ready for his fix. Fifty feet from us and my heart started to pound. My gut is nervous, but not so nervous to run away. I tell the boys, "let's make a circle, and don't break it; just keep throwing them, until you can't throw anymore. Let's go down swinging boys."

Diloreto who had been watching us, left the steps and started walking in our direction. Then he just stopped at the school property perimeter line. Damn, he looks ten times more scared than any of us. The bikers were now slowing their bikes down and doing a circle right in front of us. When I start to laugh, everyone looked at me as if I was totally fucked. They may have thought that yesterday, but my actions today have totally confirmed this.

The three bikers now got off their bikes. Hell, the biggest one, is bald with a big goatee, stood about six foot eight, and was a very solid three hundred pounds. The second biker is about six foot two and would weigh about two hundred and forty pounds. He had a white guy looking afro and a Fu Manchu. The third biker, who seemed to lead the pack, was about six foot and weighed about two hundred and thirty five pounds. He was very, very muscular and very native looking, with long jet black hair and lots of tattoos.

I yelled at Rachel to come back. She doesn't hear me. The native biker who had pointed at us, yelled at her to come back. Rachel turns around, looks at the bikers, smiles and starts to run towards us. Diloreto is now wiping sweat beads off his forehead. I tell my boys to stand down. This is my older brother Jake and a couple guys from his motorcycle club, the Hell Hounds Oakland Chapter.

Jake comes over and shakes my hand, gives me a hug and a pat on the back. Once Jake sees Rachel running towards him, he opens up his arms and Rachel jumps right into them. Jake spins her around, laughing all the while. Once he put her down, he got this real serious look on his face. He looked at the rest of my crew, then looked towards me, "Little brother, I hear you got yourself into all kinds of trouble, beating up some wops. Judging by your face, you took a few shots yourself."

"Actually these bruises were done by this fat wop at the police station. Those other guys didn't even lay a glove on me. I had them down for the count real quick. The big wop grabbed Rachel by the ponytail, and did a mock Indian chant. So I laid him out cold. My new friends here had my back the whole time. Even you would have been impressed."

Jake now walked towards my crew and eyed them all a little more closely. He got real close to Kerry, looked at her and then looked at me and smiled. He then frowned, stuck his chest out and talked to my crew. "You guys tough?"

"None of them ran when you and your boys showed up. They were all willing to fight for me." Jake just smiled, thanked my crew, and shook each of their hands. Like the dog he is, he gave Kerry a big hug and grabbed her ass and then he stuck his tongue out at me. Everyone started to laugh, even the two Hell Hounds.

The only person that didn't laugh was Diloreto. He wouldn't step off school property; but watched our every move and heard everything. Jake looked at him, snarled and asked "What the fuck are you looking at?" Diloreto just turned around and headed back inside the school.

Jake asked, "So what happened with the cops little brother?" I told him, "It was actually going alright at first; they were going to look into things. I thought maybe they would let me go for now, till they talked to everyone. The other cop said he had to take me in as there were two kids lying in hospital in a world of pain. I told him I hadn't noticed. They seemed to be resting comfortably when I left."

Jake told Rachel to put a helmet on and jump on the back of his bike. He then told me to jump on the back of the afro's bike. Before I could jump on, Kerry come up and gave me this great big hug and a little tongue induced French kiss.

Unlike my brother, I didn't grab her ass, at least not until Kerry put my hands there for me: her ass felt great! Man, I hope this girl is a "Virginity Slayer." I jumped on the back of the Afro guy's bike and the three motorcycles roared away; destination, my house.

We were about three blocks from my house and stopped at a red light. That cute little Asian girl was crossing the street. She spotted me on the back of the bike, winked at me and then waved at Rachel. As soon as we get home Rachel has to tell me who that girl is. Kerry may have my balls ready to explode, but the Asian chick gives me a funny feeling in my stomach. Funny in a good way!

Once the bikes were parked in the driveway, Rachel started to run into the house. I managed to stop her. "Rachel, do you know that Asian chick? She waved to you, at the stop light." Rachel could tell I had desperation in my voice. "Perhaps I do know her. Why, Mitchell? I thought kissy face with the big boobs is your girlfriend. Why do you want to know her name for, hey Mitchell?"

I looked at her and said, "Because I do! After all I did stick up for you and now I am in all kinds of trouble. That is what family does for each other, Rachel. You help when help is requested. Can you help me with her name?"

"My memory seems to be affected by the hunger in my belly. I think McDonalds would help me remember her name." I reached in my pockets and gave Rachel my last two dollars. And here I thought got away with the McDonald's deal.

"Her name is Lucy Thom and she is too pretty and too smart for you." Rachel then left with my last two dollars. I guess time will tell if it was money well spent.

I sat on the front porch with Jake and his two Hell Hounds buddies, and he introduced me to both of them. Jake first introduced me to the big bald guy, his name was John Derksen. He spoke with a bit of an accent. I asked where he was from.

He stated "Rhodesia, one of the last places on earth, where a white man was treated with the power and glory he truly deserves. A place where the no good Kaffir was still used for what they were truly born for; slaves, for his white master!"

There was no confusing his stance on blacks.

The second guy with the afro was Don "The Terror" Terek. He's not a full member of the Hell Hounds, he is a probationary member. They call them "Strikers." Once they have completed their eight month and eight day probation, they are accepted by the club executive and given a full patch, meaning they are now a fully fledged member of the Hell Hounds.

From time to time, strikers, unofficially of course, have been asked to carry out some illegal activities.

They could even be asked to kill for the club. Refusal to obey such an order from the club executive could result in their own death. These boys mean business!

Don came over, shook my hand and stated, "You look a lot like your dad." I was taken back, actually quite stunned. I had this funny vibe going on in my stomach. "Mitch, I was in Vietnam, to make that more specific, I was in your dad's unit. I should have been in the helicopter with your dad when he was shot down. But I was in the "Crowbar Motel" for nothing other than fighting. Your father Iggy wasn't only a great soldier, but a great human being. He always talked highly of his family. I have nothing but respect for the man's memory."

Don and I talked for another hour, until mom arrived home from school. This was just so cool, and I felt like dad was on the front porch with us. Don was telling funny stories about him. I'm sure as any kid will tell you there is a side of your parents they really never want you to see. I'm not saying it is a bad thing, but they're always your parents. There is no down time to speak of. They can't punch a parental clock and then be someone else. They are just your parents. With my family, only having one parent left, I really appreciate mom even more. Whenever I get the chance now to hear about dad, I absorb it and bank the memory.

When mom arrived home, she came over and gave Jake and me a big hug. She said she was glad that I came straight home after school. I told her that Jake and his buddies had picked us up from school.

Mom thanked them and offered to make them dinner. Jake told her, "Tonight I'm ordering pizza for all of us." He wanted to sit down with my mom and me, and discuss the whole legal matter. Mom at first insisted on cooking. Jake said, "No, you worked all day, my treat." Eventually mom agreed. I was so happy and I told mom that Don Terek had served with dad in Vietnam and had been telling me stories about him.

I saw mom's face change, her smile was gone and a tear came to her eye. "Mr Terek , I'm sure you're a nice person. One day I would love to sit down and talk to you about Iggy. I'm still grieving for him right now, and the pain is still too fresh. I hope you fully understand?"

Don just smiled back at mom "I fully respect your wishes ma'am. If you ever want to talk about Iggy, just let Jake know. He was a great man." Mom thanked him for his kind words; and with that Don and John left my house on their motorcycles

Jake, mom, and I then sat at the kitchen table and talked, while Rachel stayed upstairs and did her homework. Right off the bat mom addressed the issue of the lawyer. She just couldn't afford him. Jake told her he would pay for the lawyer. We are family here and we all help each other. I think mom was too proud for that answer. She told Jake she would take on a second job to pay for the lawyer.

Jake said he had an even better idea. He and Jerry were purchasing a gym in the North Beach area of San Francisco. It's an old canning factory and needs lots of work. With mom's blessing, I can work off his lawyer's fees.

At first mom was quiet, but I could tell her wheels were in motion. "You know Jake that might not be such a bad idea. However I don't want his grades to be effected. Are you all right with this Mitchell?" I gave it about a half second of thought. "I would like that very much. Plus a couple bucks for me as well, right Jake?"

"Yeah I don't see a problem with that, but your mom is right, your grades are a priority, Mitchell. Maybe you can start lifting weights and put some meat on those scrawny arms of yours. You will never impress the girls with those twigs that you call arms. Although the one that hugged you at the school was cute."

My face now went red. Mom asked, "What girl?" Down the stairs, came Rachel bellowing out, "Kerry big boobs mom! That's who, and he likes Lucy Thom as well!"

I looked at Rachel, "I bought you McDonalds today, and that will be the last time Rachel."

"You bought me McDonalds to tell you what Lucy Thom's name was. Tomorrow, if you don't buy me McDonalds again, I will tell Kerry big boobs that you like Lucy Thom."

Jake and mom were starting to laugh at Rachel for extorting me. Once mom was able to get herself composed, she turned to Rachel and told her, "No extorting goes on in our house. We are family and we help each other."

Jake pulled out this huge roll of money when the pizza guy showed up. The smallest bill was a twenty. He must have had at least two thousand dollars on him. I was so taken back by all the money Jake had on him. He didn't even have a full time job on the docks yet.

Jake always seemed to have a new motorcycle, or a new car. He had lots of broads and the coolest clothes. He possessed this power of some kind; whenever he would enter an establishment, he attracted attention. He hung out with famous rock musicians, knew actors and actresses, and with my father gone, Jake had become my role model. When I grow up, I want what he has. The power, the glory, the broads, the whole damn package! Perhaps I was already on the road to emulating Jake and his brothers in the Hell Hounds.

Jake told us he would come by tomorrow, when Cole Winters talks about my legal issues. For the next couple of weeks, he's going to make sure that Rachel and I are given a ride to and from school. Either Jake would do it by himself or a couple of club members from the Hell Hounds would. Surprisingly, mom agreed!

That night as I lay in bed, I kept replaying a day of nothing but highs. It started with mom straightening out Diloreto , Kerry being very promiscuous, the very cute Lucy Thom giving me the eye, and then the topper was Don Terek talking about dad. What a difference a day makes. My bed sure felt a hell of a lot more comfortable than that cold jail cell cot I slept on the night before. Life sure was good.

The next morning, true to his word, Jake and Don Terek drove Rachel and me to and from school. Most kids take school buses; in my family it is Harley Davidsons all the way. School was good. Kerry was still teasing away. Every time I saw Lucy Thom she gave me this feeling in the pit of my stomach. I seemed to be able to put a smile on her face.

Word had obviously spread around the school about my fighting capabilities. Now, having Jake and a couple Hell Hounds chauffer us to and from school got both Rachel and me respect from the other students. They were holding the doors open for us, or asking if we would like something special for lunch. Hell, we were both invited to house parties. My curfew however was putting a cramp on things. It prevented me from being alone with Kerry, the virginity slayer.

That night Winters, Jake, mom and me strategized about my legal woes. Winters brought some really good news with him. It was about the big wop Luch that I had beaten up. It seems that the cops decided to drop the assault charges against me after interviewing several witnesses.

The District Attorney and the cops agreed I was coming to aid of my sister who was actually being assaulted. However, the second wop, Tony Alfano, the fellow with the broken nose said that it was deliberate on my part, so those charges have stayed.

Winters want to use the 'pity trip' defense; my father was killed fighting for his country, which made me overprotective of my sister. Winters also suggested asking for a psychiatric assessment on me to show that I am a victim of my circumstances. Mom asked Winters what he thought outcome would be.

Winters stated, "More than likely, six months to a year in Juvenile Hall." Mom just closed her eyes and put her hand on her forehead. A couple tears rolled down her cheeks. I didn't feel bad for myself, I felt bad for mom.

Jake asked, "What if Alfano were to drop the charges?" Winters just nodded yes and said, "If he decides to drop charges, then Mitch is free. His parents, however, are pretty insistent that Mitch be held accountable for his actions, and medical expenses."

Jake said to Winters, "Go over to his parents and talk to them. Find out if they would take cash for the medical expenses and some financial compensation to drop the charges." Jake then asked, "What do his parents do for a living?" Winters said, "They own a small dry cleaning store." Jake then looked at Winters, "Go over and talk to them tonight. Tell them maybe I can send some business their way, along with some cash."

Mom just looked at Jake. As much as she would like the charges against me dropped; she told Jake, "Buying your way out of trouble isn't the answer."

I looked at mom and said, "Mom he came at me showing off. I won pure and simple! Had Luch not touched Rachel we wouldn't be sitting here. I did what I thought was right at the time. No one will ever hurt anyone in our family. Since I was young, dad has always drilled that into our heads. I didn't go start this, I just finished it!" While we are at it, "What about me taking a beating by the old fat wop cop? Mom I was handcuffed when he beat me! Where is the justice there?"

Mom said to Winters, "Try to do what Jake asked. However, I want to know how much this is going to cost. Mitchell will be paying every dime. All agreed?"

We all agreed. Winters shook all our hands and said he would go to the Alfano dry cleaning shop right away. Jake walked him out to the porch and talked to Winters for about fifteen minutes. When he came back in, he just gave me a wink and smiled. Jake actually looked a bit different when he came back in, his face seemed to have changed a bit.

Friday morning, last day of school, thank goodness. We hadn't heard from Winters in two days. We listened to the local news as mom made us breakfast. They said there was a fire in the garment district of town. A dry cleaning shop owned by the Alfano family had been burnt to the ground. Arson was suspected! We all stopped what we were doing. Mom looked at me. "Mom I was in bed sleeping all night. I swear, I am behaving myself like you asked." Jake and John Derksen then pulled up to drive us to school.

Mom told us to stay inside! She then went out to talk to Jake. I could tell by their facial expressions that it was quite an intense conversation. Jake just kept shrugging his shoulders. When mom came back inside you could tell she was royally pissed. Mom didn't even finish making our lunches. She told us to get to school now. "I'm sure your brother Jake will buy you lunch. After all he seems to have a solution to everything." Rachel and I knew not to piss our mom off. We just said to her, "Have a good day," and ran for our lives!

When I came outside, Jake just looked at me and smiled just like the cat who swallowed the canary. Deep down inside I knew he either torched the dry cleaning shop, or he had ordered it done. At that very point I knew that some of my values were changing. I actually felt good that the Alfano's shop was burnt down. Fuck with a Strongbow and suffer the consequences!

When Jake and John dropped us off at school I asked, "Where's Terek?" Jake stated he was out of town for a bit. Jake gave both Rachel and me twenty dollars for our allowance. He told us that the club was going out for a run this morning, so no one would be picking us up after school. He then looked into his crystal ball and said, "The charges against you will be dropped." That made me feel so damn good. Dad always said, "Family looks out for family."

I wanted to tell my friends about the dry cleaning shop being burnt to the ground. But I knew it was better to play it real stupid. Jake always told me, "Braggers always lose in the long run." So I acted real surprised when my friends told me about it.

Around 11:00, I was summoned down to Principal Diloreto's' office. Whenever you're paged in your classroom and they ask for you to go the principal's office, you get real nervous. All the kids just stare at you. Are they looking for fear on your face? Perhaps they want to see how tough you really are.

When I arrived outside the principal's office, I saw Cole Winters, my mom and two detectives. They were the ones who originally charged me with assault. We were all summoned inside Diloreto's office. I knew it was a good sign when the detectives asked Diloreto to leave his office so we can all talk. Man, do I love pissing that guy off! Hell, it even made mom smile watching Diloreto get so flustered. The cops asked us to sit down. One of the detectives asked to see my hands. I looked at Winters and he nodded yes. As I showed them my hands, they asked my mom, "Where was he last night?"

Mom stated, "He was at home all night and went to bed just shortly after 22:00." Mom asked, "Does this have anything to do with the Alfano dry cleaning business being burnt to the ground?" They answered, "Yes." Winters asked if I was a suspect.

They answered, "No, the description of the arsonist is a white male, in his mid twenty's. He had an afro and Fu Manchu, and was fairly muscular." I knew right off the bat that it was. His description fit Don Terek to a "T". I said nothing, but I also saw the wheels turning in mom's head. I believe she also realized who it was. Her eyes got big at one point, but she too remained silent.

Then one detective said, "With all the tragedy that has befallen the Alfano family lately, they have decided to drop all charges against Mitch. I must say the police department and District Attorney's office believe this is the wrong move to make. However, there is nothing we can do to change their minds."

For the record, someone also nailed their pet poodle to the front door of their home. Off the record they are frightened for their lives."

The detective then gave me a lecture on life as he saw it. "Mitch, one day there will be a family not so willing to drop charges against you. They won't be intimidated and you will see prison time. You need to change your ways. If you don't there will be repercussions."

They should give the same lecture to the cop that beat the shit out of me.

"Mitchell, as much as I can appreciate your father

sacrificing his life for his country, and the fact you need a male father figure to guide you, Jake and Jerry Strongbow will be your downfall in years to come. They're both very well known to the police. One day they will be behind bars. Is this really the future you want for your son, Mrs. Strongbow? He is already on the path to it."

Mom thanked the cops. She then asked, "Is that all?" The cops said, "Yes." They left the school, but not before telling me that now they know who I am and what I'm all about. From now on they'd be paying special attention to me.

I asked about my curfew. Winters said he would go and see the judge, just to make sure I wasn't picked up for any misunderstandings. I gave mom a hug and thanked her for her support. "Mom, could I please not rush home right after school? Can I please stay out to 10 P.M.?" Mom said, "Walk your sister home first, then ten is fine."

Before leaving the office, I stopped and told Diloreto, "Guess what? All charges are dropped. I guess that makes me even with all other students doesn't it?" Bastard didn't even answer me. All he did was to shoot me a dirty look. So I winked at him! Just like the other day, his face went purple. Wow, that vein in the middle of his forehead started to pulsate once again. I think he should see a doctor or something; the guy really has health issues.

At lunchtime, I sat with my friends and told them the good news. Larry told me they would have a party in his basement tonight to formally welcome me to the group. I kept thinking, hoping, Kerry would formally welcome me into her pants.

I walked Rachel home from school and grabbed a quick shower. I put on my Brut aftershave and was ready for some fun times at the Dubrowski residence. I brought this album "Meet the Beatles" along with me. Jake thought maybe I would like to listen to it while I was under house curfew. I also brought some rolling papers and a nickel bag that Jake had left me. The one item he left me that I was really hoping to use was a condom. Actually make that a couple condoms.

I was also kind of trying to get out of the house before mom came home. I heard her car pull in the driveway and the weed went down my pants. Let's hope my balls don't sweat too much between here and Dubrowski's place! It would get much worse if I had to answer a hundred and one questions from mom. Her interrogation technique was more aggressive than the cops was. As much as I would try and bullshit her, she could always see right through me.

After promising mom that I wouldn't get into any more fights, that I had indeed learned my lesson mom let me go. She even said I could stay out till midnight, but not one minute later. If I messed up I would have a curfew that even Cole Winters couldn't get me out of.

Dubrowski's place was definitely a party house. The basement is where Larry and Kerry entertained their friends. The parents stayed upstairs and did their own form of partying. Their dad was a major league drunk and the mom was always sneaking her boyfriends in and out. Yeah, this was a house of total dysfunction. It's probably why I seemed to fit in so well with the house and its inhabitants.

As I entered the basement, I was greeted with a beer from Larry, and a firm handshake. There were already maybe seven people there, and over the next hour the party maxed out at twelve people. The lights were down low and the tunes were playing. But other than Kerry and me hanging off each other, there was no real chemistry happening between the guys and gals.

I decided to pull out my weed; I hoped there weren't any pubes or ball sweat on there. I asked, "Anybody else interested?" Larry told me their dealer should be by anytime, but till then let's get high. I had at least three beers and the weed was giving me a kick ass bu*zz*. Kerry was giving me the look and the Beatles sounded great. I was really starting to enjoy the whole California scene. It was much more relaxing than being around military brats.

Then in through the door came a true brat; it was Lucy Thom who stated quite loudly for all to hear. "Who the fuck's been smoking weed here? Anybody caught cutting in on my business, I will slice their throats." Lucy now looked around the room. For some reason or other, everyone was showing some fear. Fuck she was maybe five feet tall and weighed no more than hundred and five pounds. Norm was around six foot, maybe one hundred and fifty pounds, same for Larry. Blais was about five foot ten and a solid one thirty five and I myself was six foot and around one sixty. We were all big guys for our age. What the hell did anyone have to be scared of?

"Hey little Asian Chicky Poo, that is my weed you smell. I'm not here to cut in on your territory or business. I'm just getting my buddies high. Care to join us? "Lucy then shot me a smile, "Yeah, let's try your crap weed."

I could tell right off the bat Kerry and Lucy didn't really care for each other. When Lucy ordered a very nervous Kerry to get her a beer, Lucy looked at my facial reaction. I smiled a devilish grin and Lucy's eyes lit up. Fuck Lucy was turning me on! She was this nasty person and yet to look at her pretty innocent face and petite frame, you would never guess it.

Perhaps that's what made her so dangerous and yet so damn sexy.

Eventually everyone under the influence of booze and drugs lightened up. We all decided to play "Spin the Bottle" and my personal favorite, "Three minutes in Heaven."

Lucy Thom sold Norm a dime bag of weed and a gram of cherry honey oil. That was something I had never tried before. Norm said the oil was for much later on, and he guaranteed me I would enjoy the bu**zz**. Norm and everyone else were quite surprised when Lucy decided to stick around and play the lustful games. Normally, she makes her deal and flees the scene.

Everyone is so scared of her. There's no way anyone even had the balls to ask her to leave. This intrigued the hell out of me. I asked the boys to tell me why they are all scared of her. Larry said he will tell me once she leaves.

We all sat in a circle for the game of Spin the Bottle. No one in the group seemed to be in a steady boyfriend/girlfriend situation, so it was open season for lip locking fun and adventure. My first encounter happened on Lucy's spin, as it came to rest on me. Lucy now had the choice to either kiss me, or take me into a darkened closet for three minutes. She chose to kiss me; man it was nice and slow, and soft. As I pulled away, I just stared at her. Lucy made a point of looking at Kerry and smiling.

Next lucky girl to win a round with me was Kerry. She chose the kiss as well. Kerry jumped right up, grabbed me by my collar and she hardcore French-necked with me for all to see. I think the performance was for Lucy. Kerry made sure to look Lucy's way, just like Lucy did, when she pulled away. Man, did I love it! Could there be a cat fight over me? If so, that would be a first.

Next time Kerry won, she chose to take me into the darkened closet. I barely got the door closed, when Kerry ripped off her bra and let me feel those beautiful "DD" breasts of hers. This was the first time that I have ever felt breast in the flesh. Hell, she even allowed me to kiss her nipples. I thought I was going to blow my load right then and there. Eventually, there was a loud knock on the door, our three minutes were up. I should have guessed who knocked; it was none other than Lucy Thom!

Kerry's nipples were like headlights when we walked out. The guys all noticed she had taken her bra off and I'm sure all the girls noticed the bulge in my jeans. I could have knocked over a tall building with my hard on. It was more powerful then Superman with all his strengths that night.

Lucy's turn came once again. Did I mention how I

love these games, and the whole California lifestyle? YEAH, this time Lucy also chose the closet with me. Once inside, Lucy didn't take her bra off. She had only "A" cups and couldn't compete with Kerry. Lucy however, had something better in mind. It was a first for me, in a night of firsts.

She put my one hand down her exposed pants. Lucy had me rub her vagina lips until I was fingering her. She then took my other hand, and put my thumb in her mouth. She started to suck it, while slowly pulling out my cock and giving me a hand job. I didn't need the whole three minutes. I came within a minute it seemed. Lucy then looked at me and said, "So did the crossed eyed fat cunt make you cum? I didn't think so!"

I couldn't even answer Lucy, hell I could barely talk. I was still in shock about what just took place. Lucy then told me to put my dick back in my pants. She took me by the hand and together we left the closet. Everyone was just staring at us. Lucy then gave me this real long kiss and left the party. I just stood there and watched her walk out of the party.

I didn't know what to do but turn red, when Blais and his date went in the closet next. I heard her comment, "It smells like bleach in here. Ew, did you spill your beer or something?"

Kerry didn't bother with me for the rest of the

night. This was fine with me. It left more time for some serious drinking games. Norm broke out his Cherry honey oil. It was a little harsh at first, but what a bu*zz*. Jake always drilled into my head, "Mitch, if I ever find out that you're doing chemicals or needles, I will skin you alive. Weed and hash are natural! Don't do anything that will kill your soul." He was quite serious about skinning me alive. I made a promise to him and feel I must keep it. I believed the oil would be allowed under my agreement with Jake, or rather hoped it was anyways. Man, this was great stuff.

A little while later, Kurt Wilson showed up with this bottle of Scotch. Norm, Blais, Larry, Kurt, and I started doing straight shots. Scotch is an acquired taste, I'm told. Hell, I'm not sure how many gallons it would take me to acquire it, because I hated it. Still, there was no way I was going to 'pussy out' and stop doing shots. By eleven thirty, I was really fucked up. I had cotton mouth and my balance was really off; but really, who cares? I felt my first breast, felt a warm wet pussy, and had an orgasm that wasn't self-induced. I was also introduced to oil and large amounts of beer.

It was now time to stagger home, so I won't break my curfew. I can go out again and play with my new friends tomorrow. I was kind of hoping the walk with fresh air would sort of straighten me up. I swear these sidewalks are crooked out here. My legs seemed to have problems navigating and staying upright was a chore. The fresh air however, seemed to have helped me.

As I walk into the house, my sister Pam was watching TV. "Nice eyes, Mitchell" she remarks and laughs. "Where is mom?"

"Relax, she is in bed sleeping. However she did ask me to remember what time you waltzed in here. Where the hell were you, to get those blood-shot eyes?"

Just when I start to answer Pam, she interrupts me. She says I'm talking loud enough to wake up the neighborhood. I was now trying to whisper all the while standing and hanging onto an arm of the couch for balance and support. "I was at this amazing house party, and guess what? I made out with two chicks! I really like it out here Pam, don't you?"

"You are a pig just like Jake! He treats his women like crap, and now you're starting." Talk about a party pooper.

I made myself a ham sandwich and went up to my room. Damn the munchies were in full force tonight. I lay on the bed and closed my eyes. Then it happened. A California earthquake! My bed seemed to spin out of control. I sat up and the bed stopped spinning. Wow, I lay back down and closed my eyes, and the bed started to spin again. What the hell is going here? This happened one more time, but I now kept one foot on the floor. This seemed to stop the spins, but now I don't feel so good. I lift my foot back off the ground, and the spins start once again but this time my stomach also has flipped and I staggered into the washroom. I lifted the toilet seat up and had the dry heaves. My body seemed to be burning up as I had the sweats. It must have been the ham sandwich. OK, just lay here for a minute. I closed my eyes and the floor started spinning, followed once again by the dry heaves.

The last thing I remember was this voice, "Mitchell, stick your two fingers down your throat until you tickle that speed bag thing that hangs down. You will feel much better. See what happens when you treat women the way you do? We put a curse on you!"

I just nodded at Pam and did what she suggested. I sprayed the bowl with puke, many, many times over. All I could taste and smell was that God awful Scotch that Wilson brought over. I'm never drinking Scotch again!

I eventually passed out right on the bathroom floor until morning. The only reason I woke up was hearing mom laughing at me. I couldn't convince her that the ham made me sick. Food poisoning was my defense and I was sticking to it. My defense however was shot down by the assortment of beer bottle caps mom found in my coat pocket. Never leave evidence, and never ever drink Scotch.

I composed myself and headed down for breakfast. My head was throbbing as if a school marching band was marking time. Hell, I was dehydrated. I couldn't get enough fluids into me. Mom turned to me and said, "Will that be two or three greasy green eggs, and deep fried pig's brain, or perhaps you would like it raw and runny?"

I flew back up to the toilet and threw up. I didn't need my two fingers this time to speed along the process. Eventually some dry toast, black tea and a couple aspirins did the trick. There was also the realization that I made out with two chicks the night before. It made the hangover seem not so bad after all.

With all my chores done for the day, I was set to go out and do it all over again. Mom however informed me I was grounded once again.

When I asked, "Why, I didn't break my curfew?" Mom informed me that there is a life lesson to be learned from the night before. I asked her what that lesson was.

Mom informed me, "Gluttony is the root of all evil."

Rather than argue with mom after seeing her go to

the wall for me this week, I agreed to just stay in and relax.

Around 7PM or so, Norm and Larry dropped by with my Beatles album. They asked if I wanted to hang out with them in the park. I told them I was kind of in shit and had to hang around the house for a bit.

Mom said it was cool for me to sit on my front porch with them. So we just shot the breeze. The main question I wanted answered was, "Why are so many people afraid of Lucy Thom?"

Norm told me it wasn't just about Lucy. She also has a twin brother named Ricky. Between the two of them, this is the third grade school they have attended. They were both thrown out of the other two for fighting and drug dealing. They are both into Martial Arts and Ricky is just plain nuts.

I asked, "Why would their parents allow this to happen?" Larry started to laugh, "Their dad and older brother are both in prison for importing heroin into the country and also for murder. Their mom is supposed to run a whore house in Chinatown, where Ricky and Lucy also drug deal for her."

I asked where her psycho brother Ricky was. They said he was supposedly off with mono right now, but with her whacked out family, who really knows.

Larry asked me, "What happened in the closet with

Lucy?" There was no way I could tell him. I was still hoping to score with his sister Kerry. I just told them, "Some heavy necking until I spilled my beer, then she got mad at me and left." Not sure if they believed me or not, but that was my alibi and I was sticking to it.

Before they left for the night I told Larry, "Say hi to your sister for me. If she wants to come by tomorrow, that would be cool." Just the way he nodded to me, I knew he didn't believe my Lucy story. Kerry wasn't there, but I'm sure she wouldn't have believed it either.

The next week at school I played and lived very dangerously. I tried my best to juggle Kerry and Lucy without either of them discovering what I was doing. This secretive relationship was just as much a mental challenge as it was a physical one. At this point I didn't care which one wanted to take my virginity as long as one of them did.

The biggest drawback with Lucy was I couldn't see her at night. She said since I wasn't Asian, her brother and mother wouldn't accept me. I wasn't even allowed to walk her home after school. She took a city bus to and from school. When I brought up the subject of her twin brother Ricky, Lucy assured me we would meet soon enough, so I should be prepared.

The coolest thing about Lucy was how we thought so much alike. She had no problems making money drug dealing. We even compared our drug prices for buying and selling. She showed me different ways to make our weed sales more profitable. Lucy would sell weed to the other local schools, but she would add oregano and bird seed to the bag. Hell, maybe only a quarter of it would be real weed. Sure the kids would still get high but if they knew how she was ripping them off, they wouldn't be impressed.

I was finding that Kerry on the other hand, was more of a 'Cock-Teaser' than anything. We would lie on her bed and make out, but she seemed to have a monthly period that went on forever. She would only rub me through my jeans, but she always let me feel her up. If I could put Kerry's "DD" boobs on Lucy she would be the ultimate chick. Having Kerry's home life would help as well.

One weekend Lucy asked me if I could get her some weed. She had some people lined up, but her source for the time being had dried up. I talked to Jake and he said "Little brother, if you play the game, you play for keeps. You get busted; you are on your own. No way do you let anyone know where you get the weed from; especially your mom!"

I could tell this would be Jake's one and only warning. I fuck up, that is my problem! I agreed and Jake dropped off a half pound of weed. He told me I would be just like any other of his customers. He would front me the product for seventy five dollars and I would have seven days to pay him back. Every day after that, I owed another five dollars if full payment was not made. We shook hands and there it was; my first drug deal. I stashed the weed under my bed by taping it to the bottom of my mattress. Lucy and I were heading down to Haight Asbury to move the weed that weekend.

# WHACKING IT, WEEDING IT, LOSING IT

That Friday, mom was going to my Uncle Karl's for the weekend and she left my sister Pam in charge, which was perfect. Lucy was coming over that night and we were going to divide up the weed. We planned on making those eight ounces into just over twenty four ounces with the help of a little Oregano and bird seed.

That morning I had the biggest fright of my ever young life. Pam, Rachel and I were eating breakfast at the kitchen table, when mom came in the room and said to me, "Mitchell I would like to see you in the living room please. I have just come from your bedroom and found something very disturbing under your bed." The disappointed look on her face said everything there was to say, well almost.

I replayed in my head what Jake had told me. In fact, I already had myself back in jail. How would I ever be cool in front of Lucy with mom finding my weed? My heart was in my stomach as I left the kitchen table. Pam raised an eyebrow of course, while Rachel smiled and stuck her tongue out at me. I wondered, had the tape failed and the weed fallen to the floor? Was my mom a snoop? I'm sure there are some privacy laws she must have broken. That is my room after all.

I couldn't even look mom in the eye. "Mitchell, I was cleaning your room and guess what I found under your bed?" What answer could I really give? It's for a science project! She is a teacher, not some gullible dumb ass mom. "I'm not sure, mom. What did you find?" Mom squinted her eyes and took a deep breath, "Crusty Kleenex and a soiled hand towel. Masturbation is a sign of weakness, young man, and it's also a sickness. Don't you want to have children one day? If so, you better stop masturbating or there will be nothing left when it comes time to make a baby. Mitchell, you will go blind. It's times like this I wish your father was around. I am going to ask your brother Jake to have the 'birds and bees' talk with you. I am very disappointed! From now on you will leave your bedroom door open a bit so you aren't so tempted. I'm leaving for school now and this weekend I want you to behave yourself while I'm at your Uncle Karl's."

I have just been caught whacking off, and I can't tell you how thankful I am. Come to think of it, my Uncle Karl wears glasses. He must be a big whack-off artist himself.

At lunch time, Lucy asked me if I felt like living a little dangerously. She then said she would "make it worth my while." I asked what she had in mind. Lucy replied, "After lunch we will both go to the nurse's office and complain of not feeling well. Then we will both go to my house and do the magic weed conversion."

I asked, "Is this the only thing that was worth my while?" Lucy said. "You will find out soon enough!" So, after lunch Lucy and I both suddenly fell ill and next stop was my empty house. This is just what the doctor ordered!

Lucy and I walked into my house and there was no better sound than hearing it was empty. Lucy asked where the weed was. "It's up in my bedroom." Right then and there, the butterflies in my stomach started to flutter. Lucy would be the first girl in California that I have shown my bedroom to. Maybe it was a good thing that mom had cleaned up all the evidence.

As we entered my bedroom, my breathing was starting to become erratic, and my mouth was becoming dry. Lucy looked around my room and said it was very clean. She then asked if I cleaned it or my mom. I was stuttering and stammering! Lucy asked, "Why are you so nervous?" How can this little chick be so damn cool and calm? She then asked me if I was still a virgin. I didn't have to answer. My red face said it all!

Lucy had this warm smile on her face and gave me this incredible eye contact all the while taking my shirt off; her eye contact made me feel at ease. I took her shirt and bra off. Her nipples were so dark; I just leaned in and kissed the both of them. Lucy then pushed me down onto the bed and told me to take my pants off. I did as I was told, making steady eye contact with her. I didn't blink once; neither did Lucy as she stood up and took her pants off. Lucy wasn't shy at all, she made eye contact with my rock solid cock, and gave me a smile of approval. Lucy told me to pull back the bed sheets.

I pulled them back and I held a corner open for Lucy, so she could join me under the sheets. The way she entered the bed, it was so damn graceful, almost like a ballerina. I rolled over and started to kiss Lucy, while I started to finger her. Lucy stopped me at one point and told me to slow down and be gentle. She put her hand over my hand to teach me the proper technique to use. Lucy was slowly stroking me, until finally she said those words that I have been waiting to hear all my life. "Mitch, it's time for you to get on top. Just go with it and let nature take its course, but remember slow and easy."

I positioned myself on top of Lucy as she spread her legs; she then steered my cock right into her waiting wet vagina. I thrust forward with my hips and felt every inch of her. Even in my warm wet dreams, I couldn't have imagined how wonderful this could be. Lucy was the most beautiful woman in the world. I watched her smile at me enjoying myself. This was truly a magical feeling shared by two people. All those love songs I always made fun of; well, now they all made sense to me and I fully appreciated them.

After maybe fifty slow thrusts, Lucy starting to moan and move a bit. I felt myself building up to cum, the sensation was incredible! I had no control over my body, breathing or thoughts! My body was paralyzed by the up and coming orgasm; and as I was ejaculating, Lucy was also moaning. Her face was so innocent looking. How the hell did I ever deserve to be with someone so beautiful? As I felt my cock ejaculate and the fluid shoot out, I prayed this wasn't just another wet dream. "PLEASE DO NOT WAKE UP NOW WITH A MESS ALL OVER MY LEG." I didn't wake up, this was real. I was NO LONGER A VIRGIN!!!!

I then started to kiss Lucy all over and I was laughing at the same time. Her smile was now priceless, and she was my Virginity Slayer! As I rolled onto my back, I could hear music playing and I had the most amazing appetite all of a sudden. Not even the munchies made me this hungry. I asked Lucy if she would like something to eat. She said she would rather try some of my weed. How could I say no? I rolled a joint and opened up the bedroom window. We lay in bed still naked, and smoked the joint. Man, I felt like a real cool adult. Life was good. Life was real good!

After we finished the joint, we grabbed a shower together. She was washing my balls when I got hard once again. Lucy asked if I was ready for round two. At least this time I knew where to put it and how to get it there! Lucy and I made love standing up in the shower. I am not sure if it was the pot, the steam of the shower, or just the whole damn excitement of losing my virginity; but I almost passed out when I ejaculated. I ripped down the shower curtain rail. Something tells me that I better get that fixed before mom comes home.

After, we went downstairs and I made us a nice lunch. She deserved a nice lunch, after all that was the least I could do. After we ate, naked I might add, we headed back up to my bedroom to smoke another joint in bed. Man, I like this lifestyle, the lifestyle I know my brother Jake has every day.

Eventually, I was *"UP"* for round number three with Lucy. However, this time she told me to stay on my back. Lucy straddled me and rode me like a Sioux warrior breaking in a new horse. I had my stamina game happening. Man, she was riding me hard and I loved it; until I heard a dreaded noise, *"You two are gross and I'm telling mom."* With that, I knew Rachel was home from school and Lucy and I were both caught doing the "horizontal bee bop." I went to get up, but

Lucy pushed me back down and said she wasn't done yet. Well Rachel may have taken away my weed bu*zz,* but not my hard on! Eventually I ejaculated, and shook all the while. Lucy gave me the "you did good this time" smile, and I got dressed.

I went to Rachel's room to try and talk, or bribe my way out of being ratted out. She wasn't happy with me at all. I apologized and asked those dreaded words that Rachel wanted to hear. "How much is this going to cost?" Rachel didn't react at first, which scared the hell right out of me.

I went to walk out of her room when Rachel finally said, "Wait, five dollars and next time, close your door. You two are both so gross." I promised Rachel I would pay her off by the end of the weekend. Before I left her room, Rachel said in no uncertain terms that if she has to wait to the end of the weekend, she also wants me to buy the Beach Boys "Surfer Girl" album for her as well. Regrettably, I agreed! After all, I not only lost my virginity, but damn, I had sex three times. It seemed to me that the price of doing business was well worth it.

The next shakedown of the day occurred, when my sister came home from College. Lucy and I were sitting downstairs, when Pam came in the door. She immediately started sniffing around the house saying she recognized the smell. Eventually she went up to my room then raced back downstairs, "Smoking a little grass were we, Mitchell? You and your girlfriend here, getting a little high?"

I took a huge gamble, after I introduced Lucy to Pam, I said, "Yeah, you want to smoke a Doobie with us?" Pam looked at Lucy, looked back at me and then yelled for Rachel to come downstairs. She was in her room doing homework. I didn't know what to make of this until Pam told Rachel to go to the corner store and buy us some soda and chips. Pam would give her five dollars. Now I knew she wanted to get high with us.

When Rachel came back in Lucy, Pam and I had the giggles like crazy. Rachel just looked at the three of us and said, we were all nuts, and said she is the only normal one in the family. She went back upstairs to continue her homework.

Pam said Lucy could spend the night and she would phone Lucy's mom and pretend she was our mom. It would come at a price however; it would cost me a nickel bag of weed. Lucy could sleep in my room, but I had to sleep on the couch.

Later that night while Rachel was in bed sleeping, Lucy, Pam and I turned six ounces of weed into twelve ounces. I kept almost two ounces for personal use and to sell to my new friends like Larry and Norm. Everyone else got the diluted weed.

The next day Lucy and I spent jumping from transit trolley to bus, delivering our weed and making sales all over San Francisco. I really got to see the whole city first hand. With Lucy being kicked out of so many schools she had made so many contacts, and that was a huge positive. We were charging fifteen dollars for an ounce of weed, so after we sold five ounces, anything after that was pure profit. I still had two ounces left at home.

We made one deal with these hippies. We traded them an ounce of weed for a gram of that Cherry honey oil and a dime of hash which I had never tried before but Lucy assured me I would like it. After a whole day out and about, and getting to know Lucy a little bit more; I realized that Kerry wasn't worth the time or the effort.

Lucy took me into Chinatown and we had dinner at a real nice restaurant. I then took Lucy to see the movie "Dr Strangelove." That was exactly how I was feeling with Lucy sitting beside me holding my hand; two young drug dealing lovers were we. Had you told me before we moved to California that I would not only fall for an Asian, but lose my virginity to her, I would never have believed you. Lucy made me feel alive! We have so much in common. We do our own thing and hate the establishment. We like getting high, making money and the sex, damn! Once we got back to my place, I wasn't sure what I was looking forward to more; trying out this hash, or more sex.

On our way to catch the trolley home, we walked past a bar called the "Drunken Leprechaun." We noticed all these motorcycles parked out front with Hell Hound stickers on them. Four of the bikes I recognized right off the bat, so I decided to go in and see my brother. We were stopped by this huge bouncer and some Irishman named Joseph O'Reilly who owned the bar. They both laughed and said we had to be twenty one to enter the premises. I told them I just wanted to see my brother. O'Reilly asked, "Who might that be?" Once I told him, O'Reilly started to laugh and said, "You can come in but the "Chink" stays outside." It was said without a smile and was pretty damn cold I must say.

My back was now up. I stared at O'Reilly eye to eye and said, "Her name is Lucy, and she is my girlfriend. Now, are you going to let us both in, or are you going to get my brother for me?" O'Reilly told the bouncer to get Jake. All the while, O'Reilly just kept making eye contact with me.

I have seen many career soldiers over my life that have the "Death Stare," and O'Reilly indeed possessed it. My senses told me O'Reilly was an evil person and judging my some of the scars on his face, he has seen his fair share of trouble. Jake, Jerry, Derksen, Scott Fagan who I met for the first time and

Don Terek all came out of the bar to see us. More importantly, they wanted to see my so-called girlfriend.

Derksen and Jerry just looked at each other. Jake, being a smart ass, asked me, "What happened to the blonde with the nice tits and ass?" This caused me to just cringe and Lucy started to take a deep breath; she closed her fists and got into a fighting stance.

Fagan, with a cigar in his mouth, commented, "So Strongbow, you fuck her and you need another fuck a half hour later. There is nothing to this broad." Fagan then laughed and blew cigar smoke towards Lucy.

Just when I thought Lucy couldn't rock my world anymore then what she already had, she jumped up and did a reverse jumping crescent kick and nailed Fagan's cigar bang on. This caused Fagan to swallow the lit cigar. As Fagan was gasping for air, the rest of the Hell Hounds were all laughing their asses off. Once Fagan managed to spit out his cigar, he rose to his feet and went to charge at Lucy. I jumped in the way and threw an overhand right, but it didn't connect. Damn, I thought I had timed it perfectly.

As I took a counter stance, I saw Fagan's eyes get huge, and he began grabbing the back of his head. I realized Terek had grabbed Fagan by the pony tail and wouldn't let him go. Jake and Jerry now got into Fagan's face and told him to back down or take the beating of his life. "He is family! That makes her family, got it?"

None of us could fully understand what Fagan was trying to say. The lit cigar he was forced to eat burnt his tongue. The only thing we could see was the drool coming out of his mouth. Now that was funny! Terek gave me a wink and thumbs up, and Derksen commented "At least she isn't a Kaffir".

The rest of the Hounds went back inside the bar except Jake. He looked at Lucy and said, "I like this one Mitch. She has attitude and balls to boot." That meant a lot coming from my big brother. I told Jake that we had the cash we owed him for the weed, but I felt real uncomfortable just giving him the drug money out in public.

Jake then taught me a lesson, "Mitch, only you and I know where this money comes from. When you try and hide it, you make yourself suspicious and draw attention to yourself and me. Just give me the cash. This could've been a loan payback as far as anybody else is concerned. There is no law that forbids family lending family or friend's money. Be cool little brother, never draw suspicion or look guilty, understood?" Lucy looked at me and smiled. I nodded yes to Jake and gave him the seventy-five dollars.

Jake asked, "Where are you going?" I said, "Back home to smoke some hash." Jake just smiled and said,

"Have fun but be careful." He gave me a hug and then he gave Lucy a hug, and a wink. Even though Lucy is Chinese, I truly believe Jake has accepted her as my girlfriend.

I had this knot in my stomach, and I just realized why. Damn, has Lucy even accepted that she's my girlfriend? I think I will ask her to be my girlfriend properly once we get back to my house. How can she say no? Lucy had slain my virginity not once, but three times. I might add, we get high together and both make great drug partners. I'm sure we can both kick major league ass if need be; she was Bonnie and I was Clyde.

As Lucy and I jumped on the trolley to go back to my house, we held hands and kissed hard and didn't come up for air, until air was needed. Lucy looked at me and said, "This is my stop coming up." I was confused "I thought we were both going back to my house to get high with this hash Lucy. Did I do something wrong?" Man my brain was racing; where did I fuck up?

Lucy looked at me with a tear in the one corner of her eye and said, "My mom won't let me stay out two nights in a row, she is very strict. I wish I could Mitch! I really like you and have had a real good time with you. Mitch you are a good friend." With that, Lucy gave me a kiss, jumped off the trolley car and told me she would see me at school on Monday. I was in total shock! I just watched her walk down the street until I lost visual contact with her.

Until my stop, I just sat there and replayed Lucy's last words to me, "Good Friend." Hell, I thought we were great lovers and great business partners. Besides, what is wrong with hooking up tomorrow? That knot I felt earlier had now become a cannon ball. I felt empty and confused! Women, err! So instead of going straight home, I decided to stop off at Dubrowski's house and do some partying. I needed to drown my sorrows and was also really excited about trying this hash out.

When I arrived, the usual crew was there including Kerry. She went upstairs after seeing me come in and then reappeared wearing a rather low cut striped shirt that definitely caught my attention. Larry offered me a beer and I asked the boys if they had ever smoked hash before. Blais started to laugh and asked if I had any. I just pulled out the dime of hash wrapped in tinfoil.

Larry then broke out a propane torch and a pair of butter knives. Blais went to the washroom and came back with an empty toilet paper roll. I was totally confused, but these boys didn't seem to be confused at all. Man, they were like a precision surgical team; each person was a specialist.

Larry was the torch man, Blais was the toilet paper roll man, Kurt was now cutting up the hash into small pieces, and Norm had his lighter ready to light the torch. Kerry, well I was kind of hoping she would be the *head* nurse. Like any good student, I sat back and just observed how the smoking of this hash took place.

Larry held the torch, while Norm held the butter knives into the flame of the torch. Once the knives were cherry red in color, Norm, like a surgeon, ever so delicately took the hot butter knives and gingerly picked up a small slice of hash with one knife. He then applied the second knife to the first knife as if to squeeze the hash together. Blais held the paper roll to funnel the deep blue smoke from the hash into his mouth. What a puff of blue smoke it was! Blais was coughing but gave me the thumbs up. He held the smoke inside his lungs for about thirty seconds. His eyes became glossy, and as he exhaled he mouthed *"GOOD SHIT MAN."*

Everyone took their turn, finally it was my turn and I was so eager. I wasn't disappointed! The only thing I didn't like was when I seemed to cough the smoke right up. Until it was my turn for another toke, the beer seemed to help. Damn, I really liked it! We ended up smoking almost half the dime of hash. We all sat there real quiet, deep in thought; fucked right up, but deep in thought!

Around 23:00, I called my sister Pam and asked if I could sleep over at Larry's. I had to promise I wouldn't go out and roam the streets and get into trouble. Let's be honest, I was too stoned to roam anyways. I had totally lost my legs; like my brain they too, turned to stone.

When Kerry invited me up to her room however, my legs somehow found the drive and energy necessary to walk up the flight of stairs. Once we were in her room, Kerry wasted no time taking her top off and exposing those beautiful breasts of hers. Whether it was because I was really high or the beer was impairing by judgment, I didn't feel guilty about making out with Kerry. I was hurt, mad and confused by Lucy's actions.

Jake never settled for a steady girlfriend; he always had two or three on the go at one time. I think I should like to do the same. Genetics is forcing me to do these dastardly deeds! How can I help myself? More importantly, how could I not want Kerry and her "DD" breasts?

With Lucy rescuing me the night before from the land of virginity, I was now a boy/man on a mission! Since I have indeed tasted the 'Fountain of Vagina' and it was addictive, Kerry Dubrowski was to be my next fountain to drink from. She had no problems at all letting me play with her breasts, but when I tried to take her pants off, nothing doing! I was met with a whole lot of resistance. She was either squirming away or smacking my hand and telling me to behave myself.

I was confused by Kerry's refusal to go all the way. Kerry even made sure I kept my pants on. When I tried to force her hand down my pants; Kerry looked at me and in no uncertain terms told me, "If you ever want me one hundred percent, and I mean all of me, then I want you one hundred percent, and that means NO Lucy Thom! I need your undivided attention. By the way, a girlfriend ring is a must."

Did this hash just fuck up my hearing as well? Did I hear, what I think I heard? Was that an ultimatum from Kerry? I looked up at Kerry and said "Fuck You." I jumped up out of bed, and went downstairs where the boys were still partying.

Blais could tell by the stupid look on my face what had happened and asked "Did she ask for the girlfriend ring?" *He* started to laugh, as did Norm and Kurt and even Larry. "Did you guys hear the whole conversation?" Blais just shook his head no, "She said the same thing to me." Kurt also responded "me too." I looked at Norm, "Hey man, I heard the horror girlfriend ring story from these two; so I didn't even bother." Larry shrugged his shoulders and threw me a can of beer, his mouth and face said it all; "Sisters, what can I say?"

It was around 02:00 in the morning and the boys asked if I wanted to go out and make some quick money. I asked, "How?" They said they planned on breaking into the local grocery store. I was intrigued! I had never done a 'break and entry' gig before, only read about them in the newspapers. These were my new friends and I didn't want to disappoint them by chickening out. So I said, "Count me in."

The boys had been planning to rob this grocery store for a while now. I asked, "What happens if we get caught?" Norm said, "We end up in Juvie Hall." It was a place they had all been to, except Wilson. He said he was too smart to get caught. So off we went to break into the grocery store, which was at least twenty blocks away. I had a concern with this. "Cops see five teenagers walking down the street, it will only draw suspicion, won't it?"

No one answered me, but once we were about four blocks away from Dubrowski's house, Blais crossed the street by himself. He looked inside this bright red Chevy Impala. We all stopped as Blais jumped into the front seat. His head disappeared for about twenty seconds, but once the Impala started, Blais's head reappeared. He was driving the Impala and we all jumped in as quickly as we could. As we were driving down the street Blais turned to me, "OK lazy guy, we now have wheels. You don't have to walk there and back anymore. Make you happy?" Actually, I thought it was kind of cool.

Blais took the ride over nice and easy, not wanting to draw any attention from any cops that might be out there. He parked the car a half block away from the grocery store. Wilson said he would stay with the car. Should the cops come to the grocery store, he would do three short horn bursts followed by a long horn honk. The escape route was to end up back at Larry's house, if we got broken up. No one rats out! We all touched fists and acknowledged the plan; the burglar's creed, I guess.

We circled the grocery store and Blais said the tractor-trailers parked out back by the loading docks would be our ladder to the roof. Once there, we would pry open the roof hatch. The first two up were Blais and Larry. Norm and I just kept a close watch for the cops until we were needed on the roof. Within two minutes Blais signaled to Norm and me: it was our turn to climb.

I must say I have watched many obstacle courses on base, but watching these guys scale and climb, you would think Uncle Sam himself had trained them. On top of the roof, Norm pulled out this pry bar, and we reefed and reefed until the latch was popped. Norm said, "Now we wait a couple minutes to see if the hatched was alarmed." All of us except Larry slid back down the roof; he kept a close eye out for the cops and with being up that high, we had a great view. Blais and Norm had a cigarette and when they had finished, flicked it away. The cops were a no show, which meant we were a go; it was time to climb back up.

I looked into the grocery store. Hell, there was at least a fifty foot drop. Larry shone the flashlight inside and said, "This might be a bit tricky boys! However if it was easy, this place would have been robbed by every crook in California. There are some I-beams. We could do some hand over hand climbing, until we reach the freezer. Then we can jump down on top of it, and we're in, boys. What do you think?"

Deep down I was hoping the rest of the guys would reject Larry's plan. Hell, I had already made some real decent money this weekend moving weed. I didn't need this, but I would go with whatever the boys wanted.

Blais looked, Norm looked and then I looked. Holy fuck, I wish I hadn't looked! After everyone else said, "Let's have fun," I felt my balls get real small and I had that same nervous stomach that I felt before sex with Lucy. I guarantee it will not be the same result. Blais, Larry, Norm all looked at me; one by one they stuck out their fists. Reluctantly and against that little voice in the back of my head screaming, "What the fuck are you doing?" I stuck out my fist! However, the only words out of my mouth were "Count me in boys." They all smiled at me and said, "Let's do it!"

Blais went first followed by Larry, then Norm and me. One by one, my friends made the twenty foot hand over hand I-beam walk. I grabbed on to the I-beam and thought all the nervous sweat coming from my hands would cause me to slip and fall fifty feet to my death. I know I have good upper body strength, but trying to concentrate and maneuver hand over hand, took every ounce of strength I had. My breathing was quite heavy now, and sweat was starting to roll into my eyes from my forehead. Hell, my eyes were burning, but had I tried to wipe them, I would have fallen! After the first twelve feet, I was actually starting to enjoy the whole adrenaline rush. Knowing my body wasn't going to fall, made me feel so much stronger and alive. Damn, I was really getting off on this! I really felt great. It was a high in itself to me. It was like I imagined dad felt on one of his missions, with danger all around. It's no wonder why dad made a career in the army.

I made it over to the freezer with the vocal support of the boys, and did my ten-foot drop onto it. I was patted on the back and told, "Great job!" Positive reinforcement, criminal style! After we jumped down from the freezer, we searched the store until we came upon the manager's office. The door was locked, and Norm was trying his best to pry it open. I thought it was my turn to prove myself. I moved about five feet back and ran towards the manager's door; I did a flying drop kick! The door didn't stand a chance. It collapsed with a mighty crash. I know that impressed the boys.

Once inside we tore the office apart until Norm found a safety deposit box on the desk. I'm not sure why it was not inside the safe. Norm then smashed the lock of the safety deposit box with his pry bar. Inside was at huge roll of cash; this must have been the morning float box. We were hooting and hollering at what a great score this was.

Blais started smashing the bubble gum machines, and taking all the nickels from inside of them. Norm was putting cartons of cigarettes inside garbage bags. Then we heard the sound we were hoping not to hear; three short horn beeps followed by a long horn hook.

FUCK, the cops are here! We all crouched down. Blais crawled to the front of the store, and saw two cops with their flashlights out looking through the window. They were checking for any internal movement. Blais crawled back and said the cops were out there, but there was only one car and two cops. Time to act now before more cops arrived. My natural instincts for survival had kicked in. I said, "I have a plan, a little risky, but if we get away with it, legendary."

I told the boys my plan. They all agreed it was

ballsy, but if it worked we would be legendary. I slithered to the far side of the store, with my heart pounding so hard I thought the cops would hear it for sure. I then tied two balloons to a shelf, approximately six feet in height. I then slithered back to the aisle closest to the front door. The cops were still scouring the store with their flashlights when they spotted the objects I had tied together.

They gained entrance through the front door and slowly walked towards the objects. When they were three aisles from us, I threw a can of corn right where the balloons were. The cops now split up, trying to sneak up on the object. That is when the four of us snuck out the front door. There was no sign of Wilson; guess he split with our getaway car when the coppers showed up. Now what?

Blais looked at the cop car just idling in the parking lot and said with a devilish grin "Now there is a car I have never been able to steal, till now. There is our new getaway vehicle."

My first thought was that this is totally fucked; we would be nothing but a heat score in the cop car. But Norm, Larry and Blais have no problems with this. Hey, I'm the new guy who doesn't even know his way around the city. If I don't jump in, I know I will get busted for sure.

So I threw out everything that Jake has told me about surviving as a criminal and jumped in the front seat beside Blais who was behind the wheel. Blais, like he was Bobby Unser, spun the tires and we hauled ass out of there.

For the most part, the city was dead as was the traffic, but that didn't stop Blais from driving around like a maniac. He had the siren just a-wailing and the lights a-flashing; fuck, he even took some corners so fast we went up on two wheels. I just wanted to head back to Dubrowski's and get out of this heat score, but Blais had other ideas.

It wasn't until Norm reminded Blais that the next trip to Juvie Hall, his dad said he would use him as fish bait. Blais' whole facial expression changed as he now punched the front windshield. We were about four blocks or so from Dubrowski's, when we spotted a pack of Harley's about a hundred feet ahead of us, and heading in the same direction.

I looked at Blais who once again had that maniac look on his face. "Let's have fun boys." And with that Blais pushed the accelerator pedal to the floor, and once again turned on the siren and lights. We were about twenty yards away when I saw these guys were all wearing Hell Hound patches, and they were pulling over. If either Jake or Jerry happened to be in this pack, guaranteed I will be the one used as fish bait.

Blais had the car come to a screeching halt, jumps out of the driver's side door, and gave the Hounds the finger and laughed at them.

Jerry points at Blais and says, "You are a dead man." Derksen and Kantonescu jumped off their bikes, but they are too slow as Blais jumped back in the car and winds the engine out. I put my hands up over my face, and prayed no one in the club spotted me.

Wilson was quite happy to see us when we arrived at Dubrowski's place and apologized for taking off. He said that he circled around the grocery store until he couldn't anymore; as he was worrying about becoming a heat score himself. However, he had done the job that was asked of him. Wilson had warned us the cops were closing in. Larry handed out some beers and said, "Let's count this cash."

Hell what a score, we got five hundred and twenty dollars in cash and thirty five cartons of cigarettes. What a score indeed! These guys even had their own financial plans for dividing up the loot. Wilson, being the getaway driver, was given fifty bucks. The four of us that went inside split the rest, one hundred and seventeen dollars each. Norm then started to laugh and looked at me, "Hey Mitch, that's enough money to get Kerry that girlfriend ring," and winked. I threw my empty beer can at him and asked what would it take for him to be my girlfriend? I then blew him a kiss! Man, we were all on the floor laughing after that comeback.

Wilson said, "Since the cigarettes are the only item that could tie any of us to the crime tonight, we should sit on them." Larry said they were too bulky and he couldn't hide them forever. I then stepped up and said, "I will talk to my brother and see if he can move them for us. I can't guarantee movement but I will ask him."

The one very important item we all agreed on was that because we not only pulled off a great score, but embarrassed the cops by stealing their cop car, they would want retribution, and wouldn't stop until they found out who duped them. We must not talk or brag about this to anyone outside this room. We all agreed and touched knuckles.

The boys and I stayed up all night drinking beer, celebrating our perfect score and watching the sunrise. Horny as I was, it took everything I had not to sneak back to Kerry's room. Amazing when you have an alcohol-induced brain, how your morals and values are discarded. I left Larry's house just after six A.M. and wandered home for some well-deserved rest. Once I was home, I darkened my room just like a vampire as the sun wasn't my friend right now.

I didn't wake up from my deep sleep until the sun had set. I headed to the bathroom. Every muscle in my body hurt real bad. Even muscles I didn't know I had were throbbing and aching, mostly though it was my back and hands. I put two and two together, and realized it was the hand over hand walk in the grocery store that was the cause of my grief and pain.

The excitement of my first break-and-enter, the cash that went along with it, and knowing the boys had accepted me, not only into their toking circle but also their criminal circle, was well worth the pain.

Needless to say, with mom home, I stayed in that night and got caught up on my homework. It was just another downfall of having your mom for a teacher. You can't bullshit her about lack of homework. She taught high school and knew most of the curriculums of the lower grades.

The next day at school, Lucy surprisingly was a little shy and Kerry was a cold "pussy fart" bitch! Hell, I didn't need her cock teasing grief anyways. Finally, after lunch, I had a chance to talk to Lucy. I was really hard on myself thinking where had I screwed up? I really liked Lucy and deep down wanted her as my steady girlfriend. More importantly, I wanted back inside her! The key was to talk to her, and try to find out what was wrong.

I felt that possibly I might already know what the answer might be. I sheepishly walked up to Lucy in the playground, and looked in those sparkling Asian eyes of hers. I saw her smile and I felt safe enough to talk. However, the butterflies in my stomach wouldn't stop fluttering. It really wouldn't take much for me to throw up all over the place. I heard this little voice that had been filed away in my memory banks, *"Son, sometimes you just know you are going to take a beating. You can lie on the ground and take it like a coward; or you can be a true Sioux warrior and go down fighting."* I looked Lucy in the eye and with dad's knowledge and wisdom asked, "Did I do something wrong? For some reason you seem to be avoiding me."

I held my breath and tuned out everything but Lucy. She said, "You have done nothing wrong. Remember I told you I have a twin brother named Ricky? Well, he is returning to school tomorrow and he is very over-protective of me. If he thinks you and I are more than schoolmates, he will hurt you Mitch, and that in turn will hurt me."

So, this is where whatever answer I give will either make or break whatever I have going with Lucy. If I say I will kick your brother's ass, probably something easier said than done considering his reputation, she will be mad at me because he's just protecting his sister, much like do with Rachel. Maybe I should just appreciate the time we spent together and be thankful she took my virginity. That however would be taking the easy, coward's way out, and that is definitely not me. Damn it, she truly rocked my world Friday and Saturday; this was one girl worth fighting for.

"Lucy, I can appreciate your brother being over-protective. I'm the same with Rachel, as you found out first hand. Let me talk to him, perhaps he and I can do some business, or smoke a joint and talk about it. My weed joint will become our "Peace Pipe!"

"You know Strongbow, you are different. Ricky just might like you; my mom however is a different story. It won't matter how much weed you smoke with her."

Lucy smiled and I moved in and gave her a kiss and told her to just trust me. Deep down I sort of know it will come to us fighting. I will kick his Asian ass all over the schoolyard, just like any other punk that tries me. There are no doubts in my mind about that; the key was not to maim him.

After school while walking home with Larry, Norm, Blais and Kurt I asked them what they knew about Lucy Thom's brother Ricky. The only thing they knew about Ricky was he is a bit of a head case and a martial arts expert. They asked me if I talked to my brother about moving the cigarettes yet. I told them, "Jake is coming over tonight for dinner, I will ask him then."

Jake was on the front porch having a cigar when I asked him if he could move a large quantity of cigarettes for us. Jake asked how I come into possession of so many cartons. I told him, more like bragged to him; boy did I get a lecture. It wasn't so much about the break-and-entry, and the wrongs of breaking the law; it was about my target of opportunity, and the real cost of doing business. Jake's whole philosophy was this, "With any score, you have to take the profit you make, and divide it by the amount of time you would serve in prison. Figure out if the sum of the two is indeed a crime of opportunity, or a waste of time." Hell, who would have thought that mathematics could play a major role in the criminal world.

I told Jake, "We ended up with over five hundred in cash, thirty-five cartons of cigarettes, and to top it off, we stole a cop car!" Fuck I'm not sure why I admitted to that, after just seeing how pissed Jerry was.

Jake said, "Not only was it a good score, but also a classic score." Jake went deep in thought and said he would give us thirty five percent of what the cigarettes are worth. I should tell my partners only thirty percent, as I have to also be rewarded for finding a buyer.

"Mitchell I would be a hypocrite to condemn the path you're on, or the actions that you take. If you choose a life of crime little brother, then that is your path. I can give you some words of wisdom and hopefully, you will listen to some advice from my own experience. Over the years, you will find out who the solid citizens are. It's someone who will go to the wall for you, little brother. They catch you when you fall and pick you right back up. They do it, because they know you would do the same for them."

"There are those who we refer to as lugans. Mitchell lugans are leeches! They will suck the blood from you, use you and abuse you for their own gain. They will rat you out to the cops to get off on their own charges, or steal from underneath your nose. When they feel they are losing power in your inner circle, they will try and turn the circle against you. When that happens, little brother, you cut it out just like a cancer. No mercy, no hesitation, just cut it out!" Just like dad use to say, "Those who hesitate, get wasted in battle; kill or be killed." Once again another Hallmark moment! Strongbow family values, according to Jake.

"Now that little prick who gave us the finger, the kid's a 'heat score.' He's dangerous Mitchell, the kind of kid that's just in it for himself." Jake offered up a hundred bucks cash if I would give up the asshole that had given the guys in the club the finger.

I just shook my head no. Jake shot me this dirty look for defying him. "You taught me to never rat on anyone, big brother!"

Jake asked how serious the Chink and I were. I stuck my chest out and was so proud to say, "I fucked her three times, one day alone!" You couldn't take that smile off my face with a jackhammer. Jake then came over and gave me a hug, laughed and said, "She does have moxie, good for you. Has your mom met her yet?"

"Not yet, in time. Her name is Lucy by the way, not Chink! Man, she is cute, hey? The only thing is she has a twin brother who's over-protective and supposed to be a little psycho. I'm told I will meet him tomorrow." Jake asked if I wanted some help. I thanked him but said, "Ricky Thom will be the only one needing help, by the time I was done with him."

Jake and I shot the shit for another half hour before he headed for his house in Oakland. He told me he would send over Terek and Derksen to my house. I can go with them and pick up the cigarettes.

# BROKEN HEARTS, BROKEN BONES, MUST BE LOVE

The next morning, I was excited to see my friends to tell them I had a buyer for the cigarettes. I'm once again proving my value to my new friends. I told Larry, "Some of the guys from my brothers club will be at your place with me around 5 P.M." I told the guys, "I got thirty percent of the face value of the cigarettes."

The only person that complained was Kurt Wilson. Even though I was still trying to impress my new friends, I turned to Kurt and let him have a little vocal abuse. "I didn't see your ass inside the grocery store, taking the big risk the rest of us took. Nor have you found a buyer. I will call and cancel the deal, but those boys won't be happy. Kurt, you want to piss them off, your ass will be like a cigarette; they will fucking smoke you for wasting their time. They have cash; it's a quick deal for us."

Wilson didn't like being centered out in front of the boys. Norm stepped up and said "Let's take the cash! Besides down the road, these guys will know just how solid we are, for future business deals." The rest of the boys agreed and finally Wilson also came around. We all touched knuckles and were all in agreement.

As we are standing around waiting for the bell to ring, and our morning classes to start, I see my beloved Lucy and her brother Ricky entering the playground. Lucy looked quite nervous and was reluctant to make eye contact with me. I made my way towards her and Ricky, with the rest of boys following close behind me. I can sense the pack mentality forming; they smelled blood. They had seen me pulverize the two wops, and were curious if I was going to fight Ricky, and destroy him right then and there?

I approached Ricky and noticed I have at least six inches and thirty pounds on him. I'm now starting to snicker inside! This guy is tough, what's he going to do bite my ankles? I said, "Hi" to Lucy all the while looking at Ricky. No smile, just a look that said, "I'm going to fuck you up, little Asian man." Lucy could tell right off the bat things aren't good. She tells us both, to play nice and behave ourselves.

Ricky now eyes me up and down, curls his lip and asks, did I have a problem? I look at Ricky and replied, "I'm going out with your sister, is that a problem?" Ricky nods his head, smiles and answers, "Yeah that is a problem, and I think we should solve it right here and now."

Well before I can even get "Let's Go" out of my mouth, Ricky kicks off his front foot and nails me right in the stomach. I have never been kicked that hard before. The kick instantly knocked the wind right out of me. I'm slowly starting to lean forward to catch my breath when Ricky lands a beautiful left jab followed by right hook combination. Everything is now in slow motion, as if I am watching myself in a movie. I feel my nose slide to the other side of my face and watch the blood spraying all who wanted a court side view. I'm now on my way to the ground. I catch Ricky getting ready to kick me in the head out of the corner of my eye. However, he is stopped in pre-kick flight by Lucy who yells *"ENOUGH";* and then something in Chinese, which I believe in my delirious state I actually understood.

There is now a huge crowd gathered. Principal Diloreto and several other teachers were parting the kids. Diloreto now sees me on the ground, Lucy with a firm grip on Ricky's arm and Ricky still in a fight mode. Diloreto asks Ricky, "Did he do this?" Ricky didn't answer. Diloreto now looks at me and asks, "Did Ricky do this to you?" I'm now starting to come back to reality, and look at Lucy. I can see she is worried that I would rat out Ricky and he would be thrown out of his fourth and last grade school. Diloreto now asks me once again, this time with emotion, "Did Ricky do this?"

I looked at Diloreto and answered, "I fell while running." Diloreto is now pissed but I don't care;

Lucy's smiling at me. That warm beautiful smile she possesses seemed to take away the pain in my face and stomach. A couple of teachers took me to the nurse's office, where the nurse said that my nose is indeed broken, and sent me to the hospital with one of the teachers.

At the hospital, I am introduced to one of my future drugs of choice, Cocaine! The doctor shot some up my nose, and at once the pain had subsided. He then reset my nose. Wow, what a buzz! I think maybe I like that buzz very much indeed.

I was sitting on a gurney when I heard a familiar voice on the other side of the curtains. The nurse pulled the curtains open; the voice I recognized belonged to mom. She wasn't smiling! The doctors should give her some of that fine cocaine, enough to make her smile and feel good. Mom looked right into my dilated pupils and says, "Mitchell, you will be the death of me one day."

I'm not sure if the cocaine was wearing off and my nose was now working properly, but after mom's statement all I could smell was flowers. The smell was actually overwhelming to the point it was choking me. I couldn't breathe for almost thirty seconds; my eyes were watering as if fountains had opened, and I couldn't find the tap to shut it off. My bu*zz* was now wearing off.

On the drive home, mom and I talked. Just like Diloreto , she didn't believe my story that I fell while running nor did she believe that I was sick on Friday and missed all the afternoon classes. Mom dropped me off at home and said she had 'meet the teacher' night at her high school, and I was to stay in until she got home later on tonight. Well that's sure going to fuck up my cigarette deal with Jake and his boys.

I just agreed with mom and thought once my bu*zz* cleared, I would figure something out. I just chilled on the couch and tried to think of a plan to complete the cigarette deal. I also wondered how the hell Ricky had beaten me so badly. He was so damn fast and powerful but no way was I going to end my relationship with Lucy. I'm even more determined to make it work. I looked in the bathroom mirror, and could see both my eyes starting to darken, my nose is almost three times its normal size, and it was really starting to hurt.

I still hadn't thought of a way out of the house that wouldn't get my ass fried by mom. That was until Rachel walked through the front door. She stopped laughing at my face only when she realized she had forgotten some of her homework at school. Then it hit me, my legal outing!

I phoned Jake and told him, "I'm home from

school." Within fifteen minutes, Don Terek pulled up and I told Rachel, "I have an assignment for school due tomorrow that Larry brought home for me, and I'm going over to pick it up now." Rachel fell for it. I'm not sure if mom would, but if she calls home that is the story Rachel will give her.

I jumped into the back of Don's van; he and John Derksen asked, "What the hell happened?" and if they should they seek revenge in my name. I said, "Thanks for the offer but not right now, maybe down the road." Terek asked, was it over a girl?" I just nodded my head yes. Derksen looked at me with that demented look of his, "Do you know how many wars have started over pussy? Then again, if they weren't such fun to play with, they wouldn't be worth going to war over. Too bad you lost, hey Mitch?" Don then gave my nose a little squeeze; fuck I thought I was going to pass out! Once again the tears starting rolling down my eyes. Now it was Terek's turn to razz me, "I guess she's a piece of ass worth crying over." Don and John razzed me the whole way there.

Don and John accompanied me downstairs to Larry's basement, and I gave the boys their two garbage bags full of cigarettes. Norm was downstairs with Larry and both of them said, "Hi." John and Don just growled back at them, until Larry offered them both a beer and asked if they wanted to smoke a joint. This actually put a smile on their faces. I just wanted to get back home real quick and not get caught out of the house. The five of us sat at the table and smoked a joint and drank a beer, and then another joint and a couple more beers. It was an hour later when I asked Don to drive me home as the combo of the beer, weed and cocaine was really fucking me up. I told Don, "Just give Larry the money, and they can give me my cut tomorrow at school."

Yeah I was fucked! When I tried to get up, my legs were about as stable as a slinky toy. John carried me to the van, and Don carried the cigarettes. I don't really remember the ride home, or John carrying me upstairs to my bed or even passing out for that matter. What I do remember though is mom waking me from time to time, thinking I had a concussion.

The next day at school my sister Rachel passed me a note; it was from Lucy. She thanked me for not ratting out Ricky. Lucy also said she missed me but for right now we should stay apart, until she can convince Ricky that I'm all right.

Walking down the halls of school with my nose looking as if it needed trailer lights, and my eyes belonged to a raccoon, I'm not commanding the same respect as when I beat the wops. How the tide changes! At lunch time, Norm gave me my cut of the cigarette money. Norm, Larry, Kurt and Blais all asked if I wanted them to jump Ricky. I said, "No way! Thanks for the invite but this is my battle. Besides if Lucy does miss me, I will have to find a way to make peace."

That night at the dinner table mom mentioned that Rachel and I would be starting our new Karate school this coming Thursday. Mom feels I really need to be refocused, and need that discipline back in my life. She had noticed that when I was in Martial Arts while living on base, I wasn't such an angry young man. Rachel and I both agreed.

Thursday after dinner mom drove Rachel and me to Charlie Adams karate studio. I was already a blue belt and Rachel was an orange belt. As we walked into the Dojo, the smell of sweat felt so familiar, intense and yet so comforting. The butterflies were starting to flutter, as nervous energy was now revisiting me. I loved the Dojo, it was my battlefield where I could be myself. I loved being challenged mentally and physically, whether sparring with adults or teens my own age. Having the warm blood and adrenaline flow through my veins made me feel so alive.

Charlie, after making fun of my pulverized face, showed us where the change rooms were. I exited the change house and felt a twinge in my heart. It wasn't because of the Dojo spirit and getting ready to spar, but there was Lucy Thom. Better make that Lucy Thom the brown belt, working on her Kata's. She looked so damn sexy in that gi, her eyes match her belt. Then out of the corner of my eye, I saw Ricky; his black belt also matched the new color of my eyes.

The Dojo was broken up into three different groups. I wasn't allowed in with the adults, just with the teenagers. Unfortunately my instructor was none other than Ricky Thom. After Charlie Adams introduced Rachel and me to the new group, it was time to sweat.

Right off the bat, Ricky tried to embarrass me and challenge me physically. The whole group started doing pushups on our knuckles, and Ricky made a point of positioning himself, right in front of me. We went pushup for pushup together and neither one of us would give up. We hit fifty and kept going, sixty and kept going; now just Ricky and I were the last two left. Eighty kept going, one hundred kept going. Now the whole class was watching us, eighty, one hundred, finally at one hundred and eighty two Ricky collapsed; at one hundred and eighty three my arms gave out and my face hit the ground, broken nose and all. Yeah popped my nose again, but I wouldn't leave the class; no way is Ricky going to beat me again.

Charlie checked on me, acknowledged that indeed

my nose was broken again. Then right in front of the whole class, Charlie put both hands on the bridge of my nose and manually adjusted it back into place. Damn it hurt! However no way would I admit the pain in front of Ricky, and more importantly Lucy.

Ricky had us doing more and more exercises; I could taste the blood running down the back of my throat into my stomach. I thought I might throw up a couple times. Of course whenever Ricky needed a 'Dummy' to practice a move on; guess who he picked? Yeah, yours truly! He didn't pull his body blows or leg kicks; eventually I knew I was in trouble and this glorified beating had to stop.

While Ricky was showing the proper way to throw a front foot lead off kick with an overhand right, I leaned into Ricky and gave him a head butt. Loved it! Sounded like Willie Mays cracking one right out of the ball park. Ricky hit the ground and was knocked out cold; his cheekbone was now three times its normal size. I of course acted so sorry standing over him saying, "I slipped." I'm not sure if Charlie Adams bought my act, Rachel and Lucy did not.

Charlie ended up taking Ricky to the hospital. When mom showed up, she felt so bad that she drove Lucy home. Rachel sat in the front with mom while Lucy and I sat in the back. I wasn't sure just how pissed Lucy was at me. She reached over and held my hand in the back seat, all the while looking ahead. I guess she wasn't that pissed after all.

We pulled up to where Lucy lived, and it turned out to be a freaking gated mansion. I said, "Wow look at this place. Lucy, I never knew you lived in a place like this. Look at the security, would you. Hell, it's done up just like my brother's club house, right down to the bars on the windows."

Lucy replied, "Yeah that would be my mother. She started getting a little squirrelly when my dad got sentenced to jail." I then said, "I guess I can understand that, but this place is a fortress. Lucy is your mom scared of something?"

"Mitch, my dad wasn't just sentenced to jail. They tried to kill him in there!"

"Sorry Lucy, I didn't know. Is she concerned that an attempt will be made on your family? Is this what all this security is about?"

"Yeah, something like that; at least that's her story. I think the attempt on my dad was just the excuse that she needed to consolidate her little empire. She cares nothing for family, everything is about business; we're just pawns for her to use to get what she wants."

I said, "Ah come on Lucy you don't really mean that. Your dad will be out before you know it, and everything will be back to normal."

Lucy didn't answer. She buzzed the speaker and as we drove inside, we were met by an old man smoking a pipe. He had no facial expression at all, a very cold feeling person. Mom offered to drive Lucy and her mom to the hospital if need be. Lucy came back out and so did her mom. If the old guy was cold, her mom had ice flowing through her veins. She gave a filthy look and told us to leave. "You are not welcome here." She gave Lucy a smack in the head and told her to get inside.

Well fuck you and thanks for nothing! Mom just put the car in reverse and we drove away. It was a rather quiet ride home, and my eyes were opened to a different, rather dysfunctional lifestyle. I felt so bad for Lucy. Perhaps that's why she and Ricky are the way they are. As I went to sleep that night, I fantasized about taking Lucy away from her family, to a safe place where she could be a teenager. My beautiful Tiger Lilly shouldn't be treated like some fucking disobedient animal.

Ricky didn't make it to school or karate on Thursday night. Lucy said his cheekbone was broken. After class, mom drove Lucy home once again. While at karate that night Charlie Adams said I had proved myself enough to come to a special class he has every Saturday. "They train harder and it's full contact sparring, with twelve ounce gloves." Mom said I was allowed, after Charlie told her I had great potential to advance my martial arts training as my mind and body were both excellent.

Saturday morning after watching the Coyote and Runner, and eating scrambled eggs, I had mom drive me to karate. I was set for a grueling workout and that is exactly was it was; the toughest workout of my young life. My nemesis Ricky Thom and my love Lucy Thom were there right beside me as well. With Ricky having a broken cheekbone and my nose still not fully healed, Charlie wouldn't let Ricky or I spar. However, we did everything else. I must tell you I was learning moves and Katas that were blowing my mind. I was so full of confidence now, with my overall physical capabilities and fighting prowess.

After the class I tried to make peace with Ricky after Lucy said she would make it worth my while. So, in my best native tradition, I asked Ricky if he would like to smoke a joint with Lucy and myself. Smoke the proverbial peace pipe, as it were. Ricky agreed which made Lucy happy, which in turn made me happy.

The three of us found an alley a couple blocks from the Dojo, and I sparked up the joint and passed it to Ricky. I knew he still wasn't impressed with me, as the whole time he just stared at me. He looked at Lucy. I got the message alright; no way did he want me getting close to his sister.

I wasn't sure what else to do when fate intervened;

six guys with baseball bats were approaching the three of us. I guess the bu*zz* was so good, or maybe the fact that Ricky was so focused on me, we didn't see these guys sneak up on us. They had us trapped with no exit.

This was a real bad scene. Ricky and I were all banged up and freaking high, so the odds of us taking a real kick ass beating were quite high. I wasn't so worried about Ricky or me, it was Lucy I didn't want to get hurt. As they moved in a semi circle around us, one guy approached Ricky and said, "I told you China man about selling drugs on my turf. You were warned once, now you must pay."

I looked at their ringleader who made the statement and said, "Let Lucy leave. She is innocent. If you wanna fight, Ricky and I will go at you."

As I said this, I took off my leather jacket and was preparing for battle. Their ringleader said, "I can't let the slut go, she has been dealing drugs on our turf too."

Well, Jake preached to me earlier in the week, "KILL OR BE KILLED." I was ready when I heard a couple of our enemies commenting about the t-shirt I was wearing. They lowered their bats and asked, "Where did you get that shirt?"

I forgot what shirt I was even wearing. Was this a diversionary tactic for me to lower my head? I pulled my shirt out and smiled, it was an Oakland Hell Hound t-shirt. "My brother Jake gave me this shirt, he is Sergeant at Arms and my cousin Jerry is club President." I could smell and sense fear! Their feet were now starting to shift, and their bats were completely lowered.

The ringleader stated, "How do we know you are not bullshitting us?" I didn't even have to answer. One of the six said he saw Lucy and me together outside the Drunken Leprechaun with a bunch of the Hell Hounds this past Saturday. He said, "The chick even kicked a Hell Hound in the face, and the rest of Hell Hounds threatened the Hell Hound who was hit, if he retaliated. This guy is real!"

Now it was my turn to play tough guy, "You boys say Ricky and Lucy were selling on your turf? Funny, I thought this whole damn island was Hell Hound turf. I think I should make a phone call and tell my brother Jake and cousin Jerry Strongbow that there is a new gang who wants to challenge them. Let's just call it a turf war, is that about right?"

Fear, nothing but fear was now on their faces and in their voices. "Lucy is my girlfriend and Ricky and I are partners. Should you have a problem with them, you have a problem with me and the rest of my family. I guarantee my family won't show up with just ball bats. But they may show up with guns and knives, and won't rest until you are all dead." I then grabbed Lucy by the hand and walked up to their leader and said three words that caused them all to run way, "Disappear or Die." Now that was ultimate power! Six guys with ball bats ran away from us, all because of who I am or, more like, who my family is. I didn't hesitate and I didn't get wasted.

After the three of us smoked another joint we were all well on our way. Ricky even let me hold Lucy's hand until we were a block from their house. Ricky said, "Strongbow, you aren't that bad a guy. She's still my sister, and I hope you fully understand where I'm coming from?"

I appreciated Ricky's honesty. "I have a sister too and I fully understand where you are coming from. Your sister is beautiful, man. I really dig her."

Lucy gave me a kiss which hurt my nose but I didn't mind. Ricky did give me some advice, "My mom will never accept you and Lucy going out. If she even thinks something is going on between the two of you, she will beat Lucy! If you really like my sister like you say you do, this must be kept real quiet. It can't get back to her at all. Even your brother and cousin couldn't protect her or save her from a beating."

I told Ricky, "I fully understand," and asked if we were cool. Ricky actually smiled and said, "Yes." I asked if they wanted to hook up with me tomorrow.

"Maybe we could head over to Larry Dubrowski's house and get high." Ricky said he would like that. Lucy said she would love it.

I felt so happy that the war between Ricky and me was settled. Lucy was happy too, so with that I jogged all the way home and just stayed in and did homework, which pleased mom to no end.

The next morning, I woke up with a nice smile on my face and everyone I was close to was happy with me; that made me happy with life. After breakfast, there was a knock at the front door. It was Ricky and Lucy. I asked them both inside and introduced mom to them.

Mom could sense Lucy meant something special to me. She had noticed when she drove Lucy home the past couple times, but she also knew what made her son happy. Lucy thanked her for being so nice last week and after that, the three of us headed to Larry Dubrowski's house. Larry was quite surprised to see Ricky and Lucy with me with no one in between trying to break us up from fighting.

We had just finished smoking a joint and were getting a nice mellow bu*zz* when Larry said, "Every Sunday we play pick up football at the park, just down the street," and asked if Ricky and me would be interested in playing. We both agreed and off to the park we went. Norm, Blais and Kurt were already there throwing around the "pigskin." There were twelve of us and when it came time for picking teams, Ricky was the last player picked. Well, he wasn't picked exactly he was just the last person left.

I kind of felt bad for him until we started playing. First kickoff of the game, Ricky ran it back for a touchdown. No one could match his speed or his moves; he was a tremendous athlete and it showed. It was great bonding time for all of us, playing ball and jiving to each other. At the end of every quarter we smoked a couple joints together. Lucy, Kerry, and several other girlfriends were on the sidelines, cheering us all on. There was still no love lost between Lucy and Kerry, but I didn't give a rat's ass. Lucy was my girl. Kerry had her chance and blew it. Well actually she didn't blow it and that is why she was dumped.

Over the next month or so, things were great. Lucy and I made it official; we were truly boyfriend/girlfriend and the sex was incredible. The boys accepted Ricky into the group and he was now the first pick on football Sundays. Weekends, we're always partying at Dubrowski's house. California was great and life was great.

You would think with all the commotion I seem to have caused since starting high school, the constant warnings from mom and Jake, not to mention the ever present threat of having my butt seriously kicked by him, that I would be preoccupied with staying out of trouble. But that wasn't to be the case, and in a way I blame the cops.

A month or so ago, my brother had asked me if I was interested in getting my first job. It was the same job he talked about before, when I was having my legal issues. Mom, like before, agreed as long as my marks didn't drop. This arrangement really helped my mom out, as she was the only bread winner in the house. I was quite eager to make some honest money. Dealing weed was good as you always had enough for personal use, but extra cash would help. Jerry had bought and now had possession of an old canning factory that he was turning into a gym he was calling Popeye's.

My new job was fairly physical and I had to work hard for my money, but my cousin Jerry was paying me quite well. I had to scrape all the walls down and then paint them, all forty thousand square feet, rip out old pieces of machinery, and general renovations etc. I would sleep over at Jake's house on the weekends and just go to work from there. The only downtime I had was designated for karate, school and Lucy.

Spending weekends at Jake's was a whole new way of life for me. People were coming in and out of his house at all hours of the night. Every once in a while, you would see plain clothes cops parked outside on the street watching and writing down who came and went from Jake's. The constant sounds of motorcycles going up and down the street sometimes made getting a good night's sleep not that easy. Weekends meant partying, hardcore partying, booze flowing, and all kinds of drugs.

Jake didn't mind Lucy sleeping over or me fucking her under his roof. The only rule he had was "NO CHEMICALS!" "Mitchell," he would say, "Never do anything that could kill your soul." Some of the people that would show up, you could tell by looking deep into their eyes, they didn't have a soul left. Strippers, musicians, and actors would all drop by from time to time. Jake's world was so full of life, twenty-four hours a day, seven days a week. On weekends, Jake or someone from the club would make sure I got to karate on time.

Every once in a while, Jake or Jerry would bring me to the Hell Hound club house in Oakland. This was Disney World for adults with pool tables, pinball machines, a hot tub, and a kick ass fully stocked bar; with beer machines instead of pop machines. The majority of the Hell Hounds liked me, except for Scott Fagan.

He still had not forgotten what Lucy did to him. I told Jake and Jerry many times, there was just something about that guy Fagan I don't trust. Bad vibes! Jake and Jerry would say, "It's just because of the Lucy incident." I filed that bad vibe away into my memory banks.

Don Terek was becoming very close to me, he was acting almost like an older brother. He said that he was getting married in a couple weeks at the club house. He asked if Lucy and I would like to come. I was quite excited! I have never been to a wedding before, never mind a biker wedding. I wondered if his fiancée Jeannie would wear white leather.

Don received his "Full Patch" a week before his wedding and was now an official member of the Hell Hounds Oakland Chapter. This was also his "Stag" night at the clubhouse. I was invited but Jake and Jerry drilled into my head, "What goes on in the club house, stays at the club house. Do not under any circumstances tell your friends what went on."

Even the founder and Hell Hound President for all chapters, Eric Von Kruder was present. This man exudes power! You can literally feel the energy coming off him a mile away. When you look at his weathered face with his battle scars and flaming red hair, you would think you were in the presence of royalty. He was more powerful and had more charisma than any TV or motion picture star.

I was taught to always look into a person's eyes

when you first meet them. When Jake introduced me to Mr. Von Kruder, I did exactly that. His eyes had the look of pure evil, as if he snatched the Devil's own two pupils for himself. When Eric asked me questions, I kept my answers short and respectful. I was, after all, a reflection of Jake and Jerry. Later on that night, Jake told me that Von Kruder thought I was a good kid. That actually meant a lot to me.

At one point they had Terek tied down to a chair and these strippers were naked and grinding him. They started putting their breasts into his face and when they took off his pants, the two strippers performed oral sex on him. I couldn't move. I was speechless!

Later the two strippers that had performed on Don spotted me and made their way over. They introduced themselves as Carsta and Eva Vigoda. These two sisters were both quite tall, with blonde hair and blue eyes; they were beautiful. Once I told them who I was, they started coming on to me.

They asked if I was a virgin. They wanted to know did I have a little girlfriend who could suck cock the way they did. I rather sheepishly said, "Yes." These two beautiful girls totally intimidated me, like no one else ever has; not even fighting foes. As Carsta started to rub my crotch she asked if I liked the show.

I know I'm not supposed to tell anyone what goes

on at the clubhouse and right now I don't think any of my friends would believe me anyways. Eva also started to rub me. I have never once thought of fooling around on Lucy, but damn this was too hot to turn down. Eva put my left hand on her breasts and Carsta put my other hand down her pants; and much to my surprise she had no pubic hairs. Then the unthinkable happened, big John Derksen picked up Carsta and threw her over his shoulders and said, "She has a chore to perform." Carsta looked back at me smiled and waved goodbye, while hanging off John's shoulders.

Well there was still Eva. Next thing I know that goof Fagan came over grabbed Eva by the arm and said to me, "Where is your Gook girlfriend?" He then turned and took Eva away. One day Fagan and I will go, and I will kick the shit right out of him, full patch or not! I spent the rest of the night just mingling and enjoying the whole buzz of the stag.

The next morning I was feeling a little rough, but not that bad. I'm glad in a way that I didn't end up fooling around on Lucy, although I spent many a night either having a wet dream or masturbating about what would have happened with Carsta and/or Eva.

The following Saturday turned out to be a great day for Donnie and Jeannie's wedding. I was graded from blue to brown belt in karate that morning. Lucy looked absolutely amazing, with this classy green dress that would've suited Jackie Kennedy. I wore the same suit I had when dad returned from Vietnam in a body bag. Actually it's the first time I have worn it since then.

John Derksen and I picked Lucy up a block from her house. Don's wedding was an outdoor ceremony at the club house. Jake was his best man and Jerry was an usher. None of these guys wore suits, but they were all decked out in their best leathers, Hell Hound colors and all. Even Don's Harley Davidson had soup cans tied to the back of it with a sign that said "JUST MARRIED".

As Lucy and I took our seats, Carsta and Eva waved at me, winked, and then laughed. My suit collar was now getting awful tight, as I sheepishly waved back. I didn't even have to look at Lucy; I could feel the arctic breeze coming from her. I finally looked at Lucy and said, "Friends of Jake's." I also noticed Scott Fagan looking at Lucy and me. Fuck him!

I have never seen anyone look as beautiful as Don's bride Jeannie, walking down the aisle. She was a tall blonde with good size breasts, but very small facial features. She had a radiant glow about her and sparkling white teeth; she was one classy broad. Don was so damn gruff and mean looking; I guess it is true opposites attract. Jeannie was wearing a long flowing white wedding dress. One of the strippers from the other night was playing a harp, as Jeannie and her dad walked down the aisle. Who would of thunk the stripper had that kind of talent, other than looking great and dancing naked.

It was surprisingly a rather emotional ceremony with Jeannie crying and even Don, the tough guy, wiping the odd tear away. I looked next to me and Lucy also had tears in her eyes. I too was caught up in the moment; the next thing I knew I whispered in her ear, "I love you." Whatever cold feelings Lucy had because of the Vigoda sisters were melted by my heartfelt, "I love you." Lucy whispered in my ear, "*I love you too*" and I knew all was good between us. Lucy answering back, that she also loved me, was the greatest euphoric feeling I have ever experienced, other than losing my virginity. For the rest of the ceremony we held hands and acted like love birds.

After the service, people were throwing rice at Don and Jeannie as they walked down the aisle together. Fagan came over and said out loud to embarrass Lucy and myself, "Hey Chink girl maybe you can pick it all up, take it home and feed your slant eyed family."

I had enough of him and didn't care where I was or who I was around. I let go of Lucy's hand and headed towards Fagan; this was go time. A hand stopped me in my tracks. I looked to see who the hand belonged to, and who was going to be next on my fight card; when I realized it was Eric Von Kruder. I just looked at Eric and stopped my pursuit towards Fagan.

Von Kruder summoned Fagan over. The smart ass look on Fagan's face was now gone. Jake and Jerry made their way over as well. I wasn't sure what to do. Lucy was with me and she was my old lady. If anyone was to hurt her they would have to kill me first. I know that Jake and Jerry had my back, but man Von Kruder commanded so much power over his Hounds and Fagan was a Hell Hound while I was just a fifteen year old with family in the Hell Hounds. Would Von Kruder choose one of his soldiers like Fagan over me; and would Jake and Jerry too?

Von Kruder now had two of his bodyguards beside him. They were the biggest mother fuckers I have ever seen in my life, and they were ready to strike death into whomever he decided to dispose of. Eric looked very intensely at Lucy and me, and then he swung around and grabbed Fagan by the throat. His two body guards grabbed Fagan's arms so the choke couldn't be broken.

Von Kruder addressed Lucy all the while looking at Fagan, "Young lady, are you not Fred Thom's daughter?" Lucy's face changed and her jaw dropped, "Yes, I am." Von Kruder laughed while still choking

Fagan, who was now gasping for air. "This little China doll's dad is one of my best business associates, even though he is in prison at the moment. Fagan, are you trying to fuck up my business deals, because if you are, we can turn this wedding into a funeral."

Von Kruder loosened his grip on Fagan so he could answer. He was scared, make that deathly scared, "No Eric, I'm not trying to fuck anything up. She is just a fish headed cunt who kicked me in the face last week. I swear on my life I didn't know anything about your business deals."

Eric now re-positioned his grip back on Fagan and started to squeeze once again. "You are supposed to be a full patch Hell Hound, the world's most notorious and feared motorcycle club, and a fourteen year old girl not only kicks you in the face, but in doing so causes you to eat your lit cigar. When I heard this I was waiting for someone to give me the punch line. I can't fathom how this could, would or should happen, but it did, and it will end right now. Fagan, if you so much as look at her the wrong way, I will personally slice your throat. Do I make myself clear?"

Fagan had tears rolling down his cheeks. I wasn't sure if it was from the choke or the death threat. Von Kruder let him go and told him to leave the club house, as he is taking the fun out of the wedding and he is on notice. Von Kruder looked at Jerry and repeated once again that Fagan was on notice. Jerry looked at Eric and said "Duly noted."

Von Kruder looked at Lucy and asked if she would like to dance with him. I sure as hell wasn't going to interfere and be a jealous boyfriend. I had too much life ahead of me. Lucy said she would be honored and Eric, like the classy guy he was, danced like Fred Astaire.

Lucy and I spent the rest of the night just mingling and having a real good time. We behaved ourselves as best we could, no over-drinking or too many social substances. When it was time to leave, Joseph O'Reilly, the owner of the Drunken Leprechaun, offered to give us a ride home. He wouldn't let Lucy in his bar, but he would let her in his car; some of these guys I just could not figure out.

He dropped Lucy off a block from her house and invited the both of us to his bar for lunch one day. It had to be before 7pm, as no minors were allowed after that time. Once Lucy was dropped off, Joseph asked if I had ever met Lucy's mom. When I said, "No." Joseph said, with that Irish accent of his, "She is an evil woman and she has no soul. The Devil himself lives inside of her! The devil and her meet every Sunday, when she gives him refresher courses on how to be evil. Take care of Lucy, young Mitchell. Her soul is not to be taken."

I thanked Joseph for his concern. I was quiet on the ride home, and deep in thought. I truly didn't understand what he meant, and I spent most of the night trying to replay his exact words. Jake always said, "Joseph O'Reilly is an honest man and always tells it like it is. He would back up anything he said, regardless of the friend or foe."

# SCHOOL'S OUT, WORKING OUT, TRYiNG OUT

About a week before school let out for the summer, I finished up my job at Jerry's gym. Popeye's was truly an amazing gym and I felt so good knowing I did my part in making it look that way. The parking lot was a decent size and several of the Hell Hounds taught me how to ride a motorcycle over the past couple months. I was hooked and was determined when I turned sixteen to get my own motorcycle. With the money I made from the gym and dealing, that is exactly what I was now saving for. I felt like a true Sioux warrior driving a motorcycle; the only difference, a motorcycle was an "Iron Horse".

With Lucy and Ricky as my drug partners, business was excellent. Ricky and I worked out as often as we could; we would both really push each other hard. Lucy and I were head over heels in love with each other. However, from time to time, I would see bruises or cigarette burns on Lucy's body. Every time I would question her, we would end up in a fight.

Lucy's lack of dialogue and with remembering what O'Reilly had told me, I knew who was inflicting pain on her, but what could I do? It tears me apart just sitting by idle, not being able to help. Hell, if any other human on this planet were to hurt her, I would kill them.

Every Sunday was still pickup football and weekends at Larry's house were party time. Most of the kids in our school made sure that no one in our little gang was invited to their parties. Well, fuck them! After all who needed them anyways? We were called outlaws by most of the kids from school or around town. That was exactly the way we liked it.

I knew all the guys in the local Hell Hounds real good by now. Fagan would just leave or would be real quiet whenever I was around. I would still like to go him but I respected what Von Kruder told him. I believe mom also knew I was walking a fine line between a juvenile delinquent and a normal teenage kid just trying to find his own identity. Like most teenagers, we had our own little covenant of hoodlums, our pack, where we were pulling away from the so-called family unit.

One Saturday, Blais asked us all if we would like to play a more organized football game. He had signed up for tryouts for our district Pop Warner football team, and Blais challenged the rest of us to join. I was a little surprised when my mom said she was all for me playing organized football. I guess she had the old, "Idle hands are evil hands" thing in her mind, so she encouraged me to join.

Our team was called "the Bears" and we were in a

ten team league. Trying out for the team were Herman Bauer, a true Nazi; John Walter a drug dealer; David Crowfeet, a full blooded Apache; and Connor O'Reilly, Joseph O'Reilly's nephew. Connor's parents were killed in Ireland thirteen years ago, and Joseph had been Connor's guardian ever since. Scott Kantonescu and Fraser Dalton, who had older brothers associated with the Hell Hounds, also tried out for the team.

After the first practice, we went back to Larry's and all of us hit it off really well. We all had the same thought process about criminal activities, getting high, getting laid and fighting. Throw in Norm, Larry and Kurt and we were now known as the 'Dirty Dozen'. With the new guys hanging around, it was now my turn to laugh when each new guy ended up coming from Kerry's bedroom with the horrid 'Ring Look' on his face.

Connor got his cousin Joseph to sponsor our team. I tried out for outside linebacker, as I really enjoyed hitting and hurting my opponents. By now, most of the Dirty Dozen had steady girlfriends and, for the most part, the girls all got along. Lucy, though, was a little different. She never really got close to any other girl that hung around with us. However, that was Lucy and she scared the hell out of the girls, which turned me on. No doubts about it, Lucy and I were the most dangerous couple in the Dirty Dozen.

Our first football team meeting was at the Drunken Leprechaun. We all drove our bicycles over and just like the Hell Hounds we parked our bikes all in a row out front. We were nowhere as vicious as the Hell Hounds, but we were feared by many different teenage gangs in San Francisco, and rightly so, I might add. All twelve of us were good fighters and never shied away from a scrap, either as a group or as an individual. I realized real quickly, that anyone can be tough in a gang. It's your capability to survive and still have the same attitude and principles that separates the pretenders from the rest of us.

Jake told me all about lugans and we had a few of them hanging around, until we realized what they were all about. Then, we would lay a beating on them and send them on their merry little way. One such person was named Al Berry, a big kid who moved here from New York City recently. He bragged about all the fights he was in back home. He said it was the toughest city in America. He said gangs from all over would beg him to join their gang.

Now when someone tells me how tough they are, I first look at their knuckles to see what shape they are in. If they are as smooth as a baby's ass with no damage, I know they have never thrown them to hurt. It's the same thing with scars on their face. I'm not saying they have to look like a battered punch drunk; some people are great at dodging and weaving.

However sooner or later someone will land a punch or kick to your face.

The most important facial feature I look at is the eyes. Dad used to tell me about the 'Thousand Yard Stare.' This is what he said separated those soldiers without a soul from those who fought not only to survive, but to win. Thousand Yard people enjoyed killing and weren't afraid to be wounded or to die in battle; they have already accepted their fate. They would die for each other, but not their country or their president. This logic is what we wanted from a Dirty Dozen member.

With Ricky and me really developing our full contact karate skills, we now knew exactly what it took; not only physically but mentally. I found myself never shying away from a scrap, and taking what I learned in the Dojo onto the streets. There I could really hurt my opponent and this would be a true test of what I learned. There were no practice punches or kicks, no Sensei saying stop, try it again; this was the real deal.

The more street fights I got into, the more a true adrenaline junkie I became. When I felt my heart get that first shot of adrenaline, and felt the warm blood being pumped through my veins, into my arms and legs, I was ready for battle. This made me smile; it was almost as good as sex.

It was the same rush in a sense, that I got trying to prove my manhood, and there was the high of seeing the fear in my opponent's eyes. There were those who even refused to make eye contact with me when the Dirty Dozen crashed a party. They would pat us all on the back even while we were demolishing their houses, drinking their booze and fucking their women. Eventually I could smell, as well as sense and taste, the fear coming off my opponents. It was power, absolute addictive power!

Norm heard about some private party up in Snob Hill one weekend. Some rich kid's parents went away for the weekend. Norm's cousin Gale invited a couple of us to drop by. Well if you invite one Dirty Dozen member you invite the whole gang, and that is what happened.

Blais stole a VW mini bus that actually reminded me of the mini bus Jake and I drove to hunt camp in '63. Fraser stole a Ford Falcon and off we went. The usual procedure was two people would split on a twenty-four pack of beer. When we ran out of our beer, we would just drink any other booze at the party. Anyone objected, they would take a beating of epic proportions. Lucy couldn't go to this party, as her mom had her grounded for the weekend. Her mom loved to ground her. It didn't even matter whether she was right or wrong.

While at this party, I knew by the way we waltzed in, the rich kids were intimidated right off the bat. There would be no problems if anyone tried to stand up to us. Al Berry also picked up on this and was his usual loud, belligerent self. Al was a bully pure and simple. I, on the other hand, was a warrior who enjoyed the challenge of a great scrap.

As the night went on, I noticed this really cute blonde there. She was very wholesome, with beautiful blue 'cat eyes' and a soft, shy smile. I eventually asked Gail, who was Norm's cousin, who she was and was she single? I have never once cheated on Lucy, she kept me more than happy. Plus, if Lucy where to find out I was unfaithful to her, I was afraid she would cut my dick off.

Gail told me her name was Natasha and no, she wasn't single. She was going out with this guy named David." When Gail mentioned Natasha was a Jew she said it in a very condescending manner, even though they were close friends. Enough said! I just banked her name and smile into my brain and did some more partying.

Al was starting to push people around as the night went on. He would just walk up to them and take their cigarettes, or order people to get him a beer. Al was single handily changing the mood of the party and it was really pissing me off. He was riding the Dirty

Dozen name to make himself even more of a bully.

Al also noticed Natasha and when she went outside for a breath of fresh air without her boyfriend, Al followed her. My gut told me she was someone I really wanted to get to know, and knowing the way Al was, I wasn't about to let him hurt her, no fucking way. I walked outside just in time to see Natasha pushing Al away and him laughing with a cigarette in his mouth. I told Al to leave her alone and then I told Natasha to back up a couple steps. Al just stared at me. The smile on his face was gone now. He flicked the cigarette butt from his mouth onto the ground.

I could feel the adrenaline starting to pump to my heart, blood flow to my arms, legs and fists. This has been a long time coming. I heard a voice from behind ask, "What the hell is going on?" It was David, Natasha's boyfriend. Natasha told David that Al had come on to her, and David was pissed. I was still staring down Al while making sure I wasn't in a vulnerable position with David or Al. When David asked if I was involved, Natasha answered, "No, just Al."

David now sized up the situation. There were two of us and one of him. What should a boyfriend do? He could try and seek revenge and fight us both, or just go back inside and do nothing, and lose face with his girlfriend.

In my world, I don't care how many people are involved. There are beatings a plenty coming, even if I have to take one. Man, anybody comes onto Lucy, fuck she would knock the shit out of them herself.

Al got real brave and asked David what the fuck he was going to do about him coming onto Natasha. Didn't he know who we were? David was thinking instead of reacting, so I made David's decision a little easier.

I winked at Natasha and said to David, "There is no we, this guy is on his own. I wouldn't take this fat fuck's bullshit coming onto my old lady." I'm not sure who was more confused by my statement, David or Al. I then looked at David, "I give you my word I won't get involved; you do what you feel you must."

Al shot me the filthiest look, while David just nodded his head. He believed me and charged Al with fists and legs flying. He was tagging Al with everything he threw at him. I could tell that David himself was also trained in martial arts. Al didn't stand a chance. He looked like a deer caught in the headlights. He didn't know what to do. Man, I was really getting off on Al taking a beating.

Natasha was starting to cry, although I'm not sure why. Her boyfriend was defending her honor. She should be proud and happy for him. True to my word, I just stood back and let it all go down. I heard the knockout punch come from David, a spinning reverse temple punch. Al hit the ground real hard.

David just looked at me, nothing needed to be said. I just gave him a nod of approval and said, "I told you I would keep my word and not get involved. However, the rest of these guys inside might not be so happy, seeing this loudmouth fat fuck on the ground knocked out cold. I think the two of you better leave."

David thanked me for being honest and true to my word. Natasha, well just the way she looked at me, I knew I had touched her in a caring kind of warped way. I'm sure if David wasn't there, she would of hugged me goodbye. Damn, that smile and those eyes were definitely filed in my memory banks now. She was beautiful and breathtaking; a blonde Goddess! David was a lucky guy.

Twenty minutes after David and Natasha left the party Al was still out cold, so I decided it was time to wake him up. I urinated all over Al which did the trick. As he staggered to his feet, he realized what I had done. Pardon the pun but I wasn't sure if Al was more pissed because I didn't back him in the fight, or that I gave him a 'Golden Shower' to wake him up.

There's no way was I going to waste pouring good beer on him, this asshole was not worth it. As Al was now coming to his senses, Blais, Norm and Fraser now joined me out back. Fraser looked at Al and asked, "What the fuck happened?" Al now pointed his finger at me and slurred, "That fucking Indian watched some fucking guy jump me blind and didn't help me. He stood by and watched him beat me saying, "Dirty Dozen is nothing but losers and faggots."

Fraser looked at me confused and asked why I let Al not only get jumped but didn't come to his defense after he slammed our gang. Was Fraser questioning my loyalty? Al wasn't a Dirty Dozen; he was a lugan, a loud mouth, bully lugan.

After I told Fraser my version, Al called me a liar and charged at me. It was met by a front snap kick to the groin, and an over hand right and left hook. He was out cold by the time he hit the ground. Fraser, Norm and Blais all rushed in and starting laying the boots to Al. Eventually I told the boys, "Enough, we do not want to kill him, he isn't worth going to prison for."

Norm came up with a brilliant idea. We shaved off one side of Al's eyebrow and put all this makeup on his face. We stripped him down to just his underwear, and had one of the girls give up her bra, so we could put it around Al's chest. Blais then drove Al to a gay part of San Francisco and left him on a park bench sitting upright. It was a classic payback for Al, the loudmouth lugan.

Afterwards, I came right out and asked Fraser if he doubted my story at all. Fraser said no, he was sick of Al and his bullshit stories too and just wanted to hear what his last and final bullshit story would be. We didn't see 'hide nor hair' of Al Berry for the rest of the summer.

That whole summer, I kept hoping I would run into the blonde Goddess known as Natasha. I was truly smitten by her. Infatuation? Possibly! Either way there was many a crusty Kleenex under the bed with her name on it. Even the odd time while making out with Lucy, I thought of Natasha. Whenever Lucy and I would have a fight, I wished I could run into Natasha and tell her I was available. Unlike Al, I would be the victor and lay a beating on David if need be. I can honestly say it was love at first sight with Natasha.

I learned another lesson that summer. It wasn't so much about laying a beating on someone, but having to take a beating because of your own stupidity. Jake always drilled into my head "**Do not do anything that will kill your soul**'.

So one night, Blais and Fraser showed up at Larry's house with this bag of pills. They broke into a pharmacy and stole bottles and bottles of pills, Seconal [Reds], Tuinal, Mandrax, all hardcore sedatives. Blais was passing around the pills like Halloween treats.

I thought to myself and rightly justified my logic by saying; if these pills were so bad, why would doctors prescribe them? Yeah let's take a few, and chug a few bevies. Within thirty minutes I couldn't even tie up my shoes and my speech was severely slurred. What a freaking trip man. Talk about totally wasted, not high, just wasted, fucked up wasted.

At one point David Crowfeet was so wasted he went to pee in the toilet, lost his balance and fell into the bath tub, breaking his jaw and so ending his illustrious summer football campaign. David continued to pee and made a fine mess, piss and blood all over Larry's bath mats. Scott Kantonescu and Connor O'Reilly came in about an hour after we had taken the sedatives. They couldn't believe their eyes at how screwed up we all were.

I needed a hand getting up off the sofa. Both Scott and Connor were holding me up, then decided to let go of me. I must have been faking, right? Well, it was like Paul Bunyan took his mighty axe to my legs. I fell like a mighty timber right into the coffee table, cut my head wide open right down the middle of my forehead, a beautiful two inch long gash.

John Walter and Blais decided on a contest to see who could eat more pills. They wanted to see who could out duel the other and just like the duels at the turn of the century, death was lurking, waiting to see which one would be its first victim. I honestly believe that if Larry's older sister Nicky, a nurse, hadn't come downstairs and diagnosed Blais and John as overdosed, the two of them would have died. She called an ambulance for the two of them and Crowfeet went along as well with his broken jaw. I refused treatment.

Once John and Blais were at the hospital, they had their stomachs pumped, and Crowfeet had his jaw wired shut. Needless to say, the football game scheduled for the next day was forfeited since we couldn't field enough players.

I explained to mom that I hurt myself while sparring, even though I felt wasted for almost two days. I said I thought it was the result of a punch. A concussion was my excuse, and I was sticking to it.

Nasty drugs and an even nastier learning experience for Blais, John and Crowfeet. They had suffered almost tragic effects from the 'Downers.' The only lesson they really learned was that this was a highly entertaining and almost addictive bu*zz*. I enjoyed the way the downers really mellowed you out fast, and tried to respect the effects and consequences. I now know that even if the pills are prescribed by a doctor, there are limits on how many pills you can or should take.

Other eye and mind expanding lessons learned that summer were my love of music and how chicks really dug musicians. Man, even if they were dog ugly, these musicians had chicks all over them. It was a powerful formula, almost as if they could cast a magical spell over the women in the audience. It was a spell for seduction. Chicks would go wild and lose their inhibitions. All the musicians had to do was give them the eye while on stage. Next thing you know, in between sets or after the gig, they would be getting laid. Unfortunately, I didn't have a musical note in my body.

Between bashes at the Hell Hound club house and free concerts throughout San Francisco, music became a huge part of my soul. It made me feel so alive! When I was high, the music would bring me to a sense of euphoria; they seemed to go hand in hand. Now country music, I hate that depression shit.

I also got to know some of the local musicians who were just starting out their musical careers, sort of like me starting out my criminal career. Several of us will have highs and lows, some will survive, some will die way too young, but what the hell. As long as we have fun along the way, enjoy the trip right?

The survival of my relationship with Lucy also had

its highs and lows. Lucy was full of fire which was great when it came to sex, but like fire, sometimes you felt the pain of the flames and get burned. I know her mom was a controlling psychotic bitch. She was hell bent and determined to totally fuck up Lucy's and Ricky's head. She was mentally and physically abusive to the both of them.

I wanted to get involved and stand up to their mom, but each time both Ricky and Lucy would get pissed at me. They say an abused victim will always protect their abuser! Over the years, the guilt inflicted will change their psyche into believing the punishment bestowed upon them was justified.

One day in particular stood out. I almost grabbed my hunting rifle, and was going to shoot their mom dead. Lucy showed up at my house late at night in terrible shape. She was bleeding from her nose, had cigarette burns on the inside of her thighs, and she couldn't sit down as her ass was too sore. Lucy was shaking and trembling with fear! I had never seen that side of Lucy before, and I just hugged her. I tried to get her to tell me who did this and why. She just cried in my arms for almost an hour straight. I felt my blood boiling, knowing there was nothing I could do; it was a dreadful feeling.

Lucy and I started to drift apart after that night. She had become cold! Whenever we had sex, she had to be high or drunk, and even then she would just lay there dead. It was like fucking a zombie. I truly believe a part of her soul died that awful night. Whatever happened to traumatize her, the sparkle in her eyes was gone. It was getting to the point where I felt guilty having sex with her, as I knew deep down Lucy hated it. Even foreplay was out. She would just tell me to get on top and get it over with. How could I enjoy myself knowing she dreaded it? I should have killed that cunt mom of hers that night. Maybe then Lucy's soul would have been saved.

After that night I plotted and planned how to kill her mom and get away with it. Lucy and Ricky could then move in with us and live like a normal family. But I could not do it. I really felt I failed in protecting her. Who exactly should I be protecting her from? She wouldn't tell me, neither would Ricky, but I knew. So as idiotic as this sounds, one night I just stared at the North Star, and hoped dad would come and give me advice.

I was really deep in thought just staring at the North Star, when the advice did actually come to me. Recon, do a scouting mission on Lucy, and see what the hell was really going on in her life. Having said that, did I really want to know what was going on? The truth also has a way of biting you in the ass, with no justice served. Damn it all, Lucy was well worth taking that chance. She was my virginity slayer and I loved her. Perhaps I could slay the demons that were tormenting her.

This one weekend, Lucy told me she was grounded. Perfect, well, sort of anyways. I would be able to do my scouting mission. There was a twenty four-hour Laundromat that gave a perfect view of Lucy's mom's mansion. I would be able to watch her every move. I decided to take Norm with me as I trusted him completely and I didn't want this getting back to Ricky. Just in case I did fall asleep, Norm would have his shift to observe.

Mom did a double take when I offered to take whatever laundry was too dirty to be washed in our home machine and needed to be cleaned at a Laundromat. This especially meant my football uniform and practice clothes. Mom handed me a bag and a half of laundry that needed doing. She still had one eye brow raised; she knew I was up to something, she just wasn't sure what.

Norm and I headed to the Laundromat for our special mission, that I had appropriately named "Lookout Lucy". Every mission has to have a title, another lesson learned from my dad. Norm also brought a deck of cards. As we reached the Laundromat, Norm laid his eyes on our destination for the first time. "Mitch, are you sure we got the right address?" I replied, "Yeah, we drove her home a couple times."

Norm commented, "What do you suppose they do with all those rooms?"

"Hell if I know. Moving here was the first time that we actually had rooms of our own. I'm still getting used to that. I can tell you one thing though, the security has been tightened; there's barbed wire all around the grounds that wasn't there a couple weeks ago. Makes you wonder what's really going on in there."

Two hours into our mission we spotted a long black Cadillac with darkened windows pull up in front of Lucy's. Two young, muscular Asians in suits stepped out first from the front of the car. Both men looked around before one walked to the passenger door and opened it for whoever was inside. A rather distinguished older Asian male, about mid-fifties, exited the vehicle and did a complete 360 degree turn before heading into Lucy's.

They were greeted by Lucy's mom who I had now have named the "Dragon Lady." The older gentlemen went inside with one young Asian, while the other appeared to stand guard at the car continually watching all movement up and down the street. About twenty minutes later the young Asian left Lucy's and stood on guard for about twenty seconds. The older Asian then exited Lucy's and my heart and stomach both sank. Lucy followed him out, dressed in a short mini-skirt, high leather boots, a white dress shirt and lots of makeup on.

The older Asian gave Lucy a hug and grabbed her ass. Come on Lucy, smack him! She didn't. Instead she gave him a kiss. Then the four of them all got into the car and sped away, much like my heart was doing right now. Norm just looked at me. He could tell I was hurting.

I was in disbelief at what I had just seen. I felt embarrassed and angry for being made a fool of. I was numb! Norm, like a great buddy said all that needed to be said, "Wanna get high?" I just nodded my head yes and off we went to Larry's house.

On the way there, Norm asked, "Hey Mitch, when you go to your grandfather's house on the reservation, do you sleep in a teepee?" I just stared at Norm, "Why you asking?" Norm replied, "I was just wondering what you did in the winter? I mean it would be really cool in the summer, living off the land in a tent; but winter, man that's got to be mighty drafty in there. It's not like you can light a fire in there, or can you?"

I just stared at Norm, not exactly sure how to take it. Norm realizing this said, "Take it easy Mitch, I'm just curious." With a smug look I said, "I heard this tale once about some cat that got itself killed asking questions like that." As he was saying this, I took out my buck knife and said, "I'm going to scalp you Norm!" An awkward silence was broken up by a roar of laughter from me. "I gotcha Norm."

Now realizing he'd been had, Norm says, "Fucking dumb Indian," and tackles me.

After wrestling on the ground, I managed to get to my feet. However instead of throwing a punch or two, I put my arm around Norm's shoulder and said, "Let's go smoke that joint." Sarcastically, I then said, "Indian, eh? I got to find me a name for you, white boy."

I had so many thoughts running through my head. Good thing Norm remembered to bring mom's laundry. I was quiet at Larry's place just nursing a beer. As much as I wanted to just pound back the booze, my stomach wasn't up for it. The weed was sort of dulling the pain. Then I had an epiphany that would change my whole outlook towards women.

Kerry Dubrowski showed up, and I must say was looking really good showing off those DDs of hers, and wearing skin tight jeans. Man, was it the weed? I think not. She sat beside me on the couch and whispered in my ear, "Where is Lucy?" I looked at Kerry and said, "Who cares and more importantly, who gives a fuck?"

Kerry then whispered in my ear, "Wanna go upstairs and fuck?" She took me by the hand and led me up to her bedroom. This time I didn't need to offer her a ring. Kerry stripped right down to nothing, hell I couldn't get my clothes off fast enough. I picked Kerry up and just threw her on the bed, and we fucked like animals; pure lust, nothing more nothing less. I was on top of Kerry pounding her hard, and all I could think of was, who needed Lucy? Look at me now!

Everything seemed so clear to me, girls desire me. What was I thinking being loyal to one pussy? Man, if pussy is like a piece of fruit, I want to try them all. My doldrums over Lucy were gone. I was now looking forward to getting it on with all these girls I have turned down. No more commitment, fuck that idea! No wonder Jake was always happy.

This angry sex was outstanding! When I finally ejaculated, I think there was enough force to shoot Kerry right into Oakland. Afterwards, we toweled each other off and Kerry asked, "Should we go back downstairs?" I said, "No I'm not done with you yet, but I do need to go downstairs for a minute." Kerry looked confused. I ran downstairs and came back up with a six pack of beer and a joint. She and I fucked two more times that night, and not once did I think of Lucy; at least while I was awake.

When I woke up the next morning, my head was fairly clear. The booze and weed had not left me groggy. I really had to think, did I dream about Lucy with the older Asian, or was it real? That knot in my stomach told me it was real, as real as Kerry naked beside me. Damn, we must have both passed out! Hell, now I have to sneak out without her parents seeing me coming from her room.

I didn't see Lucy until karate a couple of days later. She wasn't returning my phone calls and just hearing her mom answer the phone made my blood boil. I hated that woman with a passion. I didn't even know if she was giving Lucy my messages. Lucy could tell I was pissed at her during karate. Ricky also picked up on this. Even though Ricky and I were close, Lucy was still his sister and more importantly his twin sister.

As class let out, I didn't wait to talk to Lucy, as much as I wanted to. I still had too much anger in me and my sparring partners that night would confirm my anger by the bruises I left on them. Lucy ran after me up the street, while Ricky just walked slowly and waited. Eventually Lucy caught up to me and grabbed me by the arm. In a friendly yet concerned voice she asked, what was wrong and was I mad at her?

I lay awake at nighttime and played this whole conversation out in my head, word for word. However seeing the concerned look on her face changed everything but the anger, hurt, and humiliation I felt. Now my whole game plan had to change, well here went everything. "What did you do this weekend?" Lucy's friendly concerned friendly face now changed. "I was grounded Mitch, I just stayed in all weekend why?"

I just closed my eyes for a second and took a deep breath, "Lucy, this is the last time I will ask this question. What did you do all weekend? Your answer will determine our fate as boyfriend and girlfriend." Lucy could tell I knew something, she took a step back and covered her mouth as tears rolled down her cheeks, "You do not understand."

"No I don't Lucy, tell me so maybe I can understand."

Lucy turned and ran towards Ricky and he embraced her once she reached him. Ricky looked at me with shame on his face. I just turned around and continued to walk home and like Lucy, I too had tears rolling down my face. Lucy didn't return to karate till we were all back in school, nor she go to Dubrowski's for the rest of the summer. In fact, I never did get an explanation from her and this put a strain on my friendship with Ricky too. When the Dirty Dozen would go to parties together, Ricky would see me with other girls and I was hoping he would tell Lucy I was moving on and doing quite well without her.

What did not do well that summer was our football team. We ended up with one win and eight losses; the only stat we led the league in was penalties. Man, we were a mighty undisciplined team, although I did quite well. I was third in the league in tackles, led our team in quarterback sacks, and was fourth in interceptions.

The high school football Coach, Adam Crane, took notice of my aggression and great physical shape. I was recruited to play high school football, I was even promised the starting outside linebacker position. Now this was the first real organized team sport I had ever played.

Martial arts is person versus person; if you lose a match you can only blame yourself. It made you train harder to be stronger, faster and more furious. With a team sport, it was different. I had a hard time not getting pissed at my teammates for sloppy play or lack of having the killer instinct.

I knew if I was to play high school football, the coach had to have everyone on the same page. When I brought up these concerns to the head coach, he made me a defensive captain right away. This also caused me to train even harder at Popeye's. Jerry introduced me to several of the San Francisco Forty Niners and also Oakland Raider players, and I had a chance to work out with them. I was really inspired to excel at football. Coach Crane also came to my house and explained to mom what a good athlete and natural leader I was. Yeah, I may not be a brain in school, but my athletics were something that made mom just as proud.

# MINOR-NINER, FORTY-NINER, AND SIXTY-NINER

By the time I started grade nine, it had been almost six weeks since Lucy and I had our unofficial breakup. During that time I had fucked three other girls. For the most part, Lucy was behind me. I hadn't seen her since the breakup, however today being the first day school I would definitely see her; that would be the true test.

One other person who I had not seen since the beginning of summer was Natasha who I now know has a last name, Konstantinov. I would say I thought about her a fair amount, and I was hoping she would also be attending JFK, the same high school as me.

I also knew a new school, especially a large high school, would mean new friends, new enemies, new drug clientele and drug competition. Not to mention lots of pussy to fuck! Several Dirty Dozen members were already in high school, so I got the low down on most of the school population, including sluts, teachers, friendlies and possible enemies.

As usual, mom also gave me the, "Please don't get kicked out of school for fighting" lecture. High school would also mean more fights, as I would now have over six hundred males to prove myself to. I was also more than willing to prove myself to the same amount of females.

The whole gang agreed to meet at Dubrowski's house before first class on the first day of school. We would all walk and toke together on the way to school. We all agreed long ago to watch out for each other. If someone came on to one of us, they came on to all of us; we were tight and solid.

I also believe with me now being fifteen, working out steady at Popeye's and doing full contact karate, I was more than prepared to show my fighting capabilities if need be. The three of us that had brothers in the Hell Hounds all wore Hell Hound t-shirts to school that day. Let the competition know right away that we meant business.

As I arrived at Dubrowski's house, Ricky was already there and so was Lucy. My stomach sank and I had this lump in my throat once we made eye contact with each other. She was still so beautiful but I still felt hurt and betrayed. I just said hi and bothered with the rest of the gang.

At one point as we were walking to school, Kerry grabbed my hand right in front of Lucy. No doubts in my mind she did this on purpose. I could tell by the way that Lucy flared her nostrils that all hell was going to break lose. What was Kerry thinking? Lucy Thom is still rather psychotic. Did Kerry think because Lucy and I split that I would now protect her, or prove myself to her?

Lucy just lunged at Kerry, grabbed her by the hair and started throwing punches, with every other punch landing on Kerry's head. Larry jumped in and tried to protect his sister by grabbing Lucy. This caused Ricky to go at Larry. It was a brother-sister tag team free for all, with Larry and Kerry taking a beating.

I decided to jump in between Larry and Ricky, who were throwing punches, and sure as fuck someone landed a punch right into my left eye. By now the rest of the Dirty Dozen were playing peace maker, trying to separate everybody, until Norm yelled "ENOUGH" and hostilities ceased. I was really mad at taking a shot in the head while playing peacemaker. I was mad at Kerry for teasing Lucy and mad at Lucy for punching out Kerry. Hell, she had her chance to be my steady girlfriend and she fucked up, not me.

I was also mad at how our gang was coming unraveled. So I did what mom always asked me to do, I took responsibility; but I was anything but a quiet spectator. "We have to settle this right now, we are all Dirty Dozen. We all stick together as we all need each other. Lucy, I know you fucked around on me even while I was faithful to you. Kerry, I'm not your boyfriend, right now I don't want a girlfriend. You still wanna fuck me that would be great, nothing more than that, understood?"

"Guys, I'm sorry that I have caused dissension in our gang. No pussy should ever come between the gang again; at least not from me. Ricky if you think I'm bullshitting about Lucy, ask Norm; he saw firsthand what went on. You want to call me a liar or defend your sister's honor, we will go at it right now; but it ends right after that."

Kerry stormed off after calling me a fucking asshole. Two seconds later, Lucy also called me "a fucking asshole," and stormed off to school. Ricky and Larry started to laugh then the rest of the Dirty Dozen also joined in. They all jokingly changed their voices to pretend they were females, and called me "a fucking asshole." This laughter and mocking of me also meant the Dirty Dozen were tight once again. I was happy, black eye and all.

The twelve of us all walked on to the school ground together, laughing and talking like chicks. Larry, Ricky and Scott had bleeding noses, and I was sporting a shiner. We made one hell of a first impression on the rest of the school.

This school was huge. It had three stories to it and held twelve hundred students. Of course this meant three hundred grade nines, with several wanting to prove themselves. At lunchtime, the twelve of us all sat together and just eyed the chicks. Guys were already giving us filthy looks and we noticed which teachers had their eyes on us.

After we ate, we all went outside together as some of the guys needed a cigarette. I'm so thankful I never started that bad habit, gross. I noticed this group over by the north school fence talking among each other. That little hair that lets me know when danger is near was standing straight up. I could tell they were eyeing us up and down, seeing how tough we were. As they walked towards us, I told the boys to look alive. "We have company heading our way." The blood was now starting to pump to my heart, arms, legs and fists; my gut knew they were looking for trouble.

After the little dust up with Lucy this morning, I really felt like laying a beating on someone. I eyed up their leader and as they approached, I knew I wanted a piece of this guy big time. Their leader knew who I was. "I hear you are Mitch Strongbow, nice to meet you, I'm Pat Meyers." Pat then stuck out his left hand for me to shake. Who the hell sticks out their left hand? You shake with the right. I knew what he was up to.

I proceeded to extend my left hand and I made a calculated risk. I gambled with my martial arts training, knowing I would be faster than Pat. As soon as I saw his right hand starting to cock back to sucker punch me, I continued forward with the momentum of my left hand, but brought my left elbow right up to

Pat's jaw full force. I also knew if for some reason my timing was not right on, with Pat throwing a right overhand punch, my left elbow coming up would block his punch from connecting. I felt my elbow hit him dead on where the jaw and cheekbone meet, and I saw the pain in his eyes. I felt euphoric and as Pat was falling to the ground, I brought up my knee and landed it flush onto Pat's nose. By the time he hit the ground, the blood was flowing full throttle from his broken nose.

I didn't stop at Pat. Anyone in my circle who I didn't recognize was now receiving hard front kicks and punches. Ricky and Larry were right beside me, inflicting their own damage on these tough guy pretenders. Other than the screams for help, all you could hear was the teacher's whistles blowing, and a huge crowd chanting "Fight-Fight-Fight." Yeah baby, we were back in the saddle. The Dirty Dozen had done an excellent job proving to the rest of the school, we were all bad to the bone and weren't afraid to mix it up.

The adrenaline junkie in me had his fix once again. I was now truly becoming an addict and for my sins I was suspended only three days. However, Coach Crane pulled some strings, and I was still able to practice with the football team; he really liked my aggression.

Mom, as usual, wasn't too impressed but she didn't flip out like I thought she would. She knew all along I would get into a couple fights. Mom being a teacher herself knew how students, especially how grade nines, have to prove themselves. Her high school, James Polk, was in Snob Hill. I guess even the snobs had to prove themselves or buy their way out of trouble.

I returned from my three day suspension to word going around the school that I was also very deranged on the football field. I was given even more room in the school halls when I walked. Chicks were looking at me with a twinkle in their eyes, and wet twitching between their thighs.

That was, some girls. Not Lucy though. She had become very reclusive, her drug use was increasing, and she had dropped out of karate. There was a part of me that felt guilty, and then there was that other part that still remembered that hurt feeling, watching her drive away with the old China man. I knew I couldn't make things work between us if Lucy wouldn't tell me about her demons. Why was everything in her life so secretive? I knew who was hurting her both physically and mentally. All I kept hearing in the back of my head was Joseph O'Reilly telling me how evil her mom was.

I also learned and never forgot the true value of a

solid gang; no matter how tough you think you are, taking on anymore than two people at once was pure stupidity. This lack of intelligence and raw testosterone usually meant taking a beating extraordinaire and maybe ending up eating your meals through a straw because your jaw was wired shut.

One Friday night, I had a date with this girl Cynthia Goodman at this hamburger joint that we would hang around from time to time. The night was planned so that Cynthia and I would grab a bite to eat and then go see a movie. Cynthia was this cute, blonde, cheerleader in grade ten, kind of on the snotty side. So I was a bit surprised when she asked me out. Whether she wanted to refine me, or wanted me to corrupt her, I wasn't sure. The thing that I did know for sure was that Cynthia was very acrobatic, could do the splits, and get into all these very flexible positions. My now very sexual warped mind was intrigued, to say the least; never banged a cheerleader before.

Cynthia was already at a booth when I showed up. I sat down and although Cynthia was pleasant, she wasn't overly warm. I chalked it up to just being nervous. No biggie. As we were eating, Cynthia kept watching the front door. I asked her if she was expecting someone. She said, "No."

I, on the other hand, was expecting Fraser, Herman Bauer and Connor to show up. I had an ounce of weed down my pants for them. I just made sure I made eye contact with Cynthia as much as I could. I tried some flirting, which didn't go over to well, I might add. No damn sense of humor, no blushing, just rolling of the eyes. Let's just hope the movie doesn't suck, as I'm pretty sure that Cynthia didn't.

The only time I saw her eyes dance was when six members of the senior football team walked in the restaurant. The only player that I knew for sure was Will King, who was a city all-star receiver. Hell, this was really the only time Cynthia smiled and I know it was not for me and my good looks, wit or charm. I saw one of the six tap Will King on the shoulder and point towards Cynthia and me. Damn was I set up?

I very calmly loosened the lid on the salt shaker on our table, as the six walked towards us. I also shot Cynthia this "You set me up, and you too will take a beating" look. I tucked my fork up my sleeve. They walked rather slow, all the while trying to strut their stuff. I realized that I was in a very vulnerable position being seated. I couldn't use my feet or knees, two of my biggest and strongest weapons. "Think Mitch, think damn it!"

It was too late as the six now were right on top of us. King was leading this group and eyed the two of us. I knew not to show any fear when King spoke. "Well, what have we here? My girlfriend with some half-breed! I guess the Indian in you is trying to confiscate my white woman, is that it Indian?"

Yeah, this was going to get real ugly. She is getting a shot in the head before I take my beating. Then, as if on cue, Fraser, Herman and Connor walked through the front doors. Probably for the first time in history an Indian was glad that the Cavalry had arrived. Now I was smiling and decided to answer King in my own special way. "Too bad, King, you can't hang onto your woman like you can a football."

As King went to lunge after me, I threw the open salt shaker in his face which blinded him, I then grabbed him by the hair, used his momentum from the lunge and smacked his head right on top of the table. This action knocked him cold. The boys now joined me in the melee.

King was on top of me and I couldn't budge him off, so I rolled under the table. One of the jocks was standing right against our booth. The fork I stuck up my sleeve came in rather handy as I drove it right into his Achilles tendon. He hit the floor real hard with the fork still impaled in him. I crawled out from under the table and kicked him right in the face.

Fraser, Herman and Connor were also great fighters, and we were really starting to lay a beating on these guys. One of them even yelled at the waitress, "to call the cops, they're trying to kill us." I almost had a freaking orgasm with their cries for help.

Before we left the restaurant, I walked over to a dazed and confused Cynthia Goodman and dumped her milkshake right over her head. I thanked her for such a wonderful date, and mentioned I didn't think she was really my type. With that, the four of us left and the Dirty Dozen mystique was spawned that night. The punch up at the hamburger joint should have brought criminal charges against us all. So far we're all lucky!

Then one weekend, Blais and Crowfeet with their now fondness for bombers broke into the same drugstore they hit four months earlier. This time they weren't so lucky and they were charged with breaking and entry. Since they were juveniles, they were both put on probation.

Blais's dad dealt out his own form of punishment and broke all the fingers on Blais's right hand. His dad was a mean drunk. He told Blais, next time he would kill him if he ever broke the law again. Here's a dad that drinks heavy, drives drunk, breaks his son's fingers, and knocks the crap out of anyone in his family who questions his authority at home. Yet he expects his son to honor and obey the laws of the land. Fucking sadistic hypocrite!

A week before Rachel's birthday, we played my mom's high school, the James Polk football team.

Both teams were undefeated at five wins and no losses so the trash talking around the house had begun, all in good fun of course. I was really pumped up for this game. I was leading the team in tackles and in quarterback sacks. As both teams took the field for the warm up, I looked into the stands and noticed both my sisters sitting beside my mom.

Also talking to mom was this cute blonde cheerleader from her school. Damn, it was Natasha. My heart skipped a beat and I felt the nervous butterflies in my stomach. This wasn't just nervousness for the big game; Natasha was giving me the butterflies. As I walked towards the stands, I was now being heckled by mom's school fans.

Natasha walked by and gave me this big smile. She recognized me, but I could tell she wasn't sure exactly where she knew me from. I was hell bent and determined for her to remember me after today. I just smiled and said "Hi", as she walked by. I watched her every move. She proceeded to give the starting quarterback on the opposing team a hug.

David was the starting quarterback and unlike Natasha, he certainly recognized me. He didn't smile, he just nodded and snarled. I just took a deep breath and put on my game face. I'm going to fucking kill this guy today, might as well have the stretcher ready for him. I wasn't only focused on winning the game, I wanted to destroy these guys. I wanted to inflict the most pain I have ever inflicted on a human before. The hairs on my arms were standing up, my balls seem to shrivel and the hairs on them were also standing up. I felt so damn alive! If I could bottle this feeling, man Coca-Cola would go out of business.

After the warm up, the refs called the team captains to center field for the coin toss. The ref told me to call heads or tails in the air. As the ref tossed the coin, I didn't speak; all I could do was stare David down. My whole world was now focused on destroying him in front of his girlfriend Natasha. The ref gave me crap and asked if I was all right by not calling heads or tails?

I just continued to stare at David and said "I'm going to kill you on the field." The ref threw a flag instead of the coin and gave me a fifteen yard penalty for unsportsmanlike conduct. One of David's offensive linemen now pushed me and I pushed him back as hard as I could. One of my other team captains grabbed a hold of me, and Coach Crane ran onto the field and took me off.

We won the toss and chose to receive the ball first. Damn, I wanted to get out there and destroy David right away. Three plays later, we had to punt the ball away and I was on the punt team. I was Ray Nietzsche that day. As soon as the punt returner touched the ball, I hit him with everything I had. I knocked his helmet clean off and caused him to fumble. Kurt Wilson picked up the fumble and ran the ball in for a touchdown. I just stood over the downed and hurt punt returner and pointed to David, that he is next; which was greeted by boo's from the home team's fans.

Mom told me later that night she was quite embarrassed that so many people hated me by the end of the day, especially with me being her son. Yeah, well fuck them too!

As the game went on, I felt stronger and stronger. I had two bone jarring sacks on David and every chance I could, I would hit him after a throw; sometimes I would get called, other times I would get away with it. My seriously demented aggression was definitely getting not only into David's playing abilities, but also into the rest of his team.

The more the fans booed me, the more determined I was to play harder, nastier; I was obsessed with beating their school. At halftime, we were up 17-3 and the refs took Coach Crane aside and they told him, as much as they appreciated my tenacity, these were all still just kids, school kids, and if I continued to play shall we say, too close on the edge, they would toss me from the game in the second half.

Coach Crane just told me, the refs were now going

to watch me a little more closely; DO NOT change my style but don't put the team in jeopardy. I guess David's coach also realized I was the key to our team's success mentally and physically, so they had to change up their game plan.

The second play of the third quarter, I sacked David so hard I could feel the oxygen leave his lungs as I hit him. He was hurt and had to be helped up and off the field. I just stared at Natasha as she showed concern and rushed onto the field to see if her boyfriend was still alive. I think if hanging was still allowed, I would be on the gallows pole waiting to dance like a dead man!

This last hit brought more boos, and swearing. Their fans screaming how they were going to get me after the game. I think I even saw mom at one point booing me as I came off the field. Rachel just shook her head in disgust at me, while Pam was laughing at how I had so many people wanting to hurt me. David did return with five minutes left in the third quarter. This time they had a special play designed just for me.

I was so obsessed with hurting David, I made a brutal mistake, I lost focus on my own survival. As the ball was snapped, David faked the hand off and handed the ball to the wide receiver coming around, almost a reverse. I knew the wide receiver would then throw the ball down field to David. I know this play, how stupid do they think I am?

I looked eye to eye with David and mouthed "I've got you." I didn't finish the last syllable, as the full back blindsided me in full flight. I felt my brain actually bounce side to side, and everything then went into slow motion. I heard a popping noise when my body hit the ground. I tried to get up at first but was unable to, all I could focus on was cheers of joys come from the home team fans. I was still trying to get to my feet but I felt like Bambi on the ice; I had the whole crazy legs happening. This wasn't good, but no way was I going to show any pain or fear to my opponents.

I staggered off the field like a drunk. My shoulder was really hurting and I couldn't move my arm. Coach Crane was yelling at the refs for the non-call hit on me. The fans were now really enjoying the chance to heckle me. The team trainer took me inside the dressing room. As I was starting to regain my senses I knew I was hurt real bad, but I had to go out and finish the game. There's no way I could let my teammates down.

The trainer examined me and said I was going nowhere. I said, "Like fuck!" Well, all it took was a push on my collarbone; it stopped me cold in my tracks. I got a real cold sweat to go along with the intense pain. By now my mom and sisters had made their way into the dressing room. Mom asked if I was all right. I said I was fine.

The trainer said, "He's not fine, he has broken his collarbone and he should go to the hospital right away." He would tell the ambulance people that are at every game that their services would be needed.

I looked at the trainer and in a very firm voice said, "I'm not leaving until the game is over." Mom told me, "Quit being such a tough guy, you need to go to the hospital." I told my mom, "I can't let my team mates down; I will go after the game."

The trainer put my arm in a sling and I made my way to the sidelines. Normally, when a player is hurt they are greeted by a nice round of applause, no matter if they were home or visitors. These guys, man, they were still booing and shouting obscenities at me. True to my word, I stayed right until the final whistle and a win for JFK.

I walked towards David as both teams shook hands and told him, "Great game." I was being genuine. I told him with Natasha standing beside him, "I hit you with everything I had. I salute you from one warrior to another. I'm looking forward to the next time we play each other."

David was shocked but still thanked me. He also said he had never been so beat up before. We left everything on the field that day, there's nothing to be ashamed of. Natasha was pissed at me, but she looked so damn cute with this frown on her face. She looked at me really sincere now and asked "Does your shoulder really hurt?"

Time for a little bragging, "I broke my collarbone, hurts a little." Natasha now raised an eye brow and said "Good game" and slapped my bad shoulder real hard. It was good thing I still had on my shoulder pads or I would have passed out.

In a very painful voice I said "Thanks" and walked towards my mom. "I really need to go to the hospital now, and by the way, how well do you know Natasha?" There were tears rolling down my cheeks from the pain and my legs were once again rubbery.

Mom looked at me and said, "Never mind her! Aren't you in enough pain, Mitchell?" Well, it was finally nice to see Rachel laugh. My pain brought her to laughter and they call me the sick one in the family. Pam was quite upset at me being hurt, as she was going through school to be a nurse.

At the hospital, the doctors had to cut my jersey off me as I couldn't move my arm at all. When it came time for taking off my shoulder pads, the doctors had to 'dope' me up first. I recognized that bu*zz,* bombers. Very high grade bombers, more like morphine; I liked this bu*zz* very much.

As the doctors were examining me, all I could talk

about in my drug induced state of mind was, "How I love that blonde girl Natasha. I'm going to marry her and have all kinds of grand kids for my mom." The doctors also found I had broken a rib and wanted to keep me overnight for observation.

After mom and my sisters went home, I just stared at the North Star and had a conversation with dad. I told him how proud he would have been with me today, being a true warrior on the field. I really missed him a lot. Uncle Jack was supposed to be taking Jake, Jerry and myself hunting next week back on the reservation; I really felt dad's presence. Morphine also helped make the feelings a little more surreal.

The next day I was discharged from the hospital. The doctors said I couldn't play football for at least six to eight weeks, which meant no more regular season games. The playoffs were still a possibility though. Coach Crane brought me the game ball and said I deserved it. I even made the local sports section, with a story of how I played with reckless abandon and how I was the most hated person in Nob Hill.

Lucy pleasantly surprised the hell out of me and dropped by to see how I was. This was the first time we have had a normal conversation, without yelling and screaming at each other, since the first day of school. I was quite touched and when she went to leave, I asked her to stay and told her that I missed her. By the time the sun set that night, Lucy and I were boyfriend and girlfriend once again. It took away some of the pain in my body; it did not stop me from thinking of Natasha though. There's just something about her I can't shake; and speaking of shaking, I really enjoyed the pain killers the doctors prescribed for me. What a great bu*zz!*

The next day when mom and my sisters were at church, Lucy dropped by and did her best Florence Nightingale routine. She was actually showing a warm and caring side of herself, something I have never seen before. One thing led to another and I tried to mount Lucy. My cock was more than willing but between the broken collar bone and ribs it was a no go. Too much damn pain, so Lucy like a good girlfriend give me a sponge bath, with her tongue.

The next day at school, I felt like a professional football star. All these students were asking me how I felt and what a great game I played. Even teachers who didn't have too many good things to say about me complimented me on the game and what a brave soldier I was. Several girls wanted to give me their phone numbers, but I had decided to stay faithful to Lucy, at least for now anyways.

As much as I enjoyed the compliments, like anything in life where there is good, evil is sure to follow. I was now in a very vulnerable position being semi-disabled. I had made a few enemies and I could sense payback might be coming my way. The drugs for killing the pain also made me a little more paranoid than normal.

At lunchtime I spotted at least four different people I had punched out, including Pat Meyers and his crew just staring at me and talking to each other. With most of the Dirty Dozen away on a field trip and just Lucy and Kurt Wilson and me at our table, things weren't good. Eventually Meyers and several of his boys walked towards our table. I held a butter knife under the table, and I swear I would stab him right in the balls. Meyers looked at me and said, "You aren't so tough now are you?"

I was squeezing the knife real hard now, but he was still too far away to stab. Lucy now stood up and told him to fuck off. I know Lucy and Wilson would have gone at them no problem. We would have lost, but their bravery was very commendable. Well, time to gamble! "I can still beat the fuck out of you with a broken collarbone and rib, how about we meet after school at O'Leary Park?"

Meyers told me how he was also going to fuck Lucy after he was done with me, as he and his crew walked away. Wilson and Lucy both asked, "Are you fucked?" The meds must be affecting my brain capacity and judgment as the three of us are bound to lose, and lose real bad. I looked at them and said, "Trust me" and headed to the payphone. I made three phone calls and then headed back to class.

After school the three of us headed to O'Leary Park. Perhaps it was the meds but I wasn't nervous. I was actually looking forward to meeting Meyers. What a true punk coming on to me, disabled as I was. As we entered the park, I didn't like what I saw. Meyers and about ten of his buddies were there and just the three of us. It was still too quiet, damn maybe my gamble would only bring me failure and the beating of my life; time to stall this beating. I talked nonsense until not only did I hear Harleys roaring towards us, but I also saw several 'Devil Dogs' carrying baseball bats in hand.

The Devil Dogs are a street gang for the Hell Hounds. They are vicious and once they have proven themselves to the Hell Hounds executive, they then strike for the Hell Hounds. Their leader was Johnny Kantonescu. This guy was huge; he's also the first person I met that did steroids.

Johnny was a regular at Popeye's and he was also Scott's older brother. Fraser Dalton's older brother Caleb was also present. Meyers and his crew were now terrified and rightly so. Jake and several patches and strikers for the Hell Hounds also came flying into the park; time for me to get cocky. "Meyers, you know what that sound is? It is the sound of a pale horse; do you know who drives a pale horse? DEATH, yes death rides a pale horse." I told Lucy to back up, this is going to get ugly.

She didn't back up, she just stared at a terrified Meyers and started to scream at him. "So are you still going to fuck me Meyers? You are not going to fuck anyone for a while." Lucy kicked Meyers' right in the nuts; bang on Lucy, a perfect front snap kick. As Meyers fell to his knees, I could tell by the color in his face Lucy had done some damage. Meyers covered his balls but he had his mouth open and was moaning in pain. Lucy kicked him right in the jaw, you could hear it break. Man, I love this girl! "No moaning you little faggot! Remember you are supposed to make me moan?"

Kantonescu told Lucy to back up as Jake walked towards Meyers. "This is my little brother, you so much as even look at him the wrong way I will kill you and your family. Do I make myself clear? You other faggots here understand what I am saying. Johnny, send a message to the rest of these guys." Jake backed up and the Devil Dogs starting to lay a beating on each of Meyers buddies. Jake walked over and told me to keep Lucy, she was outstanding. He gave her a hug then he and the Hell Hounds jumped on their bikes and left.

The Devil Dogs didn't stop their beatings until everyone was on the ground moaning in pain. Kantonescu walked up to Meyers and said, "In case you forget what Jake told you, here is a reminder." He pulled out his switchblade and went to cut off the top part of Meyer's ear. Kantonescu was only stopped by the sound of sirens.

This made the Devil Dogs flee the scene and that was also our cue to try and leave the park. Before we exited the park, we were stopped by the cops and questioned. I said, "I'm incapacitated, my girlfriend weighs maybe hundred pounds and Wilson can't take all these guys down. Let's be real here, we just heard some commotion and wanted to see what was going on."

The dumb ass cop agreed with my statement and let the three of us go. That was the last time Meyers or any of his friends played tough with me. Word also spread around the school, giving me more room to wheel and deal drugs. Times were indeed good.

A week later was Rachel's birthday and as tradition would have it, this always coincided with the annual trip to the hunt camp. Mom was at first very apprehensive, I was still in a sling and nursing my injuries. She was worried that I may not be able to take care of myself. This would be the first hunt since dad died, and was so important to me. I felt such a strong sense to head home to the reserve. I knew I couldn't fire a rifle but it was the bonding time between all males in the Strongbow tribe I needed.

Hell, I had to promise mom I would bring up my average in all classes at least ten percent and when I did arrive home, I had to catch up on all homework before I went out with my friends. Mom finally agreed and talked to the principal and explained how important hunt camp was to the Strongbow family men; the principal reluctantly agreed.

I paid a visit to the household of Theodore Barone, Teddy to his egg head friends. Ted was the smartest kid in grade nine, but had serious issues about girls. He couldn't score with a prostitute carrying a roll of twenty dollar bills. I didn't come alone. I showed up with Jane Cooper.

She's one of the girls who hung around and serviced the Dirty Dozen. I learned this lesson courtesy of the Hell Hounds. These broads have self-esteem issues, so you keep them high and praise them. They will drop their pants and you can then have your way with them. So I told Jane, "I have a business deal for you, if you are interested." Jane replied, for a quarter bag of weed she was very interested in my business proposition.

Ted's mom answered the door and she looked at us as if Jane and I were Mr. and Mrs. Satan themselves.

When we asked for Ted, she invited us both in. I guess maybe with me wearing a sling, how dangerous could we be? Ted's mom yelled upstairs for Ted to come down as he had company. She asked what the nature of our visit was with her Theodore. I told her, "I need help in math and the teacher recommended Theodore." His mom smiled and praised her son's effort and brains.

Theodore came downstairs and was shocked to see us both standing at the landing of his stairs. Jane was actually very well put together, "DD" breasts and always loved to show off her cleavage; quite tall with long flowing blonde hair. I myself have gone several rounds with Jane and have always been impressed with her capabilities in the bedroom.

I asked Ted was there a quiet place for the three of us to talk. Ted just stared at Jane and she worked it well. I had to ask him once again and then he said, yes he has a tree-fort out back was that good? "Perfect" was my answer.

As the three of us were walking to the tree-fort, Ted tripped over the garden hose; he couldn't take his eyes off Jane's bouncing chest. This plan was going to be easier than I first thought. Once inside the tree-fort, I had to physically put my hand on Ted's head so he could look at me in the eyes and pay attention to my deal. "Ted, I have a well-paying job for you with some fine incentives. I'm going away for a week, and I need you to do my homework for me. I will pay you twenty dollars for the week's homework that you'll do for me; I will pay you up front, Ted."

Ted's face kind of squinted and said, "That is wrong, sort of like cheating." I said, "Ted, you like Jane don't you? Now she has a boyfriend but told me how attractive she thinks you are. She wants to kiss you, but isn't that cheating too Ted?"

Poor Ted. I thought he was going to have an anxiety attack, now that Jane was starting to unbutton her blouse. Ted was catching flies with his mouth open staring at Jane's cleavage. "Ted, obviously you really like Jane. I know Jane also wants you to do my homework for me. Isn't that right Jane?"

Jane now circled her lips with her tongue and said to Ted, "I can't tell you how sexy that would be Ted, if you did Mitch's homework. It really turns me on, a rebel like you going against the rules. You are a rebel aren't you Ted?"

Ted was now nodding yes and just staring at Jane. "Yes, I will do your homework, I promise."

"Ted, I'm so glad to hear that. I will give you and Jane some time alone, as she would like to show her appreciation. One more thing Ted, if my grades come in at a B, Jane will also reward you once I'm back in school, won't you Jane?"

Jane said, "Yes of course but right now I need some quality time with Teddy the Rebel. Would you climb down and wait for me on the grass below the tree-fort?"

"Of course I will, be careful Jane, he's a rebel" I climbed down the tree-fort and searched for the North Star. By the time I spotted it, which was all of thirty seconds, Jane was on her way down. I looked at her puzzled, "Jane, you were supposed to give him a hand job weren't you?"

Jane just shook her head, started to snicker, "I didn't have to do anything Mitch. I let Ted touch my breast and he blew his load right in his pants. I didn't even have to touch his dick." Jane and I laughed all the way home. Poor Ted's dick was as quick as his mind. Egg heads, don't you just love them.

# HALLOWED GROUNDS

As the leaves turned color every fall, I knew this sign meant that hunt camp was just around the corner. This has been a Strongbow family tradition for decades and decades. Even before the invasion of the white man from Europe who hunted for a blood sport, my people would hunt for survival. Every part of the animal would be put to use, for food, clothing or blankets. Young warriors would also hone their skills for future battles with their enemies.

This hunt camp, my biggest enemy is the memory of dad. I never felt so close to him as I did at my first and only hunt camp two years ago. Tragically, he was taken away from me last year; make that all of us. Even now, his presence was still very strong at hunt camp. So Uncle Jack, Jerry, Jake and I flew up to the reservation for hunt camp. On the ride up, Jerry, Jake and I smoked a joint beforehand; throw in some booze on the plane and it was one carefree plane ride. I don't think Uncle Jack was too impressed with us. I think perhaps he should have a drink, mellow out and enjoy the ride himself.

Once we arrived on the reservation, we all paid a visit to dad's grave. A headstone had been erected. No one talked; we were all deep in thought. Much as I wanted to allow that tear that was building in my eye to run down my cheek and release the pain I was now feeling, I could not. I was a young warrior standing amongst great warriors and I knew dad would want me to be strong and brave. Showing any signs of weakness like crying would be an insult to his memory and the rest of the warriors buried here.

With my broken collarbone, I was unable to fire my rifle or use a bow and arrow. I must admit I was kind of moping around and feeling sorry for myself. I could blood track but not kill a deer, what kind of warrior was I?

Grandfather had a long talk with me about how every person in the tribe has a role to play; not all could be warriors. This fine balance kept Sioux tribes alive during bad winters, or summer droughts, or when the white man tried to starve the Sioux nation. If the entire tribe didn't buy into the team concept, disaster and death would follow.

My grandfather really took me under his wing and taught me how to gut and clean a deer without the sight of blood; how to sharpen a knife that could straighten a pubic hair, and also how to throw and defend myself using it. He then taught me how to use different plants for survival in the wilderness, what plants could be used for medicine, or what plants were poisonous when applied to the tip of my arrow to bring quick death, or prolonged agony until death finally takes over. Grandfather not so much taught me these lessons, as much as he opened up my mind and warrior senses to a new level. I'm sure if dad was still alive, he would have taught me these things. Then again, my grandfather taught him, so he is truly the master.

As we walked through the fields, grandfather pointed towards an object on the ground, and yelled at me "Poisonous snake." I froze at first, and then took a step back trying to give my brain time to determine the extent of the danger. Grandfather looked at me and asked me why did I take a step back.

"With me being wounded, I couldn't kill the snake. He was a lethal threat to the both of us."

My grandfather smiled, "Mitchell, when you see potential danger you go back to your primitive instincts. You must decide either to fight or to take flight. But there was no snake Mitchell. It was just a piece of wood. I planted into your subconscious the threat of danger, and you reacted accordingly; to either fight or flight. Did you like the adrenaline rush Mitchell? Did you feel full of life?"

"Yes I did like it!" When I fight, I live to feel my heart pound, to feel the warm blood rush to my muscles. I love to see what my opponent has to offer. Did all my training come in handy? Just knowing that I am up for the battle gives me confidence.

Grandfather listened to every word I spoke, he

listened to the tone of my voice and how I would get excited about fighting. "You are a warrior young Mitchell. To be a great warrior should be the only goal of a warrior. Your father and brother are and were great warriors. Watching your eyes and reaction and thought process Mitchell, I truly believe you can be the greatest warrior in our family since Red Cloud. At fourteen, I watched you kill a mountain lion to save my life. Others at that age would have frozen or run away; you didn't! Mitchell, you killed that animal instinctively. However what I see and sense from you is great anger and loss of direction. I will correct that and point you in the right direction."

The first lesson he taught was, never see what my opponent has to offer, never respect that he has trained hard, and see if he is stronger or faster than you. *"You must destroy your opponent right away."* My grandfather had me hooked and convinced. I listened to every word he said, and knew the knowledge he was teaching me would be an invaluable tool in my life.

Man, the teachers all through my whole life have talked bullshit topics, math, reading; and who gives a rat's ass about the Bedouin society? They were all pussies anyways! I was out in the great outdoors learning how to hunt, fish, and survive off the earth and almost a kind of "Dark Magic."

Grandfather was teaching me all about the 'Hearts and Minds' of all men. Why they do the things they do, and what makes us go back to our primitive roots. He taught me how to sense and conquer fear before it becomes an enemy. If you allow fear to take a hold of you, and determine if you fight to live; you will never survive. You will curl up and hide like a coward, waiting for your enemy to eventually find you and beat you like a dog with fleas.

Then one cold frigid night grandfather said, "We are going on a 'Mystic' journey in the woods." We packed our gear and rode our horses out. My grandfather wasn't only a great warrior, he was also a 'Shaman' and this would be one hell of a mystical field trip. I'm positive they didn't offer these in my high school.

We rode our horses for about ten miles from hunt camp; the sun was just starting to set so we gathered up our firewood for the night. That is when grandfather passed me this item which appeared to be a chili pepper. It was sort of sweet tasting at first, it was Peyote and this was to be my first hallucinogenic trip.

Grandfather didn't get me high to enjoy the **TRIP**. He used the Peyote as a way to further open my mind to his teachings, and the ways of the Great Spirit 'Wakan Tanka;' teachings about the natural world we are chained to. As the night went on and darkness surrounded us, the effects of the peyote made life and death so crystal clear.

As grandfather talked, I couldn't look at him, I was drawn to the dancing flames of the fire. How massive and pure the sky looked. It was a full moon and the stars were the brightest I have ever seen in my life. When I saw a shooting star, the trail from it shooting across the sky seemed to control my breathing. I would breathe out in time with the star, and once the stardust had disappeared, I could breathe once again. I have never felt so at one with the universe, or so alive. Knowing that as much as I may feel cooped up and smothered in San Francisco, there is a whole world out there to be discovered mentally and physically.

As the night went on, grandfather didn't stop his teaching. He taught me how to embrace the peyote and whenever he spoke, for some cosmic reason the message was filed way deep in my brain. He talked for almost ten hours straight, but I absorbed it all. Whether for use now or further down the road, the message was clear; makes you wonder if this is this why the hippies call it a trip? Is this the best part of the journey?

I couldn't speak for hours, until I finally found the mechanism that seemed to control my brain, thoughts and voice so I asked him, "Why did dad have to die and leave us?"

"Mitchell your father's body may have left us and this planet, but his memory and spirit will always live with us and through us. Don't you ever think, is this what dad would have done?"

"Yes I do actually."

"See he lives through you. Do you ever talk to him and ask for his guidance?"

"Yeah I do."

"And that guidance comes through for you does it not? We are all going to leave this natural world for the spiritual world. You are reborn there Mitchell. One day when I leave the natural world, you can ask me for guidance and advice. I, like your dad, will always come to you whether consciously or subconsciously. Your dad died in battle like all great warriors should die."

My grandfather's words helped ease a lot of doubts and pain I have been suffering through since dad's death. As the sun rose, I felt like I have been cleansed and indeed this was a new day; more importantly a new awakening. I never really looked at grandfather the same after that night. I think before I just took him for an old man, who could hunt and fish, and was one hell of a cook. I see him now as an enlightened person and healer of my soul; I also see dad and myself in him. Had I too stay on the reservation for the rest of my natural life; that too would have been fine with me.

On the plane ride back to San Francisco, I was very quiet, just reflecting on what grandfather had taught me. Jerry and Jake were getting drunk and Uncle Jack just shook his head and smiled at me from time to time. I was just in another zone, another realm but I really liked where I was at.

I was a hell of a lot more relaxed and content than on the ride to the reserve, when I was drinking with Jerry and Jake. Now I was high on life itself. I didn't need the booze to enjoy my life. The plane was starting to shake and rumble and the 'Fasten Seat belt' light came on. Man, the turbulence was even turning my uncle a lighter color pale than normal and he, like dad, was in the Airborne.

I was calm and I was at peace and the true test of this happened when we hit an air pocket and dropped a couple thousand feet in a matter of seconds. I sensed my dad and grandfather's hands on my both my shoulders telling me, "All will be fine." After the yelling and screaming from the frightened passengers had ceased, Uncle Jack just looked at me. "The old man got through to you didn't he?"

"Yeah he did," I just smiled and looked around at all the weak humans, now whimpering and some still crying; even the tough Jerry and Jake were shaken up a little.

Within a week of being back, mom, my karate instructors, and even Lucy all noticed the change in me. Physically, my collarbone was healing ahead of schedule; spiritually however I was in a different place. Mom said I wasn't so angry and easy to fly off the handle now. I really thought things out, and wasn't so quick to react.

In karate, my breathing and striking techniques were very fluid and lethal, it seemed to flow evenly. Lucy, yeah I think she dug I had increased stamina while fucking, and wasn't just a bull rider. Things were good.

Rachel asked, "Did aliens come down, and take you away?" She didn't recognize the new me, she liked it but it kind of freaked her out.

Even the Dirty Dozen noticed I was getting real quiet and deep in thought when I was high. I tried to explain to them I found a whole new way of tripping; however they just thought I was fucked up.

I still hated school and skipped as many classes as I could, but when I walked down the halls, I did so as not to intimidate people. I knew deep down inside I can kick anyone's ass in the entire school; why flaunt it and set myself up.

# SATURDAY, OCTOBER 30, 1965

Not sure how appropriate it is to have the City Football Championships on 'Devil's Night,' but that is when the big game was. This was also my first game back since I broke my collarbone and rib. As luck would have it, we are playing mom's school for the championship; yeah the same bastards who were responsible for my injuries.

This was also Natasha's school and I would get another crack at mutilating her boyfriend David, their star quarterback. The last game I hit him with everything I had. Now after being reborn and refocused from my time on the reserve, I will play even stronger and more fiercely. Losing is not an option. Besides, we beat them soundly last time.

A bunch of the Dirty Dozen were actually quite pissed that I stayed home the night before and rested up for the game, as Dubrowski had quite the party. Hopefully, my party will be hoisting the championship trophy and maybe more than just a smile from Natasha. On the way over to the stadium, I hooked up with the Dirty Dozen at Dubrowski's. A couple of the boys were pretty high by now. Normally I wouldn't give a rat's ass, but damn it, I wanted to win this game.

So like a preacher on his soap box, I blasted the

boys, "There will be enough time after the game to get high. We play to fucking win; do you guys not realize the magnitude of this game? 'Championship' boys!"

Blais told me to mellow out so I lost my temper and threw him into the wall. Well, so much for the new me being composed. Even Lucy lost it and told me, "It's just a game."

"I broke my collarbone and a rib; this isn't just a game for me. My revenge will be to annihilate these cocksuckers on the field. This is war and we won't lose!" With that, I just stormed out of Dubrowski's and walked to the game by myself. I was really losing focus, not sure who I was more pissed at, Polk High or the Dirty Dozen for getting wasted.

I got to the stadium about an hour before kickoff, so I walked the whole field and tried to visualize myself making play after play. I tried to embrace the 'Pigskin-Battlefield.' Coach Crane just shot me a smile. He knew to let me be; I was getting on my game face and into my killing zone. I pictured what my ancestors went through at the battle of Wounded Knee and the Little Bighorn. I know they too would have been just as mentally prepared, unlike some of my unfocused teammates getting high.

I saw Natasha on the sidelines and just the way the sun shone on her, I knew she was a total goddess. When she started walking towards me, that's when I felt the most nervous energy all day; not for the upcoming game/battle, but for her. "How is the shoulder tough guy?" she asked with a smile on her face.

"I guess after the first time I hit your boyfriend David, we will both find out."

Natasha looked around and said in a very sincere warm voice, "I never got a chance to thank-you for what you did at the party, so thanks."

"You know if you were my girlfriend, I would never let you out of my sight. That incident never would have happened with Al; and you are very welcome, and damn you're also cute." Natasha now blushed and started to play with her blonde hair, I had to ask her, "You and David still a heavy item?"

Natasha just smiled. She didn't know how to respond. She knew that I liked her, and I truly think she either felt the same way; or perhaps I had intrigued her. "Yes we are still seeing each other." *As* Natasha answered, she put her head down. She wasn't happy with David and she never replied about being a heavy item.

Whether it was having my game face already on; I felt mighty brave and asked, "Could I come 'Trick or Treating' at your house tomorrow night?" Natasha just looked at me and realized that I was different than most people in her life. "It is my birthday tomorrow, I will want a gift."

"Sounds like a plan. Listen, I have to get in the locker room and get dressed. I really like talking to you, you are cool and cute, and as stupid as this sounds, I'm going to dedicate my first sack to you. Just don't tell David, pretty sure he wouldn't like that."

"I think you're right, Mitchell Strongbow. Thanks, you are cool and sort of cute also," she said with a laugh.

"What do you mean, sort of cute?"

"Have a good game and try not to get hurt this time; OK, you are cute."

I just smiled and walked to the dressing room. She is by far the cutest girl in California. She has no flaws at all, except having a boyfriend. Hopefully, I will hit him so many times he'll be so butt ugly; she will have to break off with him.

As I was putting on my equipment, I heard rowdy noises coming from the hall; this told me the Dirty Dozen were seconds away from entering the dressing room. Fraser looked at me and asked if I was done with my PMS mood swing.

I just looked at the boys and said, "If you think I was hard on you guys, wait till I get out there and nail these fuckers."

Blais told me I was fucked and came over and we shook hands, "Strongbow I'm glad that I'm on your team and not playing against you. You're one fucked up miserable Injun, aren't you?" I just nodded and let out a Sioux warrior howl followed by a wolf howl. All was good with the boys and me.

Coach Crane gave an inspiring speech before the game; we were prepared mentally and physically. I did some light contact drills leading up to today's game. No matter how much pain I might be suffering through, there was no more tomorrow; I had the rest of the year to heal. We left the dressing room with fire breathing from our noses and ready for battle.

We finished first overall in the city, but Polk High got to call heads or tails. I did bring something to the coin toss. I just stared at David and smiled like a raging lunatic; no words were spoken and I knew this spooked him, as he stuttered while calling tails. I knew I was in his head already. They won the toss and chose to receive the ball.

As we walked back to the sidelines, I just embraced all the fans cheering us on. To my surprise I saw Jake, Jerry and several other Hell Hounds in the stands, sitting beside mom and my two sisters. Natasha was already cheering on Polk High with her pom-poms, and Lucy was still pissed at me for my outburst at Dubrowski's. Fuck her too. Time for battle!

It took me two plays before I recorded my first quarterback sack. I hit David real hard causing him to fumble the ball and Fraser recovered it. On the way back to sidelines, I just looked at Natasha and was nodding my head; that sack was for her as promised.

One of the biggest differences I found in this game from last game was that I wasn't expending extra energy on theatrics and verbal confrontation. I let my play on the field do my talking and I had so much more energy and focus. I was reading and following the play of the opposition so much easier. By the end of the first quarter, I was double-teamed.

Their coach had their fullback # 39 Clark do nothing but try and stop me from getting to David. He was a dirty cocksucker who broke my collarbone and rib last time we played; a couple times he went right after my knees. Coach Crane countered with Bauer and me doing stunts and crossovers. It was working from time to time, but the more time David had to set up, the more time he was burning us long. Blais and Wilson were still stoned and were playing like shit, and as calm and focused I was trying to be, that fullback was going to pay.

I called Jake down to the sidelines and asked if he had his brass knuckles on him? Jake just smiled and passed me them ever so discreetly.

We scored to get the game close; it was now 21-17

for Polk High. On the ensuing kickoff, I saw that their halfback was lined up against me in my down field lane. Our kicker nailed the ball long and hard. Clark's mission was obviously to try and knock me out of the game.

As we hustled down to tackle their kick returner Clark and me just ran at each other like two runaway rail cars; chuga-chuga-chuga. I saw him stutter step and I knew he was going to chop block my knees. Hell, I didn't even need the brass knuckles. I just kicked him right in the face as hard as I could, as he was heading towards my knees. With his full momentum and my full force kick, all I heard was the sound of his neck snapping back, and saw his teeth flying all over the field. He was out cold even before he hit the ground. The blood from his mouth sprayed farther than any Bart Starr pass.

There was a hush over the crowd as the ambulance came on the field to take him away. I guess Clark wasn't so tough after all, pussy! The refs missed the whole play, but the fans of Polk High didn't miss a thing. Once again, I was public enemy number one. As much as my grandfather may have taught me to be humble, well at least to a certain degree, I fucking loved being the villain.

Fights were now starting to break out in the stands. How did I know to look where Jake and the Hell

Hounds were sitting? It seems those boys didn't take kindly to Polk High supporters wanting to hang me. The refs told both teams to go in the dressing room, and the final 4:20 left in the half would be added to the second half.

Football appeared to be secondary to the fighting in the stands. The cops even had to be called to break up the fights. It was pure bedlam. All we heard were sirens, and then more sirens. I wanted to go in the stands and join in the fun, fighting and festivities, but Coach Crane dragged me into the dressing room and said, "Our fight is on the field not in the stands."

As we came out to start the third quarter I was still being heckled. All it really did was to make me play harder, even though my shoulder was now starting to hurt a bit. With Clark now out of the game, I was able once again to hit David often and with impunity. Like the villain after every sack, I looked towards Natasha and then taunted the Polk fans.

By the time the fourth quarter came, we were still losing by three points 24-21. I had a career game so far with six sacks and seventeen tackles, including eight for losses and two forced fumbles. With just over five minutes to play, I made one of the biggest brain farts that I have ever committed on the playing field. I threw the whole sportsmanship word right out the window.

David went back to pass on a third and long play. I found myself with a clear path to his blindside and I hit him with everything I had. I managed to stay on my feet while David went crashing to the ground; the football went flying straight up in the air. I caught the ball and ran it in for a touchdown. I was so pumped we now had the lead. I was mobbed by my team mates in the end zone. Whether it was me really digging this whole villain act, I didn't hear the cheers from our fans; all I could hear were boos coming from the Polk High fans.

I kept the football and as I strutted past their bench, I saw Natasha just staring at me with this really cool look of intrigue; yet also a look of hatred on her face. Her loyalty may have been to David, but that seductive yet bewildered smile on her face was for me. So instead of going to my bench, I strutted over to Natasha and presented her with the football and said, "Happy Birthday." Needless to say, all hell broke out once again.

I was charged and jumped by half their bench, it was a good thing I had the brass knuckles with me. I just kept swinging and kicking with psychotic abandonment. With at least twenty guys charging and wanting to kill me, I took quite a beating, and subsequently cost us the game. Our school was disqualified for me instigating the fight. Bottom line, I cost us the Championship.

After the cops broke up the melee I looked to the stands, but mom and my sisters had left the stadium. I figure Jake and his crew must have been escorted out of the stadium, so we all went back to Dubrowski's to lick our wounds, and celebrate Devil's night. I guess I made sure we couldn't celebrate the Championship Football Crown.

I sat in the corner trying to drink my beer with a very sore jaw. The Dirty Dozen and Lucy were all mighty cold towards me. What had triggered me to be that very angry person once again? Was it Natasha? Perhaps it was the sweet addictive taste of power, or getting off on other people hating me. I'm not sure, hell it was probably a combination of everything.

It took Lucy about fifteen minutes to walk over to me; I could tell she was pissed. "Who was the fucking blonde bitch you gave the ball to? Are you fucking her, Mitch? Was the ball a token of your love to her?"

I just looked at Lucy and smiled like a true freaking jerk. When I didn't answer her right away, she smacked me right in the face; damn that really hurt my already throbbing jaw. I just blew Lucy a kiss, which was met by a punch to my face, make that several punches; until Ricky jumped in there and dragged her off me.

Lucy called me "an asshole" and said, "I got everything I deserved today." She stormed out of the basement and I believe, headed home. I guess I'm not getting laid tonight, although performance issues could be a factor anyway. I asked Blais if he had any of those "Bombers-Seconal-Reds?" I really needed to just pack my bags and take a trip from reality.

It was now Blais's turn to lose it on me, "You cost us the fucking game! Now you want me to help you forget what you did? Fuck you Mitch! You come in hours earlier and give us all shit about us trying to mellow out before the game; and focus on the bigger picture of winning the game. Then you cost us the game. Maybe you should have had a toke with us. What the fuck were you thinking giving that broad the ball? This I have to hear!"

There was now dead silence. You could feel the animosity brewing to the point of almost epic proportions. At first I didn't answer, not because I was being coy; I didn't really have an answer. Bauer, Dubrowski and the rest of the Dirty Dozen agreed with Blais, they also wanted to hear my explanation, why the fuck did I give the ball to Natasha and cost us the game? Norm was the only person in the gang who knew how much I really liked this girl; I sure as fuck couldn't tell Ricky.

Bullshit with a hint of truth; there always has to be some truth for the bullshit to be believed. "When I was at the reserve a couple weeks back, my grandfather taught me how to get into people's heads, especially on the battlefield; to me the grid iron is indeed a battlefield. The blonde who I gave the ball to was the starting quarterback's girlfriend. I was just trying to get him off his game. I wanted him to have his game focus all screwed up. I wanted him to hate me so bad he couldn't complete a pass, take a hand off or read our defense; in theory it worked. I guess I didn't expect the whole team to jump me. By the way, thanks guys for jumping in there and saving my life."

Norm was the first one to come over, and called me "an idiot" in a joking manner. He noogied the top of my head which I might add, also really hurt. Come to think of it everything was hurting. That was without a doubt the worst beating I have ever taken in my life.

Blais had no Bombers but Fraser had some real smooth hash with a real kick ass bu*zz* to boot. Around midnight, I decided to head home. I had the munchies and really needed some rest, my body was hurting. Norm also decided to walk home with me, "You really like that chick don't you?" There's no sense in insulting Norm's intelligence, besides he is the only person in the gang that I can trust right now about Natasha.

"There is just something about that girl. When I see her I just get all warm, fuzzy and goofy. I have never felt that way about a chick before, not even Lucy."

"Listen, my cousin Gail is good friends with her. She is a Jew, you know?"

I started to laugh, "Your cousin Gail said the exact thing to me about her being a Jew. It's not contagious being a Jew is it? Fuck, it's just a religion man! I'm telling you man, she just does it for me, big time. Actually I need a favor from your cousin, tell her I will give her a couple of joints. It's Natasha's birthday tomorrow, find out her home address, I have to give her something for her birthday."

Norm now stopped and looked at me in the eyes, "Yeah, sure. You have a concussion or what? Is your brain not working right? Or are you just plain fucked?"

"My brain is fine, thanks for your concern, see what you can do." Norm just nodded yes and said o.k. but no promises.

When I arrived home, mom and Pam were still awake watching TV, Mom wasn't impressed with me. "You know Mitchell, Principal Stewart from my school told me after your shenanigans today that I can no longer teach at Polk High. Mitchell, you cost me my job."

As serious as mom looked, I could see that it took

everything in Pam not to smile. This gave it all away that my mom was just bullshitting me. "Don't worry mom, after today I have been hired to be a wrestling villain, you no longer need to work; one more reason for me to quit school."

This was met by an even nastier frown and a raised eye brow. I know when the one eye brow is raised that I have pushed mom to the limits, usually a smack upside the head was coming next, and after today I have seen and felt enough slaps upside the head to last a lifetime.

"I'm kidding, all I did was to give a girl I really liked the football."

Mom took a deep breath before replying. She chose her words very careful just like a teacher, or was it a concerned mom, I wasn't sure. "Mitchell, do you really like Natasha Konstantinov that much? What about Lucy? She seems like a nice girl."

"Lucy is a nice girl. But Natasha, there is just something about her."

"Then why did you embarrass her in front of her whole school and her boyfriend? He is probably not very happy with her right now. I hope their relationship doesn't end over your immature stunt today. Start thinking about the others you hurt; not just the macho jerk inside you, Mitchell."

Damn I never thought about it that way. If David hurts her I will get that game ball and stick it right down his throat. Man all of a sudden, the bruises on my body seem so unimportant. What the hell was I was thinking? I have to make it up to her somehow.

Mom made me a sandwich, gave me a couple aspirins and told me, "Think next time. Think of the bigger picture, and the consequences of your actions."

The next morning when I woke up, the previous day just seemed like a dream; make that a bad dream. It started with blowing the Championship game, then mom's comments about embarrassing Natasha, not to mention Lucy just losing it on me. Truly a Devil's Night to remember.

I received a phone call early that morning that I was hoping would at least change one of my many screw ups. Norm called me to say, "Natasha and her family are having dinner to celebrate her sixteenth birthday at Agresta's." It was a fine upscale Italian restaurant; a restaurant where Jeannie Terek was also the assistant manager. This was good. No make it, this was really great news, better than I had hoped for.

I jumped up out of bed and realized that no matter how positive this news was, I could barely walk; damn I was hurting. It took everything in me just to make it to the breakfast table. I sort of had an idea but I really didn't want to screw up again with Natasha so I asked my sister Pam for help.

She gave me a couple of ideas and so I put my plan in motion. I wanted to go down and see and wish Natasha 'Happy Birthday', however, physically I was in no shape to do so. I'm sure that David will also be there, so I called Jeannie Terek and told her I need a huge favor.

After telling Jeannie my story she said she wouldn't let me down and she would do her best. All day I just watched the clock move slowly, time was now joining my body in agony, as it was moving so damn slow. Shortly after 21:00, the phone rang at home. It was Jeannie. I stopped my candy treat handouts and gave my post to my sister Rachel. Ever so nervously I asked Jeannie how it went.

"First off Mitchell, she is a beautiful young lady, you weren't lying to me. I can see why you would want to please her. She arrived with her family and boyfriend; I told her after they were all seated, that we had a special treat for her in the back. It's a manger's surprise for those celebrating their Sweet Sixteen. I took her in the back and handed her a dozen long stem red roses. She seemed confused at first and then she asked me, how did we know it was her sixteenth birthday. I told her a little birdie by the name of Mitchell Strongbow told us, and he thought you might like this better than a football."

"And what did she say?"

Well Mitchell she went redder than the roses themselves; she was deeply touched. She made me swear not to let her family or her boyfriend know they are from you. Natasha said, "You are still an asshole, just not that big an asshole." She said this while laughing though. She did say, thanks Mitchell, you are sweet; she then got scared and asked if you were in the restaurant. When I assured her that you that you were at home, she seemed relieved.

"Why would she be relieved over that? I thought she would want to thank me in person."

"Mitchell, I'm sure with her parents and boyfriend sitting there, they wouldn't be so happy to see you. It puts the heat back on her; you do know she is a _"

"Yes, a Jew."

"Does she know your mom is German?"

"Mom teaches at her school. I don't see the big problem with it."

"Some of the boys in the Hell Hounds may not think the same way as you; some of those boys are pure Aryan. Anything not white and Christian, they hate. Just keep that in mind Mitchell."

"Thanks Jeannie I will, and thank you so much for what you did for me today. I owe you large."

"No problems honey, actually you owe me twelve dollars for the flowers."

Money well spent. I went to sleep that night after pleasuring myself thinking about Natasha. I wondered if she felt the same way about me. Did she make me part of her wish while blowing out the candles on her cake? Was I the last thought on her mind before bed? I hope so, she was my last thought.

# DEATH REVISITED

December 1965. Over the next couple of months, things were pretty good in my life. Most of the students in my school forgave me for blowing the championship game. At Polk high, they still have a hangman's noose in the hallway with my name on it. Screw them too!

Lucy and I were fighting a fair amount, sometimes she would disappear for a whole weekend at a time. Her actions just led me to have multiple affairs on the side. It made me feel better that other girls enjoyed and appreciated my company. I wasn't totally sure what was going on, although I had an idea. Whenever I broached the subject, we would just fight.

Speaking of fighting, I was now a senior brown belt in karate and a familiar face at Popeye's throwing around the iron. I was up to a very solid one hundred and eighty five pounds and almost six foot two.

The drug dealing business was good and working part time at Popeye's gave me a legit cash flow. I was saving up my money to buy a motorcycle. Jake said he could get a deal on this Sportster from a guy in the club. I hadn't seen Natasha, but I did receive a thank-you note given to my mom, but destined for me.

*"Mitch, thank-you very much for the flowers, they're beautiful. The thought and preparation you put into this was*

*very sweet and appreciated. To say I was surprised is an understatement! You aren't as mean off the field as you are on it. Should David and I ever breakup, I would like to thank you in person."* Natasha!

As tempting as it would be to go to her house and see her, I couldn't. I listened to what mom said. Jeannie Terek also reminded me Natasha can get in touch with me if she really wanted to. I also believe her last line in the note left the door open for me if she and David ever did break up.

My grades at school were just enough to show I was passing school, not much more. School was just like doing time until I could get a full time job. Other than sports, getting high with my buddies at lunchtime, and sex with different skanks from time to time, school was just a waste.

# TUESDAY, DECEMBER 21, 1965

December Xmas break and every night was a party at Dubrowski's. Tonight, Lucy and I tolerated each other. Hell, even the Dirty Dozen were sick of our constant hardcore fighting with each other. Between being drug partners and her getting back into karate, we still spent a fair amount of time together, and if we ever broke up for good it would hurt us both in the long run. Damn, we sounded like a married couple who only stayed together for the kid's sake.

Blais and John Walter asked, did I want to do a score; a break and entry. I asked, "Where?" They replied, "Schwab's drug store." I turned them down for reasons which I kept to myself. Number one was they have broken into this drug store at least three times this month alone; the place has to be a major league heat score by now. Number two, they eat their loot; they just both want more 'bombers.' If you ask me they were both starting to become pretty addicted to the bloody things. I liked them every once in awhile, but these guys couldn't go more than a day without them.

Once Blais and Walter started injected the 'bombers' we all knew no good would become of it. Then again if I had lived in Blais's house, I too would have found a way to escape the madness. His dad was a raging alcoholic. It seemed whenever his dad would get pissed at the world that normally meant Blais would be the whipping boy. He took a fair amount of beatings, and like his drug addiction, the beatings were also becoming more frequent.

In my world, if you want to do a score for large cash, let me think about it. Doing scores just to get high, it makes no sense, no thanks. The next morning I was told the phone was for me, it was Norm. "Hey man, Blais is dead."

I'm thinking that sometime last night Blais must have pissed off Norm somehow, and now Norm wants to beat him up for it. "What did he do now to piss you off Norm?" I said jokingly.

"No seriously, Blais is dead. He and Walter broke into Schwab's, and the cops were watching the place the whole time. Blais and Walter spotted them. Blais jumped right through the front window to escape, and you know Blais, he could run like a thoroughbred. He did get away from the cops. The problem was he sliced a major artery in his leg. I guess while running and hiding from the cops, fuck man he bled to death!"

"I got to call you back Norm, I have to let this sink in. What's everybody doing and where's Walter?"

"Walter's in jail. We are heading over to Dubrowski's, you coming?"

"Yeah, let me get cleaned up and I will head over,

see you there man".

As I was showering, I kept replaying what Norm told me over the phone, and yet it still wasn't sinking in. Blais was dead! I couldn't eat breakfast as I had no appetite at all.

Once I arrived at Dubrowski's, the mood was very somber; we were all truly in shock. The girls in the crew were very emotional. Some were crying, even normally cold-hearted Lucy was upset. The atmosphere reminded me of my house when my dad died. Death had found a way to creep back into my brain.

I had to numb those emotions. They were starting to rise to the surface once again and can't say I like them returning. It took about five, maybe ten, hell I'm not even sure how many joints and shots of Jack Daniels. I became very deep in thought. I didn't want to discuss my feelings with any of my friends as much as they seemed to want to open up.

The booze was causing them to open up, and tell tales of Blais and his ways. How there wasn't a car in California he couldn't steal. How he liked to get really high and speak his own language that only he understood. To me, he was dead, never to come back; just like my dad, DEAD!

The day of the funeral, Mom knew I was hurting. She also knew she would have to give me a lecture about how living the life of a criminal isn't all glamorous. However mom knew now was not the time, so she gave me a hug instead. Mom said she loved me and would see me tonight. It was Christmas Eve, but today, that meant nothing to me.

The Dirty Dozen minus Blais and Walter met at Dubrowski's before the funeral. We all needed to get high and have a few drinks beforehand.

Once we were at the funeral parlor, a couple of the boys were asked to be pallbearers. I was asked by Blais's mom and out of respect for Blais, I accepted. I also noticed Blais's mom had a fat lip and a swollen eye. I guess now that Blais is dead, his dad must now take out his frustrations on his mom. I'm sure she is getting blamed for his death, as that bastard could never blame himself.

The whole time during the service, you could tell his dad was piss drunk. He kept giving all of us the dirty eye and mumbling under his drunken breath. The rear doors of the church opened. It was John Walter; he must have made bail. I was happy to see him as were the rest of us, except Blais's dad. It's a good thing looks can't kill or I would have to stay in my suit for Walter's funeral. I can only imagine how shitty Walter must feel right now.

After the service they had a lunch in the church basement. Blais's mom and sisters were real thankful for us paying our respects. Blais's dad came marching over with his chest stuck out and this scowl on his face. He was looking for trouble and headed straight for Walter. This was going to get ugly and this was not the place, nor the time.

He grabbed Walter by the throat and blamed him for Blais's death. Blais's mom tried to pull her husband off Walter, and he gave her a backhand upside her head that sent her sprawling backwards. I couldn't take him or his drunken abusive ways anymore.

I grabbed Blais's dad by the hair and drove him face first into the wall, "You killed your son you fucking bully. You beat him so many times that he would rather die than get caught by the cops and take another severe beating from you. Blais is gone, but I'm not. If you ever hit his mom or his sisters again, I swear I will come back and kill you myself. I don't care if I get arrested by the cops, you will still be dead! Understand?"

Yeah I got his attention all right. Blais's dad now started to cry uncontrollably. I just stormed out of the church basement and headed back to Dubrowski's with Lucy right behind me. I was more pumped about hitting Blais's dad, than any quarterback sack, including David. He truly was a piece of shit bully. Did he really think that because he gave Blais life, he could control it, manipulate it? He beat him like a dog, his own flesh and blood!

Whether it was just wishful thinking or not, I truly felt like Blais was coming to me and saying, "Thanks Man". No Blais, thanks to you, I'm a better person for knowing you. Shits and giggles brother, you will truly be missed.

One by one the Dirty Dozen came back with their girlfriends to Dubrowski's place. Walter came up and thanked me personally, which was nice. I just told him, "It was the truth, whether that fucking drunk wanted to hear it or not."

Blais's death actually made us a tighter group. I think we really realized we had two families in life, our blood family, and the Dirty Dozen, now minus one member. We all looked out for each other, and for the most part treated each other with respect. Perhaps we gave each other that certain missing ingredient that our family couldn't give to us. I actually didn't get drunk or too high that night. My head was pounding, an anger migraine I guess, but just being around the Dirty Dozen was medicine enough to help ease the pain of his death.

Christmas brought me one of the biggest thrills of my young life. Jake showed up around 10:00 with one of his girlfriends, Liz. It struck me kind of strange that Jake was driving this older style Harley and Liz was driving Jake's car. As Jake brought in box after box of gifts, we were all blown away with his generosity.

The first big box was for Rachel. It was a whole collection of Funk and Wagnall's encyclopedia's. The next box was ten albums and a Hi-Fi player for Pam. Mom got a mink fur coat then came my turn. I received a box as small as a large pack of cigarettes, damn was it a watch? As I opened it, Liz and Jake just smiled at me. It was a set of keys.

I was confused as I already had keys to Jake's house, and I had keys for Popeye's. Jake said, "Those keys are for that motorcycle in the driveway." I felt like doing back flips. I looked over at mom and my legs lost whatever power and strength they had in them. I know she will tell me to give Jake back the keys. I dropped my shoulders, took a deep breath and looked towards mom once more.

"Mitchell, go outside and start up your motorbike."

"Really mom, you don't mind?"

"I don't mind at all son, just be responsible."

Must be the spirit of Christmas affecting mom's brain; she is OK with this? As we went outside I was just shaking. I turned the key over and jumped up and came down to activate the kick-start. I fell on my ass. Everyone couldn't stop laughing at me; myself included. I was just so damn happy, my own Harley

Davidson. A 1957 Ironhead 900cc Sportster, painted black with a Springer front end and lots of chrome. What a sharp looking bike, and it was mine. I was still in shock over mom allowing me to have the bike.

After Jake left, mom, in her own little conniving, scheming way, told me straight out the deal on the bike is this. "When you get your report card in March, each percentage point below seventy; means you would lose use of your bike for a week. If you average sixty-five, you would lose the bike for five weeks. You have to pay your own gas and insurance on the bike." I was up for that part of the responsibility. The grades aspect however, was a shrewd move by a shrewd mom; always the teacher.

The only sort of advice, well, ball busting, that Jake gave me, was to make sure I was not too high or too drunk to operate the bike. It isn't a toy and will come back to bite me in the ass, if I don't respect the dangers. The cops in and around San Francisco and Oakland hate bikers. Don't give them a reason to confiscate my bike. I guess if I want to be treated like an adult, I better act like one at least around the cops and my mom.

It took a couple days because of the Christmas holidays before I could get my bike insured. One of the first people I wanted to show the bike to was Blais. As I drove down his street something just didn't sit right with me. When I hit the four way stop sign five houses away from Blais's, I realized he was dead. Fuck me! How could I have forgotten that?

I went for a real long ride on my bike to try and clear my head. I felt so alive just driving along the coast, and the freedom was a natural high in itself, and perhaps a cleansing. My native roots seemed to be coming to the surface as I felt like an eagle just soaring high above to clouds, and those clouds were the death of Blais. From that point on, whenever I need to clear my head naturally, and the heavy bag or sparring opponents, weights or even a fuck-fest didn't work, I just jumped on my bike and went for a long brain clearing ride. I also felt a real sense of power while riding my bike. It's as if it made my arms and chest bigger somehow.

Every once in a while, I would drive to where I was a hated person, yeah, Polk High. It wasn't only mom's workplace, but also where Natasha attended school. After several scouting missions, I finally figured out what exit of the school Natasha would use. I would park across the street and when I would see her leave through the doors, I would swing around on my bike and make eye contact with her. I would have approached her but she was never alone. She's was with David or a bunch of her girlfriends, or she would leave with this other male; not sure who he was, as sometimes David was also left with them.

When Natasha was just with her girlfriends I would make sure I got their attention by just driving real slow by them, and then revving my bike and gunning it out of there. Her friends didn't have a clue who I was, but Natasha sure as hell did. She would blush and smile and when she did that, I could tell there was something still in her eyes for me. That something was real.

# SPRING BREAK, BONES BREAK, HEART ACHE

Report card time! Was I worried about losing my bike if my marks dropped below the minimum of seventy percent average; beset by my shrewd mom/teacher? Hell no. I had several students on my payroll to make sure my marks were exemplary. Not so much as to draw suspicion onto myself, but just enough to keep everyone happy.

Like mom being shrewd, I too could be shrewd, and sometime ruthless, to those not wanting to help me to keep my marks up and my ass firmly planted on my bike. I would rather use gentle persuasion and compensate through cash or weed, but every once in a while I would have to lay a beating on someone. Shit happens, as they say!

During the school March break, the biggest full contact karate tournament in California was taking place right here in San Francisco. My Sensei had enrolled me to fight in the tourney; Ricky and Lucy would be my corner personnel. They had fought in so many different tournaments over the years, their experience and knowledge would be invaluable.

We should have had home court advantage, but as luck would have it, all my fights in the preliminary rounds were at Polk High. Yeah, mom's school, where

I was still public enemy number one in many people's books, not just students, but several teachers too.

The event was to take place over three days. Friday night, all day Saturday, then the championship rounds on Sunday, if you made it that far. I had trained very hard for this tourney; it was a true focal point in my life. After losing the city championship in football, this was one championship I needed to win. I was going to dedicate this whole tournament to dad and Blais.

Jake knew how serious I was about the tournament and enlisted the help of Caleb Dalton. He wasn't only a full-fledged patch of the Hell Hounds, but he was also a member of the 1960 USA Olympic boxing team. Caleb really taught me how to increase my hand speed and would push me so damn hard at Popeye's gym I would sometimes collapse from pure exhaustion.

My Sensei was neither a traditionalist Karate fighter nor teacher, and had no problems with me learning the different fighting techniques, strategies and training methods.

On the first day of the event I woke up very focused and determined. I had a real good breakfast, went for a run, then I did lots of stretching and meditation. I felt really good and knew my chances of winning were excellent. Top eight just wasn't good enough, second place wasn't good enough, and failure was not an option.

Now in this competition, there were two hundred and fifty six other opponents. I calculated it would take eight wins to be State Champion. There's that math again. I'm sure my opponents are also thinking the same thing. Fuck them! Just wait till they get a look at me!

Mom picked up Lucy and Ricky on the way over to Polk High. The only thing mom demanded of me was that there wasn't to be a repeat performance of the Championship football game; no hot dogging, stay focused and try my hardest. I assured her that I would make her proud that I'm her son. That's the least I could do, especially with all the shit I had already caused at her school.

Just like on the way to the football stadium, I was also quiet on the way to Polk High. Lucy asked me, "Is there anything wrong?" I said "Just getting into the zone babe." I wanted to say the Kill Zone, but I don't think mom wanted to hear that; nevertheless, that is truly how I felt.

As we entered the school for my first time, I could feel the energy emanating from all the competitors. A part of me wanted to know the exact location of Natasha's locker. I just wanted to get a feel or whiff of her, to feel close to her. Lucy stopped us and said,

"Look over there."

It was the Polk High trophy case and upfront was Polk Highs latest addition, the San Francisco City Football Championship trophy. A trophy that, because of my fuck head actions, I basically handed to them. Enough of the love sick feelings for this girl; time to get in there and kick some major league ass.

Mom, Pam and Rachel all took a seat in the stands, while Lucy, Ricky and I searched out our sensei, Charlie Adams. Once we located Charlie he told us my schedule for the tournament. It was a 'sudden death' tournament. As soon as you lost a match, you didn't fight again. I have never fought in a tournament like this before. I have fought in "Double Knockout" where once you lost two matches you were done. Then again, this was for the California State Championships and it took me two other tournaments just to qualify for this tournament, both of which I won.

I was in the sixteen to seventeen year olds, blue to brown belt, and from one hundred and eighty to the two hundred pound category. I weighed in at a very solid one hundred and ninety-seven pounds, just three pounds to spare.

I had almost forty minutes until my first fight. That's a long time for nervous energy to build up, but right now I'm focused. I went up into the stands and asked mom to show me her classroom. Mom and everyone else were totally shocked, but mom said with a pleasant smile, "Of course, Mitchell." I told everyone else to just hang tight. "I will be back."

Part of my reasoning was this; the energy coming from my opponents and the fans was starting to make me nervous. I wanted to stay focused and grounded. That is what mom does for me so well, she keeps me focused and grounded. We went up two flights of stairs to her classroom. As we were walking up the stairs I could feel every single muscle in my legs, they were ready for action. My breathing was under control and not erratic; all systems were a go.

Once we were inside my mom's classroom, she showed me her curriculum and some of the class projects her students were working on. I stopped at this one certain collage of works and tried to consume the feeling and emotion of it.

Mom walked over and smiled, "Is there a reason why this work interests you so much, Mitchell? Wait let's see, who did this? Hmm, Natasha Konstantinov! You really do like her don't you, son? She asks about you from time to time."

I felt my stomach sink and my breathing was now becoming erratic, "Why didn't you tell me this before mom? What exactly did you say I was doing? Mom, you didn't tell her about Lucy, did you?" Before mom could answer, someone else had entered the room and was clearing their voice.

"Mrs. Strongbow, I thought I heard voices out in the hall. I just wanted to make sure no juvenile delinquents had found their way into our classrooms." It was Principal Stewart with a smart ass remark, "Wait, a juvenile delinquent has made his way into one of our classrooms."

I just looked at mom and heeded her advice about behaving myself at her school. Perhaps the fact that I was able to fluff off Stewart's derogatory comments was a real good sign that I'm indeed very focused for the competition. Mom, however, couldn't help but fire a volley back at Stewart.

"Principal Stewart, my son here has this new move where he can kick an apple right off the top of your head, sort of like William Tell. As luck would have it, I do have an apple on my desk. Would you mind?"

Stewart didn't know what to say, he just got all shifty eyed on us, a true sign of weakness.

"Mom remember the last three people I tried it on all ended up with broken jaws, and they were all shorter than Principal Stewart here. I'm not sure that is such a good idea, but I'm up for the challenge if you are, Mr. Stewart."

"That's fine Mrs. Strongbow. I will just take your

word for it, carry on."

Once Stewart left the classroom, I asked once more about Natasha. "No Mitchell, I didn't tell her about Lucy." Mom took one of those breaths and thought very deep about what she was going to say next. She knew the next set of words from her mouth might hurt me, but dad always believed in all of us being brutally honest with each other. Don't purposely hurt a family member, just be honest.

"You know Mitchell, you are absolutely right, she is a lovely girl. But right now you have a tournament to win. Let's talk about Natasha on Sunday after you have won the Championship trophy and are State Champion."

"I would like that mom, I would really like that a lot, yeah time to kick some ass. Sorry mom, I mean win."

"No Mitchell, you need to kick some ass to win, that's fine son." Damn, could mom be my "Wing-Man/Person"? Soon find out, I guess.

My first opponent was this tall, sloppy looking, curly haired kid from Hollister; he looked more like a dopey farmer. As the refs called us in to explain the rules, I just gave him the KILL look. Hell, he didn't even flinch, no facial expressions at all, was he trying to fuck my head up? We will soon find out.

Now the rules and equipment for the tourney are this, full headgear, mouth guard, eight-ounce gloves and safety kicks, which are just like gloves for your feet, and a jockstrap with cup of course. The ref can stop the fight at his discretion, three knock down rule, can't be saved by the bell. Three rounds in total and each round is three minutes. Three judges will grade the fight, and if it is a tie after the judge's scores, then a fourth round will be granted. This also takes place in a ring. Caleb really worked with me on how to cut a ring off, how to fight my way off the ropes and how to protect myself while on the ropes.

As I was pacing in my corner waiting for the bell to ring, I could really hear my family and friends cheering me on. Waiting for the damn bell to ring, it couldn't come fast enough. Then I heard that sweet sound 'DING'.

I just growled as I strutted towards my opponent with my hands up and tried to figure out his foot work for my own timing. He must be a farmer as he sort of galloped towards me, the same momentum the whole time. When he galloped and landed on his front foot, I used his forward momentum against him. He was putting himself in a very vulnerable position. I lunged towards him with a front snap kick, right off the front foot. It connected full force, and as he dropped his hands, it exposed his head. I then nailed his head with a lightning quick left jab, and a right over hand punch and followed up by a left hook to the head. He was now falling backwards and I threw a roundhouse kick that nailed him right on the side of the head. My kick went full leg extension, and combined with full power making contact, he was knocked out before he hit the canvas.

The ref jumped right in and pushed me to my corner so no more damage could be inflicted. WHAT A RUSH! Ten seconds of controlled anger released in a fury combined with my ability to beat my opponent into a bloody unconscious mess. I loved it and so did all my supporters who were cheering me on, including this blonde girl now sitting beside mom.

Wow, what a secondary rush it was to see Natasha in the stands, clapping and cheering in approval of my rather decisive victory. I wanted to run up into the stands and say hi to Natasha, but Lucy would kick both our asses and I was genuinely concerned for Natasha's safety. There's been enough blood spilled already tonight, without bringing more trouble. Lucy can be one very demented Asian bitch, and with a black belt around her waist, she certainly knows how to hit to hurt.

When I left the ring, I didn't look at my Hollister farmer still lying on the canvas. Caleb Dalton taught me to never look at a severely beaten opponent. "If you let the damage inflicted upon him bother you then you yourself become soft. Next time you won't be so ruthless, or you will try to hold back, and not beat your opponent senseless." That is exactly what I did. I didn't look back! I only watched my supporters coming down from the stands to congratulate me. I must say it felt quite euphoric.

I guess the biggest difference between a victory in karate compared with a victory in football is the plain and simple fact you are alone in the ring. Competing in full contact karate, you can only blame yourself for failure. Like a warrior, I take great pride in this aspect of the sport. I'm responsible for my own actions and the extra training sessions in the gym. The ability to pay the price, whatever it might be. If the price is too high, fuck it, just do it, no prisoners baby, no prisoners. You must stay focused and never show fear, that is the key!

In football, you have ten other bodies on the field with you. Should someone not perform their job well, the other ten can lose the game while still playing their heart out. You have to rely on so many others. As I know from personal experience, sometimes you can't even rely on yourself.

Much to my chagrin, Natasha didn't leave the stands. I was at first confused until I saw her boyfriend David, also in a gi, walking towards her. Damn, let's hope we get a chance to meet in the ring and battle against each other one more time.

With the fights in San Francisco, I must have had close to fifty supporters here. My next fight wouldn't happen for another thirty minutes, so Charlie kept me away from my supporters. He told me I have to stay focused. The only person from outside or Dojo he allowed to go back in the warm-up/dressing room area was Caleb Dalton. Charlie was asking Caleb about different training and strike techniques. They seemed to get along really well; that meant good Karma for me.

My next opponent was from Long Beach. He looked like a surfer, but judging by his nose and that stare, he has been around. Caleb picked up he was left-handed while watching him warm up. I hate fighting lefties, screws up my whole timing, but I had two inches and maybe about fifteen pounds on him.

Caleb and Charlie both agreed that until we know how fast this kid is, to use my feet to keep him at bay. Counter punch him and hit the left side of his body. Try and get my feet into a position on the outside of his right foot so he can't set up that left hand of his. Ricky said that was a good idea. He watched him knock out his last opponent with a real hard overhand left. He will want me to walk into it and then throw that big left to hurt.

As we both walked to the center of the ring to

receive the ref's instructions, I could tell this kid wouldn't be an easy win like the Hollister farmer. As the bell rang, he came charging right at me, and I did as instructed. I set myself up to counter punch and kick, while staying outside the perimeter of his knockout zone.

I could tell this was starting to frustrate him. I switched myself to a south paw, and he started getting really frazzled. My jab was quicker than his, and with this being my strong hand, my blows were starting to do some damage. He acted like it wasn't hurting him, but I knew better. The blood coming from his nose, and the dark marks under his eyes, told me I was inflicting damage. He couldn't stop my jab, especially when I used it with a front snap kick.

As the bell rang to end the first round, he was frustrated. Both the body and mind must work in harmony to succeed. He was going to fail miserably in the second round. Charlie said I was doing great, but he believed my opponent will come out charging as soon as the bell rings.

Time for the game plan: it was brilliant, dangerous but brilliant. "DING" as expected, he took two little steps then charged at me. I was ready, charged at him and did a flying scissor, and while in mid-air, landed a strike right on the side of his neck. We both hit the canvas real hard. With me, it was a case of momentum; he was knocked out cold.

I know I promised mom no 'Hot Dogging' but I was so damn pumped. When I rose to my feet and saw him out cold, I let out a huge loud battle cry. My supporters were also going wild, even mom was showing some real emotion, "That's my boy!" Yeah mom, I'm your boy alright and I'm happy I made you proud enough to shout it out loud. I don't think I have been doing that enough lately, even Rachel was happy and showing emotion.

Just like the last match, I didn't watch to see if my opponent was all right. With this being my last fight of the night, I jumped right into my mob of fan support. I truly felt like a rock star being mobbed like this. While being hugged and congratulated I looked, and three rows away were David and Natasha. She was smiling right at me while giving me the thumbs up. Hey, she was also sporting a thumb ring; major league turn on I might add.

David didn't take so kindly to Natasha's positive actions towards me. He abruptly grabbed her by the arm and tried to whisk her away. She didn't like this and neither did I. I ran up the stands until I caught up to them. I also sort of blacked out. I could sort of hear mom yelling at me to stop, but I was in a full rage mode. With several Dirty Dozen and Hell Hounds following right behind me, my back was more then covered. David had about a dozen supporters with him including his parents.

We eventually all met in the parking lot. This wasn't going to be pleasant for them. The Hell Hounds and Dirty Dozen were all buzzing off the fights and the pack mentality was at a feverous pitch. I was yelling at David for his treatment of Natasha, when mom grabbed a hold of me and said to just calm down. Charlie Adams said the same, "Caleb, hell he just wanted to beat someone."

He grabbed her by the arm and told her to leave, just like a fucking rag doll. "Why don't you try that with me and see what happens?"

There was quite a crowd, including officials from the California Karate association, and now at least six cops. Hell, even a local television crew was filming the brouhaha. David didn't answer me and Natasha was crying. One of the Karate officials told me that if I start anything I will be kicked out of the tournament. The cops also said, "Anyone fighting will be charged."

Mom then offered Natasha a ride home but she said she was fine. "Mitchell, Natasha says she is fine. Let's just call it a night, shall we?"

I wanted to beat David so badly, but between the cops, camera crew and the Karate officials present, I had a hell of a lot to lose. I know how bad I felt when I cost us the football championship. I did dedicate this tourney to my dad and Blais. I walked up to the Karate official and told him in no uncertain terms, "I want David as my next match."

They knew the hype between us would be good for selling tickets. "How does nine o'clock tomorrow morning sound?"

Now that put a smile on my face. "Let's go guys, tomorrow he takes a beating." The hooting and hollering reached an even higher decibel; tomorrow will be my payback.

Charlie Adams told me to go home tonight and stay focused. "Don't let the anger towards David make you lose focus on winning the tourney." As much as I agreed with Charlie, my stomach was a burning pit, full of vengeance. I wanted to destroy David. It made winding down and falling asleep extremely difficult.

I lay in bed with my heart still racing and noticed the North Star was especially bright. Was dad also incensed and wanting me to seek revenge on David? I found the more I just got into my 'Box Breathing' techniques, the more focused I was on the North Star and the more of a calming effect it had on me. Eventually my heart rate was back to normal, my thoughts and head were clear, and I was now starting to drift in and out of consciousness. I fell into a very deep and very sweaty sleep.

When I finally woke up the next morning, the bed was soaked from my sweat, but my brain and body was fully rested. That burning pit in my stomach was gone and I was ready for another day's battle.

As we arrived at the school gym, you could feel and sense the buzz in the air. The hype that the organizers had hoped for was there, and the gym was maxed out at capacity. This was all for two people to pound each other into submission. They wanted to smell, see and even taste the blood that day. We were two local kids bringing out the worst in the San Francisco community. However, I was hoping it would bring out the best in me, the warrior in me.

I believe I know why dad made a career in the army; knowing the battle was coming was better than an orgasm. I felt so alive, goose bumps up and down my arms, the blood rushing to my muscles; my will and hard training will determine if I win or lose this battle. My brain was also very focused, thinking of every single move David might use to try and defeat me in battle.

I was in the dressing room ten minutes before we were scheduled to fight. The fans were stomping on the bleachers, all in rhythm. Yeah this was better than the football championship; this was just me and David, no one else. Charlie told me to stay focused and not let my emotions work against me. This fight was against David my opponent, not Natasha's boyfriend.

As we exited the dressing room, supporters from both sides were rooting for their person to win. The Dirty Dozen clan was among my supporters, and there were also at least ten members of the Oakland Hell Hounds, along with their girlfriends. No doubt about it, my supporters would have won the rowdiest, gnarliest looking crowd. They were a regular Motley Crew, I must say, and I fed off them.

David had his Jew friends and egg head supporters. They wore their blazers while my supporters wore leather. The whole of us against them was now about to happen.

As the ref brought us together, I just stared down David. I had at least two inches and maybe ten pounds on him; this would be to my advantage. When the ref told us to keep it clean, I purposely fucked David's head up. I said, "Have good match David, all the best," with a big sincere smile. I could tell by looking in his eyes he was confused. He was expecting the beast in me to be cursing and swearing with fire and brimstone coming out my nostrils.

As I walked back to my corner, waiting for the bell to ring I saw Natasha; she had a front row seat. She seemed nervous! Natasha looked at David then gave me a sheepish smile. The tournament officials were sitting right beside her. They were both ear to ear in smiles; it was a complete sell out.

"DING", as David and I walked towards each other I totally blocked out the crowd mentally. I didn't want to look at Natasha until I was standing over a knocked out David. We both threw some jabs and some kicks, just measuring each other up. We were getting rid of any nervous energy.

David was nervous, his breathing and body were not in sync with each other. So I was now purposely starting to telegraph my moves, to let him get confident and come in for the kill. After a minute of me telegraphing everything, I purposely threw a left jab, but not full extension. As David stepped in to throw a double left jab, he leaned in just enough for me to land a perfect roundhouse kick to the left side of his ribs. The kick connected full force and I could hear David wheeze in pain and the air leave his lungs as he collapsed to the ground. I just glared over him as the ref pushed me back.

He was hurt as he lay on the mat in pain, but just like in football, he didn't stay down. He was up on his feet ready for more of a beating. As we engaged once more, I noticed he was now fighting defensively, protecting the left side of his ribs, and that is where I went again. David tried to keep me from getting near his ribs by using a steady barrage of front kicks designed to keep me away.

However, I was too quick and once I was able to get passed his kicks I let a barrage of punches fly to his already injured ribs. This was followed by a right uppercut. David hit the mat once again. The blood from his broken nose sprayed me as he hit the ground.

David impressed me by getting up once again. I wasn't sure if it was stupidity or courage. Either way I was going to make him suffer, and for the rest of that round that is exactly what I did. I inflicted just enough force with my kicks and punches to sustain the pain without knocking David out or beating him into submission. He had to pay for what he did yesterday to Natasha, and this beating was now dedicated to her.

I let the bell end the round to save David from taking any more of the beating. In between rounds, Charlie and Caleb told me to finish off the fight, and David. Charlie said I would need my energy for the other fights of the day. If I was successful, there would be three in total for the day. I agreed with them but I wanted to hurt David some more. As far as I was concerned, there was lots of pain and suffering still to be inflicted upon that boy.

"DING" as David left his corner, he was scared, not nervous. I think he knew deep down he was going to lose this match. He just wasn't sure how much more of a beating he was going to take. I'm sure if he truly knew how much more of a beating I had planned for him, he never would have answered the bell for this round.

Every kick and punch I threw was finding their target. I was now very confident of my victory. I could hear my supporters cheer with every punch and kick thrown. Each time I would land either, there was hooting and hollering. David's supporters were now very quiet; I could sense they were feeling David's pain.

There was also a feeling of euphoria. Just like in football, I liked being the villain. I even tempted fate at one point, and let David land the odd punch and kick. I would mock him and just shake my head no at him. No David, no that didn't do anything at all, try it again. I really liked when people don't like me and his supporters just freaking hated me. I liked it when my supporters had that pack mentality fueled by me inflicting pain upon my opponents.

Twice during that round, David collapsed to the mat in pain, and twice the ref asked if he was all right to carry on. Both times, David wouldn't submit or give in to losing the match, and once again the bell announced the end of the round. The five minutes of pain for David has finally halted.

Charlie and Caleb really blasted me now. "If he

lands a lucky punch and knocks you out or cuts you real bad, you are fucked. Never ever tempt fate like that, remember this is a tourney. Mitchell, you will need your strength and all your endurance to win the whole damn thing. End this fight within the first thirty seconds of the next round."

I looked at Natasha, she didn't look very good; neither did David's parents. Even mom had that look in her face. I was hot dogging for the sole purpose of inflicting pain upon David. Yeah, time to end this, mercy kill now.

"DING" David was still protecting his left side, so I did what any battlefield warrior would do. I set him up for the final blow. The final kill! I must have thrown at least ten roundhouse kicks to his sore ribs, until I saw him drop his guard to protect those ribs. Then, I threw the perfect roundhouse kick to the right side of his head. It landed with my leg at full extension. By the time my leg was recoiled, David was on his way down to the canvas, knocked out cold. I knew I hurt him pretty bad with that kick.

That's it, no more show boating, no more playing it up to the crowd. Even my supporters, after they stopped celebrating my victory, knew David was in real trouble. When the doctors jumped into the ring, Caleb and Charlie abruptly took me to the dressing room. Natasha was crying in the front row. I felt like shit for making her cry. I just wanted David to pay for rough housing her. She mouthed "*YOU ASSHOLE*" to me.

Seeing David lying out in the ring with his eyes rolling back in his head, and having Natasha so pissed at me, was really fucking me up.

After twenty minutes David left the ring and went to the hospital for observation. He would live. He had a concussion, but wouldn't fight another day. I, on the other hand, would have my second fight of the day in less than two hour's time. I really needed to smoke a joint and get mellow. So after I did a real long stretch out and most of David's supporters had left the gym, I went in search of a joint to smoke.

Most of the Hell Hounds left after my match, but Jake stuck around as did most of the Dirty Dozen. I was greeted with much fanfare. Mom was happy that I won and didn't get hurt, but I could tell she was upset about David lying there out cold.

Mom said that easily could have been me and not David. I told her, "I never set myself up to be hurt." Mom just nodded. She said that she had some homework to do, and seeing we are in her school, this was the perfect opportunity to get caught up. She would see me in a bit. Perfect.

Herman said he had some weed on him. I told him, "Let's go for a walk to the park and smoke the joint."

So Norm, Jake, Herman, Ricky and Lucy and I went to smoke the herb.

As we were sitting around just getting mellow, Herman the true Nazi voiced his opinion on the match. "I'm glad you smoked that fucking Jew kike, too bad you didn't kill him. Did you see his Jew girlfriend crying? Hell, you should have also knocked her out cold. Kikes!"

I just looked at Herman and didn't say yes or no, I should knock him out for saying that about Natasha. Norm just looked at me. He knew she was something special to me, even if it was from a distance.

Perhaps Jake picked something up from me being quiet, as he asked, "Little brother, you are pretty quiet, all OK?"

"Yeah, I'm all right. I just want to forget this past fight and get focused for my next fight."

After about a half hour at the park, we all decided to head back to the school gym. I had the munchies and needed some food to give me the strength for the next bout. Thirty-two fighters now remained in the tourney. I know my next opponent has also won three matches, so he had to be good, and he was. Yes my work will be cut out for me.

He was a tall and very muscular Kaffir from Los Angeles. Caleb watched him destroy his last opponent and said he was a lefty that threw his punches like pistons non-stop, and he threw them to hurt. Now Caleb and Charlie's job was to build up my confidence, all the while keeping me focused. They also had to find a way to beat my opponent; I hate fighting lefties.

As the Kaffir and I approached the ring, we just eyed each other step for step, until the ref asked us to approach. The Kaffir had quite the stagger in his walk. Was he flat footed or just fucking with my head, and my game plan? I guess we will find out soon enough, maybe sooner than later.

As we got right into each other's faces, I could smell the watermelon coming off his breath; I wonder if he could smell the weed coming from mine. Speaking of which, my bu*zz* for the most part was gone. The ref had to separate us while giving instructions, then the Kaffir decided to push me backwards. He was strong all right. I just snarled at him. I could tell right off the bat he was a bully. There's no way his bully antics are going to intimidate me; you are going down like the rest.

"DING," Just like a bully, my opponent came right at me throwing punches. I just covered up and tried to counter punch him in between some well-practiced bobbing and weaving. There's no way that could he keep up this pace for two or three rounds.

Caleb and Charlie told me to get off the ropes and into the center of the ring. However, my opponent had other ideas. This guy was really good at cutting off the ring and not letting me use my feet. I'm not used to being overpowered, this was something very new and I sure as hell didn't like it. It was screwing up my concentration, and I could hear my supporters yelling at me to do something.

I was, for the first time in a very long time, anxious and worried. Were all the beatings I have giving out over the years now coming back to haunt me? Was it the effect from the joint we smoked early in the day causing the bu*zz* to inhibit my fighting skills? Who fucking knew!

What I did know for sure, was that if I didn't do something fast I would be going down for the count. I almost felt smothered by the barrage of punches and kicks being thrown at me. I couldn't breathe! I panicked, I came at my opponent recklessly and he nailed me with a left hook. I never even saw it coming, but damn I sure felt it. I saw stars!

I felt my brain toggle back and forth ever so gently, then my legs muscles lost all control and down I went. I just lay there, trying to figure out what the hell was going on. Am I late for school? Why are these lights so bright? Did I get high and pass out at some strange place? Seconds become minutes! I tried to give my head a shake, and finally realized the reason why I'm down on the ground in the first place. My brain was given one hell of a shake.

The true test of a warrior is when your heart starts beating for revenge. The savage beast in you, perhaps in my case an Oglala Teton Sioux warrior, brought me back to my senses. I don't quit, you don't submit to your enemy. I want to fight, fight to win! I took a standing eight count. The ref asked me if I was I was able to continue. **"FUCK YEAH",** was my response.

I knew my opponent would come charging right in and try and finish me off once and for all. His mistake! I purposely let my guard down so he would go right after me. I could tell he thought in my semi dazed and confused state, I was ripe for the picking. Time for a dangerous gamble; damn right, it was.

He went for my head with another left hook and I nailed him right in the sternum with a solid one two combo. As he now leaned over in pain, I let my legs do what they do best. I nailed him with a side kick right to his jaw. I'm not sure what happened next, his mouth piece that came flying from his mouth or hearing his jaw break. He was done!

This time I did raise my arms in victory while standing over my fallen opponent. Caleb jumped in, picked me up and hugged me. My supporters were going crazy with enthusiasm over my 'come from behind' victory. I'm sure my dad was very happy with my victory. I felt his presence in the ring, helping me get up off of the ground when I was knocked down. Thanks, dad.

Charlie and Caleb checked me thoroughly in the dressing room to make sure my opponent hadn't inflicted any serious damage to my brain. They both commented on my heart and desire to win, and how they were both proud of me.

I had less than an hour before my next fight. This time I wouldn't partake in any toking sessions. Let's just blame my panic in the corner on the weed. I left the dressing room and was stopped and mobbed by my supporters, including the 'Wizard' who was the Hell Hounds main drug dealer. Wizard offered me a little help, saying, "These magic pills are called 'BEANS', and they will make sure that you never run out of energy."

I asked what they had in them. Wizard said "SPEED". Jake was beside him, so I knew I had my brother's permission to take them. "Thanks Wizard, but I want to win this tourney fair and square." Wizard then told me, should I change my mind, just let him know.

Jake said I was making everyone proud with my fighting skills and never giving up. He was worried about me taking a beating from the last guy.

Derksen just patted me on the back, "Good victory over that Kaffir."

I went outside to get some fresh air and gather my thoughts. Lucy informed me she couldn't watch me fight anymore today. She has relatives coming from out of town and her mom is forcing her to spend time with them.

I was madder at her than my last opponent, "Another rich Uncle, Lucy? Like the one who left cigarette burns on you, or the other uncle who left belt marks around your neck?" Lucy didn't answer me, she just called me, "An asshole" and left. I looked at Ricky. He said, "Sorry", and chased after his sister. One day I will find out exactly what is going on, then I will take action. God help them all if what I think is going on, is actually going on. Hell has no fury like a 'warrior on the warpath, and that is exactly what it would be.

Jake just shrugged his shoulders and took me for a walk and talk, "You know little brother, when any of my women piss me off, I just go out and find another pussy to play with. Don't ever get tied down to one pussy. I really like Liz O'Malley, but I'm also playing with at least three or four other women on the side. The key is never to flaunt it, make each one feel special, as each one is truly special in her own little way."

Jake's talk made me feel better. So who was the first pussy I thought about? Who else could it be, but the beautiful Natasha my one and only. I could see being a one woman man, if ever given the chance, maybe in time.

Charlie and Caleb eventually caught up with the boys and me. They stretched me out real hard while giving me the lowdown on my next opponent. He was an Asian from San Bernardino, with real fast hands and feet. He was the perfect point's fighter and so far with his speed, no one had really tested his jaw.

Well, my last two opponents I sent to the hospital by testing their jaws; this guy would be no different. Too bad Lucy left. Maybe he is also a long lost relative she would have to entertain. This kid being Asian, it would be a good way of taking out my frustrations and I was ready.

Caleb figured this Asian kid would come out "hot dogging," and playing it up to the crowd, just like he did last time. Caleb told me to go right at him. He might land a few, but let's test that jaw right away. As we walked to the ref this kid seemed more interested in the crowd than me. Bad move!

"DING" I purposely walked real slow and lethargic towards him. He was bobbing and weaving and doing all this quick handwork. I saw him look towards the crowd for approval; that was my chance to check out his jaw. He charged in and I landed an over hand right flush to his face. I hit him so hard I think my pinky finger just picked his nose clean.

He fell like a construction crane and was out cold. I just calmly walked back to my corner. Before my supporters could even cheer, everyone in the audience fell silent. Hell, a one punch knockout! The one and only punch to land in the fight was also the one and only punch that mattered.

As I was being congratulated by my corner, we all heard a loud and thunderous sound; Harleys, and more than one of them. I just figured it was either more Hell Hounds or some Devil Dogs. Nope, that thunderous sound turned out to be several members of the "THUNDER" motorcycle club, Bakersfield Chapter. The Hell Hounds and the Thunder were rivals. Eight full patch members and several of their girlfriends and hang-arounds were now present.

Jake, Jerry, and their members were now starting to gather and talk. This also caught the eye of the police who were now trying to get in between the gangs. Caleb left me with Charlie and headed to hook up with the other Hell Hounds. Combined with Devil Dogs there were close to thirty people; this would be a total massacre in favor of the Hell Hounds. Too many witnesses to start something here, and too many civilians present.

As I left the ring to join the Hell Hounds, I noticed one of the tourney fighters head towards the Thunder. They must be his supporters. He was a very stocky muscular fighter, and the name on the back of his gi was Da Silva. Well, according to the fight scoreboard, he was going to be my next opponent. Fate? Could be, but to me he was just another victim.

I know to both gangs it would be a Thunder versus Hell Hound fight. Jerry led his gang members towards the Thunder. There was now a real buzz in the air just knowing there might be more blood spilled between these two hated rivals than all the matches in the ring combined.

There were only four cops present, but within minutes it seemed every single cop in San Francisco was now in the gym separating the two gangs. The many civilians inside were now starting to leave in fear of what might happen next. This was truly a powder keg just waiting for the spark to detonate. Charlie caught up to me and told me, "Don't do anything to get disqualified from the tourney."

I have to give the tourney director credit for his ability to semi-defuse the situation. He actually walked between both gangs and started to speak. "In one hour from now we have a Da Silva versus Strongbow match to see who will advance to the semi-finals tomorrow. I hope both sides will agree that any hostilities will be settled in the ring only."

Jerry agreed, and their club president also agreed. Jerry looked at me with a smile and asked, was I ready?

"He is going to spend more time on his back than a Hell Hound Splasher at a gangbang." Jerry and Jake both started to laugh and rubbed the top of my head and said, "Good boy."

Caleb and Charlie took me into the dressing room to strategize against Da Silva. They said from what they both have seen, Da Silva is a brawler. He's a very powerful puncher, with good kick strength as well, and surprisingly fast for a kid his age. Kid, hell, he almost had a full beard happening.

Was I nervous? I wasn't nervous about fighting Da Silva. I was more nervous about losing and letting down the whole Hell Hound club. I just tried to be really focused mentally and physically.

After thirty minutes or so, the dressing room door opened and three bodies walked in. It was Jake, Jerry, and National Hell Hound President Eric Von Kruder wearing a full-length black leather jacket with club colors. Von Kruder looked at me rather stoned faced and said, "Mitchell, you are not only fighting for your family name, but for all the Hell Hound Chapters in North America. You must win this fight. These Thunder are the lowest form of human filth. They should all be annihilated off the face of the earth, but the law won't allow it. Mitchell, are you ready to kill this cocksucker, son?"

"Yes I am. I won't let anyone down. I will fight to the death if need be." Von Kruder liked my response, gave me the thumbs up, and left the room with Jerry. Jake stayed behind. "Your mom is a little upset thinking you might really get hurt against this kid. I assured her you are a Strongbow, and as a Strongbow our destiny is to fight; that is what we do well. She didn't respond to my words, Mitchell, should she be worried?"

"I am a Strongbow just like you said, Jake, and that is what we do, we fight. Tell her not to worry. Da Silva's mom is the one who should be worried. I need this fight, Jake. I need it to prove to dad that I am a warrior. I know he will guide me through this match. Von Kruder being here, this must be important."

"Yeah, with Eric it is a big thing! He hates the Thunder. Any chance we get, anytime we can! Should we seek revenge or lay a beating on them, you know he would be here. This match is huge, Mitchell."

I saw a little fear in Jake's eyes, or was it a little worry? Was it for my safety or a Hell Hound issue? I didn't ask. I know the Hell Hounds are also his new family; perhaps a part of me didn't really want to know the answer.

After Jake left the room, Caleb and Charlie went over a game plan against Da Silva. They told me to stick and move, attack like a cobra snake, and then get out just as quick. "Try and wear him down." That was the pre-game fight plan. However, as I have learned over the course of the tourney and what dad also taught me, be prepared for anything and adapt to all situations on the fly. Before we left the dressing room I asked my dad for support, guidance and strength.

As we left the dressing room and headed for the ring, the ovation for both fighters was deafening. I was getting goose bumps! I looked to the crowd, found mom and gave her the thumbs up. She just smiled and returned my thumbs up with one of her own.

As I scoured the crowd it was truly a carnival atmosphere, with more Thunder in the stands than earlier on. There were also more Hell Hounds, and more cops, lots of cops separating the gangs. Hell, even the local television crew and a beat writer for the local newspaper were looking interested in the upcoming match.

As Da Silva and I approached the ref for his instructions, he started to growl at me. He meant it too! I just hoped he had his rabies shot already. I had at least three inches on him and I also noticed he had a bit of a gut. A spare tire tells me if we go to the final round, he's in trouble. With my hard road and cardio training, this will be a bonus for me.

As I walked back to my corner I just nodded to Jake, Jerry, and Von Kruder all seated in the front row. Terek yelled at me, "Make your dad proud, boy." You are so right and I will make him proud.

"DING" as the bell ring Da Silva charged right at me. He walked right into my front snap kick followed by a left hook and a hammer of an over hand right. He was stopped cold in his tracks, but he didn't go down. His eyes were glazed over but I could tell he was just pure evil, not to mention psychotic. Most men, never mind teenagers, would be out cold. Why the hell was he still standing? I backed up a bit and started throwing kicks to his body, real hard kicks,

I thought the ref might stop the fight, but he wouldn't go down. Then, like a man possessed, he charged at me and forced me into the corner, all the while he was throwing punches to my head, real hard punches. I learned from my previous match, do not panic, bob and weave or try and muscle my way out of the corner. He was too strong to bull over so I just covered up and waited for an opportunity to punch my way out, or kick him hard enough to hurt him,

I was pinned in too close to use my feet. Hell, at one point he stomped on my left foot, so I kneed him right in the thigh. That sent him to the ground in pain, dirty cocksucker. I can play that game too. The ref took a point away from both of us, and gave us both a warning to abide by the rules or face disqualification.

Da Silva was back on his feet. He was pissed right off and was starting to scream at me. Keep it up and waste that energy and lose your focus you fat fuck. "DING" end of the round. He kept mouthing off in between the round, a loose cannon for sure.

"DING," as Da Silva now came towards me quite a bit slower, I just smiled at him. Then he got real dirty. He threw a round house kick, and as I lowered my left hand to block it, he spat in my face which blinded me for a second. That was all he needed. He charged at me and landed a right cross, the hardest right cross I have ever been hit with in my life; make that the hardest punch ever. I felt my legs go and down to the canvas I went. Da Silva then tried to come in and finish me off while I was on the ground.

The ref jumped in at that point and kept pushing him back. What a dumb fighter he was! His corner kept yelling at him to go to a neutral corner, but he was in a kill mode and didn't hear a word they said.

He must have wasted at least forty seconds doing this. I would have been declared knocked out if he would have gone directly to the neutral corner, instead he gave me time to clear my head and refocus.

I was back on my feet and I knew he would come

right at me. Normally I would've been able to out maneuver him no problem, but I believe he broke a couple of my toes when he stomped on them. My movements were now hampered, but like dad always said and drilled into my head, "Adapt to all situations."

I just blew him a kiss and waited. When the ref said "Fight", he came right at me in full flight. This time I spun around on my good foot and threw a reverse punch which landed solidly and broke his nose. He was hurt but still hadn't gone down. With him sucking blood into his stomach I went to work on that spare tire of his; kick, kick, kick followed by uppercuts when he tried to go inside on me. I still couldn't knock him down. So I took a gamble and decided to start kicking him not only in the gut, but nailing his arms as hard as I could. His brain or lack of one I might not be able to damage, but his body I could and would destroy. In the last remaining ninety seconds of the round, that is exactly what I did.

As the bell rang to the end the round, he was hurting real badly. His corner spent the whole time trying to get some blood flow back to his arms. He wasn't yapping at me between these rounds, just staring with much hatred and confusion.

I went back to my corner. Caleb said he will come right at me. His arms won't last more than thirty seconds before exhaustion sets in and the bruising will disable them, so I needed use my feet to keep him at bay. Charlie checked my toes and said at least two were broken. He told me to bite down real hard on my mouth guard and he will reset them. 'CRACK', they were reset. Thank God this is my last fight of the day.

'DING,' as Da Silva came in charging and throwing punches wildly, he was exposing the rest of his body. Make no mistakes about it, I not only was scoring and landing at will, I was doing some serious damage. Thirty seconds later Da Silva could barely keep his arms up to defend himself. Normally I would take it easy on my opponent until the ref either stopped the fight or the bell rang.

Da Silva wasn't only associated with the Thunder, he was a dirty fighter and needed to be schooled and tuned up. So I refused to let up. I could see his biceps turning purple and bruising, he had a mouse under both eyes, and his jaw was open, trying to suck air through his mouth with his nose broken. Oh well, sometimes stuff happens.

As much as I tried to tune out the supporters, every time I landed a big punch or a big kick, the cheers were deafening. The hooting and hollering made me thirst for more of his blood. It became like a fix for me. Eventually the bell put an end to the beating. His corner crew jumped in and helped him to his corner. A doctor came into the ring to take a look at him, but was pushed away by his corner. They were humiliated by the beating.

The ref called us both to the middle of the ring to announce the winner. Da Silva couldn't even get off the chair in his corner as I was announced the unanimous winner. The ref raised my hand and I felt so damn good. I won not only for myself, but for my whole family and my extended family, the Hell Hounds. I didn't bother going over and telling Da Silva good fight as it wasn't a good fight. He was a dirty fighter and received everything he deserved.

As I left the ring every Hell Hound, Devil Dog and family member mobbed me with congratulations. Terek, Jake, and Jerry carried me into the dressing room like some conquering hero returning from an epic battle. I guess that is what did happen though. Von Kruder came in the dressing room and said I made the club proud. I will always be remembered for my fearless battle and ultimate victory. One other thing, if I wasn't too tired there was a beer with my name on it back at the Oakland clubhouse.

My mom and sisters didn't come in the dressing room.

I saw them smiling on my way to the dressing room, although I'm not sure if mom was smiling because I won, or survived.

After Charlie and Caleb took my gloves off, Caleb noticed I broke a knuckle on my right hand, my power hand. I didn't even feel it break with the adrenaline flowing so strong during the fight. I had one hell of a black eye from the right cross, two broken toes and I was freaking exhausted to the point where I felt like throwing up.

The tourney director came in and said that was the fiercest fight he has ever seen in a three-day tourney. Was I all right to carry on to the semi-finals? I just nodded yes. He said, "Well, get some rest and be back here in fifteen hours." I would be fighting this tough, lanky black kid from Inglewood named Jules Winston. He had knocked out every opponent in the first round so far.

I showered, and as I was getting dressed I started to feel some of the pain now that the adrenaline rush had left my body. As I left the dressing room the gym was pretty empty. No Thunder left, although a few cops were still hanging around though. I wonder if they were expecting the same battle between the two gangs, as Da Silva and I had just gone through in the ring.

My mom and sisters came over and gave me a big hug. Norm and Crow asked if I was still going to this concert at the Fillmore that I have been looking forward to all month.

I told them I was too tired. I just wanted to go home and get some rest. Normally they would be shocked to hear this. Even mom laughed at how this was the first weekend since we moved to California that I haven't gone out at least one of the nights.

The boys said they would have some fun for me and would see me back here tomorrow.

Charlie gave mom some liniment to put on me before bed. Charlie said, "It will help ease the pain in his muscles." I was actually surprised that Jake, Liz O'Malley, along with Don and Jeannie Terek decided to go back to our house rather than go to the clubhouse right away to celebrate my victory.

Once home I went into the freezer and broke out several ice packs for my broken and battered bones. I think maybe me just lying in a frozen snow bank would've been easier and more effective.

Liz was a trauma nurse and she came over and started to rub the liniment on my back, arms and leg muscles. She had fiery short red hair and stunning green eyes. I'm not sure if was just the pain, along with Liz's soft and gentle touch, but when she was rubbing my thighs, I was getting aroused. She was like Florence Nightingale. Liz just had that nurturing thing about her. Once she noticed I had a hard-on, she just raised her eye brows and smiled. I know she was one of Jake's girls, and almost ten years older than me, but damn she was really turning me on. I wanted to go more than a few rounds with her.

Jake then walked over as I was still hard and Liz was still rubbing me. I was so damn embarrassed, but what could I do? I put a pillow over top of my pants, actually more like over my crotch area. When Jake asked did I want to join him and Don on the front porch to smoke a joint, I said, "Just give me a couple minutes, I'm still trying to stretch things out. Once all the liniment is put on I will be right out."

As Jake and Don went to the front porch, Liz said she was done. I thanked her and as I was getting up, she decided to have a little fun at my expense. "Mitchell, do you have a bone out of joint in your groin area? Let me just check that out for you."

I went so red, redder in fact then Liz's hair. "I'm fine, thanks a lot Liz." As I went to get up still hard, Liz did a quick look around, grabbed my cock and gave it a little twist and laughed. Man that really fucked me up.

Liz went to go wash her hands and I went to the front porch to join Jake and Don for a toke. I was still hard so I just walked real slow and hoped they didn't notice. Jake asked if I was all right. I said, "Just sore muscles and broken bones."

Once I had a couple tokes I started to relax, along

with my joints and muscles. I was really starting to hurt, and as much as I wanted to talk about my great victory and ogle Liz some more, I had to go to bed. I truly needed a good night's sleep in the worst way. I needed my muscles and broken bones to mend as quickly as possible. Man, I made it to the semi-finals, and I get to fight another day. That day is tomorrow against Jules Winston from Inglewood.

I don't remember falling asleep. I didn't even hear Jake or Don fire up their bikes when they left. I just closed my eyes and saw Liz's sultry smile. The only person who could truly knock me out was Mr. Sandman. It was time to put me away for the night.

I had slept a very solid ten hours when Rachel came in to wake me up. As I opened up my eyes, I felt like I was in a car accident. Everything hurt. The broken knuckles had made my hand swell in the night. My broken toes and even my eye was killing me. I know my nose wasn't broken, but it hurt, hell even my hair hurt. It almost felt like a hangover.

I remembered Charlie saying I had to start pumping fluids into myself as soon as I got up. I hobbled down the stairs and mom cooked a real kick ass breakfast of oatmeal and scrambled eggs; a fighter's breakfast. I was pounding back the water and once I was properly hydrated, I felt almost normal.

The previous night after the fight was like a dream

state. Did Liz really grab my crotch? Did I smoke a joint with Jake and Don? It was all a blur, a freaking blur!

Mom was concerned about me carrying on in the tourney. "Mom, I have too many battle wounds not to continue, I will be fine. Charlie and Caleb won't let me fight if they truly feel I will get hurt and can't defend myself. I will be fine." I hope!

As we arrived at the school gym for another day's battle, the sun felt real good. I stayed outside for a bit before going in, just trying to get my game face on. Much as I tried, my body was really hurting, so many of my weapons wouldn't be as effective as normal.

My right hand had never failed me, but now I could barely make a fist because of the swelling in my hand. My broken toes made my balance not the greatest. I must say, for the first time in my life I doubted my body's ability to fight. This was a very eerie and frightening feeling and I didn't like it.

Just then two of my senses seemed to bring out the warrior in me; sight and sound. I was starting to feel alive. I heard Jake and a whole complement of Hell Hounds on their bikes headed to the gym. They were headed to see me fight, which made feel fearless, especially knowing after last night's brawl that I did have it in me to win.

I saw three girls approaching the gym entrance. As

they got closer I felt my stomach get those butterflies again. I felt full of life again. It was Natasha and a couple of her girlfriends. "Morning ladies, are you here to see me fight and win?" Yeah I was back to being, pardon the phrase, "Cocky" and no way would I show any pain while talking to them. Natasha stopped, smiled and said, "Actually we are here to see you get beat, and end up on your back."

"Well if you want to see me on my back, I assume you will be on top riding me?" Natasha's face went beet red, her eyes got real big and she started to laugh. Her friend called me a pig and they stormed off into the gym. Natasha just stood there still in shock at what I said to her, still blushing and smiling. Her friends came back, grabbed her by the arm and said, "Let's go inside, he is gross."

Jake and Liz were the first two from the club to greet me. They asked how I was feeling. I said I was ready for another day's battle." Jake answered "Good boy" and Liz just smiled at me rather seductively. Yeah she did grab me last night. It's all coming back including my hard on. I better get to the dressing room and get prepared for my fight. There are way too many distractions out here.

As Caleb was taping my right hand it really hurt, and I would flinch from time to time. Caleb assured me that once the bell rang, I wouldn't feel any pain.

Like hell, I thought. Charlie taped my toes and said the same thing. They had me do some real intense exercises to warm up, and once I broke a real hard sweat I actually did feel better.

Jules Winston, he was the only person stopping me from advancing to the finals. We had the second fight of the day, and the other semi-finals have already been determined. I didn't want to know who won, or anything about him. My focus was Jules.

He had knocked out every opponent in the first round so far. Lightning quick punches and kicks, great ring presence and a veteran of tourney fighting. He had won his title for the past three years. He had almost two years of age on me. Man, it was getting harder to clear the doubts of my fighting abilities, injuries and the whole tourney psyche out of my semi fogged brain. I meditated for a bit, and then Charlie said it was time.

As we entered the ring I knew I wasn't on my game. I looked for familiar faces in the stands. Natasha, the Hell Hounds, Liz. Man, I was looking at Liz a little differently now. I couldn't find where my mom and sisters were sitting.

Damn it Mitch, concentrate on Jules! As I went through the ropes, I could hear Jules quoting scripture from the Bible, "Was I the tyranny of evil men?"

What the fuck was that all about? This wasn't going

to be good. As the ref gave us the instructions, Jules just kept talking away about how he was the shepherd. I had no concentration except for my aching bones, joints and muscles. I wasn't ready for this, and I was scared, really scared.

"DING" I sort of hobbled towards Jules. He asked was I the "GIMP": whoever that is. Jules struck first and struck often, he was tagging me with every jab and kick. I was in tremendous pain now. Even trying to block his punches hurt my already broken right hand. Caleb yelled at me to be less defensive and fight.

This was just too much for me. My breathing was becoming very erratic and my hands and feet felt like I was carrying twenty pound weights. I had no energy, and no focus. Jules came in a landed a double pump jab, followed by a right roundhouse kick to my head. I not only felt but heard my nose break as I was falling to the ground. I was basically in a dog position. I could see the blood from my broken nose drip onto the mat.

At last I felt it 'CHUG-CHUG-CHUG' that sweet addictive adrenaline pump to my heart. Suddenly I felt no more pain in my body. I was now able to tune out the supporters in the stands; all I could see, feel and sense was Jules. It was now time for me to get aggressive.

We both just charged at each other. I got the sense

my body was back in sync with my brain. I was landing punches and kicks against Jules. It was now hurting him. Yes Jules, you may be the shepherd, but I'm the one with the staff in my right hand and whacking you with it religiously; now that is tyranny! The only thing saving Jules from losing the fight was the bell signaling the end of the round.

As I walked to my corner Charlie asked, "What took so long for you to get interested in fighting this guy?"

"He had to piss me off, and breaking my nose pissed me right off."

Charlie reset my nose and said I'm good for maybe another round, not sure about two. Get rid of this guy quick! I just nodded yes all the while just staring at Jules. I'm the only opponent so far in this tourney to last beyond the first round with him.

"DING" Jules came out dancing and weaving just like a ballerina. I charged him into a corner and started landing body kicks and head shots with my fists. They were finding their mark and eventually Jules went down. My gut told me he wasn't that hurt though. When he looked over to his corner, I knew exactly what he was up to. He was playing 'Possum.' He wanted me to come in hard and reckless, to try and put him away. All the while I knew he would be lining me up with a counter strike to knock me out.

Well, time for my counter strike. I moved my shoulders forward and did a quick in and out leg lunge. Jules went for it and walked right into an overhand right, followed by a left hook, right cross and round house kick, to his left side of his jaw. Down he went, and this time he was out cold!

This victory was more a mental win than a physical win. I just stood over Jules until Caleb and Charlie came in and congratulated me. My supporters were more than enthusiastic shouting, "STRONGBOW-STRONGBOW-STRONGBOW."

It was nice hearing my name chanted. Jake was ear to ear with the smile, as was Natasha. If David could only see her now, what would he think? One day she will be mine. I know it, and feel it!

One more match and the State title was mine. Yeah I was feeling so confident. Had there been any doubts in my fighting abilities, this last victory dispelled any doubts I might have.

On the way to the dressing room, Jake came up to me with Liz beside him, "Hey little brother, I would say let Liz rub some more liniment on you. I hear it is used to take away swelling in your muscles."

Liz said, "It seemed to cause swelling in another muscle." I didn't know what to think or do next, damn she ratted me out! "It's OK little brother, she gives me all kinds of swelling too." Wow that was kind of freaky. I think he was OK with it?

As I was taking off my hand wraps and safety kicks, Charlie had the ice packs ready for the wounded areas which seem to be growing with each fight. Caleb worked on my nose and said I wouldn't be as cute, but then again I was never really that cute to begin with, so no big deal.

Much to my surprise, mom and younger sister Rachel came in the dressing room. The first words out of mom's mouth, was typical. "Are you all right Mitchell?"

"I'm fine mom, what did you think of my last match?"

"You did really well, your father would be proud of you. Mitchell, are you sure you are well?"

"I'm fine, one more fight and the title will be mine, and then dad will be proud."

Rachel just commented on how the dressing room really stank of B.O. My mom said she would let me be, told Caleb and Charlie to look after me, and kissed me good luck. Rachel said I was too sweaty and smelly to kiss, but wished me good luck just the same.

It was now time to get down to business; final fighter, final match in less than one hour. He was a tough street fighter from the east side of LA, half black and half Asian. Tobias Chong was his name, a no nonsense fighter with a straight forward attack. He could take a punch and a kick, and hit to hurt with decent hand and foot speed.

With this being the Championship fight there was now five rounds instead of three. So what was our game plan? Simply knock the fucker out! Don't give him a chance to knock me out first. Pretty simple if you ask me, but right now I needed some air.

As I left the dressing room I was kind of hoping to actually get a chance to talk to Natasha. I felt so alive around her and yet grounded at the same time. I didn't see her anywhere, but I did get a whiff of someone smoking some weed. Where there was weed being smoked, I'm sure I knew someone that was smoking it.

I walked towards where the smell of the burning evil hemp weed was coming from. There was a circle of at least twelve people, and those people were a bunch of the Dirty Dozen and a few of their girlfriends. They were all happy to see me, as I was to see them. Herman offered me a toke. I passed and said, "I need all my smarts for the next guy."

I told the boys I was dedicating this match to Blais and my dad. No one said anything, everyone just nodded in approval. I asked Norm had he has seen Lucy or Ricky. He answered "No." This was my biggest fight ever in full contact karate, and my girlfriend still wasn't here. I wasn't impressed at all.

Eventually most of the Oakland chapter of the Hell Hounds came cycling in led by Eric Von Kruder and Jerry. As they pulled in, also watching the spectacle was Natasha and her two girlfriends. When it came time for all of us to go inside, we walked past Natasha and her girlfriends.

I stopped and said to her, "Sorry I disappointed you and didn't end up on my back. I'm just a bastard that way," and gave her a wink.

Jeannie Terek recognized Natasha, "Hi sweetie, remember me? I still think you two would make a cute couple."

Natasha's eyes grew big as she was recalling Jeannie. "Agresta's and the flowers, right?"

"That's right sweetie. Would you and your friends like to come and sit with us and cheer Mitch on?" Her friends were so damn straight, hell you could tell they were scared shitless of the Hell Hounds. Natasha answered, "Maybe," but her friends said, "NO." That was nice of Jeannie to try and help me out. Natasha thanked Jeannie and said she was going to sit with my mom and sisters.

Everyone took their seats and true to her word, Natasha did sit with my mom and sisters. I went into the dressing room to prepare for the fight of my life with my broken nose, broken toes, and broken knuckles. However the one thing not broken, and could never be broken, was the fact that I was a Strongbow.

I was a true Sioux warrior ready for battle. I meditated and visualized my every move and counter move. I felt the adrenaline starting to slowly pump to my heart as I was warming up. I didn't feel any pain in my body and my breathing was now in a proper mode. I was ready and before I left the dressing room I said out loud, "This is for you dad, and you too Blais. Give me strength if need be."

As I exited the dressing room my eyes were now fully focused on Tobias Chong, who was already in the ring. The crowd was already tuned out of my head. I didn't even bother to see where all my supporters and family were sitting. There would be time for that soon enough.

Tobias and I just stared at each other while warming up in the ring; he was hard core, no doubts about that. As the ref explained the rules we just stared at each other. Death stares! I decided to fuck with his head some, "Have a good fight man." He flinched, I saw a weak side. He didn't know what to do next, "Same to you man".

"DING" Tobias came out to touch gloves as a sign of respect for each other; which I guess was his turn to fuck me up. Was he setting me up for a sucker punch? What the hell, we both touched gloves and the fun began.

Tobias landed a few, I landed a few, just measuring each other up, and feeling each other out. With it being a possible five round match, I had to pick my spots. Every time Tobias threw a kick to my body, I would block it with my elbow. I knew that sooner or later, his feet would start hurting real bad. If I can take away his kicking game, he won't be as lethal.

Tobias didn't give me too much to work with offensively. He never set himself up to be hit with combinations of kicks and punches. I might sneak in the odd first punch or kick, but never two in a row. He was a very slick, quick, a hit and move fighter. "DING" end of round one.

Caleb suggested I try and cut the ring off, and use my more powerful upper body strength and start to pound him relentlessly.

"DING" round two. I take Caleb's advice and go right at Tobias, trying to cut the ring in half or pin him in a corner. He is just so damn quick. Time to adapt, think of what his next move is and get there before he does. I throw a double left jab and know he is going to back up right side, so I throw a roundhouse kick, right where his body should be. MISTAKE!

Tobias comes in with a right hook that lands solid,

solid enough to daze me. I stagger against the ropes and try and get my legs back. They're doing the rubber chicken right now. I'm real close to going down. Tobias starts to unleash a flurry of body blows and shots to the head. Then it happened, something I thought was only a legend.

Damn his legs are double jointed. He goes to throw a roundhouse kick to the left side of my head, I get my gloves up to protect the area he has targeted, then like a magician his knee stays on course, but his shins reverse and his foot lands square on my now open right side of my face. He does this move four more times. My legs weren't strong enough to properly counter, so I collapsed to the canvas. I managed to struggle to my knee, and then took a kneeling eight count as I tried to clear my head and get my leg muscles working once again.

I have now decided to stay in close. At least close enough that Tobias 'Crazy-Legs' Chong can't bewilder me to the point of a defeat. I am now sure Tobias knows what my game plan is. As I move in close, I'm met by a fury of punches. A few of them find their mark but I'm now going toe-to-toe with him, and punch-for-punch.

Some of his punches are losing steam, or are delivered with only half his normal energy. I'm hurting him more than he is hurting me. I managed to land a right cross and a left uppercut, and down to the mat went Tobias. He is hurt, six, seven, eight, he is not getting up. "DING" he is saved by the bell, lucky bastard.

Caleb and Charlie both told me I have to fight unorthodox for the rest of the fight. From time to time go south paw, throw punches even off balance. This guy is a textbook fighter, and well-practiced in normal fighting. Anybody reckless and off the wall, he has never practiced or trained for. Well, off the wall is my middle name.

"DING" time for some unorthodox fighting, go down swinging and in ill humor. Round three was just as insane for the both of us. Twice he knocked me down, and twice I knocked him down; neither one of us cowered. We just kept throwing and kicking the whole time, both of us were inflicting damage on each other. From this point on, we will see who has trained harder, who is a warrior, and who has the true heart of a Champion.

"DING" round four. My arms were starting to cramp on me a bit. I could feel the acid burning every time I threw a punch. Those broken knuckles of mine were banged up. I was never sure if I had a complete fist made when I threw a punch, my hands were that swollen! The first eight punches of each round that landed just killed, then thankfully numbness set into my fist.

On a positive note, being able to block Tobias's feet with my elbows right from the opening round made his kicks now few and far between. Whenever I did block them with my elbows, you could see the pain written all over his face. I needed that pain to affect his battlefield thought process.

Tobias just wouldn't give in and lose the championship over pain. One of us had to be knocked cold or the ref would have to stop the fight. Perhaps it was the warrior in me or just my body and brain releasing natural pain killers. I was determined to fight to the death if need be. "DING" round four was over. One round left with three minutes to go.

As I sat on my chair, Charlie and Caleb were giving me instructions for the final round. They both agreed it was too close to call if it went to the judges hands, and never ever leave it to the judges. I had to knock Tobias out once and for all. I'm sure in Tobias's corner they are telling him the same thing. As I am sitting on the chair just trying to gather my thoughts, I can hear Sioux battle drums beating in the background; this inspires me!

"DING," just like the first round, Tobias comes out and wants to touch gloves. However his face looks different, something isn't right. I see his face grimace in pain and his shoulders drop, and notice he pulls back his gloves before they can touch mine. Cocksucker, he's now trying to do a spinning reverse punch. The pain on his face is unmistakable. All his weight going to his battered foot gave him away.

I duck as he is coming around and I land a roundhouse kick right to his head. With his momentum and my momentum colliding full force, Tobias is about to be hit with the same power as a locomotive. 'BANG', he is stunned by my kick. I let my fists do the rest of damage as Tobias leaned against the ropes. I'm now truly pissed and angry, and serious anger is now being thrown in my fists. The only reason Tobias is still on his feet, is because of the ropes holding up his battered and bleeding body. I don't stop my barrage until the ref jumps in there and signals the match is over.

Even when Caleb and Charlie come in to lift me up, I still want a piece of Tobias. I have complete tunnel vision towards him. Man, he went from a worthy opponent to scum, just like Da Silva.

Eventually Charlie gets me to relax and let the anger and frustration go, with these easy words. "*You are the Champ Mitch. No one in California is better than you. Mitch, you're the Champ! Nationals are next.*"

Jake and several Hell Hounds and Dirty Dozen were now mobbing me. Then it hit me, and I went ear to ear with a smile, which I might add hurt like hell, but that was pain well worth it. I looked to where mom was sitting. She, along with my sisters and Natasha were all standing up and clapping. It's been a long time since I made mom smile like that. Seeing Natasha smile and clapping for me was almost as good as the trophy I was about to receive.

As mom, my sisters and Natasha made their way down from the stands; Von Kruder came in the ring and said, my presence was requested at the Oakland clubhouse for a party to celebrate my victory.

When Eric Von Kruder invites you to anything you better show up. To refuse his invitation would be a slap in the face, not only to him, but also to Jake and Jerry. Eric was very powerful. He wasn't only the most powerful leader but also a founding member of the Hell Hounds. I answered with the only words that could be spoken. "Of course I will and thank you." I have been at the clubhouse several times, just not ever there for a huge monster party, and damn sure not a party in my honor.

As I leave the ring, mom gives me a hug and tells me how proud she was of me. Hell even Rachel gave me a hug and said she's happy I'm her brother. Pam is always more emotional, and just hugged me while crying tears of joy. I just stared at Natasha and as I smiled and gave her a wink, she turned beet red.

"How is David doing? I hope you know it was

nothing personal, he was just another opponent. I did what I had to do."

"First off, congrats Mitch, and thanks for asking about David. He has a concussion, broken nose and his jaw is swollen, however not broken. You really can fight can't you?"

My euphoric high of winning the California Championship brought out the courage to ask Natasha out to celebrate my victory. I have accomplished so much this weekend, every battle I have won. I now had the courage to finally ask her out. "Some things or people are worth fighting for. I just got asked to a party that is being thrown in my honor. I was wondering, would you like to come with me as my date?"

Her smile told me she wanted to go but her eyes told another story. Her friends standing beside her would've ratted her out to David. Then again, even more reason to ask her, dump David and be my girl. Natasha said, "I better not, I have school tomorrow, but thanks anyways."

She didn't mention anything about David. One day we will go out and I will show her what a real man is all about. Mom then mentioned that I also have school tomorrow, and could use some rest and good night sleep.

Jake put his arms around me and my mom and

said, "We are having a party for Mitch at the clubhouse in his honor. I am sure he will need at least a day's rest from all his fights. I'm also sure his school would give him the day off. After all how many of their students are State full contact Champion?"

Mom agreed, as long as Jake was responsible for my actions. Jake said he would take care of me. I thanked Natasha for coming and said, "Maybe another time." She answered back, "Yeah, maybe another time." Then her girlfriends dragged her away.

I told Jake I just had to shower then I would be right out. John Derksen said I could ride on the back of his bike to the club house. I asked, "What about my trophy?" Von Kruder said he would put in on the back of his bike.

As I was showering I was still in shock that I had actually won the whole tourney. Once the adrenaline rush started to wear off, every punch and kick that landed and every broken bone was now starting to hurt like hell. Washing my hair was truly a chore, not to mention all the bumps on my head, but this pain was well worth it.

As I was drying off I heard Charlie thank Caleb for all his help. Caleb then invited Charlie back to the clubhouse for the party. Charlie thanked him but said, "That wouldn't be such a good idea."

Caleb looked confused and asked, "Don't you

party?" Charlie answered with a smile, "I party, but you don't know what I do for a living, do you Caleb?"

Caleb's eyes now got big, "You're not a cop are you?" Charlie nodded his head. "Yeah, I'm a cop."

Caleb made sure there was no one else in the dressing room. He walked over to Charlie, shook his hand and said, "For a cop, you aren't that bad a guy." Caleb then left the dressing room.

I walked over and also thanked Charlie for his leadership and coaching. Charlie also thanked me. I was his first ever state Champion. He told me we are going to take a week off of training, to let the bones mend and give my body a chance to heal. Then we can get set for the USA open in Hawaii in four weeks from now. I asked if Caleb could also go with us. Charlie's answer was, "Why not?"

Before I left the room, Charlie said he wants the trophy at the Dojo this Tuesday to show all the other students, "This is the result of hard work and dedication."

As I went to leave the gym I was stopped by a local television crew and was interviewed, then by a local newspaper sports writer. There was no way my helmet would fit on my head. Damn, it was getting mighty big all of a sudden.

Eventually Derksen came inside and yelled at me,

"It is time to leave Mitchell, time to celebrate your victory little brother." Derksen even tried to pick up the rather cute newspaper writer and asked if she wanted to come to a party. She looked more scared than most of my opponents, right before they knew I was going to knock them out.

As Derksen and I were driving over the Oakland Bay Bridge on our way to the Oakland clubhouse, I felt real special, knowing that I made so many people proud of me today. The one person who didn't share in my victory was Lucy.

After spending little time with Natasha, I now realize that Lucy and I are going to split up once again. It will probably be real soon, and this time for good. How the hell could she miss this? She is a black belt in Karate; she knows how important these tournaments are. I'm supposed to be her boyfriend, where the fuck is she? Who knows and right now, who cares. It's party time.

As Derksen and I cycled in through the front iron clad gates, I almost felt like a celebrity in the Hell Hounds with everyone giving me cheers. Jake brought me over a beer, I looked at him and we tapped beer cans. "This is for dad and Blais." We both then did the Airborne "Currahe" call back to each other, and took a drink in their honor. I must say this beer tasted awful damn good now that I was the victor.

After a couple beers, my hands were really starting to throb and swell. Caleb checked them out and said I had at least two broken knuckles, but that trophy sort of kills the pain, doesn't it. After a couple more beers, several tokes on the old bong pipe, and recapping each victory out loud, hell the pain was starting to go away.

I felt kind of guilty not partying with my own gang the Dirty Dozen, but Caleb's brother Fraser was the only Dirty Dozen member allowed here. Caleb being a full patch Hell Hound made it alright. Fraser and I were pretty tight anyway, that was until Fraser told me something, "Mitch your old lady, Lucy, is nothing but a fucking whore."

Normally I would have started to swing at Fraser. Whether it was because my hands were killing me or I was exhausted, I did nothing, I just sat there semi-stunned. "What makes you say that Fraser?"

"She has not been around all weekend has she? Where do you think she is man?"

"I'm not sure man, do you know?"

Fraser I could tell was equally split with his demons in telling me, but Dirty Dozen look out for each other.

"You know I have nothing to gain, and I would never go out of my way to fuck you over, bro. I'm not telling you this to hurt you, or fuck up your head after your tremendous victory. Herman and I saw her in Chinatown and this old guy was all over her. She didn't push him away man, she was dressed like a whore, Mitch."

"When you say all over her, like what?"

"Like a lion on a fresh piece of meat, they're necking and he had his hand up her skirt man."

"Did she see you and Herman at all?"

"No she didn't. Sorry bro, they're Chinese gangsters Mitch, or Herman and I would have laid a beating on them."

Well that sort of took the wind out of my sails. Then a new wind come blowing my way, the key word was blowing. Jake and Jerry came up and said I should check out the brand new hot tub installed in one of the play rooms, "it's all set up for you," they said. A bunch of the boys from the club started to laugh. I knew they were up to something.

Liz walked by and told me to be careful, that the hot tub could have crocodiles in it, but as a nurse she assured me, the soothing jets and warm water will help my joints, all my joints! Liz then grabbed my crotch and laughed. I'm now more intrigued than ever. I walked into the room with the hot tub. The only light that was shining was coming from candles, and they shone upon two great looking blondes, Carsta and Eva Vigoda, the two Hell Hound strippers and club 'Splashers.'

Eva told me to get undressed and get into the water, don't be shy, they won't bite. Eva said she couldn't guarantee that statement though. Damn, I just looked at the girls with water up to their neckline. I was in a blissful state of shock.

Carsta then stood up. She had to be at least six feet tall, but that wasn't as shocking as the fact that she was completely naked. Then Eva stood up and she was wearing the same amount of clothing as her sister. They both walked over and undressed me all the while necking with me. Each one then grabbed a hand and escorted me to the hot tub, where the necking turned into heavy petting.

All the while I kept having these flashes of statements from Jake saying whenever one of his women pissed him off he would have another one ready to go. Combine that with what Fraser just told me, and the feeling of freedom and power I was getting from the Vigoda sisters, I wanted to hurt Lucy.

I need to let my brain and self-confidences know that I can score not only with her, but I can score with other chicks. No more of her disappearing. I enjoyed the two older sisters and the hot tub, and I enjoyed myself more than once actually.

As the night went on I was fucked right up, so Jake and Liz drove me home. It was just shortly before two in the morning when we pulled in the driveway. I don't really remember going to bed, all I do recall was that the steps seemed to be harder to climb than normal.

The next morning I felt like I had been in one hell of an automobile accident. My head was foggy and groggy, and not just from the booze and weed. My body hurt from head to toe. I felt every single muscle and joint aching, some more than others. Just like a car's engine sparkplugs firing in perfect sequence, my joints would also fire up in pain. I looked at my alarm clock and it was almost noon and even though I had just awoken, I was still very tired, very, very tired.

Only two factors brought a smile to my face, my Championship trophy at the foot of my bed, and reminiscing about making it with both Vigoda sisters in the hot tub, damn now that was cool. I just stared at my trophy. I had to touch it just to make sure I wasn't still dreaming. Yeah, it was real, I did in fact win the State Championship.

When I went for a leak, there was bit of blood in my piss. Guess that's to be expected when your kidneys take some serious physical beatings. I staggered to the shower and tried to come alive via the magic water from the shower head and for the most part it worked. I went downstairs to get some grub, every step I felt my muscles tighten and burn. My broken toes didn't help my balance. I felt like a drunk coming down the stairs. I grabbed something to eat, went out back and smoked a joint, then crawled back into bed. It was almost 13:00 and I didn't wake up till the next morning when mom said it was time for school.

As much as I wanted to just stay home and recoup, my mom said, "The principal phoned and said they are planning something for you. So you have to show up with your trophy," and show up I did.

After third period they had a special ceremony for me in the school auditorium. Just like the school board to pat themselves on the back, every teacher and trustee was taking credit for my victory. The whole thing was so fucking phony. I'm the one with broken bones, sore muscles and joints, and these guys and gals are taking credit.

I just bided my time, bit my tongue and thanked the people who really counted, Charlie, Caleb and just to embarrass Rachel, "For all you single boys out there who may think my sister Rachel is cute and sweet, well she is the true pit bull in the family, not me." I also made sure to thank Ricky Thom, but nothing for Lucy.

It was nice of the school that a plaque will now

hang in the school trophy case, but I still felt I was being exploited. This school was always so quick to expel me for my violent tendencies, now they are honoring me for controlled violence. I guess maybe the brightest spot was actually seeing Vice Principal Nash, who hates me, have to present me with the plaque. I knew it just killed him inside to do this.

After school, as is tradition, a bunch of us Dirty Dozen headed back to Dubrowski's to smoke a couple joints. Fraser and I were shooting the breeze when Lucy and Ricky came in. Lucy seemed to be pissed at me, and as much as I wanted to lose it on her, this was not the place. Besides, how dare she be pissed at me, she's the slut!

The sight of Lucy now sickened me. I told Ricky I would see him at karate tonight and it took everything in me not look at Lucy. Even though I made out and had sex with the Vigoda sisters, make that had sex with the Vigoda sisters a couple of times, this was only after hearing that Lucy was out whoring around on me once again.

At Karate that night, I was hit harder than by any of my opponents during the tourney. An official from Full Contact Karate California was in the office talking to Charlie. I was told by Ricky there was trouble, and Charlie and the official have been yelling at each other and I'm at the center of the dispute and yelling. I knocked on Charlie's office door, Charlie asked me ever so sheepishly, to have a seat.

He introduced me to Brian Morton, the official from Full Contact Karate California. I thought maybe they were arguing about paying for flights and accommodations for Caleb. I wish it was something that simple. Morton pulled no punches, "Strongbow, I am going to ask you something and I better hear the right answer. Did you take performance enhancing supplements? To help you win the State Championship?"

"I took nothing! I won my title fair and square through hard work, great coaching and the heart of a warrior."

Morton didn't like my answer. He asked to see my hands and feet. I looked at Charlie for direction. Charlie just nodded yes to me; so I showed him my battered and broken feet and hands. "Are you telling me son, you fought this tournament with all these broken knuckles and toes, and took nothing to help you win? I saw them break your nose. I saw punches that should have knocked out most men, never mind a sixteen year old. I hate being bullshitteded to."

Now my back was up, "I am not bullshitting you. I fight to win not lose! Who complained about me?"

"I'm not at liberty to divulge who complained. Are you willing to take a blood test, to check for any enhancing drugs in your bloodstream son?"

"What if I say no, does that automatically make me guilty?"

"You say no son and you lose your Championship, and you don't get to fly to Hawaii for the National Championships. It's up to you son."

"I always thought in America you were innocent until proven guilty. Now I know why the hippies hate the establishment. I spilled enough blood in the ring, what's a little bit more? Yeah I will do a blood test. Then I want an apology, and to be left alone to do what I do best, fight."

"You prove me wrong son and you will get that apology. First though, you have to pass the blood test. I have this requisition, and it has to be done tomorrow at the latest. And I have to also be present when the blood is taken."

I took his requisition. I know I'm clean but man I'm pissed. As I left Charlie's office Ricky asked me, "What was all the yelling about?" After I told him, Ricky said I should tell him to just stick it up their ass and sue them for slander. I promised Ricky I was telling the truth, and I took nothing to help me win the tourney. Hell, I even turned down the Wizard's offer of 'Speed' pills. I told Ricky I needed some air and was going for a bike ride. "Tell Charlie I had to split and will contact him tomorrow after my blood test."

As I was firing up my bike Lucy tapped me on the shoulder and asked if she could go for the ride with me. Hell just what I need, more grief. "I need to go for a ride alone, actually make that be alone for ever. We're through."

I revved my bike and did a burn out, then fled the scene. I just drove up the coast and tried to clear my head. I was shifting gears, with my broken knuckles and toes still hurting. However, I felt free as an eagle; make that a wounded eagle. The drive did in fact clear my head. I knew what my next course of action would be.

When I got home I talked to mom. I assured her I hadn't taken anything to help me win the Championship. She then phoned her brother and my uncle, Karl who as luck would have it, is also a lawyer in Sacramento. Aunt Sandy said he was in Los Angeles on business. She gave my mom his phone number at his hotel in Los Angeles, but there was no answer.

Mom, like she has always done in the past, assured me everything would be all right. She said "Get a good night's sleep and don't let it worry you. You won the tournament fair and square and justice would be served."

That night I couldn't sleep. This whole drug test, and the unwarranted accusations of me cheating to win the state Championship, to me ending my relationship with Lucy once again kept me awake. I have put lots of time, heart and blood into both of these ventures and yet both are causing major grief in my life. Nothing comes easy does it?

The next day, Pam went with me to get my blood tested, and to offer support. Brian Morton was also there as he said he would be. It was a rather painless procedure; perhaps this was an omen of things to come. When the blood work was complete, I headed back to school. Morton told me, should there be a problem he would be in touch with Charlie Adams. He said he hoped there wasn't a problem, as I would be a favored fighter in Hawaii and would make California proud.

Pam being a hippie of course gave Morton an earful about being the 'Man'. All of us Strongbow's, regardless of gender like to state our opinion; Pam and Rachel through brains and vocals, Jake and I through brawn and brawling. I'm sure as soon as I see Lucy I will be using my brain, vocals and brawn. I won't brawl with her, mom did teach me some manners. But that doesn't mean I can't call her a cunt or whore though.

Once at school, I actually tried my best to stay away from Lucy. I figured I had enough on my plate with the drug controversy. All went according to plan until school let out and I saw her sitting on my bike. She wasn't smiling and she was smoking a cigarette which totally grossed me out.

So do I go against mom's advice and just cuff her upside the head, and then ride away? Nah, that would be cowardly, anyway I had something to say. "So I see you started smoking behind my back, anything else you started behind my back Lucy? Wait that's right, you are also whoring around on me once again!"

This statement caused Lucy to flick the cigarette right at my face. This was followed by an irate temper tantrum and denials of her whoring around on me. Fuck, I wanted to break her face! It took everything in me, and I mean everything in me, not to hurt her.

"Fuck you Strongbow! You're the one who spent the night at the clubhouse with all the whores that hang around there. I also hear that blonde Jew is your new fan. I hear all, Mitch."

"Well I heard you disappeared in the back of a limo with the same rich Chink as before. Uncle Incest, is that his name?" Lucy tried to slap me in the face. I blocked her attempted slap and spun her arm behind her back until it started to hurt her real bad.

"At least the blonde Jew came and saw me fight, and win. Where the fuck where you? Wait we already established that answer haven't we? I'm so sick of you and your secret life Lucy, no more. I needed your support this past weekend, well no more. We are through for good! Now do I break your arm or are you going to behave yourself?"

By now a crowd was gathering around. The first loud mouth tough guy that says or tries to act like a hero will take the beating that Lucy should be getting. Most people in the school knew I was more than just a little whacked in the psychotic department, so the crowd looked on with anticipation.

No way was there going to be a white knight in shining armor to come and save Lucy the dreaded Asian damsel in distress. They all knew she ripped people off with drug deals and that she was a whore and a bully to the other girls at the school. Some of the crowd obviously wanted to see her take a shot or two upside the head and experience the suffering she has inflicted upon others.

Lucy knew with a crowd present I wouldn't do anything too stupid. This knowledge made Lucy get even braver, as well as stupid, by taunting me. She called me a tough guy picking on a girl, and followed that with, "Where is your blonde Jew whore now?"

Now I'm pissed and past my breaking point; how dare she insult Natasha? I picked up Lucy and carried her kicking and screaming over to the school trash dumpster, then threw her in. Bruno Sanmartino would have been proud of my body slam.

As I walked towards my bike, some students were laughing and clapping. One male teacher didn't find it so funny, put his hand on my arm and told me to stop. I looked him in the eyes and told him if he didn't take his hand off me, he could join Lucy in the dumpster. As he was explaining to me that I was in real trouble, I just blew him a kiss and jumped on my bike. I needed to clear my head and compose myself.

As I drove off the school grounds, all I could think of was Natasha. I hauled ass over to mom's school, hoping I would get a chance to see Natasha alone. I just need ten minutes with her, just to tell her how she makes me feel.

I looked into her eyes during the tourney and they couldn't disguise the fact that she too felt something for me. Now it was time for my brain to find a way to display my heart and soul. Hopefully, Natasha will embrace my attributes and give me a chance to prove myself. Maybe let her see the softer, emotional side of me, not just the warrior she witnessed, destroying my opponents.

The final few students trickled out of the school, but no Natasha. I was so desperate to see her! Had I known where she lived, I would go and ring her door bell. I just drove around different neighborhoods, hoping to catch a glimpse of her. I hit all the local hamburger joints and nothing, so I decided to give up my futile search and head to Dubrowski's.

I pulled up to a traffic light, and something told me to look to the left. There was a jewelry store and the girl dusting off the display cases looked like Natasha. I tried my best to focus on the blonde girl inside just as the light turned green. The driver of the car behind me wasn't impressed with the fact that I was still sitting at the green light and began to hit his horn. He hit it several times and was now also starting to swear at me. He called me a punk and said, "Move your bike before I move it myself."

Where's the dumpster when you need it? I put down my kickstand and walked towards the idiot in the car, when I heard *"Mitchell"*. Damn, that angelic voice I recognize. I don't even have to turn around. The butterflies in my stomach told me that voice belongs to Natasha.

I halted my forward motion towards the loud obnoxious driver against my warrior upbringing, as I truly wanted to break the loudmouth's jaw. After all, I had just promised myself that I would show Natasha my compassionate side. I really wanted to win her heart and soul. So I walked back towards my bike and pulled up right to where Natasha was standing.

Those beautiful hypnotic eyes of hers are once again smiling and dancing, as are mine. Her smile is contagious. "What brings you down here Mitchell?"

"I never got a chance to thank you for your support at the tourney. Do you believe in luck?"

"Yeah, a bit I guess. Why?"

"At one point I thought I had nothing but bad luck. During the tourney I felt it starting to creep up on me, with several of my bones breaking. Then I felt a great change come over me, but I couldn't figure what was different and what was causing my luck to change."

"Then I happened to look in the stands and I saw my 'Good Luck Charm.' She had these gorgeous blue eyes, the long blonde hair of a goddess, and a smile like 'Helen of Troy.' That was the lady with the smile "that could launch a thousand ships."

Natasha's face now went beet red, and her neck all blotchy. Suddenly her face changed, as if someone had sucked the joy right out of her. A middle aged male approached us, while staring at me the whole time and asked Natasha, "Who is the Shagetz?" This was followed by, "is he being a Shmendrik?"

"He is fine Barry. Mitchell's mom is one of my teachers and he is just looking to get her something for Mother's Day. Relax already."

Barry, wearing all these chains and rings, knew I was up to no good. He gave me the look and then went back inside the jewelry store.

"I'm sorry if I got you into any trouble. Who was that guy? Please tell me he is not your dad and what exactly was he calling me?"

"Barry is my step-father, and he was speaking Yiddish. You are a non-Jewish jerk."

I started to laugh, "I guess me being invited to a family dinner is out of the question?" She started to laugh and I felt the courage to ask her out once again. "Natasha, how do you feel about dinner then, just the two of us?"

Natasha's eyes got real big and her smile was starting to get smaller. Her eyes almost showed signs of pain, she took a slow breath and an even slower exhale. "Mitchell, how do I explain this without hurting you? I really think it is so sweet of you asking me out, but I have a boyfriend. He's Jewish and I know it shouldn't matter, but with my mom and Barry it does. David's family and my family are very close. His parents are like an aunt and uncle to me, and have been for as long as I can remember. I just can't go out with you, I'm sorry Mitchell. I have some really cute non-Jewish girlfriends who might interest you."

I stopped Natasha in her tracks as this was a conversation I never wanted to hear. "I don't want anyone else but you. The first time I saw you, I wanted to know everything there was to know about you. I just…"

Fuck I never got the chance to say, "I just want you as my one and only," when Barry came back outside.

This time Barry had a cigar in his mouth and started to walk towards us. He had attitude. "I know your type, nothing but trouble. She's a good girl with a nice boyfriend. I think you should leave. I have connections. If you start trouble."

I guess if I started to knock the shit out of Barry, it probably wouldn't leave the best impression with Natasha. "No trouble here Barney, I'm just leaving."

This made Barry really mad. His face was getting redder than the heater on the end of his cigar. *"It's Barry, not Barney!"*

At least my sarcastic name slip and slam made Natasha smile. I decided to just go with it, "OK Barney Rubble, I'm leaving, say hi to Betty for me." Sadly I fired up my bike and revved up my engine, all the while forcing a smile at Natasha. I gave her a wink goodbye, laid some rubber right in front of the jewelry shop, and sped away. I went directly to Dubrowski's house. Man I needed to get high and have a drink or ten.

As I drove down to Dubrowski's place, I replayed in my mind what I heard Natasha say about David and her upbringing. Her eyes and smile told me something entirely different, and I just know I'm right. For now, I will just admire her from a distance, and if fate wants us to be together; fate will make it happen. I have done my part, ever so boldly if I say so myself. Something tells me she's worth it.

At Dubrowski's, news of my episode with Lucy and the trash dumpster had already made its way there. I was called the 'Garbage Man' all night. I was pissed at first, but the higher and drunker I got, the funnier the whole episode became.

I officially declared myself single and available. Had Kerry Dubrowski been home, I would have fucked her that night and thought of Natasha the whole time. I just got severely wasted instead.

The next day Charlie Adams left a message for me to bring a pair of swim trunks to the Karate studio. So after school, I headed over. Charlie said we have less than a month to train for the fights in Hawaii. Since I have broken toes and knuckles I would train in the water, as the resistance wouldn't bother my broken bones.

This should be fairly easy, but after about twenty minutes of training, Charlie got real pissed and lost it on me. "I know you like to party Mitch, but this is a onetime chance for the United States Championship. If you want to party and waste my time with your half ass effort, let me know now!"

I guess with me still hurting from kicking it down the night before, it showed in my piss poor effort.

"I'm just tired from school, and I guess this blood test thing is dragging me down, zapping me mentally and physically."

"Mitchell I can smell the booze coming off you. Hell you aren't even of age to drink, it's a school night and you're wasted. If you dad was still alive, he'd kick your ass, wouldn't he?"

Now my back was up, "Well he's fucking dead isn't he?"

"I see your dad's spirit in you Mitchell. I see that same tenacious look in your eyes, as I saw in your dad's eyes when we were in Korea. Your dad will never be truly dead as long as you are alive. Quit trying to kill your spirit, as well as his spirit with booze and an undisciplined lifestyle. Mitchell, you have so much potential and so much unfocused anger. Let that anger be your focal point of training, let it fuel your desire to win. I never saw your dad lose a fight or ever even think of giving up, and you know why? Because of his family, he wanted to come back to you guys and be a part of your lives. Mitchell, embrace your dad's spirit and what he stood for. You always say you are a Sioux warrior, well start acting like one!"

Charlie was right, my dad would be kicking my ass for training this half-ass hard only to flush it all down the toilet by partying too hard. The biggest battle of my life was yet to take place in Hawaii. So back into the pool I went, throwing punches and kicks against the resistance of the water. Here I was surrounded with water, yet I was unbelievably thirsty and sweating profusely.

After two hours Charlie told me to call it a night, go home and do some shadow boxing and abs. I thanked him for his "Pep" talk and he thanked me for training so hard. I didn't bother to go to Dubrowski's. I went straight home and did some more dry land training.

I did this hard core training for two more days, then on the Friday Charlie left a note for me at home and told me not to bother bringing my swim trunks. Great finally some sparring. I guess he figured my knuckles and toes had healed enough.

As I walked into the Dojo, I had quite the skip in my walk. I felt real good about my training and was ready to take it to an ever higher level. Caleb Dalton was already at the gym in Charlie's office, but he wasn't smiling when I came in. Brian Morton was also in the office as I walked in. The air was stale and the tension, hell you could have cut it with a knife. The hair on the back of my neck was now standing straight up. I knew something wasn't right. What now, more unfounded accusations? Am I older than what I say I am, or a higher belt?

I looked at all three but I wasn't sure who to ask

what was going on. Why is everybody so damn gloom looking? I still wasn't sure which one to talk to. I knew if it came from Brian Morton, I might not like what he'd say. "Charlie what's going on?" I must say my voice was trembling a bit with unsure emotions.

"Your blood test for drug use came back Mitchell, it came back positive."

I was confused. I didn't take anything to help me win. "What the fuck did it come back positive for? I am fucking clean!"

Brian Morton now looked at me and said, "You tested positive for Cannabis Sativa, do you know what that is son?"

"No I don't but I'm sure it is something bad right?"

"You tested positive for having Mary Jane, marijuana, hemp or whatever you kids call it nowadays. It was present in your blood Mitchell, any idea how it got in your bloodstream?"

I looked at Caleb first, then Charlie. "I don't mean to disrespect you Charlie, but if I tell you, will I get arrested?'

"I'm your Sensei in this Dojo, not a cop"

I trusted Charlie, "I smoke pot from time to time. It helps me relax it doesn't give me an edge over anybody. Hell, I smoked once before a fight, and it just fucked me up more than anything. I didn't use it again during the tournament."

"I appreciate your honesty under these trying times, but Mary Jane makes people have super human strength. It turns them into killers and they can't feel pain. I'm sorry son but you are disqualified."

Caleb was now getting pissed and addressed Morton's absurd theory. "Have you ever smoked weed? Where the hell do you get your information from by the way? This kid trained his fucking heart out, broke bones and spilled his blood all over that fucking ring. Now you won't let him fight because he smoked a little weed?"

"I'm truly sorry but I have superiors to answer to and the rules are the rules and Mitchell clearly broke them."

I felt like throwing up and I broke out in a cold sweat. Is this actually a fucking nightmare? Someone please wake me. I have suffered enough.

Brian then asked, "Can I have our State Championship trophy back?"

Caleb now sprung up out of his seat and told Brian in no uncertain terms, "That is the kid's trophy. He has broken toes, knuckles and his nose. You want that trophy you, go through me. With any luck all you get out of it is a few broken bones and not a fucking broken neck."

Brian looked at Charlie and said, "I have just been threatened and you are still a cop, regardless of what you promised the kid."

Charlie told Morton, "Sorry did you say something? My hearing is not the greatest tonight. I must be coming down with "get the fuck out of my Dojo."

Caleb now started walking towards Brian, who was indeed intimidated and left the Dojo very quickly and even importantly very quickly without my trophy.

As I sat in the chair, I replayed everything that had just unfolded. I was still in a dreamlike state, my body couldn't move, even my thoughts and words didn't line up correctly. I just sat back and listened to Charlie and Caleb talk about a possible appeal. I finally came out of my induced state of shock, and did what I thought would have made dad proud.

I looked at both Charlie and Caleb and said, "No appeal! Charlie you have been an inspiration and like family ever since we came out to California. I know my dad would have smiled upon you for your guidance and wisdom. However, you told me the other day I had dad's spirit in me. This tournament is not worth your job Charlie. Make no mistake they will go after your job as a cop and I can't let that happen. I just realized how those dicks over at Karate USA are going to fuck us all up. I appeal, but with me testing positive for weed and Caleb being a full patch Hell Hound, don't you think at a certain point they will go to your supervisors? They will ask about the company you keep or how is it I'm doing weed and you can't even tell? I can also see them pulling your teaching license Charlie. I couldn't live with either. I'm sorry Charlie."

Caleb smiled at me and gave me a wink for my decision and showing maturity. 'Mitchell you have grown into quite the adult over the past year. I'm touched that you think more of my job and this Dojo than your own personal gain. Do you think if we asked for another blood test you will be clean?" I just shook my head no. Caleb looked at me and said "Now what?"

"Are the Vigoda sisters around? I think I need some tender loving care. Oh yeah, I also need to get wasted." Caleb said, "He knows where they are stripping right now. Let's go see the fabulous Vigoda sisters."

Charlie shook both our hands and asked me, had I forgotten something? I was confused. "Your championship trophy Mitchell. You earned it, you keep it! I will tell Morton someone stole it, hell I will even write the report myself."

As Caleb and I were almost at the door Charlie

asked if I was still going to train, as I'm so close to getting my black belt.

"Are you sure you want a weed demon like me around? Yeah, I'll be back, Charlie. I just need some time to clear my head."

Charlie said "Fair enough." I strapped my trophy on the back of my Harley, and Caleb and I headed to the Drunken Leprechaun and the Vigoda sisters for some tender loving care.

I stayed on my bike while Caleb went inside the Drunken Leprechaun, and looked for Jake and the Vigoda sisters to come outside. The Drunken Leprechaun was a 'Heat Score' to the cops, and the different religious groups who have tried in the past to shut it down. The 'Go-Go' dancers and topless waitresses were accused of lewd and unruly behavior.

Joseph O'Reilly had the joint crammed wall to wall. He hired only the finest young local musicians. It was basically the Fillmore West with a liquor license and slutty broads working inside. Damn, I couldn't wait till I was old enough to drink inside. Then again, the Oakland Clubhouse was everything like the Drunken Leprechaun and no one cared how old I was.

Jake came out with Don Terek and asked, "What the fuck happened?" I told him, "I don't know man." He was pissed, he actually wanted to go and skin Brian Morton alive, as did Don Terek. I explained that

Morton was just following orders. Jake then said to call my Uncle Karl in the morning. He also wanted to know, "does my mom know what was going on?"

I told Jake I was really embarrassed to tell her, I tested positive for weed and I'm now disqualified. Can I at least enjoy the weekend? I'm pretty sure I'm going to be grounded until I'm at least twenty one years old. This has been a rough week already, breaking up with Lucy and then being told, "Thanks but no thanks," by Natasha.

Jake had a sympathetic laugh and told me, "No problems little brother. Being grounded until you are twenty-one years old is a long time. Let's have fun this weekend shall we?"

And fun we had, at least from what I remember. I think I lost a few brain cells that weekend. Jake went back to finish his beer, and came back outside with those two 'goddess of sin,' the Vigoda sisters. Carsta jumped on the back of my bike right between myself and my trophy, and the four of us then headed to Jake's house.

Before we kicked it down I phoned mom and asked, "Could I spend the weekend with Jake?" After Jake told her, "everything was on the straight and narrow," mom agreed. Then it was bottoms up for a bottle of Tequila and the Vigoda sisters.

I have never had another couple in the same room

as me having sex, never mind it being my older brother. However after several shots of Tequila, a couple joints, and the girls and Jake doing some coke, which I really wanted to try myself, I got into it with Carsta.

There's still no way that Jake would allow me to partake of a few lines. He told me once again, "Don't do anything that can kill your soul little brother, cocaine will kill your soul."

I asked Jake, "What about your soul?" He made no bones about it. He was going straight to hell; he didn't have a soul left. When Jake told me this, I could just tell by the dark shark-like eyes, his soul was truly gone, and yet he wanted my soul to live. I guess that was the big brother in him, looking out for me now that our dad was dead.

Just like at the Drunken Leprechaun, the girls were dancing and striping for us. They were doing simulated sex acts on each other for us. Damn this was hot. Somehow it managed to take my mind off the week from hell. Eventually Jake and I were swapping sister for sister. I don't remember falling asleep or more like passing out in the spare bedroom. I woke up and I quickly realized that tequila gave me one of the worst hangovers I have ever experienced; but what a night, I think.

Jake told me, "Grab some grub," as the Oakland

club is going on a run to Anaheim and I'm invited courtesy of Eric Von Kruder. I didn't feel like eating but a seven hour bike ride would be hard on an empty stomach, never mind on a hangover. Carsta and Eva made us some breakfast and then we dropped them off at their apartment building and headed to the Oakland Clubhouse.

This was a 'Snowball Run' which meant along the way, we would be hooking up with several other Hell Hound Chapters and 'Puppet Clubs'. At the Oakland Clubhouse, there were already sixty members from the San Francisco and Sacramento clubs. It was the first anniversary of the Anaheim Chapter and no one knew how to throw a party quite like the Hell Hounds Motor Cycle Club.

Also along for the ride were John 'Mad Dog' Kantonescu and several members of the Devil Dogs. John always liked to put me in a bear hug every time I saw him. John was getting stockier, and at the Popeye's he was the official bench press king at just over five hundred pounds.

I'm sure if Morton were to test John, he would have something in his blood to disqualify him. I still can't believe it. I'm hoping no one brings up me fighting for the USA championships. Hell, if there is ever a motley crew that could understand me getting fucked over by society or the 'Man', these guys would understand.

As we left the Oakland Clubhouse, we were over one hundred strong. It was quite the spectacle not only visually, but also the deafening sound. It was more than enough to wake the dead, and a little extra to shake the cobwebs of my Tequila hangover.

Our first stop was the San Jose Hell Hound Clubhouse, where close to two dozen members were awaiting our arrival for the journey. I already know a couple of the San Jose members, as my Cousin Val's boyfriend George is a full patch, like Jake. George is also a 'Crazy Eight' and club executive; he is their Vice President.

George is what you would call a hard core biker, old style 'Rebel without a Cause.' He lives hard and plays hard. George served in the Korean War and when he came home, he killed a man in a bar fight. He did seven years in prison where his reputation grew as a person not to fuck with. He would slice your throat from ear to ear, or as George loves to call it, "A grin under your chin." Unlike John Derksen or Kantonescu, he wasn't the biggest in stature, but you just knew that George was all business when pissed off or pushed to the edge.

George and most of the older Hell Hounds were like official older brothers to me. They always looked out for my best interests and gave me advice on everything from drug dealing to women issues. The only advice I couldn't ask for or really talk about was my infatuation for Natasha. I heeded the advice from Jeannie Terek about Natasha being a Jew and the fact that most of these boys are hardcore Aryans.

George was pleasantly surprised to see me along for the ride and came over and gave me a big hug and official Hell Hound handshake. George congratulated me on winning the California Championship and asked, "When are you leaving for Hawaii?"

I told him once we get to Anaheim I will tell him the story, about how I got screwed out of winning. I told George I needed a beer to explain everything.

George said, "Fair enough," and off we rode.

The Hell Hounds Motor Cycle Club had twenty chapters throughout California, and at least the same amount of 'Puppet Clubs. We drove down the coast to Anaheim and rendezvoused with some other chapters. I was amazed at how much respect each member from different Chapters had for each other.

I guess in many ways the Hell Hounds had similarities to that of dad and his army unit. No matter what part of the country they come from, they were all 'Brothers in Arms' and had the same outlook on life.

In the army it was a fight to the end knowing the

guy beside you in a foxhole was willing to do the same for you regardless of the odds. With the Hell Hounds they, like my dad's army unit, lived life on the edge, but they were really gangsters who wore leather and rode Harley Davidsons. But who was their war with?

Anybody who interfered with them making money was in trouble. They were either into drugs, prostitution, loan sharking, protection and even muscle for hire. The Hell Hounds provided a lot of muscle for the Battaglia Mafia family. I guess in many ways they were like mercenaries, just very organized and they flew their flag with the Hell Hound patch.

Jake took me aside before we left San Jose and he reiterated his stand with me doing hard core drugs. "Mitchell, never let anything kill your soul." He told me there will be others along this journey who will offer me everything from Speed and Heroin, to LSD and MDA. I won't embarrass him amongst his brothers and take some of these drugs, as he would be forced to kick my ass all over the whole state of California. I can smoke as much weed I wanted, and drink all the booze I wanted, just nothing that would kill my soul. I was really getting right off on being around the club and the whole Snowball run; so I respected my brother's wishes.

As we left for the Pacific Coast Highway, George

Paiement told me to ride beside him. We drove for just over three hours. The cars on the highway were clearing a path for us, whether from fear or from curiosity. We stopped off in Moro Bay for lunch. There were at least fifty members from the Bakersfield Chapter already at Whiskey Joe's and they had set up a BBQ for us. This was also the half waypoint of our journey.

Jake told me to stay close to him. He wanted to introduce me to members of the different chapters. Some of these guys looked like pirates, scruffy, with long hair and long beards. Some of them you would think the only time they ever had a bath was if they accidentally fell into one. Others you could tell were just plain evil with no sense of humor, real hard core killing machines, and some wearing the crazy eight patch.

As we were eating lunch and having a couple beers, the local cops began patrolling the perimeter of Whiskey Joe's. There were maybe ten cops, and I would say we were close to about two hundred riders by now, two hundred riders who all hated the cops with a passion.

Eventually the cops made their way onto Whiskey Joe's property with shotguns in hand. There was one cop who seemed to be in charge. He asked to speak to Eric Von Kruder. He introduced himself to Von

Kruder as Captain John Kowalski of the San Luis County sheriff's office. I have to give this guy credit. He had balls, although maybe not much in the brains department however.

Walking into the lion's den, even though this was a public setting, wasn't exactly smart. With so many Hell Hounds here, the cops would be swarmed and killed. Who would testify about what they saw? A waitress making minimum wage, how about the cook or bus boy? There would be no witness. Should they tell what they saw, those witnesses would be found in the ocean, floating face down, accidental drowning of course.

Von Kruder hated cops, so when Kowalski came closer to talk to him, Derksen, Terek and Kantonescu circled Kowalski. This caused some of the other cops to cock their shotguns. Just to show that he also had big balls. Von Kruder walked towards Kowalski and asked, "What's the problem?" Von Kruder got right in his face, hell Kantonescu was starting to growl. I was just absorbing the tension in the air. I saw several Hell Hounds ever so discreetly pull out some of their own weapons. Blood is going to spill and people on both sides are going to die.

All you could now hear was more and more sirens headed towards Whiskey Joe's. Jake told Kantonescu to stand down! Von Kruder reiterated his initial question, "What is the problem?"

Kowalski wanted to know where we're headed and how long we are planning on staying here at Whiskey Joes.

"Me and the boys are headed to Disney World, you wanna join us?"

Kowalski now still looking directly at Von Kruder said, "I think me and my boys would be more than happy to give you and your boys an escort out of my county. How does that sound?"

"I think we can find where we are going on our own."

"This is the way I see it. Moro Bay is a nice quiet community and I like to keep it that way. That is what the tax payers expect. I see several of your boys have been drinking, and some look pretty stoned. I'm sure if we checked every rider for proper ownership and insurance, and of course also making sure none of these bikes have stolen parts on them, along with the smell of booze on their breath, you might not see Disney World until Mickey fucking Mouse officially retires. Do you understand what I am saying? I'm sure a call to the California Highway Patrol for assistance would bring a prompt response, don't you? I don't want to bust your balls, just leave my fucking county and all will be well."

The last thing Von Kruder wants to do is lose face, especially when it comes to the cops. He knows that if Kowalski wants to be a real dickhead, he will have every member stopped, and searched. I'm sure at least twenty five percent of the bikes would be impounded, and the same number of Hell Hounds thrown in jail for drinking and driving. Hearing more sirens approaching us wasn't a good sign. As much as Von Kruder would've liked to rip out Kowalski heart and eat it, the brains that made him National President knew better.

Von Kruder looked around and surveyed the scene, then looked back at Kowalski. "We are just about done here anyways. I think you should buy yourself and me a drink for the road. Then you can escort us right out of your beautiful, quaint little county. How does that sound Officer Kowalski?"

Kowalski then ordered the bartender to put two shots of Jack Daniels on the bar. The bartender did as told and Kowalski passed one of the shots to Von Kruder. Kowalski then tapped his shot glass to Von Kruder's and muttered, "Frozen Chosen."

Von Kruder's eyes got big and answered back, "Frozen Chosen. So you are a Leatherneck! I thought you had big balls; now I know for sure you do."

"It was a lifetime ago wasn't it? You don't remember me, do you Eric?"

"Can't say that I do, Fifth Marine?"

"No Seventh Marine! Hell I think my balls are still frozen, but we did what we had to do, didn't we?"

"Yeah we did" then Von Kruder did a Marine Corp grunt, and several other Hell Hounds who were also in the marines grunted back. This kind of blew my mind. I thought for sure there was going to be a battle royal going to happen. These two sides had nothing in common with each other.

Turns out they did have one thing in common; their love for their country, and the battle at the Chosin Reservoir in Korea proved it. Damn that was over sixteen years ago. I remember dad telling me about that battle, as he also fought in the battle. Von Kruder talked with Kowalski for another twenty minutes, and then we all headed for our bikes, and gladly welcomed our escort out of San Luis County.

Our next stop was Long Beach. We hooked up with over one hundred full patch members from the three different Los Angeles chapters. Along the way, we've hooked up with probably close to three hundred motorcycles. Von Kruder purposely had us drive by the Thunder's headquarters in Los Angeles. We drove by real slowly and I think we caught the Thunder's attention.

We had several different police forces following us the whole time. Two of the local Los Angeles TV stations had their cameras taping us as we drove through Los Angeles. People on the through ways would stop at the over passes and watch us drive by. It was one hell of a show of force! The procession seemed to be stretched out for at least a mile.

This is also been the furthest I have ever driven on a motorcycle and Anaheim can't come quick enough. My ass was numb, hell even my balls felt funny. With my broken knuckles and toes still not fully healed, my hands were starting to swell and shifting gears hurt; and my back was also tightening up. However the power and strength that came with the snowball run was making the pain all worth it.

Within thirty minutes, we pulled up to the Anaheim clubhouse. They had the outside all painted in Hell Hound colors; with the three-headed Cerberus painted on the side of the clubhouse.

As we parked our bikes Jake reminded me of our little talk. He also told me to hang with people I knew well, in case shit hits the fan. There already were cops going around taking down license plate numbers. He doesn't want to be my babysitter, and if I fuck up, this will be my last run ever with the club. We made our way inside the gated clubhouse and enjoyed our first sip of beer.

That night the Anaheim Chapter threw one hell of a party. Go-Go dancers in cages were hoisted ten feet above the ground, and they had this upcoming band playing; they were a bunch of UCLA film students. Judging by their performance, they should all quit school and make this their full time job.

The singer was totally wasted and quite frankly, he was insane, with really bizarre lyrics in his songs. The women loved him though and man they were tight. The strangest thing about this group compared to other groups, was that they had no bass player. Instead the keyboardist played two organs at once; one organ was the band's bass. Who the hell needs this fucking British Invasion? These California rockers are what the USA needs to be back on the top of the charts.

We chowed down on roast pig, lobster and of course all the beer we could drink, not to mention all the shot glasses of booze one could hoist to their mouth. There were broads everywhere, probably one chick for every ten guys and these girls were all willing to do whatever anyone asked. With me being a non-club member, I would end up with sloppy tenths never mind sloppy seconds. Think I will pass!

There were three people that intrigued me though and I wasn't sure if I was going to pass or not. These three were tattoo artists. I have always been fascinated at the thought of getting my own tattoo. I don't want something that other people have inked onto their bodies. I want my own tattoo. Jake has several and dad had a couple of them. I'm not sure what mom would do if I ever did come home with one; something to think about though.

The further the night went into the early morning hours, the more I realized how fucked up I really was. I kept my promise to Jake and stuck to just weed and booze. It was tempting to get really high and expand my mind. The thought of dropping some LSD was made even more tempting, knowing that it was forbidden, I wasn't allowed it.

Almost like Adam in the 'Garden of Eden', being told he couldn't have the apple. Well that 'Purple Double Barrel Microdot' was my apple. But should Jake ever did find out, I would be joining Adam, either in Hell or Heaven. Yeah Jake would kill me, and whoever gave me the LSD.

The only thing I knew for sure was the design of my tattoo. I crashed that night in my sleeping bag watching the stars, at least stars I could see anyways. My vision was pretty fucked up once I lay down. The spins started and I knew what I had to do next. I walked to a quiet place and stuck two fingers down my throat. Nothing was coming up but dry heaves. I truly felt the earth and my body spin. What the fuck was this? Maybe someone spiked my drink.

That was until I heard laughing. Kantonescu picked

me up like a rag doll and now had me in an airplane spin. Hell he had me spinning around and around, and several other club members were having a good laugh at my expense. There was no way was I in any shape to stop the laughing. Kantonescu was making me the brunt of several laughs until the beer Gods took it upon themselves to seek revenge on him.

I puked all over him and everyone within a six foot perimeter. This made the club members who weren't being sprayed with puke, laugh even more uncontrollably. The club members who were at first laughing at me were now being sprayed with puke. Damn, they must have mistaken me for someone else, as all I heard was "Jesus Christ." Now tell me is that a bit of a oxymoron or what, calling Jesus Christ at a Hell Hound bash?

Don Terek hosed me down, damn that water was cold and it sobered me up real quick. Don told me, "This is what they do once you get thrown into county lock up. Get used to it!"

I apologized to Kantonescu for puking all over him. I did say it with a bit of a laugh, and I'm sure if I wasn't Jake Strongbow's little brother, I would've taken the beating of my life.

I crashed pretty hard that night. I'm sure the only reason why the booze was and weed. The night having a date with the dawn didn't stop the partying.

This was a twenty-four hour bash.

Now whether or not it was several Hell Hounds doing their Hound howl all night long while I was dreaming, I'm not sure. However, it came to me in my sleep what my first tattoo would be. Soon as I had some grub, I went looking for Jake to tell him of my tattoo plan, and at the same time also asking for his blessing.

With Jake being an executive in the Hell Hounds, he got to sleep inside the clubhouse, while the rest of us slept outside like peasants. He also had this fairly hot broad lying in bed with him. "Little brother, you aren't going to puke on us are you?"

"No Jake, just don't put me into an airplane spin." Jake laughed, "I was wondering, are these tattoo guys real good?"

Jake now smiled, "So you are thinking about getting a tattoo? What about your mom?"

"I think she will be all right. Dad had tattoos and this is my money and my body."

Jake nodded his head in approval, jumped out of bed and said, "Let's go and see these tattoo artists." Jake tracked down the Anaheim Hell Hound Vice President Wayne Walsh and asked, "Which one of your tattoo artists is the one you would recommend?"

Walsh came down to where the tattoo artists were

now getting setup for their work and introduced us to Buck Jones. Buck has done Walsh's last four tattoos. He told Buck to take care of us.

Buck was a big man who didn't smile, he just did his work and he did it well. Buck asked what I wanted. I told him, he nodded his head the whole time and then he said, "Give me ten minutes to draw it up."

Jake smiled he liked my idea for the tattoo. Buck came back and he showed me tattoo on paper, it was a wolf's head wearing a Nazi SS helmet. The same helmet I wear while driving my motorcycle: the same helmet my grandfather wore during the war. It looked so cool. The only change Buck recommended was to make the eyes of the wolf red. Perfect! Buck took out a razor and shaved what little hair I had on my upper chest; the tattoo would be roughly six inches long by four inches wide.

The whole process took around ninety minutes; ninety semi-painful minutes I might add. It was a weird feeling, almost like a burning rather than a stabbing feeling; I was surprised by that. Because I drank so much beer the night before, I was bleeding pretty good while the work was being done.

Tattoos don't hurt so bad going down on the skin, but when the tattoo gun would go up against the grain of my skin, damn that hurt! Every time I made a face in pain, Jake would laugh and take another sip of beer.

I asked for a beer. Buck told me, no I'm bleeding enough. I think he might have almost twitched a smile muscle, telling me "No beer!"

Several of the Hell Hounds from Oakland and San Fran that I knew were commenting on how good my tattoo was looking, great choice and great design. It meant a lot. Von Kruder was very impressed with my choice, and let me know it.

I was told by Buck to "keep it covered for the first hour, and then slowly remove the protective bandages."

I took off the bandages after an hour and it looked sharp, real sharp! I'm sure my grandfather and dad would have liked how I put both my heritages into one tattoo. A heritage that I am proud of. Hopefully mom feels the same when she sees it herself, for the first time.

It was now just shortly after noon and a bunch of the Oakland Chapter decided to check out Disneyland. I liked the rides there myself and was hoping to pick up a chick. Hell, at least she would be cleaner than the sluts here and I really needed to get laid. I asked Caleb could I come along. Then I heard a growl and this raspy hoarse voice. It was Kantonescu. "Do you also puke on rides?'

"Only if I am sitting beside you John."

Kantonescu now growled and chased me all over the Clubhouse grounds. I was laughing so hard he almost caught me. Fear and knowing that one of Kantonescu bear hugs could break my ribs, kept me running until he was all tuckered out, and I knew things were safe, for awhile anyway.

Two dozen of us headed to Disneyland, the full patches were wearing their colors. We were all given a fair amount of space while walking around the place. No one complained when we butted in line, no matter how long the lineups were. Any complaint would bring an instant beating.

The local girls were also giving us the eye, some were 'Jail Bait' but this one red head working the concession stands was making 'come fuck me eyes' to me. She reminded me of Jake's girlfriend Liz O'Malley; just a younger version. We did a little flirting and when she had her break, she came right out and asked me to fuck her. I didn't even ask her name, I didn't really care, I just wanted to fuck her. So she led me in the back to the private washroom and we fucked like wild animals. As I was cumming, I heard a disturbance coming from outside.

I knew if all hell was breaking out who would be in the middle of the action, if not the cause of the ruckus. I pulled up my pants and had a look outside. Sure as hell, it was Kantonescu and the members of the Oakland Club. They were fighting a bunch of niggers. I ran right over and dropped kicked the first nigger I saw, and then I noticed two niggers were on top of Kantonescu. I went over and drilled one right in the side of his head. That sound when I made contact I knew all too well. I heard his jaw break, and he hit the ground real fast.

Kantonescu picked up the other nigger and threw him onto the rail tracks below, where a bunch of cars from the roller coaster ride ran over his body. He was decapitated instantly, and his blood was everywhere. That was the first time I have ever seen anyone killed. I just stared at the body which was now shaking, even without its head.

Kantonescu grabbed me and said, "Let's get the fuck out of here." I just looked at him with disbelief, what the fuck just happened, a dream, a nightmare? Kantonescu then yelled at me and the rest of the boys, "To flee." We could now hear sirens in the background. I didn't think, I just did what Kantonescu told me, we all ran to our bikes and fled the scene.

Not all of us managed to evade the cops, as I saw Fagan tackled to the ground. My novice motorcycle skills were now going to be tested. I just kept up to Kantonescu and Terek as best I could. We were all driving like madmen up and down alleys, back roads, and even going down one way streets the wrong way till we were out of the city limits.

I realized that with me punching and kicking the niggers at Disney, whatever healing may have started in my knuckles and toes had now regressed. I believe that I've re-broken them all over again. Going back to the Anaheim Clubhouse would've been easier for me, as the pain was affecting my ability to control my bike. However, that was out of the question. The cops would be looking for us; we're too much of a heat score. So I drove in pain the whole time, hoping I wouldn't become road rash or worse.

Lucky for us, Don had served in the army with a guy who lived in Lancaster, and that is where we headed. For the whole two hours on the road we didn't stop. We just drove normal, so as not to draw attention to ourselves all the while checking our rear view mirrors for the cops.

As we pulled into the driveway, Don's friend came outside, probably wondering who the hell was paying him a visit. His friend Victor Diaz knew we were in trouble, just the way the three of us kept looking around. Don asked if we could hang at his place for a bit. That wasn't a problem with Victor. He suggested we put all three bikes in his garage for the time being, keeping them out of sight from the cops.

It gave us a little time to gather our thoughts, until the heat was off. Don didn't tell Victor what kind of trouble we were in exactly. He just said we were in a whole world of shit. I asked could I have ice packs for my knuckles and toes. We all had blood sprayed on our clothes.

Victor didn't have a legitimate job, lucky for us. He earned his living smuggling drugs from Mexico to the United States. We told Victor we needed to get back to San Francisco without the cops stopping us, and we're willing to pay cash. This made Victor smile. He told us to hang tight while he made some phone calls.

After about twenty minutes or so Victor came back and said he had a plan to get us home. One of his business partners uses his tractor trailers for smuggling drugs; he would put us, along with our bikes in the trailer. We could drive right by the cops, along the coast till we hit San Francisco. The cops would be stopping bikers, not truckers. It will cost two hundred bucks and a favor in the bank. Don agreed.

Personally I felt that Kantonescu should have to pay the whole two hundred bucks; he was the killer, not us. However when you run with a club, you all help each other out. Even though Don and I didn't kill the nigger, we're all accessories to the murder.

Victor said we would have to wait till nightfall. Once it was dark, we were good to go. As we sat eating dinner, the murder made the top story on the news. Victor just looked at us and smiled. Kantonescu stressed out, took exception to Victor's smile and asked, "What the fuck you smiling at?"

Victor stood up and called Kantonescu a prick and ungrateful. He told him that maybe he should just find his own way back to San Francisco. Don jumped up from his chair and told Kantonescu, to"just fucking chill! We're all brothers sitting here tonight. Everyone is cool and safe."

"You bring this clown into my house and he thinks I'm one of his flunkies. Let's see how he gets you out of this pickle!"

I could tell Victor wasn't impressed by Kantonescu at all. I asked John, "How about we go outside and get some air?" Reluctantly, Kantonescu came outside with me. "John, mellow out man, this guy is going to help us."

John had his mouth like Elvis, you know that little curl in the lip thing Elvis did. "I don't trust any fucking Spick, they will sell you out for a fucking taco."

It made me laugh to think of John being such a racist. Next thing I know John got even more serious, and looked me right in the eyes. "The question is will you ever sell me out? You saw what I did, are you solid? The gas chamber is no friend of mine."

This guy has to cut out all the freaking steroids he does. His brain is getting way to weird. "John I'm solid, you know my family. You also know the values Jake has instilled in me. Death before dishonor right John?"

John may have nodded his head, but his eyes were pure evil. It wouldn't surprise me at all if he just fled into Mexico by himself. At this very moment, that would be all right with me. As the sun went down I sat on the porch, and closed my eyes for a couple minutes. I was hoping that when I opened them, I would be in Dubrowski's basement and this was just some weird drug induced trip.

I heard what sounded like a large truck pull up out front of Victor's house. That knot in my stomach that wouldn't go away told me it wasn't just a dream, but a fucking nightmare. I saw Johnny Kantonescu kill someone and now I'm an accomplice to the murder. However, what I said to John was real, 'Death before dishonor', never rat.

Victor told us our ride has arrived, time to get ready and leave. The driver of the truck didn't speak any English. He looked like a true Bandito with scars on his face, scruffy looking and gold front teeth. As he came inside, John was really giving him the up and down look. He said something to John in Spanish. I have a feeling it wasn't something very pleasant like nice to make your acquaintance. More like what the fuck are you looking at?

Don, however, did speak Spanish and told the Bandito in Spanish, "Let's get going." So Bandito backed his tractor-trailer in the driveway and opened up the back doors. We put all three bikes inside the trailer. I didn't like the way that Bandito was looking at our bikes. John and Don's bikes were custom motorcycles, worth a fair amount of cash. Mine was, well mine was mine.

Bandito said the three of us had to go in the trailer with the bikes. Hell, all of a sudden he can speak some English, what other surprises does he have in store for us? Don said, "No, one of us will be riding in the front with you."

The Bandito said we look like the bikers the cops are looking for. Should we get stopped, he would be better alone.

Don looked at Bandito and said, "The deal is now off." After much hesitance, Bandito agreed to one of us being in the front. Don pulled rank and said he's riding up front, as he doesn't look like Kantonescu and he's who the cops are looking for.

Should the Bandito change his mind and decide to do something stupid like go to the cops, or decide that our bikes are worth more money than what he is being paid and takes us to a non-friendly gang, we could be killed for our bikes.

Don took Kantonescu and me aside and said, "Should things go wrong on the way home, do what you have to do to survive." Don admitted he too had an uneasy feeling. Ever so reluctantly, John and I jumped into the trailer with the bikes. As they closed the doors on us it went black, jet black. I had this real uneasy feeling, almost like someone closed a casket lid on us.

As the truck drove out of Victor's neighborhood, I told John about my uneasy feelings. He told me I was just a scared kid. I reminded him of what he said earlier, "That you don't trust Mexicans, as they will sell you out for a taco. John I may be a bit scared, but please trust me on this one; things just don't feel right. I got a real bad vibe from 'Bandito.' My dad, grandfather and Jake always taught me to go with my gut instinct to survive; things aren't right."

Whether it was because I was Jake Strongbow's kid brother or not, John finally agreed to trust my gut instinct. We took out some the motorcycle tools we carry for road trips, a ball peen hammer and put some ball bearings in a sock; we had created a little improvised weapon.

We always carry ball bearings while on the highway. Why, you ask? A car cuts you off, hell you throw ball bearings at them, or throw the ball bearings in the air if the car is behind you. It will land on their windshield. I hoped Don was also starting to have bad vibes about Bandito.

Instead of going up the coast like the way we arrived, the Bandito said, "There are too many cops. We will go west along highway 395, almost parallel with the Nevada state line. Less cops that way."

After an hour on the road, we stopped, not sure why. Don came to the back of the trailer and said, "Bandito is using the payphone to tell his old lady he won't be home till tomorrow." Don didn't totally believe him.

I told Don my fears. Don agreed and told John he has a 38 snub nose pistol tucked up under his gas tank. We didn't have enough time to get Don the 38, as Bandito now made his way back to the truck. He wasn't happy to see us talking, another red flag.

After the doors to the trailer were closed once again, and we were back on the road; John searched and found Don's 38 snub. Now we just sat back, waited, and tried to relax. I say kind of relaxed, because between the bumpy road and the uncertainty of Bandito, relaxing was the last thing on this journey back home. For southern California, it was freezing in the trailer of the truck. This also set off a 'Red Flag' in my head.

I'm so glad my grandfather taught me how to

survive during my last visit to the reservation. I was looking for anything unusual, even though we were inside the dark trailer. I started to pace and Kantonescu told me to just mellow a bit. I felt like a caged animal at the vets. As soon as they opened up the trailer door, Kantonescu and I would be put down. I knew I was right!

Yeah I was younger than Kantonescu in age, but not in street smarts. I always remember dad telling me that, "bad things happen to bad people." I watched Kantonescu just murder someone. Was he truly a bad person? Was I in the wrong place at the wrong time, with the wrong person who was clearly a bad person? I know I am right. There isn't even a thought of being wrong.

After another hour of driving, all of a sudden the road seemed to have a different surface, bumpier then smooth. We then we heard a loud bang. Was it a blown tire? The truck and the trailer now started to veer all over. Kantonescu and I were being bounced around like a pinball. He yelled at me to grab onto something but it was jet black inside the trailer. Why wasn't the truck slowing down if we had a flat tire?

The trailer was now as stable as a slinky; you could actually feel when the trailer was airborne from time to time. This was truly one hell of a ride. As sick as it may sound, the adrenaline rushing to my heart made me feel like I just took the most perfect designer drug and was enjoying the best part of the trip. It meant there was a good possibility we were all going to die.

Time seemed to stand still. I no longer felt the trailer in the air; I no longer felt any movement beneath or beside me. Suddenly I flashed to my dad and my grandfather hunting. It wasn't my Strongbow grandfather, but mom's dad, the one dad killed during the war. They both looked at me and said I'm too young to hunt with them, it's not my time yet. Then they both laughed at me, and the vision of them went away, and I came back to reality.

The trailer was starting to flip, and I began to feel the movements of the trailer again. I could smell the gas coming from our motorcycles, being spilled all over. The noise was deafening. It was now getting really scary. I just hung on for dear life until it came to a rest. Once the dust settled, I realized the trailer was now on its side.

Even though my vision showed I wasn't to die, I was scared shitless of being left a quadriplegic. To me it was worse than death itself. I yelled at Kantonescu and asked, was he OK? "I think so, I'm not really sure, and my ribs are hurting. How are you doing?"

"I'm fine, just real dizzy and I feel like puking. Damn John, why is it you make me always want to puke around you?" As I started to laugh, I realized my ribs and neck were really sore. I walked toward the sound of John's voice ever so slowly as my legs were really shaking.

We both heard someone yelling from a distance, they too were in obvious pain. Kantonescu couldn't find the 38 snub nosed pistol. Kantonescu was rubbing his ribs and cursing, meanwhile the voice was now getting closer to us. There was a bang at the door of the trailer, a very weak bang. The voice asked, "Are you all right?" It was Terek.

Don said he couldn't get the doors open. All the flipping has jammed the doors shut. Kantonescu started to growl. He walked towards the doors and told Terek to stay clear. With a mighty kick, Kantonescu kicked the trailer doors wide open and then fell to the ground in pain. I walked to the open doors and saw that Terek had been hurt; he had blood all around his shoulder area.

"Don what the fuck happened?"

"Fucking Bandito shot me in the shoulder. As much as I would like to sit and talk about it, we should get the hell out of here."

Kantonescu asked Don where was Bandito now? "I shot him in the head, he's dead." Kantonescu now nodded with approval over Bandito with a bullet in his head.

We picked up our bikes, but quickly realized that my bike wasn't able to be driven. The handle bars were broke in two. We siphoned what gas I had left in my tank. It was decided with Don being shot and not able to drive, he and Kantonescu would drive together on Kantonescu bike. I would drive Don's bike.

Don looked at both of us real serious. "The Bandito was taking us to be killed for our bikes. Where he was taking us I'm not sure." We looked around into the desert and Don said, "Whoever was going to take our bikes and kill us is still out here somewhere. We have to get out of here."

Kantonescu asked, "Do we even know where we are driving to? We could be going deeper into the desert and could run out of gas trying to get out." Don said he needed medical attention soon. He had slowed down the bleeding; but not stopped it.

I decided it was time to show these guys that I wasn't just some scared teenage kid who would fuck things up for them or get us all killed. I looked towards the stars, and could tell by the different constellations which way was home. Kantonescu and Don both looked at each other and smiled. Don said, "Jake and your old man would be proud of you."

Don apologized in advance to me for what he was about to do. I thought to myself, he isn't going to kill me now that I have found our way out of the desert, is he? Don grabbed a rag and soaked up whatever gas was still in the bottom of my broken motorcycle's gas tank. He then dipped a second rag in the gas, lit the second rag and set the trailer on fire. We drove to the truck where the dead Bandito's lifeless body was. Don lit the truck on fire, then asked me to lead the way home. That is exactly what I did, just like a Sioux warrior on a hunting party.

The burning truck with Bandito inside lit up the night sky as we drove out of the desert. Within a couple minutes I saw the fireball from the explosion in my rear view mirror. A couple of seconds later we heard the actual noise of the explosion. With canyons in the desert, the echoes of the explosion seemed to go on for minutes, bouncing from bank to bank.

After about twenty minutes of driving through the desert I found us highway 395. I looked at the stars and we headed north until we met up with highway 108, where we stopped just to check on Don's wound. He was starting to get cold and flush looking; I thought maybe he was sort of going into shock. I checked his wound and the bleeding had stopped.

Kantonescu also didn't really look that great either and he was real quiet. I knew he was hurt, just not admitting it. Once I knew we were OK to carry on, Don said, "This highway will take us to Stockton. I have friends there who will take care of us and make sure we get back to Oakland."

Kantonescu then piped up, "Your last set of friends tried to kill us. Hopefully these ones will be a little nicer!" No one laughed, we just headed towards Stockton.

We arrived in Stockton in the middle of the night, so it was still dark outside. Don was now going into shock over his blood loss and trauma to his shoulder. I told Kantonescu that Don needs to get to a hospital now; he is going to die if he travels any further.

Kantonescu said he also has some contacts in Stockton that will make sure we get back to Oakland. "You show up at a hospital with a gunshot victim, the cops will be all over you. Remember, we are heat scores right now."

"John, Don is going to die unless he gets immediate medical attention. Oakland is out of the question." Johnny Kantonescu is not the type of person you would normally argue with. The last guy who argued with Kantonescu is now headless. But Don has been like an older brother to me, and I couldn't ever face Jeannie again knowing I let her husband die.

"Listen John, the cops are looking for you, not me. Just take me to where the hospital is and I will take Don inside myself. I will take my chances with the cops. I won't rat anyone out! I will say we were north in Sacramento and Don was shot on the highway by someone in a pickup truck. Trust me!"

"You got balls kid. Not sure about brains, but you got balls. You make sure to tell Don that I did NOT abandon him."

"I promise, John. Just let them know back in Oakland that we are in trouble here. Maybe get a hold of Jeannie Terek and let her know Don has been shot. See if you can somehow track down my brother or Jerry."

"Your brother and Jerry both have brains as well as balls, they will figure we fled the scene. You did good Mitch, must be a family trait."

I felt like a man, not some teenage kid. "I am a Strongbow, I am a Sioux warrior." Never had that statement ever felt so clear, either in my brain, heart or coming from my mouth.

John put Don on my bike, and then John drove us right up to the hospital. He nodded at me and drove off into the night. I drove right up to the emergency ward and yelled for help and within seconds, doctors, nurses and yes, the police came outside.

They took Don inside and after a quick exam said they were taking him right up to the operating room. I wanted to go up with Don but the cops detained me as expected. I used my brains and looked at the one cop and said, "I need to see a doctor! I had to dump my bike once we were shot at and I don't feel that good."

The cop agreed that I looked pretty beat up as well, so he finally agreed for me to see a doctor. However the cop said, "I'm not leaving your side during your exam by the doctors." As they were examining me, the cops were still trying to question me. So far it was just uniform cops. They didn't bother me. Detectives however were a different breed.

I told the cops, Don and I were driving down from Sacramento, and this pickup truck pulled up beside us and fired shots at us. The one thing I did do was to give them a damn good description of the shooter. Who did I say he looked like? I gave them the exact description of Blais MacDonald, God bless his soul. I know the cops would continually ask me questions, about the shooter trying to get me to catch me in a lie. Blais was perfect.

The doctor told the cops I had re broken my knuckles and toes, had a bruised sternum, bruised ribs and had re-broken my collarbone plus I had a concussion. I really played up the sore head and didn't want to talk to the fuzz. The doctors asked the cops to leave me alone, and then the doctor gave me a shot of morphine to kill the pain.

The cops thanked me and said they would pass

along the information I had given them to the detectives. I'm not sure if they believed me or not, and after this insane weekend, I didn't give a rat's ass; I was more worried about Don Terek .

I closed my eyes in my hospital bed and tried to get some sleep. However, the disturbing events of these last hours I know won't allow me to sleep. Kantonescu murdering the nigger at Disneyland, driving in the back of the tractor trailer, the flip flop and roll ride from hell, then Don killing Bandito before he had a chance to kill us. As if that weren't enough, my motorcycle was destroyed in the accident, and then I had to watch the flames light up the desert, knowing my bike and Bandito were in those very flames. Yeah sleep was not going to happen. Damn that morphine was a nice buzz. Too bad it couldn't shut my brain down, or so I thought.

I'm not sure how long I was in La La land from the morphine, but I heard strange noises from outside the hospital. The sound seemed to be coming from the night skies. It sounded like fire breathing dragons flapping their massive wings and spewing their venomous flames throughout the ominous black sky searching for their next victims to mutilate. I could once again sense danger.

I stumbled from my bed and looked outside, but it was just too dark out to see, then my other senses seemed to kick in. My hearing picked up several heavy set men headed down the hall and my gut told me they were headed towards my room. Their boots were making the noise. I imagined turn of the century, dark hooded executioners headed towards the cell of the victim they plan to decapitate next. Did these executioners ride over on the backs of these fire breathing dragons?

I realized I was too stoned and too beat up to think straight or fight off my opponents, whoever they were. Hell, just walking to the window was a challenge. I tried to stand and prepare myself for my fate, with one arm in a sling, and my other with fist clinched for the fight.

I heard the evil voices of the executioners in the hall coming closer and closer. I felt like throwing up. I was frozen with fear, my mind and my body wasn't in unison with each other. I had to sit on my bed as I thought I was going to pass out. What should I do? What would dad or Jake do? Was I now being punished by the devil himself for being involved in the two murders? Was my soul or life to be paid for my participation? I was starting to freak out and couldn't stop it. I was now back to being a scared teenager; this trip I didn't like.

As the evil voices stopped outside my room, I could feel their evil aura pulsating right through the door. I felt like hiding under my sheets like I did as a child, thinking the boogeyman was in the hallway. I heard them laugh; could they sense my fear? Did this fear amuse them? Was my life and soul that easy to take?

I heard and saw the hall light now coming through the opening crack of the door. My mouth was dry, and the hair on my arms and testicles were standing up in fear. The door was starting to open more and more. I felt the air being sucked out of my lungs; death was present and there was nothing I could do about it. I just closed my eyes and waited to feel the pain, and the inevitable wrath on my body and soul. I was hoping and praying it would be quick and relatively painless, but then what fun would that be for death? With my eyes tightly shut in fear, I was ready to accept death.

"Strongbow! Hey, Strongbow." Shit the death executioners know my name! This knowledge meant to me that I was indeed their target. I was unable to talk, unable to answer them. Perhaps if I didn't acknowledge the voice, they would leave me to live. I heard a woman's voice, "Mitchell, are you all right hon?"

Was this a trick by death? Did it want me to open my eyes, and face my punishment for my sins? I felt a hand on my shoulder and the woman once again reiterated, "*Mitchell, are you all right?*"

I opened my eyes. Hell, it was Liz O'Malley and Dick Coltrane, Vice President of the Oakland Hell Hounds. I was never so happy to see friendly faces in my life. Liz looked like an angel sent down to calm my fears. I was shaking. Liz hugged me and said it would all right, they are here for me. I could've cried something which I haven't done since I can't remember when, and definitely not in front of Coltrane and the other members of the Hell Hounds that were now in my room.

Dick told me that Kantonescu told them how we were betrayed by Bandito. I knew better to even divulge about the Disney murder, even though I was still flying high. Dick also told me he was mighty proud of me making sure Don made it to the hospital, and that Jake and Jerry would also be proud.

When I asked, "Are Jake or Jerry back yet?"

Dick said, "No". However members are slowly making their way back. The cops are questioning everyone about the murder at Disney." Dick asked me what I knew about it.

Was this a test? I said, I knew nothing, I was banging some broad. When I finished up banging her I was told to get on my bike and flee the scene.

I didn't ask why, I just did as I was told.

Dick just nodded in approval and said, "Good boy."

Liz was sitting beside me on the bed rubbing my back. Her hands were so soothing and so warm. You could tell by her touch she was a nurturer. I truly felt at ease. I also was getting another massive hard on, which I tried to hide with my blankets.

Liz already told Jake about me getting aroused by her earlier at my house, and with a couple Hell Hounds in the room it wasn't what I would call a romantic setting.

Liz told me she was going to drive me home. She talked to the doctors and they agreed to release me into her care, seeing that she's a trauma nurse. I told Liz, "I don't want to go home. Mom will be really upset seeing me like this."

Liz agreed and said we could go back to her apartment, and hopefully Jake will be home soon. We can then come up with a story that won't get me grounded until I am sixty-five years old.

Before we left the hospital, I wanted to go up and see Don. Liz agreed and as we went to the recovery ward, I ran into Dick Coltrane and the other Hell Hounds once again. There were a couple of uniformed cops and a detective waiting to interview Don. Jeannie Terek was also present and she came over still sobbing and gave me a hug, and thanked me for taking Don to the hospital.

I asked how Don was doing. She said, "He lost a lot of blood and there might be some long-term shoulder damage, but he should be all right." This made me feel as good as winning my karate kickboxing championship.

The detective came over and said he had a few questions for me before I leave.

Coltrane walked towards the detective and me. "He has answered all your questions". You could just feel the tension in the air.

"I just have a couple questions. I'm not too sure about the answers he gave to the patrolman".

Liz looked at the detective with a real pissed off look on her face. "Mitch has a concussion and has had a shot of morphine. Whatever answer he will give you right now will be while he is in a drug induced state. His answers will be under the influence of a narcotic, and may not be accurate of events of what happened. Now if you will excuse us, I am taking Mitchell home; he needs his rest."

The cop wasn't too impressed with Liz, "And what is your name?"

Liz just smiled at the detective. "Am I under arrest for anything?"

Liz just stared at the cop who mirrored her look

and said nothing.

"Yeah, I thought not, now I'm taking him home".

Coltrane ordered two Hell Hounds to escort us to Liz's apartment. A motorcycle escort home in case Bandito's men had somehow followed us from the desert. Now that was cool. Well, at least to Liz's apartment anyways.

Liz and I were alone in the car on the way to her place. The more I looked at her, the more I appreciated what Jake saw in her. No, it wasn't just because I was high from the morphine; she was beautiful, stunningly beautiful. Liz had short red hair, a petite body and the brightest, warmest smile I've ever witnessed. I just stared in awe at her. Eventually she asked. "Why are you just staring?"

"I'm staring because you're so beautiful, Liz!"

I witnessed her cheeks turn the same color as her hair, bright red. "You Strongbow boys certainly have a way of charming the ladies, don't you Mitchell?"

"I'm serious Liz, if I was Jake I would marry you."

Liz laughed, "Glad to hear the morphine is still dancing in your head. Thank you Mitchell, that's very nice of you."

"From the first time I saw you Liz I thought that, and I wasn't high. Please, my mom calls me Mitchell, can you call me Mitch instead?"

"OK Mitch, you are very handsome yourself, you must have all kinds of young girls after you."

"I do all right, I find most chicks my age are nothing but a pain in the ass. They just whine and whine. I like older chicks actually, less games and less whining."

Liz started to laugh, "And how many older chicks have you been with?"

"The Vigoda sisters." Even though I was still really high, I knew not to mention that Jake and I had both done them the night before the run to Anaheim.

Liz didn't comment about the Vigoda sisters, at first anyways. She knew they were club dancers and whores. Even though Liz was with Jake, she was different, almost like they were from two totally different worlds. After a couple of minutes Liz asked me, "No one your own age interests you?"

"There is a girl I really like, I really like her a lot, I think about her all the time. Do you promise not to tell Jake about her?"

Liz was curious now, "I promise Mitch whatever we talk about stays between us."

"She's Jewish. I know Jake, and the Hell Hounds only like Aryans. I'm afraid they would hate her or hurt her; and I won't let anyone hurt someone I care about."

"Well if you like her that much, then you should pursue her Mitch. My family doesn't like Jake or his lifestyle, but that doesn't stop us from seeing each other. Out of curiosity, was she the blonde girl sitting with your mom at the Karate Tournament?"

I seemed to come out of my very fine bu*zz* for the moment, "Yeah, that was her, what did you think?" Every guy wants approval of his girlfriend or at least a girl he thinks is really special.

"Well Mitch, I really think she is very pretty, pretty enough that I remembered her. What does that tell you? Now that I think about it, when I saw you two talking I saw her face light up and she had this amazing glow. You must have brought that glow out in her Mitch. She really likes you, Jewish or not. I really think you should pursue her, that's my advice."

"Thanks Liz, Jeannie Terek also liked her."

"That's two of us that agree you should go after her."

I thanked Liz for the advice, and then I got quiet for a bit. I was replaying the last conversation I had with Natasha. How she felt it wouldn't work between us; fuck nothing comes easy does it.

After an hour or so on the road, we arrived at Liz's apartment. I thanked the two Hell Hounds for the escort. They both agreed we weren't followed. I could see the sun was just getting ready to rise. Once inside Liz's apartment, I parked my sore ass on her couch. I asked Liz did she have anything to drink. I really needed to wind down some more.

Liz advised me that booze and morphine wasn't a good idea. I asked did she have any weed we can smoke. That she did have, and my nurse proceeded to roll up a joint. However, before we sparked it up Liz lit a few candles, put on Van Morrison's 'Blowin Your Mind' and that is exactly what the album did in combination with the weed; it blew my mind.

Liz and I just sat on the couch together and watched the sun rise holding hands. We were both quiet, really quiet. I was thinking about the madness of the past twenty four hours; not really sure what exactly Liz was thinking about. I looked at her and ran my hand down the side of her face ever so gently.

She cradled my hand in between her shoulder and face, looked at me and smiled. Was this a signal to pursue my lustful desires? I just put away any thoughts of right and wrong with Liz being Jake's girlfriend, and I did what came naturally. I was still really buzzing from the morphine. Throw in the weed and my close encounter with death. Yeah I'm going for it, damn straight.

I ever so gingerly leaned into to Liz and started to bite her on the side of her neck. I could tell by the heavy breathing and her erect nipples showing through her top that Liz was enjoying this. When Liz asked what I was doing, I didn't answer; I just kept on my mission of seduction. I was so aroused! I would say as much as when Lucy took my cherry, so I put Liz's hand on my cock. She began to rub me through my jeans, as I did the same in her groin area, until she said, "No!"

I stopped and looked at Liz confused until, she told me to take my pants off. There were no mixed signals about that request, and busted collarbone and all, didn't stop me from dropping my pants. My hands were shaking a little and I wasn't sure if it was from the drugs or just being so excited about Liz and me getting it on.

Liz then told me to lay flat on my back on the couch and she began to perform oral sex on me. Just like the Van Morrison album, Liz blew my mind. I've had at least a dozen girls perform oral sex on me, but none of them compared to Liz; she was outstanding. If performing oral sex was an Olympic event, she would win Gold. Each time I thought I would ejaculate she would stop, then slowly build up my sensations all over again. Liz was like a machine, a perfectly well executed machine, and her moving parts knew exactly what to do.

Once I finally did ejaculate I shot everywhere, all

over Liz's hair, her face and even up her nostrils which caused her to gag. Damn, I think I even hit the other side of the room fifteen feet away. That isn't the only thing that went away. The pain from my injuries ceased during the oral session.

After Liz grabbed a towel and cleaned herself off, she did the same for me. Liz then had a serious talk with me. "Mitch, your brother Jake can never know about what just happened, he would never understand. Jake, as you know, has a wicked temper, so please Mitch, never mention anything about this."

I looked at Liz and promised her I wouldn't ever mention this to anyone. I then told her she was fabulous. Liz laughed, thanked me for the compliment and said, "You aren't such a little brother after all. That little Jewish girl gets a look at what you are packing, she will be impressed." At first I didn't get it, but once I did I felt awful damn good. Liz covered me with a blanket on the couch and off she went to bed.

Before I closed my eyes for the night, I realized how much my life has changed in the past twenty-four hours. I would never be the same person as before. I have witnessed heinous acts of crime, was slated to be murdered myself, then I had sex with my brother's girlfriend, and now Jake might just kill me. I wished I could just open my eyes and be back in Dubrowski's basement, and this was just a bad trip.

The next afternoon was when I finally woke up. Was this just a bad dream? And where the hell was I? The morphine was still dancing in my head, making everything kind of foggy. I tried to get up off the couch, but the pain in my body told me it wasn't such a good idea. I have never felt so much pain in my life; I could barely move. It felt like the worst case of flu ever, right from my body aching to the head hurting, and an inability to think straight.

My sense of smell was still working as I smelled coffee brewing, and bacon and eggs cooking. I heard the Beatles being played on the turntable and then Liz walked by wearing just a teddy. Things are coming back to me, including some 'morning wood'. She stopped and asked, "How are you feeling?" However after seeing my 'Woody' she snickered and said, "Your brother will be here very soon. You'd better lose that, and remember what we talked about last night Mitch."

More things are coming back to me, everything but feeling fine. I asked Liz if she have anything for pain. She told me the hospital gave her some codeine for pain. Praise be for pain killers. I popped a couple of codeine pills against Liz's recommendation that one would do the trick. Perhaps I took more than one not just to kill the pain, but to kill the memory of the day before.

Liz and I ate breakfast, and just as the buzz was

kicking in from the codeine, Jake was knocking at the door. I felt a little nervous, and Liz looked at me before she opened the door. I just nodded to her yes. As Jake came inside he wasn't smiling. He looked at Liz, and then he just stared at me. Did he know? Could he tell? If I can sense danger, can he sense when his woman has been unfaithful?

Jake told Liz to go to the corner store and buy him a Dr Pepper, and "take your time getting back." He wasn't smiling and he didn't ask her nicely. He barked that order to her. Liz was nervous and she did as she was told. Jake walked over to me after Liz left; he still wasn't smiling.

"So tell me everything that happened". So much for concern and how you are doing, glad to see you are alive, he was pissed and I was now getting really nervous; especially as the buzz from the codeine was getting more intense. I tried to speak but I was starting to slur and stammer, "What the fuck is wrong with you, boy?"

"I'm kind of fucked up Jake, I have had a rough day or two, and I took some pain killers about a half hour ago." I then took a deep breath, part of me wanted to cry. I could feel my voice quivering as I was talking. "You're making me nervous, Jake. Can you sit down and relax a little?"

Jake nodded his head and said, "Sorry little brother,

I keep forgetting you're just a kid. I'm sorry all hell broke out around you. What exactly happened? And leave nothing out."

I told Jake the whole story and left nothing out. For some reason even though I was high, I could go into great detail about every single incident to a tee. I did of course leave out Liz blowing me on the couch. I mentioned how nice Liz was in taking care of me last night and I felt safe in her hands.

I asked Jake about the fallout from the murder. He said, "The cops all up and down the coast are pulling over every person who rode a Harley and taking them in for questioning. The cops have a description of Kantonescu, but with so many Hell Hounds and puppet clubs in the United States they would have a hard time determining the true culprits." Jake also said, "You did real good making sure Terek made it to the hospital, and the story of the phantom shooter.

"Little brother no matter how many years go by, you have to etch that story into your brain as if it was real. Terek's buddy who recommended Bandito will be taken care of. No one hurts anyone in my family. I'm glad you're alive, really glad." Jake then came over and gave me a hug, "Maybe you're not such a kid after all. You saved Terek's life. I was told this morning he'll pull through. I also heard you lost your bike, don't worry. Your deeds and bravery will not go unanswered."

"So what's going to happen now, Jake?"

"Kantonescu will disappear for a bit. Just stick to your story and next time they call you in, call me or Jerry, and have a lawyer present. The club has their own lawyer, do not call your Uncle Karl; the less your mom knows the better. I'm going to have Liz drive you home. You have to tell your mom the same story as you told the cops. The more you tell the story, the more you and everyone else around you will believe it. I know you don't like to lie to your mom, but this a double and very shortly a triple murder. Sometimes we lie, no, make that deceive, to protect the ones we love, Mitch. Are you cool with that?"

"Yeah, I'm cool. Glad to hear Terek is alive. Other than Disney and the desert, I had a good time. My tattoo is healing nicely, kind of itchy though." Jake had a look and laughed. Liz knocked at the door. Imagine having to knock at your own door, and ask permission to come inside. Great in bed, obedient and had a great job; man Liz was cool.

Jake said he had to go to Stockton to see Don Terek . He asked Liz if she could drive me home once I came down a bit from the codeine and please explain to my mom the reason I'm taking legit pain killers.

Liz agreed, Jake came over and shot Liz a hundred

dollar bill and told her to buy a nice mini-skirt and top for taking care of his brother. That gesture by Jake made me happy; she came through for both of us.

After a couple hours, Liz drove me home as Jake had requested. She didn't ask if I spilled the beans to Jake about us getting it on. I guess she'd know if I did; she would've taken a beating and not be giving a hundred dollars for a nice new outfit.

As we pulled up to my house, I thanked Liz for everything, before we went inside. She was truly amazing. I hope one day Jake would appreciate her as much as I do. Mom seemed quite shocked by Liz driving me home and could tell I was injured. I asked, "Could the three of us sit at the kitchen table, as I have some bad news to tell you?" I also said it was best if Pam and Rachel didn't hear the story.

As much pain as my body was in, lying to mom and seeing that she was this upset pained me even more. I knew she could never hear the truth. Once I started to tell her the same story I told the cops, the floodgates opened. Liz tried to comfort mom by her rubbing her back and reassuring her, "It's all right now, and he's safe. His dad must have been watching over him."

After about an hour of talking, mom was finally coming to terms with my near-death experience. She said my dad would have been proud, that I made sure

Don Terek received life-saving medical treatment. She also said, "Maybe for the next little bit, you could just hang around your own friends." How could I argue with her? I knew agreeing to her wishes would stop the crying and worrying about me.

Liz said she had to go work the 'Graveyard' shift. I walked Liz to her car, thanked her once again and gave her a hug goodbye. I didn't want to let go, she felt so calming and yet so hot at the same time. I just looked into her mystic green eyes; damn I wish I was ten years older.

Liz's final words before she left were, "Mitch you're a good kid, but like your mom said, hang around with kids your own age. Hook up with Natasha, she would appreciate you, honest! I'm too old for you." Nothing comes easy does it?

I popped a codeine pill that night and puffed a joint laced with some good quality cherry honey oil. As I lay in bed before drifting off to sleep, I never realized before how good I had it at home. I felt so safe and loved by mom and my sisters. I'm not sure why it almost took a near-death experience for me to realize this.

I missed the next two days off school, because I was still hurting really bad from the accident. I did however mange to make it over to Dubrowski's place each night. I felt really naked having to bum a ride over; I really missed my bike. I put in an insurance claim and hopefully I'll be riding again very soon. The nice weather is coming and I don't want to go back booting around town in mom's 'Woody Wagon'. Not exactly what you would call a babe magnet.

At Dubrowski's, I didn't tell anyone the truth. I had to keep to my story the same for all ears, you never know who may rat you out in the future. It was hard, but because it involved a triple murder it was so surprisingly easy.

After spending the weekend with grown men, and my own near-death experience, I also realized just how young the 'Dirty Dozen' were. We should be enjoying our youth while we still can. We should be enjoying our youth, our innocence, while we still can. Being naïve was still a reality, something I should appreciate, and so that is what I did.

We smoked our pot, drank our beer and talked about what chicks at school were worth banging, or at least which ones actually put out.

I wasn't sure at this point if I even wanted a full-time girlfriend. Liz blew my mind being so kind, the Vigoda sisters were nasty and would do whatever you requested sexually, then there was Natasha. She was a teenager and so young in her ways, compared to Liz and the Vigoda sisters, and yet she was unattainable. She was the girl I truly desired, and in time she will be mine; my gut, head and heart tells me so. I'm not even thinking about Lucy these days, why should I?

I think most of the guys thought my motorcycle accident must have affected my brain. I was going perhaps a little soft on them. At one point during the night, I just closed my eyes and I mentally put myself back in the trailer bouncing out of control. I wanted to sense that fear, that near-death feeling once again! Once I obtained the fear, I opened my eyes and there I was, back with the Dirty Dozen in Dubrowski's basement. There were no ruby red shoes worn and I didn't have to click my heels twice. I just wanted to really embrace a part of my life that means so much to me. Getting high and drunk with my friends in Dubrowski's basement, that was my Valhalla.

When mom and our family doctor both felt I was ready to return to school, I had to check in with the school office first. Vice-Principal Nash wasn't a fan of mine at all. He would, from time to time, remind me how I lost the school's football championship with my foolish behavior, and of course how I was just a thug.

I know it must have killed him to have a school assembly for me winning the State Championship in Karate. He would love to kick me out of his school, so I tried my best not to give him the satisfaction. Not only because it pisses him off, but for my mom.

So when I checked back in with my doctor's note, he asked to see me in his office. Fuck me. More grief! OK Mitch, take his bullshit for mom and that is exactly what it was. At first, I told him I couldn't tell him anything as it's a police investigation. I was hoping he would just back off, but he did not. He enjoyed seeing me uncomfortable.

Eventually Nash told me if I brought any trouble to the school I would be expelled. I kept my mouth shut, agreed with him and went to class. I was quite proud of myself, and hopefully mom would be proud of me too.

The next couple of days I really tried my best to live this new life, appreciating life and friends and family. The simple things I have taken for granted since we moved to California. Just like dark storm clouds on the horizon, I knew eventually the clouds would burst into flames.

# The Week From Hell: April 18, 1966

You ever have one of those weeks where you keep asking yourself, "What the hell else can go wrong?" You get a headache that even Mr. Adolph Von Bayer couldn't anticipate or cure.

It has been a week since my near-death ride from hell, and as much as I'm really trying this new attitude about life, I knew sooner than later I would fall back into my old ways. I felt like a caged tiger at the zoo. People would provoke me knowing the steel bars would keep them safe. However like any wild animal, steel bars wouldn't hold me back for very long.

# MANIC MONDAY

Monday at school, Scott Kantonescu, who was John's younger brother and a fellow Dirty Dozen member, kept asking me, "What happened in Anaheim? John seems to have just disappeared off the face of the earth." The more I said, "I don't know," the more pissed Scott got with me.

As much as I appreciated Scott being concerned at his brother's whereabouts, there's a reason why John had to disappear. The tension was getting so thick it was starting to divide members of the Dirty Dozen. I guess Scott could tell I wasn't being totally honest with him. Regardless, I promised my brother I would keep the same story; the safe story.

Norm, Crow, Fraser and I were having lunch at the Millionaire restaurant when Scott, Herman and Connor came and sat at our table. I could tell by their eyes and the smell coming from them, that they just finished smoking a joint and had a couple beers. Scott just stared at me the whole time and yet said nothing. As much as I tried to ignore him, the more I felt myself getting pissed off at him. Herman, being the big mouth Kraut he can be when drinking too much booze, started up about how we are all supposed to be tight with each other, trust each other and support each other.

I knew where he was going with this. I wanted to tell Herman and Scott, "If I tell you what I know, someone from the Hell Hounds club would put a bullet in both your heads, and then mine." I couldn't say anything. I was kind of hoping that Fraser would have clued in somehow, seeing how his brother Caleb is a full patch. I wasn't getting the full support I was hoping to receive, so I stood up looked at Scott and said, "If your brother wants you to know where he is, and that he is all right, he will do just that, now leave me the fuck alone."

With that I just got up and left the restaurant by myself, and headed back to school. Had my hand and collarbone not been so busted up, I swear I would have broken Herman's jaw. As I was going back to school I still had the pain from the accident impeding my walking. My arm was still in the sling, but being so pissed I really didn't feel the pain.

My hearing wasn't impeded however! I got a block from the school when I heard a police siren give a quick wail and someone yell, "STRONGBOW." I stopped walking and a cop car pulled right up in front of me. Now what? Was I being arrested for the murders in the desert and Disney? I closed my eyes and tried to remember what Jake said if I was questioned by the cops.

I opened my eyes, and it was Charlie Adams! He

seemed shocked to see me so banged up. I told him the whole safe story, then Charlie told me some more bad news. My appeal to fight for the United States Championship in Hawaii was turned down, and this was the last and final appeal. Charlie also said I was now officially barred from any future tournaments because of testing positive for drugs. Charlie apologized and asked if I could drop by the club one day this week. He had something for me that just might cheer me up some. I thanked Charlie for the bad news and said I would be by later in the week.

Those dark ominous clouds in my life that have been lingering in the distance; are now starting to let their presence be known. I can see flashes of lightning; no thunder yet, just lightning. I'm also starting to feel droplets of rain, the storm is coming; will I be ready for it?

I was maybe twenty steps from the school doors when I saw Lucy Thom. I was too beat up physically and mentally to run away from her, not so much to run away in fear, just avoidance from her bullshit. Lucy stopped me and asked if I was all right. She then proceeded to give me a hug, which I guess wasn't as bad as I thought it would be. She asked me did I want to go smoke a joint with her. I should have said no, but I really needed to wind down, get mellow and forget, so I agreed. Next thing I knew we made our way back to my house, got high, and fucked all afternoon. Perhaps there was a silver lining to those storm clouds after all. I was lying in bed while Lucy was getting dressed, before she headed home. I decided to maybe eat my pride and ask her out again. She did take my 'cherry' after all, and besides, the way Scott Kantonescu and Herman were earlier today, I think I might stay away from Dubrowski's for a bit.

Then I heard that clap of thunder, "Sorry Mitch, you dumped me and I have moved on already."

I was a bit confused and laughingly I asked what did she mean by moving on?

"I have a new boyfriend, in my life Mitch, I am seeing Donald Brewer. He goes to Polk High, same school as your little blonde Jew girlfriend." Now I am really confused. "So what about what we just did?"

"I was horny. You have always been a decent lay, not the first time I fucked around on a boyfriend." She smiled ever so vindictively at me! I tried to get out of bed and smack her upside the head, but my injuries made any movement painful and slow. My mouth, on the other hand, was working just fine. I don't think I have ever sworn so much at one person in my life. I need a Seconal.

# TOONIE TUESDAY

    Pam drove me to school this morning. For the first time since I moved to California, I was feeling kind of alone. I was being shunned by several Dirty Dozen members because I wouldn't reveal the location of Scott's brother John, which I honestly don't know. Lucy just gave me the final payback, ending our relationship. Natasha was still just a schoolboy crush, who had already told me, "It wouldn't work out between the two of us." Damn, this was before we even really got to know each other. Hell, those were just my personal problems. Then of course my motorcycle was destroyed. I couldn't partake in any more full contact Karate tourneys, and fighting was my addiction! No charges could be laid and you could still lay a beating on someone, plus the training involved was also very addictive. Yeah, right now, life was really starting to suck.

    After first period Norm saw me in the hall and could tell I was really bummed out, not only physically but mentally. So like a good friend he asked did I want to go for a walk, talk and most important, a toke. Now that is what I wanted to hear.

    As we were walking around puffing the joint, I felt like I had to tell somebody what had happened, but I know Jake wouldn't be impressed, nor would Kantonescu or Terek. They would be sitting in an electric chair, waiting for the switch to be turned on if I talked.

Norm looked at me and said, "I guess whatever happened with Scott's brother John, it must be real bad?" Now, of all the guys in the Dirty Dozen, I trusted Norm more than any of them.

"It was real bad! John is all right and in time I will tell you everything, just not right now." As a good friend, Norm let it drop and said he would back me. Now that is what I wanted to hear more than anything.

I was in sitting in second period with one hell of a bu*zz* from the weed and the painkillers from the night before when I was called down to the office. Something told me when the speaker in the room cued, that it was for me. "Mrs. Harper, can you have Mitchell Strongbow come down to the principal's office please?" Yeah I will go. What the fuck, why not? Now who wants a piece of me while I'm down?

As I entered the office, there were two guys in suits talking to Vice-Principal Nash. They identified themselves as Detectives Tom Aylmer and Jerry Duff, homicide detectives from Anaheim. Well, right then and there, I felt like throwing up my breakfast. My bu*zz* seemed to have intensified even more, dry cotton mouth and slits for eyes; for once I was hoping for an after school detention.

The two detectives asked if I was willing to go with them to a station in town. They said that they have a couple questions that needed answering. I said, "Sure, what station as I want a lawyer present?"

Just like cops, I was given the old line, "If you have nothing to hide, why would you need a lawyer?" I may have been young and pretty high, but I wasn't stupid and was very quick on my feet. "I have been taking pain killers since my accident, and I would hate to answer anything wrong."

Both cops looked at each other. Tom then said "Relax Mitchell, you aren't under arrest, just a few questions."

Fuck them! "You want me to go downtown and be questioned, I want a lawyer present, or I stay here in school. Perhaps I might even go home sick; my shoulder is really starting to bother me."

The cops knew that unless I was put under arrest, they had no rights to question me. They decided to allow me to have a lawyer present while questioning.

I called Cole Winters, who is the Hell Hounds official legal counsel, and asked him to meet me at the downtown Police headquarters. Cole agreed. Before we left the principal's office, Nash told the detectives what a bad kid I was.

Tom said, "No, he is just exercising his rights."

Jerry agreed with Nash. They were already playing 'Good Cop-Bad Cop' before we were even downtown. Even buzzed out and all, I picked up on that.

Once down at the station, Tom and Jerry took me into an interview room. Tom offered, whatever I needed, he would get for me, like a soda or water or cigarette. Jerry was being a real jerk asking me if I was a big man, a tough guy?

After about ten minutes of cop foreplay, there came a tap at the door. It was Cole Winters, thank God. Cole asked to talk to me in private for a couple minutes. Tom and Jerry agreed. I went to say something and Cole pointed to the glass mirror and told me it was a one-way mirror where they can watch everything we are doing; they can also hear our conversation.

Cole was briefed by my brother and Jerry. He told me to use the safe story and if everything comes up that can incriminate me, he will step in. The key, said Cole, was not to volunteer any information. They will try and trip me up, so a simple yes and no will do.

Showtime I guess as Tom and Jerry came back in the room. Tom-"Do you know why we are here talking to you Mitch?'

"I'm not sure."

Jerry-"We had a murder take place at Disneyland while you and other Hell Hounds were in town. In fact, we have you in the park and at the crime scene, where the murder took place."

Cole- "Is my client being charged for murder, or is he just a suspect? Are you two fishing or just cutting bait?"

Tom- "We know he is just a kid, wrong place at the wrong time. I would hate for him to spend the rest of his life behind bars. If he were to tell us who did the killing, I'm sure he would have his whole life ahead of him."

Now I'm getting a little scared.

Jerry- "Do you know Mitch, that the State of California has executed 193 people, including four women in the gas chamber? Just because you are a youth doesn't mean you would be spared the gas chamber." I can feel my asshole tightening up, and I'm officially scared shitless.

Cole- "Quit intimidating my client, is he charged or not? If so, I would like to see what evidence you have."

Tom- "Look Mitch, I'm pretty sure you didn't do the killing. My partner, on the other hand, thinks I'm wrong. If you were to tell us everything that happened, well then we would know for sure that you were just an innocent bystander. By the way, how did you get so beat up?"

I looked at Cole and he told Tom and Jerry, "A motorcycle accident."

Jerry- "Are you sure this wasn't from the fight at Disneyland?"

Cole- -"My client received medical treatment in Stockton California. He drove up to Stockton General Hospital. Do you think he could drive that far, from Anaheim to Stockton, with a broken collarbone? There is a police record filed with the Stockton police."

Cole left out about Terek showing up with a bullet wound. He knew Tom and Jerry would check out this part of my story, and they would come back and question me some more. This would give Cole more time to talk to different parties about my alibi.

Tom, "So Mitch, we have a witness that puts you at Disney, same time as the killing took place. We want to hear your version."

Cole interrupted Tom, "How reliable is your witness that it was Mitch?"

Tom- "You just got a tattoo of a wolf wearing a Nazi helmet on your chest the day before?"

Cole just looked at me, and I nodded yes. The only person that knew this was that chick that I fucked while the fight was going on. I don't think she saw me join in the fight. I think she said she had to get cleaned up, time to gamble, what the fuck.

"Yeah I was at Disneyland."

Tom- "And what was your involvement during the fight?"

"I didn't get involved in the fight, I was fucking some broad. When I came outside from her back washroom I was told, 'To get on my bike and flee the scene'."

Jerry, "Who told you to flee the scene?"

"I can't remember. It was total madness! I just followed everyone else, jumped on my bike and took off. I'm not even sure what the hell went down. I did what I was told to do."

Jerry- "You mean to tell me that you didn't participate in the fight. You expect us to believe that?"

"It is the truth. Ask the chick I was banging, I don't even know her name."

Tom- "Can you tell us what members of the Hell Hounds you left Disney with?"

"I don't know any of these guys, there were so many different chapters there. I'm not a member I just went on the run with my brother Jake. I honestly don't know any of the guy, I just met those guys this past weekend."

Cole- "This is true. Mitch isn't a club member, and he's not striking for the club. Mitch doesn't have a criminal record; he has family members in the club. He was just in the wrong place at the wrong time. If you don't have any more questions, I'm sure my client would like to get back to school."

Tom and Jerry just looked at each other. Tom asked that I don't leave town, and he will check out my bike accident story with the Stockton police. I asked if I was free to go. Jerry said, "Yeah."

As Cole and I left the station I asked if Tom and Jerry had interviewed anyone else yet. Cole said I was the first.

I asked, "Why me first?" Cole said, I was young, naïve and would be scared, if anyone would give up more information or squeal on anyone, it would be me.

I did quite well but Cole made sure that I understood that if I'm picked up again for questioning, to call him right away; don't answer anything without him present. I agreed to his request.

Cole drove me to school against my wishes, I wanted to try and track down Jake. Cole told me to keep my nose clean, stay away from club members, as the cops are watching everyone's movement, try and act like a normal teenager not a Hell Hound wannabe and make sure I stay in school and attend all my classes.

I told Cole I would try my best. I pleaded never to mention me being interviewed by the cops around my mom, or he would be an accessory to my murder after mom kills me. Cole laughed and agreed.

Cole dropped me off back at my school. My head was really starting to throb with all the tension of being questioned. I'm not sure how much of what I said the cops believed, and for the most part I told the truth. The last thing I ever wanted to do was screw up and implicate any of the Hell Hounds with the murder. I just wanted to be cool, and a solid citizen with club members, not just some teenage punk.

I had to check in with the office before going back to my class; damn I already missed lunch. With this headache starting to build, some food would either help, or make me hurl; screw it. I'm going to see the school nurse and go home. Nash said I didn't look sick to him what seemed to be the problem?

"I don't feel good, I feel like I might throw up."

"Balderdash Strongbow! You'll say anything to get out of class. What did those two detectives want to talk to you about?"

I was really feeling sick, and I'll be damned if I let

Nash know what the detectives wanted me for. "I really don't feel good, please let me go and see the school nurse."

Nash went to open up his mouth again, to question or scold me. I felt the floor start to spin, my stomach flipped and I free based puke all over Nash. With his mouth open, I nailed him good, he ate some and began to puke all over the place, all the while screaming at me. I wish I had a camera, it was classic! I felt like a sniper, my aim was true; Nash was indeed nailed from head to toe.

The school nurse called my mom but she couldn't leave, and I was really too weak and light-headed to drive home. I called Liz O'Malley and she said she would come right over and pick me up and then drive me home.

I felt so cool walking down the school halls with her, she was so damn hot. As luck would have it, it was between periods, so the school halls were full of people, including that Asian whore Lucy Thom, who just stared at Liz and me.

Just like on the drive home from Stockton, Liz looked stunningly beautiful. I just stared and smiled at her and promised I wouldn't puke on her.

Once home, I was hoping lightning would strike twice with us. I asked if she would like to smoke a joint with me. Liz looked down at my crotch region she could tell I was up to no good. She asked me to have a seat on the couch. God, here we go again, maybe not such a bad day after all. Before I sparked up the joint Liz said she had to talk to me about something. I already know what she is going to say. "Don't tell Jake, this is wrong etc."

I looked at Liz as she took my sweaty left hand, and put it into her left hand. "Mitch I'm your brother's girlfriend. What we did the other night, I'm not very proud of; it really has bothered me. I know you are a mature teenager, but you're still just a kid. You can't have these thoughts and sexual urges for me, it's wrong, it's so wrong! So I'm asking you, please don't come onto me anymore. I would love to still be your friend and confidant about other girls if you need advice, but that's it. I'm sorry."

I felt so embarrassed, so ashamed of myself. I didn't even feel like smoking the joint now, I just wanted to go sleep, and think that this was just a dream that went wrong. Fuck, nothing comes easy does it?

I sulked around the house till bedtime. My battered body and broken bones seem to hurt even more as the day went on and my head felt like it was going to explode. Tonight's sleep aid was a couple of aspirins, a kick ass joint, one codeine pill and a Gravol.

# WHACKY WEDNESDAY

The next morning when my alarm went off, I slammed it with such force I cut my good hand wide open. I was starting to bleed pretty good but I didn't want to get out of bed. I didn't have the strength mentally or physically to take on the deeds of the day. If Monday and Tuesday were an example of the rest of the week, perhaps just lying in bed would be a good game plan. However bleeding all over my sheets was not a good plan; mom would kick my ass for that.

I received a phone call at the breakfast, it was Norm. He was sick and wasn't able to make it to school. He needed a favor. Ricky Thom was supposed to meet him at school to front him a quarter pound of weed. Norm asked if I would pick up the weed after school and drop it off at his house. He had customers lined up waiting for the weed.

I asked, "Why not just get Ricky to drop it off at your house before school?" He said, "Ricky had already left for school when I called his house."

Logic would say I'm more than just a heat score right now, and I should say no, but Norm has been the most solid of all my friends. How could I say no or turn my back on him? He hasn't turned his back on me ever, so I reluctantly agreed.

I was running a little bit behind so I didn't get a

chance to see Ricky before the first bell. I would catch up with him after first period in the smoking area. First period class was history which I must say I enjoyed. We were studying prohibition and how so much money was made from the sale of illegal booze. We were focusing on the war between Dion O'Bannion and Al Capone.

I heard one hell of a commotion coming from the hallway, dogs were barking and I heard several police radios going off. Fuck was I now being arrested for my involvement in the murders? Where is Vice Principal Nash? I felt like throwing up again. Then I heard a sound that sort of eased my nerves; the cops were popping open lockers.

An announcement came over the school sound system for all students to stay in their classrooms. Fuck it was a drug raid, I know it. Then it hit me. Ricky brought in a quarter pound of weed for Norm. Unfortunately for Ricky he'll get busted. Fortunately for me I was late this morning or the weed would be in my locker. Maybe my luck was changing after all, for the good.

At lunchtime I called Norm to tell him that there was a huge drug bust at school, and I never got a chance to see Ricky before it went down, thank God! Then much to my surprise I saw Ricky Thom walk by with Lucy. I called Ricky over; Lucy gave me the finger and kept walking. I told Norm I would come over after school. I didn't feel like talking business over the phone. Norm agreed.

"Rick, Norm is sick. I'm supposed to pick up the weed for him. You must have forgotten it, or you would be in jail right now, you lucky fuck!"

Ricky got real serious looking. "I had the weed in an empty locker. The cops found it but the locker isn't assigned to anyone. As far as I am concerned Norm still owes me for the quarter pound, but seeing at how he is sick and you were supposed to come through for him, you owe me forty bucks."

I could tell Ricky was quite serious, "The transaction was never complete Rick, the goods were never delivered."

"Norm was supposed to meet me first thing this morning. I was there. If you were filling in for him, where the fuck were you?"

"First off, Norm called you this morning to say he wouldn't be at school. I'm doing him and you a favor. What is the big hurry to unload the weed?"

"The deal was to take place before school. I had the goods and was on time. You and Norm better figure out who is going to pay me for the weed."

Now I was getting really pissed. If my arm wasn't in a sling, I would knock Ricky out cold. "Fuck you

Ricky! No deal, goods not delivered, all part of doing business. Sometimes you take a loss, sometimes you make a profit."

Ricky then said something to me that had I been carrying a gun I would of shot him in the head. "You know Strongbow, I find it kind of strange, or is it coincidental, that you get taken away by two detectives yesterday. Today, here you are back in school and it gets raided. Did you rat out people to get off a charge? are you a RAT?"

I lunged at Ricky with only one semi-healthy arm and swung to knock him cold. I wanted to break his jaw for even suggesting I was a RAT. Ricky weaved just enough to get out of range of my punch, he countered with a flurry of punches to my head. I vaguely remembered being thrown back from the momentum of his punches, right into a row of lockers.

I'm not sure how long I was knocked out for, but I woke up in the hospital emergency ward. A doctor had his little flashlight blazing into my eyes. He asked, "Did you know where you are?" First answer was Stockton.

"Try again son."

"Anaheim?"

"One more try son."

"I hate guessing games Doc, how about you tell me. I've had one hell of a fucked up week. What kind of damage has been done?"

"Well son, you have a broken nose, your collarbone appears to still be OK and I would say a concussion. Do you know how this happened?"

I thought for a second real hard, did I dump my bike? Was I jumped? It took a couple minutes to remember exactly what happened. Ricky, fucking Ricky, he will pay. "I fell at school Doc, being feeling kind of queasy ever since last week. I actually threw up at school yesterday, yeah I must have fallen."

The doctor said he was going to order a batch of tests, just to make sure they didn't miss anything, while examining me in Stockton.

After a couple hours of tests, and then that old friend Novocain was shot back up my nose. The doctors reset my nose and said I had a pretty decent concussion, and I should just take it easy for the rest of the week.

That to me meant no school, yippee.

Mom, like the last time I had my nose broken, was quiet during the ride home. Damn, it just occurred to me, Ricky Thom has now broken my nose twice. That is two times too many! I will have revenge. Not by ratting him out but by an old fashioned beating.

Well tonight I went to sleep with a little Novocain bu*zz*, a codeine pill and a couple tokes off an oiler joint. The biggest pain in the ass, and I mean the biggest, was the fact that someone had to wake me up every four hours. With me having a concussion, not even sleep comes easy.

# THURSDAY

I must say, waking up every morning and feeling like shit really sucks. Every morning for the last five days, it's a new ache and pain. Today my nose feels and looks like Rudolph, after tangling with the Abominable Snow Man; red and sore. Ricky Thom will pay for this. Normally I take great pride in laying a beating on someone and never asking for help, this time I'm willing to call in favors if need be.

Actually, I would like to fire bomb his house. That way Ricky and Lucy would both be dead and that cunt mama san of theirs, the dragon lady, would be killed. That's right, kill the whole damn family. Hey, I'm smiling once again, even if it hurts my face.

I staggered downstairs and realized I had the house to myself. So I sparked up a joint before breakfast. Sugar Frosted Flakes always tasted better stoned, it's GREAT!

The phone rang around 10:20. It was the insurance company, and good thing I was home. "Mr. Strongbow, its Mr. Clinton from Fidelity Insurance. Mr. Strongbow, we have a little problem with your claim for your motorcycle. In your statement to us, you state you left your motorcycle purposely at the side of the highway miles from civilization. You basically abandoned your motorcycle. Is that not correct sir?"

At first I thought the weed combined with Tony the Tigers sugar rush was causing my inability to follow Mr. Clinton's conversation. "Yeah sort of, but I didn't purposely abandon my motorcycle. Don Terek and I were shot at by a passing vehicle. Don was hit, and I lost balance of my bike and dumped it, lost control of it. When I picked myself up from the road, I saw that Don needed immediate medical attention and my bike was no longer able to be driven. So I drove a shot and severely wounded Don Terek to the nearest hospital on his bike, the only means of available transportation."

There was now a couple seconds of dead air.

"Mr. Strongbow I have read the police report. Are you a member of the Hell Hounds?"

I was now starting to get really pissed. "I'm not a member, but if I was, what would that have to do with my insurance claim?"

"Actually it has a lot to do with your claim. You would be considered a 'High Risk' and your rates would be adjusted accordingly. Right now I see you as a member or associate of the Hell Hounds, and this makes you subject to fraud while filling out your insurance information. This could possibly make your insurance void and make coverage unavailable for your motorcycle accident. Fraudulent claims are on the rise Mr. Strongbow, and my job is to sort out these fraudulent claims. To be honest with you, there is just something about your story I don't believe, and this will affect your insurance claim."

"Are you saying that Don wasn't shot, because right now he's lying in a hospital bed in Stockton? I'm sixteen years old. Do you really think the Hell Hounds would make me a member? My brother is a member and Don is a family friend. What would you want me to do, leave him on the side of the road to die? You dumb fuck!"

"Mr. Strongbow, there is no reason for that kind of language."

"FUCK YOU, yeah there is a reason for this language." CLICK.

"Hello-Hello" bastard hung up on me. I'm still paying for half that bike. What the hell do you pay insurance for in the first place? Damn, I'm pissed. As I stood to hang up the phone, I had one hell of a head rush and my legs were real shaky; I had to go and lay down on the couch.

I woke up completely drenched from head to toe. I didn't even sweat this much training for the Karate Championships. I was shaking and edgy, and my mind was still foggy. The fear from the dream I just had was clearer than reality itself. I could even taste fresh blood in my mouth, and the stench of death was everywhere. I ran to the washroom and threw up. I guess I had been repressing the nightmarish Snowball Run, but my deepest fears were realized in this dream.

After my stomach had settled down, I grabbed a long shower, and just let the stream from the shower pulsate the back of my neck until the tension seemed to have dissipated. As I was drying off, I heard the doorbell ring. My normal reaction was just to go and see who it was but after this dream I was kind of nervous.

I went to my room, grabbed my baseball bat and slowly approached the front door, ever so cautious. As I walked towards the door, I listened for any unusual sounds and tried to hear if I recognized any of the voices coming from outside on my front porch. I slowly pull the curtains back; it was Norm, Fraser and Crow, thank goodness!

After I let the boys in, we discussed the little problem of Ricky Thom wanting to be paid for the drugs that were confiscated by the cops during the raid at the school. Crow also told me that Scott Kantonescu is still whining it up about his brother John, and how I have something to do with him disappearing. It seems Scott and Ricky teamed up, and they're now allies against me.

This is the first time there has been a true division in the 'Dirty Dozen'. Time to call big brother Jake and get a few issues resolved. I also needed advice on how to deal with the insurance company. I hate having to call Jake for this shit, as I take pride in fighting my own battles. However, I'm too busted up physically and mentally. I need help, and that is what family does, they help each other.

To be honest, I have no idea how to deal with the Kantonescu issue. I've never been involved with a murder and the murderer going into hiding. I never learned that in history class. Capone just whacked who ever pissed him off. I think Capone had the right idea.

The boys and I smoked a couple joints and I told them I should be back at school tomorrow unfortunately as my mom is getting real pissed at me being home so much. I thanked them for their loyalty and understanding.

I haven't heard from Jake in over three days, so I called Jerry and asked if we could we could hook up. I needed some advice. I never discuss business of any sorts over the phone, especially now! I'm sure the cops have the lines at his house tapped. I know the phone at the clubhouse is tapped for sure, fucking cops.

Within twenty minutes Jerry came by for a visit and talk. He already talked to Cole Winters and said I did well. He said Jake is away on *business*, and he's not sure when he would be back. I never asked what *business* meant; some things are best not to know. I explained to Jerry that I'm not whining, but I can't handle certain aspects of my personal life without help. Jerry is family and I need direction.

After telling Jerry my problems with Scott Kantonescu and Ricky Thom, Jerry assured me he would handle my problems. They would now be his problems, and rest assured they will disappear or Scott and Ricky would disappear. I knew beforehand that this might be Jerry's solution to my problems. Even though I was tight with Ricky and Scott, my broken nose and concussion from Ricky and the endless talking behind my back now made the possible solution very viable. I wonder if the 'Death Dream' was a premonition.

As far as the insurance screw around for my motorcycle, Jerry suggested I talk to Cole Winters once I get official paperwork from the insurance company denying me my claim.

I went to bed that night and I tossed and turned a fair amount. I was actually terrified of having another 'Death Dream'. I was also sort of fearful that Jerry would have someone from the club kill Ricky and Scott; not sure if I could live with that. Why the fuck did I tell Jerry this in the first place? I finally popped a Valium and drifted off to sleep.

# FREAKOUT FRIDAY

Wow, I woke up fairly clear headed, no nightmares and no headache. I was also starting to be able to breathe out of my nose. I felt so good I didn't even put on my sling; yeah the shoulder was also feeling better. I must say I had a very positive attitude stepping out of bed.

Breakfast tasted good, even Rachel was nice and wasn't sarcastic to me. Mom was singing Etta James and Pam seemed to also have a spring in her step. Pam dropped Rachel and me off at school. As Rachel and I were walking towards the front doors, some boy said "Hi" to Rachel, and her face went beet red as she answered "Hi" back. Damn, they liked each other.

Normally I would have growled at the kid, but today I was in a great mood so I just smiled at Rachel, raised my eyebrows and said, "Don't let me catch you two doing a kissy face."

This was met by one hell of a punch to my bad shoulder followed by, "YOU'RE AN ASSHOLE." I was laughing and grimacing all at the same time. Damn it hurt, but well worth embarrassing Rachel.

At my locker, Scott Kantonescu approached me and said his brother John called him last night, to say that he's all right, just away on business, and said to apologize to me.

I told Scott, "That's cool, lunchtime you can get me high." Scott agreed. I'm glad we're cool with each other.

After first period, I was hanging with the boys in the smoking area, when Ricky Thom approached us. Ricky asked how my nose was. I said it was getting better. I wasn't sure what Ricky would do next. Was he going to swing at me again?

"Look Mitch, I'm sorry man. I never should have swung at you. I know you're solid man I was just really stressed out about the drug bust. We're even man! Don't worry about paying me back for the quarter pound. Like you said, cost of doing business right?"

I'm not sure why Ricky had a change of heart. I'm sure it has something to do with Jerry getting involved. So, do I be a total dick or let it go? What the hell. Today has been a real good day and Ricky and I have been real close, so I'll let it go. But next time he pisses me off, I will break his nose; forgive but never forget. We all agreed to meet in the woods at lunchtime for beer and weed just like every Friday.

Damn, the lunch bell couldn't come fast enough. Off we went to do some socializing in the woods. I'm not sure if all the drugs I've been taking all week for pain made my bu*zz* more intense; but I noticed it seemed I had to pee more often than normal. I also noticed wetness on the end of my penis even before I pissed. When I did piss, it burned a little bit. Strange, must be the meds, booze and kickass weed. It was a good feeling, the Dirty Dozen all getting high together again, once again we were tight.

As soon as we got back into school, I realized I was really buzzed out. My eyes were really hurting, I had a bit of the 'Weebiles' happening, and I had to go piss again; damn this is the third time in the last hour. This time when I pulled out my penis, it was really wet at the end, covered in a creamy milky substance, sort of green in color. When I tried to piss, damn it burned; something just ain't right.

Before I went into class I asked Crow if he ever had any of these symptoms. Crow laughed and asked have I been playing with any dirty, filthy whores? Crow told me I need to go to the venereal disease clinic, as I have sexual disease.

What the fuck. Isn't that what killed Al Capone? It was some sort of sexual disease. Now I'm not sure what I am, pissed or frightened! Whose face comes to mind right away? Lucy Thom, that little fucking dirty filthy whore, she gave me this and I know it.

I'm sitting in Geography class doing everything but paying attention to my teacher. I feel buzzed right out, my penis is now burning, and I want to slice Lucy's throat. The teacher asked me a question and I didn't even clue in she was talking to me. She asked me the same question once again and I just looked at her like a deer caught in the headlights. She asked if I was all right.

I said, "I have to go and see the school nurse right away."

My teacher agreed and as she's writing out my hall slip, the classroom speaker cued, "Mrs. Edwards, can you have Mitchell Strongbow come to the Principal's office, please?" Hell, not the cops again? Damn things started off really decent this morning, but in the last half hour things are back to normal; insanity.

As I'm walking down the hall I wondered what the cops wanted now. I thought I did really good answering their questions last time. I peeked into the office first but there are no police present. Strange, maybe my luck is turning again.

Vice-Principal Nash greeted me as I came in to his office. I peek in and still no cops inside. Nash is a goof, him I can handle, even if I'm still fairly bu*zz*ed out. I can tell by Nash's ear to ear smile, he is going to try and fuck me somehow; he is just too cheerful.

"Mr. Strongbow, it really pains me to say this, but we noticed you missed school on Monday afternoon. I talked to your mom earlier, and she assures me you should've been in school the whole day. I'm going to suspend you for the rest of today and also for

Monday. I'm sure it really bothers you being suspended, doesn't it?"

What a sarcastic bastard! Actually I'm the one who is smiling from ear to ear. Monday is the day Lucy and I hooked up at my house; yeah the day she gave me the 'dose'.

"Now Mr. Strongbow you might want to wipe that smile from your face. It's now my turn to smile. You are nothing but a thug and a bully! You like flexing your muscles but they don't impress me. As you know it pained me to no end, when Principal Higgins made me, of all people, organize a school rally for you for winning the State Karate Championship. However, Mr. Strongbow, I've been informed that you've been disqualified for illegal drug use."

"Mr. Strongbow, with the current drug crisis, in my opinion, taking over the youth of this country, I'm going to use you as an example. I'm planning an assembly in your honor! I will take down the plaque that was put in the school Hall of Fame, and instead it will be put in the brand new Hall of Shame! You will be the first inductee Mr. Strongbow."

Nash continued, "I don't know just what kind of an educator your mom is, because if her parenting skills are anything like her teaching schools she will be unemployed very soon. You and your family will be living on the street with the rest of the vagrants and unemployed bums. What do you think of that Mr. Strongbow?"

I sort of blanked out. I don't even remember getting up out of my chair. Everything went into slow motion, just like in the movies. Nash was starting to laugh, standing not even three feet from me. I threw a hook with my good arm. It connected directly on the side of Nash's head, and his glasses broke in half, as did his jaw. I just stood over a now knocked out Nash and then I heard the screaming from the secretaries in the office.

I turned around and knew this wasn't good. I left the office, turned to my left and saw four men in suits headed my way. Two were Tom Aylmer and Jerry Duff, the two homicide detectives from Anaheim. The other two I didn't recognize. What are the cops doing here so fast?

I saw Aylmer point at me, and then one of the secretaries ran out into the hall, screaming to stop me. I knew I was I fucked, feet don't fail me now. I tried my best to take off. I was really hoping my knowledge of the school grounds would help me in my getaway. Alas, I was high, drunk and my penis was burning, not to mention I was still really hurting from the accident.

Duff caught me within one hundred feet of the office and tackled me to the ground. As we're wrestling on the ground, Aylmer stuck his .38 snub nosed pistol in my face and asked, did I wanted to die? Reluctantly and wisely I stopped wrestling around with Duff. I was handcuffed and taken to San Francisco police headquarters.

Once at the police headquarters, Aylmer turned me over to the San Francisco police and I was charged with assault for knocking out Nash. I almost felt like a VIP. Three different police forces were chomping at the bit to talk to me. Aylmer and Duff were from Anaheim's Homicide unit, McBurney and Miller from the Los Angeles Homicide unit, and Church and Maxwell from the San Francisco juvenile squad. I told all six of these cops, "I'm not talking to no one until my lawyer Cole Winters is present."

Until Cole arrived, each set of cops tried their best to get me to open up and spill the beans. They could tell I knew much more than what I was letting on. I was a youth and they tried their best to scare the hell right out of me. McBurney and Miller showed me pictures of Bandito, with a hole in his burned out face. That was mighty gory I must say. They wanted to know how my motorcycle ended up in a truck, being driven by a deceased and burnt to a crisp Bandito. I said, "I have no idea."

At first I thought about shutting up until Cole came, however I would've just looked guilty. Keep to the same story I've been telling all along. I have told so many people the same story, I actually believed it myself. I was even willing to bet I would pass a lie detector test.

Once Cole arrived, McBurney and Miller came back inside and started to question me in front of him. McBurney found it just too damn coincidental that Bandito had a bullet take out the whole one side of his face and that same size caliber of bullet was also in Terek's shoulder.

Cole jumped in at that point, "Perhaps the same people who shot Terek also stole Mitch's motorcycle. It was dumped on the side of the road. And they could have put the bike in the back of Bandito's truck, and drove away. Bandito must have pissed them off enough and they killed him with the same gun. Obviously the killer is still on the loose. Do you have any other evidence of my client being involved with the murder?"

"Not at this time", answered Miller, "However Mitch is a person of interest." I leaned into Cole and whispered a question. "My client would like to know what kind of shape his motorcycle is in?" said Cole.

McBurney said, "It's a write off."

I asked McBurney for a number, so I can pass along the information to the insurance company. They gave me a phone number, but before they exited the room, Duff and Aylmer also came inside. Perhaps they sensed desperation in this case.

Duff started, "Your client is going to be charged with aggravated assault, and even though he's a first time offender. I'm going to make sure that the District Attorney's office is made well aware of the fact that he's involved with the Hell Hounds motorcycle club and is being investigated for a double homicide. I'm willing to bet you won't get probation. You will serve time, son. You might not get out until you're twenty-one years old. Your teenage years spent behind bars. Are you ready for this? Ready to be ass raped on a regular basis? You won't be the same person you came in as, son."

"I'm sure that between the Anaheim and Los Angeles District Attorney's offices, we can talk the San Francisco office into having these charges for assault dismissed. Just tell us what we want to hear son. We know you're not a killer, you're just a kid. Wise up kid, these adults will sacrifice you for their own freedom. You're nothing but a useless kid to them and you will be sacrificed. Mitchell, you go to jail for this assault and your whole future will be flushed right down the toilet. No one will ever hire an ex-con."

Aylmer chimed in, "This is your only chance to live a normal life son, just tell us who did the killing at

Disney and who shot Bandito, very simple. No one will ever know the information came from you. I understand you have family in the club, but I truly believe your brother would understand. After all Mitch, family's more important than the club to Jake, isn't it? You're more important than other club members, are you not Mitch? Would your brother sell out his own blood over members from the club? Would his loyalty lie with them or you?"

This cop was good. I had to really think smart. The cops, along with Cole and I, went around in circles for another couple hours. They tried every angle to get me to open up, building blocks to get me to spill the beans. I just stuck to my story. A couple of times when I did go to answer, Cole grabbed my wrist and answered for me. They tried their best to make me feel like shit. They would say Jake or Terek is going to rat me out, and I should take the deal before they do. Even though they normally don't execute minors in California, with me being linked to several different murders the District Attorney's office just might make an exception."

Hell at one point, Aylmer and Duff even threatened to charge me with the rape of the girl at Disneyland. I told them it was consensual. They agreed but said because she was only fifteen; it is still statutory rape! "Going to jail for rape isn't a good thing, no matter who my brother is. I would face death every day behind bars."

"Fuck you; I'm a year older than her. It was consensual."

Cole could tell they were desperate. We were into our sixth hour of questioning and I was starting to wear down. The whole rape threat shook me up more than anything. I have always prided myself on seduction by wit and charm; win their hearts and mind. Once I win both, I know their body will follow; never seduction by force. Yeah, that really shook me up.

Finally an exhausted and frustrated Cole asked the cops if they were going to charge me for anything right now. No one answered him. "Then we are done. You know how to contact my client and me. He has answered all your questions truthfully, and in great detail. We are now going leave?" All four cops said they would be in touch probably sooner than later. Don't leave town.

As Cole and I stood up to leave Church and Maxwell, two of San Francisco's finest stopped us and said, "Not so fast, our turn to ask questions." My head now truly felt as if it was going to explode. I felt worse than any hangover I have ever endured. I gave my statement of the events in Nash's office acknowledged that I punched him in the head, and gave the reasons why, as if that even mattered.

Cole also told me that Aylmer, Duff, McBurney and Miller would be on the other side of the glass watching my body language and vocal tones. So I was as forthcoming as I could be and I signed my statement. The whole ordeal took about forty minutes.

Cole said I did real well, but there was one problem that he could see right off the bat. "Those cops watching through the two-way glass now know that your mom means something very special to you. Next time you are brought in for questioning, they will use her to get at you; keep that in mind Mitchell. It's all part of their game."

Cole told the cops we had money set aside for my bond, so when can we see a judge for a bond hearing?

Church said, "The judge left about twenty minutes ago, you will have to stay in lock up until Monday morning."

Cole turned to me and said, "You'll be staying at the taxpayer's hotel all weekend, better known as Juvenile Hall. Keep your nose clean in there and I'll see you Monday morning for your bail hearing."

I asked could he let my mom know where I am, as well as Jake. Cole said, "Will do," and then he left.

Church then took me down and had me fingerprinted, picture taken and took down all kinds of information about me. I even had to tell them I had a tattoo on my chest. All the while he kept trying to make small talk at how I should help out Aylmer, Duff, McBurney and Miller with their investigations. I was so mentally drained I said what only I needed to be said.

I told Church I was real hungry. He told me, no problem he would get me something.

Maxwell then said, "No way!" good cop-bad cop. I told Maxwell, "Fuck off!" He punched me in the gut, followed by Church telling him to back off. Now I just want to crash, so I'm saying nothing more.

Eventually I was taken to a cell block. Friday night in San Francisco lock up. The place is full, all kinds of people already in here. I'm given my own cell, one over from the drunken tank; so much for sleeping tonight. Every twenty minutes or so the cops were bringing in a new drunk and everyone was fucking loud, yelling, screaming and banging on the bars. The odd fight broke out in the drunk tank. I was so tempted to ask to be put in there myself so I could knock out whoever was pissing me off. With only one good arm, maybe it's best to having my own cell.

Finally it seemed that all the drunks in the city were eventually locked away and passed out for the night. Now I could go to sleep. Unlike past nights I didn't have the luxury of several aspirins or a joint of weed, and there weren't any valium or codeine pills either. Tonight the only thing new was a steady drip of a green milky substance coming from my penis; nothing comes easy, does it, except the 'Dose'.

I was awakened by some huge cop in uniform. He passed me a cheese sandwich for breakfast and said he'll be taking me to Juvenile Hall in about ten minutes. The bread was rock hard and the cheese didn't smell the best, but this was the only food I had seen in almost twenty hours, so I ate it.

I was put in the back of a paddy wagon and driven to Juvenile Hall. It must have been a rough night in the city, as there were still fresh pools of blood in the back of the paddy wagon and it smelled like piss and booze.

Once I arrived at Juvenile Hall, I was taken to this area known as the 'Bull Pen', where I was processed before being taken to my 'Pod'. More photos were taken and I was fingerprinted once again. As I'm sitting in the bull pen, I see other juvies eyeing me up and down, seeing if I'm a tough guy or not; can they prey upon me or not?

Now I was a big kid for my age, working out steady at Popeye's, and with my martial arts capability I was ready for whoever would challenge me. My shoulder was feeling much better. Perhaps I might get a chance to see just how good it is very shortly. I know Cole told me to behave myself, but I also know what dad and Jake drilled into my head. 'Kill or be Killed.' never hesitate, as he who hesitates gets wasted.

I was taken up to Pod 3-C Right. This was used mostly for short term offenders that are either close to being released, or as in my case, offenders waiting for a bail/bond hearing. I was given a comb, toothbrush, and a small container of tooth paste; I guess that's all you really need.

The head guard read me the riot act before I was taken inside my pod. He basically told me, "don't be stupid", I have a bail/bond hearing on Monday so don't blow my hearing by acting up. Logically he made sense but logically I should never have knocked out the Vice-Principal either. But I'm a Strongbow, and I was defending my mom, as dad would've wanted.

As I walked into my Pod all eyes were on me. I was a piece of fresh meat, the new kid on the range. Was I going to be tested, did I show any signs of weakness? Fuck no! In a strange and psychotic kind of way, I wanted to punch out the toughest guy and rule the Pod. I'd heard stories of how things were run in a detention center, and whether it be a juvie hall, jail, or even prison, only the strong survived.

As I was eyeing up my future combatants I heard someone yell 'Strongbow'. It was John Walter, fellow

Dirty Dozen member. I haven't seen John since he was busted with Blais for the drug store break-in. This was good, someone I trusted to watch my back. John and I shot the shit while others in the pod just looked at us. There were a couple Mexicans and Asians, about half dozen blacks and maybe ten whites; no one that intimidated me.

I asked Walter how things have been in here for him. He said it wasn't bad until he was transferred down to this 'Step-Down' pod. These three guys have been pushing him around, knowing that if he gets into a fight with them he'll lose all his good time served and will have to do more time behind bars. Walter said two of the three have done their full sentence so they have nothing to lose; they have a definite release date. The only way they would get more time was if he ratted them out. Walter isn't a rat, no way.

When I asked, "What do they like to do?"

Walter said, "They would come over and take my food, or cigarettes. They are just bullies."

"I hate bullies. You have my back, right?"

"Don't fuck up your bail hearing, man."

"I won't be bullied and I don't give a fuck where I am." I could feel myself getting very aggressive again. If I was going to be challenged and turned down a physical confrontation, I would fail as a human and a

Sioux warrior. Three of them want to pick on a fellow Dirty Dozen member; let's see how they do with two of us.

Walter and I had just started playing some Euchre, when the three bullies approached us. This big but flabby red-headed kid was the leader of the three. The second kid looked Italian, maybe Portuguese, and he was fairly stocky. The third kid I could tell was just a tag-a-long; he was only tough with his buddies. He was a pretty boy, no scars on his face or on his knuckles, teeth were also too perfect; he would hightail if his friends started to take a beating.

I made sure when I sat down that I left myself room to throw a kick if necessary, until I could get up on my feet and fight. I also kept at least ten playing cards held real tight. Dad taught me years ago. How to maim or even kill someone with playing cards. Yeah, I guess dad was no Ward Cleaver. We did things just a little different in my household.

Red came up to us at the table. He was eating an apple and in-between bites he asked if I was a tough guy.

"I'm the toughest and meanest motherfucker you have ever met." Pretty Boy started to laugh, so I looked at him real serious, "After I knock out your boyfriends here, I'm going to fuck you right up the ass, pretty boy. By the way, I have this green puss coming out of the end of my dick, what do you think of that? We're gonna use it to lube up your ass." That stopped his laughing.

I looked at Red who was now going to take a bite of his apple. "Do you like magic tricks, Red?" I could tell he wasn't too amused with me as he snapped off a bite of his apple. Show time. I sprung up out of my chair, grabbed my own apple, and tossed it into the air. As it was on its way down I came across with the playing cards in my hand and sliced it. I retrieved the apple after it hit the floor; it had been sliced to the core. A simple twist of the wrist separated the two halves. I could tell my hand speed really stunned Red. "Next time it will be your throat. The jugular is a lot easier to slice up. Now do yourself a favor and fuck off before I make apple sauce out of you!"

Red didn't answer me. He and his two buddies just went back to their table. Red just sat there, still in shock. I blew 'pretty boy' a kiss; he never looked at me for the rest of the weekend. This Pod was now mine to rule, even if, hopefully, it would only be for the next forty-eight hours. No blood had been spilled and no chance of fucking up my bond/bail hearing. The only casualty was just an apple core split in half.

Later that afternoon my reputation was solidified by one of the guards. It was just before dinner when this big, and I do mean big, black guard came over to the table I was sitting at. I didn't know him from 'Jack Shit' but he certainly knew me. "Hey Strongbow, what the fuck are you doing in here? Shouldn't you be training for the United States Championships?"

I just looked at this half man, half beast. "Do I know you?"

"I saw every one of your fights boy. Man you can throw 'em. I saw you knock out everyone you faced. Why are you in here boy?" This guy was even bigger then John Derksen, there was no way I was going to insult him

"I knocked out my school vice-principal. He insulted my mom real bad so I knocked the fucker out cold. I can't fight for the States Championship because I tested positive for having weed in my system so the bastards disqualified me."

"That's a real drag man, being in here is also a real drag. Man you gotta smarten up, a life of crime is no good. Strongbow, you have so much potential with your fighting skills, use that aggression towards something else man. Anyways I know you're a tough kid, but you act up in my pod, I will kick your ass, understood?"

"Understood."

There seemed to be something else bothering John. I asked him what else was up. He didn't really seem to be himself.

"Mitch, do you blame me for Blais's death?"

"No man, why would I do that? Blais's old man is the one with blood on his hands. Blais was so scared of taking another beating if he was caught. It's bad luck that he just happened to slice a vital vein in his leg. You just happened to be with him when he died man. John, you got to let it go. I also believe Blais's old man would have eventually beaten him to death. Bad luck was Blais's downfall and contributed to his death."

I truly believe what I said, although I'm not sure how much John believed me. That's something he's going to have to sort out on his own, as I have enough shit in my life to worry about. I told John I'll see him shortly on the outside. He told me to have a cold beer and hot broad waiting for him at Dubrowski's.

I did what the guard said and I behaved myself. Before I knew it Monday morning was here and I was in the back of a paddy wagon on my way to the bail/bond hearing. What didn't behave itself was the damn dose. Every time I pissed, it burned. As soon as I'm released I have to see a doctor.

Handcuffed I was escorted through the back of the courtroom. Mom, Jake and Liz were in the front row. Cole sat beside me once it was my turn. Cole told the judge I had no prior convictions, had been under a great deal of stress, and had been on pain killers at the time of the assault, thus my judgment was impaired. I didn't pose a threat to the community.

The judge didn't appear to like the look of either Jake or me when he asked Cole if there was a father in my life. Cole told the judge that my dad died fighting for his country in Vietnam. The judge's face seemed to relax a bit once Cole told him about my dad.

Bail was set at fifty dollars. I was given a twenty-three hundred hour curfew, and he wanted a copy of my medical chart for my next hearing along with the list of prescription drugs that I'd been taking. Cole agreed, Jake had the cash and before I knew it, I was released to mom's custody.

I thanked Jake for posting bail and told Liz I had to talk to her about something. Mom just raised her eyebrow.

"Mom, trust me you don't want to hear this, just trust me please."

Mom agreed and said she would meet me outside in the car. Jake asked what was so important. I'm not sure big brother trusted me around Liz, so I talked in front of the both of them.

"I think I have the dose. What should I do?"

I told Liz the symptoms and she told me there's a

free clinic every Tuesday and Thursday, they would take care of me. Jake just shook his head, but he was smiling at least. I thanked both of them and said, "I better go with mom."

Jake told me to keep my nose clean because mom was pretty upset. I agreed. Jake then said he and Liz would be by for dinner later on that night.

The drive home was really tough. In my mind I was defending mom's reputation but every time I tried to bring up why I did what I did, mom said, "Not now Mitchell."

Those were the only words spoken by her and it was tearing me apart inside. A piece of me wishes I would have just walked away from Nash, but then another part of me wishes I would've sliced his throat. Just breaking his jaw and knocking him out wasn't good enough; nothing comes easy, does it.

After dinner that night Liz took Pam and Rachel to the show. I knew it was my turn to face mom's wrath. I also knew she had Jake in her corner, which is kind of strange. I know Jake would've put a bullet into Nash's head if he pissed him off as much as he pissed me off.

Mom started first, "Tell me your side of the story, son." I did as instructed, word for word, nothing fabricated. I not only told the verbal story, I told her how he hurt me emotionally deep inside, slamming her that way.

I did what dad would have done.

Jake jumped in "Dad wouldn't have hit him Mitch, remember what dad preached? Sometimes you have to use your brains over your brawn. I'm sure the old man would have been proud how you defended your mom. However, you set yourself up to lose by hitting him. Life is a war; sometimes you lose a few battles. Sometimes you just have to walk away and wait till the enemy puts his guard down, then you attack! Brute force isn't always the answer. Damn it, Mitch."

"I'm sorry to both of you."

"Mitchell, I'm an educator, and you attacked someone in my profession. Word gets around the school board real quick and as much as we women have made gains in the teaching profession, it is still the 'Old Boys' network who actually run the school board. I'm honored that you defended me, but you can't go around beating up everyone who agitates you in life. I have also tried to call in every favor I can, and it hurts me to say this, but the school board has suspended you for the rest of the school year. This will now put you two years behind everyone else your age, Mitchell. I can guarantee that Nash will make sure you have to find another school for next year. He may also call in favors to have you suspended indefinitely from any school in the Bay Area. Mitchell, you need an education son. It's the key to your success in life, not how well you can beat someone up."

We talked for a bit longer. I knew better then to argue about anything, just take my lumps like a man. Once Liz came back with Rachel and Pam, mom thanked Jake for his support and then she went to bed. She didn't look good at all, very worn down.

With mom in bed and Rachel doing her homework, Jake, Liz, Pam and I smoked a joint on the front porch. Pam busted my balls about how mom's been crying ever since I attacked Nash.

Not sure if I've ever felt so low in my life.

I woke up the next morning to an empty house. It was a really weird feeling. Normally I like the house to myself, but this was a real cold, lonely feeling. Everyone was in school or working.

Cole told me I wasn't allowed near the school grounds so I couldn't even see the Dirty Dozen until nighttime; the twenty-three hundred hour curfew was also hard.

Around noon, I received a call from Cole. It seems Nash went to the District Attorney's office and told them I'm suspended from school. The District Attorney said they talked to the judge and I had five days to find a full time job, or my bail would be revoked.

Cole told me the District Attorney's office used the old "Idle hands are evil hands" theory and the judge agreed. Damn, Nash was really getting to me, but I learned from what mom said last night. "Just walk away and be the bigger person."

I informed Cole that I work part-time at Popeye's on the weekends. Cole said, "Not good enough! They want a full time job, and they want a written statement from your employer on proof of employment."

I said I would work on that today. Right now, it is time to see what the hell this green ooze is coming from my penis once and for all. I took the bus to the free clinic. It was in the Haight Ashbury district. Lots of hippies hanging around there. Make peace not war, fuck them all too.

As I went to go inside I heard a female calling my name, and when I heard that voice these little butterflies in my stomach started to flutter. I turned around to see who was calling me. It was Natasha wearing this tie-dye t-shirt; she looked like one of the hippies.

"Mitch, what brings you down here?" She looked at me with a smile and a glow in her eyes, but I knew if I told her was there to get my dick looked at because it was seeping green ooze, that smile and glow would disappear real quick.

"My brother Jake, his girlfriend Liz volunteers here

periodically. She's a nurse. I was going to ask her if she wanted to go for a coffee if she was working." Damn I'm good on my feet at times. "If she isn't working, would you like to go for a coffee?"

"I would really like that, Mitch."

So I went through the motions, walked inside the clinic and was back out in thirty seconds. "Liz isn't working; where is a good place for coffee?"

Surprisingly Natasha took me by the hand and led me to the coffee shop a couple blocks away. I was shocked by her physical contact. Did this mean she and David broke up? The owner of the coffee shop asked for cash up front before he served us. Bastard, but I kept my cool and didn't cause a scene.

Once the owner served us our coffee Natasha commented to me, "What a fascist pig, man. He's like the rest of the establishment, trying to keep the youth down."

I laughed, "You sound like my older sister Pam. The man this, the man that. He probably has a family to feed. I don't dig his scene, but that's his gig right?"

Natasha stuck her tongue out at the owner when his back was turned to us; that made me howl. Then there was a moment of silence. We just looked deeply into each other's eyes until Natasha's face started to turn red. I was going to take Liz's advice and make my move for her. "Can I tell you something really personal Natasha?"

"Sure you can, but call me Tash if you're going to tell me something that personal." She took my hand and said, "I'm here for you. What's on your mind?"

I took a deep breath, all the while knowing there are just some things I could never tell her. "I've had the week from Hell." I paused and looked away. "In the past week I was almost killed. I was shot at while on my motorcycle. The bullet missed me but made contact with a friend of mine, who almost died and is in a hospital in Stockton. I crashed my motorcycle during the shooting and it was stolen as I took my friend to the hospital. I broke my collarbone once again during the shooting when I dumped my bike, so please don't punch me this time."

Tash laughed and promised she wouldn't punch me like she did before.

"I had my nose broken by another friend, over a deal gone wrong. I knocked out the vice-principal of my school and broke his jaw because he was degrading my mom, who is so pissed at me right now. I spent the weekend in jail, found out I'm suspended for the rest of the year, and the insurance may not pay for my bike. Then to make matters worse I was also suspended and stripped of my California Karate Championship because I had some Mary-Jane in my system. As a result there won't be any fighting in Hawaii, which was a lifelong dream. But you know what, seeing you here today wiped away all those bad memories, Tash. You've turned around all the negativity of the past week with that positive aura of yours."

Tash's eyes were starting to swell up with tears, "Your mom is a great person and a great teacher. Why would the Vice Principal say those things?"

"He said those things to hurt me. I guess it hurt me so much it ended up hurting him, but in the end it was mom who it hurt the worst. He was always a dick to me. I hope his jaw never mends properly and he talks like Daffy Duck. Hey speaking of Daffy Duck, how's your step-dad Barney Rubble doing? He didn't get mad that I was talking to you did he?"

"He's such a square, don't worry about it.

Tash and I talked for almost an hour. Her smile and beautiful blue eyes were helping erase the memories of a shitty week. The only time I was reminded of how crappy things were was when I had to go pee; the burning was getting worse. I have to get into the clinic and get treated, this can't wait any longer. I don't want to end up like Al Capone and have my brain meltdown on me.

Tash and I left the coffee shop, and I walked her back to the rally site where the other hippies were.

Once we were back I asked her was she still seeing David. I had to know!

"Mitch you will be the first person I call if David and me break up, I promised you that. We are so different, and yet in many ways so much alike. I really do enjoy your company."

I just smiled at Tash; I know her words were genuine and sincere. "I'm looking forward to the day the phone call comes, saying you're single." I wanted to kiss her so bad! I'm sure if there weren't so many people around, Tash would've given in and indeed kissed me. I can feel she wants to get closer, but I'm sure her moral values would stop her right now.

I told Tash while I'm down here I should get the doctor at the free clinic to have a look at my shoulder; yeah good cover story. Before I walked away Tash leaned in and gave me a hug goodbye. I didn't want to let go of hugging her, as I felt her positive life force embracing my battered and tortured soul, but I knew I had to. I needed to get my burning, puss oozing cock in for repairs and quick!

I just eyed Tash the entire way to the clinic, and she eyed me. I'm telling you with 100 % certainty, she'll be my girlfriend one day. I walked inside the clinic, took a number, sat down and filled out the proper paperwork. I used an alias, as God forbid anyone finds out I have, or had, the dose. The name I came up with was none other than Willie Hertz. I just sat on a chair and waited to hear my name or alias name called.

As I sat back I reflected on my time with Tash. I was falling for her big time. She was my drug, my addiction! The more time I spent with her, the more I wanted to be with her, all the time.

Then I heard my alias being called. *"Hertz, Willie Hertz,"* followed by the nurse also cursing as she finally figured out what my alias meant. The now agitated nurse took me into a room and asked what seemed to be my problem.

I told her and she told me, to drop my pants while she put on rubber gloves, and had a look for herself.

After examining me she said, "Stay here, the doctor will be right in."

When I asked her what she thought it was, she didn't answer. She just shot me this dirty look.

A couple of minutes later a doctor came in, had a look himself, squeezed a little bit of the green ooze out and then asked me if was I was straight.

I was confused by his question until he asked if I was a homosexual.

"Fuck No!" was my very abrupt answer. Whatever impure thoughts I had about Tash were very quickly dashed. The doctor reached down and pulled out the longest and biggest Q-Tip I've ever seen. "What is that for Doc?"

"I need to take a swab to see what exactly we are dealing with here."

I gulped and asked ever so sheepishly, "Where does the swab need to come from, just the top of my penis right? That Q-Tip is pretty damn long."

"No son, it's going right down your pee spout, all the way down. See what happens when you don't use protection and you play with dirty girls? Unless you want this again I really suggest you start to wear condoms; cuts down the odds of any sexual transmitted disease."

As the Q-Tip was slowly put all the way down my pee spout, it took everything in me not to pass out or have an anxiety attack. The doctor then asked me as he pulled the Q-Tip out, "How many sexual partners have you had in the last two weeks?"

I answered, "Three."

He said he would like their names so they can come in and be tested.

I had to think real quickly; no way could I mention Liz. If Jake ever found out I gave his girlfriend a sexual disease, he would kill us both. The only real name I gave was Lucy Thom. I honestly believed all along it was her that gave me this fucking God awful disease.

The doctor left the room for a bit, and came back in with this big freaking needle. If the Q-Tip didn't almost get me to pass out, this needle will do the job. I hated to ask where the needle was to go, but human nature is human nature, so I asked.

When the doctor said, my ass, whew, did I breathe a sigh of relief. The doctor said I have gonorrhea and to come back in a week for another needle.

He promised, "No more Q-Tip test," and he made me promise I knew the value of a condom!

After the Q-Tip dip test, your damn right I knew the value of a condom. Before I left, the receptionist at the front gave me a care package containing a six pack of condoms.

The next morning I received a phone call from Mr. Clinton at the insurance company. "Mr. Strongbow, "I have some bad news for you. I received a phone call from a Detective McBurney. They've found your motorcycle in the back of a burned out tractor-trailer. This was also a major crime scene! Since you didn't have fire insurance on your bike, your claim is now going to be denied."

I really wanted to tell Clinton I was going to drive down to his office and let him know how close he is to joining Bandito, but being out on a bail bond, that probably wasn't a good idea. "Why are you insulting my fucking intelligence. I do have theft insurance, correct?'

"Yes you do."

"If my bike wasn't stolen, it wouldn't have ended up in the back of a burned out tractor-trailer, now would it? You also talk about this being a crime scene. I already know that. McBurney and his partner grilled me for almost seven hours on this. They told me that one guy in the truck had his brains clean blown out of his head. I guess you could say he was allergic to lead! You're not allergic to lead, are you Mr. Clinton?

Clinton just snickered in a funny way. I could tell I was getting his full and undivided attention, "Now Mr. Clinton, I also understand you are located in the beautiful city of Anaheim. I heard there was a gruesome murder their last week at Disneyland, did you hear about that Mr. Clinton?"

"Yes I did."

"Guess how I heard about that murder, any idea? You're a smart man."

Clinton was now starting to stutter. I could smell the fear coming through the phone. "I'm not sure what that has to do with your insurance company, or your claim for that matter."

"Two of your finest detectives, Aylmer and Duff,

were here asking me about my connection to that murder. Damn, two different police forces, two different murders. How crazy do you suppose they think I really am to kill both of those people?

"I only get crazy when people totally piss me off, Mr. Clinton. However you're well on your way to driving me there, denying my claim and starting to piss me off. Now I've just spent the past weekend in jail here for knocking someone out and breaking their jaw. He wasn't even close to getting me as mad and crazy as I'm right now. I really think you should reconsider my claim, Mr. Clinton. Call me crazy, wait don't do that, you never know what may happen next. I do expect next time I hear from you, that it will be good news, Mr. Clinton."

I hung up the phone, and yes I think dad would be proud that I used my brain to intimidate Clinton. I can always deny the conversation if the cops want to talk to me. Clinton can't deny the fact that I have been questioned about both murders though.

Jake came by later on and said Cole informed him that I have to find a job within five days or my bail-bond would be revoked. Jake said, "Don Terek was so impressed and thankful for you saving his life. He could get you a job at his motorcycle repair shop, but Don has a criminal record and that would be deemed as unacceptable."

"So, lucky for you, Jerry is a union leader with the Longshoreman's Union. He can get you a job in Oakland working on the docks.

Jake said it's really physical work and it is night shifts only, from midnight to eight in the morning. Cole is going to the District Attorney's office to find out if a 23:00 curfew can be waived for this job.

I gave Jake the low down on Clinton and the insurance fiasco. Jake laughed but also reminded me, "A murder investigation is no laughing matter." He said, "For now, let Cole handle Clinton. You never know if the cops are going to tape the conversation."

Jake got this big smile on his face and asked if I wanted to go for a ride on the back of his bike. He said Don Terek is home and has asked to see me. I was more than happy to go and see Don; glad he is finally home.

Once we arrived at Don's house and we walked inside, I had the same feeling of accomplishment as when I won the California karate championship. Seeing Don alive and knowing I had a huge part in this made me feel real good, a very warm feeling. Don had his shoulder in a sling, looked a little pale and was still in obvious pain. He thanked me for saving his life and for showing great leadership in getting them safely out of the desert and him off to a hospital. "You know, Mitch, your old man trained you well. He would've been proud of you stepping up, being a good soldier and leading the way. I owe you bro."

I thanked Don, and also for the job offer, but Cole Winters said the judge and District Attorney's office would shoot down that idea.

When we were there I found it kind of strange that Don never offered me a beer. He let Jake help himself but no beer for me. I saved his life and he's worried because I'm a minor? Even when a joint was being passed around he told Jake, "None for Mitch." Hell, did Don have an enlightening?

Before we left, Don commented about how the insurance company was giving me the gears. We also talked about the murder of Bandito and the murder at Disneyland. Don couldn't stress enough that I keep the same story for the rest of my life. McBurney, Miller, Aylmer and Duff all visited him in the hospital, took a statement, and so far so good.

As Jake and I got up to leave Don said, "Here catch," and threw me the keys to his 1965 FL Electra Glide. "I can't drive it until my shoulder's healed. I hate for her to just sit there unappreciated. Hang onto her for me until we get the insurance issue straightened out, or until I'm able to ride again, but there are a few rules with borrowing Lola."

These guys all name their bike after some broad.

"# 1, no driving while loaded or if you're too high, and every Sunday Lola likes to be bathed and waxed. Are we clear on that? If you bring her back and Lola looks abused or misused I will personally kick your ass! Now, is your shoulder good enough to handle her?"

"Yeah I believe so Donnie and I promise you, I will take great care of Lola."

Lola was a lot heavier than my old Ironhead, but she drove so smooth. I decided to go for a run to Davis right through Napa Valley and just enjoy the feeling of being on the road again. I also decided to tempt fate and drove very slowly past Tash's jewelry store, hoping she was outside and maybe ask if she wanted to go with me. Unfortunately I didn't see Tash, just Barney Rubble, her step-dad, who gave me a dirty look, damn.

A couple of days later I heard from Cole. The judge agreed to our request to have my curfew waived and I was allowed to work on the docks. However, days off meant the curfew was back in place. The judge said he was greatly disappointed by the school board's decision. I also had to promise to return to school come September, and I agreed.

# ACT LIKE A MAN – WORK LIKE A MAN

I was only sixteen years old, a couple weeks from my seventeenth birthday, but I was a big tough kid, well over six feet tall and around one hundred and ninety pounds. I won the California full contact Karate Championship, had a right hand that would knock out a freight train, and lifted weights on a regular basis at my cousin Jerry's Gym, 'Popeye's.' I had also been involved in two murders, so yeah I was ready to join the working world, even if I was pushed into working by the court and school board. Wait, that's right I knocked out the Vice-Principal of my school, and that's why I'm now forced to work, which suited me just fine as school is really such a drag.

My cousin Jerry, the Chapter President of the Oakland Hell Hounds, also happened to be a union rep for the local dock workers in Oakland. He got me the job working the night shift from midnight till eight in the morning. I've spent many nights partying all night long, so I'm used to staying up late; this should be no problem.

Friday night I packed up with my steel-toed boots ready to work. Mom packed me a lunch and said to be careful. The only thing pissing me off about starting today was a house party at Kurt Wilson's. That was a first. None of us ever went to Kurt's house as his parents were deeply religious, or so we were told, though not by Kurt so who really knows. I also heard Kurt had an older sister who was just as much a mystery as his parents. Yeah, he certainly kept his private life quiet, maybe a little too quiet.

There's also a party at the Oakland Clubhouse tomorrow. They are having a fund raiser to help Don Terek while he's off work with his bullet wound; that should be fun. Throw in the Vigoda sisters with a six pack of condoms and I'm there, but instead I'm headed to the docks for my first day, or make that night, of work.

I parked my bike which drew the attention of my co-workers; Don had Hell Hound decals on his bike. They were there to not only show he was a full patch with the Hell Hounds but also to make sure that if anyone thought of stealing this bike, they would face the wrath of the Hell Hounds. Bike thefts are a great way to make a living, but stealing the wrong person's bike is a great way to die.

I knocked on the foreman's office door and was told to come in. He was a hard-nosed, cigar chomping, heavyset Italian, Bruno Valeri was his name. I could tell he wasn't expecting a new worker for his crew. He called his lead hand into the office and asked did he know anything about me starting today. Hey, maybe I'll be able to make the party at Wilson's after all.

Bruno wasn't impressed that I was only sixteen. He asked, was I healthy? I said, "I'm still nursing a shoulder injury". Yeah that went over real well. On a positive note he said that if I had the same work ethic as my Uncle Jack and Cousin Jerry, he would be happy to have me on his crew. Bruno asked, "Are you afraid of heights?"

"Not at all," was my answer.

Bruno grabbed me a hardhat and said, "Let's go for a walk and talk." Let me tell you, for a fat cigar smoking guy, Bruno was in not bad shape. I was impressed as we walked up and down all fifteen cargo cranes. Each crane was about twelve stories high; no doubt Bruno was testing me. Was I afraid of heights? Could I keep up with him? I passed both tests with flying colors. Bruno even had us on top of this one crane and then we walked right to the end of the trolley bridge, suspended out over the water. He asked what I thought.

"I really dig this, great view man." I always remember asking dad, could I go with him and learn to parachute? Now I truly appreciate why dad liked jumping from a plane so much, and why he signed up for Airborne; that adrenaline rush from being up so high and the view was outstanding.

After we walked up and down each cargo crane, Bruno took me to the workers' lunchroom. As I walked in I was eyed up and down by all. It doesn't matter whether it's a new school, new sports team, jail or a job, you are eyed to see whether you are threat, a good person, a jerk, or the nicest guy since Jesus H Christ himself. The key is how you handle yourself once you open your mouth.

Dad and Jake both taught me to always sit back and observe all, listen to their thoughts and opinions, see who is strong, who is weak, who can be trusted, and who can't. Check out the cliques and take it from there. I was a teenager among all these men, ranging from mid-twenties to late fifties, so keeping my mouth shut for now goes without saying.

I was put into a work crew of four people. We were the 'riggers' for the Oakland Docks. It was very physically demanding work but there was some down time. However, when a cargo crane had cable problems we had to jump into action. Each minute a crane was delayed cost one thousand dollars. When we weren't working on a cargo crane, we had to get cables ready to be threaded and these cables were made from really thick steel wire.

I'm no stranger to hard work. In the past I trained really hard for the Karate Championships, but nothing prepares you for pulling cables and climbing up and down the cargo cranes. It was real hard physical work. I was also taught how to use a torch, not just any torch, but a six-foot, hand held torch.

As the night went on fatigue became a bit of a factor; partying all night into the morning was a hell of a lot easier than working. My steel-toed work boots felt like they weighed fifty pounds each by the morning and the bottom of my feet were also starting to throb. My shoulder that was injured almost two weeks ago was in agony. I couldn't raise my arm above my head by the dawn and my fingers were also starting to swell.

I wondered how the party at Wilson's was going. I'm sure they were having a better time than I was. Oh well, tomorrow is the party for Terek at the clubhouse.

As the moon was approaching the end of its shift and dawn was beginning her shift, I had never seen a sunrise like that before. I was never so happy to see the morning sun. It was a rather humbling sight, not only for sore eyes, but also for everything else that was sore on my body.

The guys in my crew said I did a good night's work and asked if I wanted to go for breakfast with them. It was a custom on every last shift of the work week. I guess that was their way of welcoming me to the crew, I was hoping it also meant I was accepted as one of them. I agreed with a smile and thanks.

For the most part I was quiet at breakfast. To be honest, I was just freaking bagged tired from working. A couple of them asked how my cousin Jerry was doing. I never mentioned I was related to him, but I guess word travels quickly on the docks. I felt more alive after breakfast. The coffee also helped, but I knew I had to get my rest for the party tonight. So I told the boys I would see them Monday night.

The house was already empty by the time I got home; everyone had gone to school or work. It was kind of weird that people actually work through the night and now they must sleep through the day. I felt wide-awake after my shower so I just lay on my bed and had a couple tokes off my pot-pipe. I don't even remembering falling off to sleep, it was that fast. Once my body and mind knew it was time to rest, I was gone.

When I woke up, I didn't know where I was or what time of day it was. The clock showed it just shortly after five. Did I have school? I was clueless. It took me a couple minutes before I came to my senses. I definitely had to go to the washroom. It took all my strength just to get up out of bed. I didn't feel this damn sore after the Karate tourney or the trailer accident. My fingers hurt so much that even trying to clinch a fist hurt. Hell, my thighs, feet, gut muscles and shoulder were all seized; damn, this working for a living sucks ass. I was still really tired, sort of dizzy almost, so I figured I would crash for maybe another half-hour, then get cleaned up and head to the party at the clubhouse.

My next awakening was after eleven at night. Same as before, I woke up bewildered and hurting. Mom and Rachel were watching television as I staggered downstairs. Mom came over and asked if I was all right as I didn't look that good.

I told her I didn't feel that good and could she make me something to eat. She agreed and said Jake and Don phoned and were wondering where I was. Mom also told me, "I tried to wake you several times, but you didn't budge, stir, nothing. Just a little moaning in pain and that was it." I ate a fried egg sandwich, watched a little television with them, and then went back to bed.

I dragged my ass for the rest of the weekend. I apologized to Don for not making his fundraiser, but I was so done in from working. I think from now on, I'm really going to try and get an education; this working for a living really sucks. How the hell are you supposed to party and have fun, when you are tired all the time?

# HAPPY BIRTHDAY TO ME

Friday May 13, 1966, my seventeenth birthday. Normally I would be all hopped up to celebrate it. But I also had my final hearing for the assault case. Would I be blowing candles on a cake at home tonight or would I be asking for a cake with a file in it?

My body was finally getting used to the grind of working on the docks. Things were good down there; at least as good as a night shift worker went, although most of the money earned went to my lawyer Cole Winters. I was given the night off from work because I had court first thing in the morning. Everyone in my family was to show up in support of me.

At breakfast that morning, I was given gifts from my family members. Jake and Liz ate with us. I really dug the support from everyone. I might not be with them by the time the day was done so it was really appreciated. Mom handed me a present after everyone else had given me their gifts. I was a little perplexed as mom said with a smile, "it was from a secret admirer."

I opened up the gift. It was a tie-dyed t-shirt, like the hippies wear. Inside the box was a note, *"You don't think I could forget your birthday, seeing how you remembered mine."* It was signed Natasha Rubble. This note, the thought and the gift, put a nice smile on my face. I now felt good about my chances in court, damn,

Natasha Konstantinov remembered.

Before we went inside the courthouse I just took a deep breath, hugged mom and said, "Sorry." Mom smiled back at me and said, "All will be fine Mitchell".

As I was sitting beside Cole I felt more and more at ease, while the judge was reading several documents that the doctors had written about me. They were all about painkillers and the effects they can have on people. For some reason, the judge was really going over them thoroughly. Also in the courtroom was Vice-Principal Nash.

In the previous court sessions the District Attorney had tried to portray me as the next Al Capone. I was nothing but an out-of-control juvenile delinquent who resorted to violence when things didn't go my way. Cole did a great job in portraying me as a fatherless teenager whose dad died in battle for his country. He said I was belittled time after time by Vice-Principal Nash, who seemed to take great pride in taking away my self-esteem.

Cole also had medical testimony from the doctors in Stockton, stating that if it wasn't for me, Don Terek would have died. I was a true hero, and the stress caused by that week from hell, along with the painkillers, climaxed my anxiety into a rage against Nash, who I saw as nothing more than a bully.

Then the judge asked me to stand as he read his

verdict, "Mitchell Strongbow, after much careful consideration I find you guilty of aggravated assault. Even though this was your first criminal conviction, which leads to probation, I'm really torn in my decision. An assault upon an educator, in my opinion, is a very serious offense. I truly believe the educators in our society, more so now than ever before, have to shape and mold our youth's minds for the future, not Timothy Leary trying to poison their drug-induced minds. However when I take a look at your educator Vice-Principal Nash, and you Mr. Strongbow, you're no different than Hoffman and Leary. I have asked the San Francisco school board for any incidents involving you and other students."

"Mr. Nash, please stand before me. The defense and the school records show that you are indeed an agitator and abuse your position of power, but that doesn't condone what Strongbow did when he flexed his muscles."

"Mr. Strongbow, "I am sentencing you to six months' probation. The revised terms of your current curfew will be part of your probation. You must be enrolled in school this upcoming September, and you will maintain a seventy average in school. Should you fail on either one of these requirements, you will do the remainder of your probation in Juvenile Hall."

"I'm also not very happy with you, Mr. Nash. I will

be writing a letter to Bill Bain, the President of the San Francisco school board, about my findings towards you.

"Mr. Strongbow, I believe you have the potential to become a good, upstanding citizen in this community. I also believe you have potential to not only stand in front of me again, but before the adult judicial system. I'm giving you a chance to redeem yourself, to change your life around Mr. Strongbow. In the long run the final decision is up to you."

The judge asked my mom and Jake to stand up. "Mrs. Strongbow, as I look at you I see an educator and mother trying her best to raise her children without their father, and I commend you on your actions. However, I firmly believe with all my years spent on the 'Bench' here, that Mitchell's brother Jake will be his downfall. All children look up to their big brothers, especially with no other father figure in their lives."

"Jake Strongbow, do you want the best for your younger brother? "

Jake answered, "Of course I do!"

"Then be a positive figure in his life, not a negative one. Your lifestyle is your own, chosen as an adult. Mitchell is still trying to sort out his own destiny in life. With his mother trying to teach him to be a fine upstanding young man, for your brother's sake, don't interfere with her teachings."

Jake just nodded at the judge. His face was red with anger, but he knew to bite his tongue.

"Mitchell, do you understand what I just said to your brother and mother?"

"Yes I do sir,"

"Very well then, I hope for your sakes that I never see you standing before me again. I want to see your report card and school marks the last Friday of every month. I'm very serious Mitchell! This is your one and only chance to redeem yourself in front of the courts. failure to do so will result in time spent in jail." The judge slammed his gavel down and I breathed one hell of a sigh of relief.

My mom and sisters hugged me, as did Jake and Liz. As we stood on the court steps I kept hearing a song in my head playing, "I Feel Free" by Cream. Great song, great feeling.

Jake said he and Liz were going to split as they had things to do. He would really like to take the whole family out for a birthday/no jail time dinner tonight at Agresta's, where Jeannie Terek also works, his treat.

Mom said, "Sounds good 18:00 at Agresta's it is."

Jake also said that birthday or not, Donnie Terek is

feeling strong enough and misses his Lola. Don would like his bike back so just drive it to Agresta's tonight as he and Jeannie are coming along to celebrate my birthday. Reluctantly I agreed. I knew it had to happen sometime.

I hugged mom and both sisters and thanked them once again for their support. I also promised mom, "This has been a lesson well learned, and I will never get in trouble with the law again."

Mom said she was glad to hear it, and yet saddened that it took standing in front of a judge to learn what she has been preaching all along.

With everyone doing their own stuff, I looked at Lola, and decided I could use a nice long ride. Yeah you guessed right, I drove by Natasha's parent's place in hopes of seeing her. I wanted to thank her and ask did she want to go for a long ride with me. Natasha, however, was nowhere to be found; damn school!

As I headed out for my ride along the coast, I really appreciated what a beauty of a bike Donnie owned. It was a shame to have to give it back so soon. One day soon I will buy another bike, with or without the insurance company approving my claim. That is, of course, once I pay off my now destroyed bike and also all of my lawyer's fees. What the hell, Cole kept me out of Juvie Hall.

# SUMMER 1966
# "TURN ON, TUNE IN, DROP OUT"

"Turn on, Tune in, Drop out", this was the slogan for the summer of '66 not only in San Francisco, but also across the whole country.

For that slogan to truly mean what it implied, each person would have his own version of what it meant. The origins of this statement come from the man who made it famous, Timothy Leary.

Leary wanted the youth of America to 'Turn On'. He meant go within, to activate your neural and genetic equipment. Become sensitive to the many and various levels of consciousness, and the specific triggers that engage them. Drugs were one way to accomplish this end.

'Tune in' meant interact harmoniously with the world around you - externalize, materialize, express your new internal perspectives.

'Drop out' suggested an elective, selective, graceful process of detachment from involuntary or unconscious commitments. 'Drop Out' also meant self-reliance, a discovery of one's singularity, a commitment to mobility, choice, and change.

Unhappily, my explanations of this sequence of

personal development were often misinterpreted as he meant 'Get stoned and abandon all constructive activity.' And I have to admit, even though I had a disdain for hippies other than Natasha, I agreed with Leary. Even though I hadn't tried LSD, at least not yet. I was having enough fun with my dope and women; love the women. A fine piece of ass was just as good as any drug, and as just as addictive.

San Francisco was becoming a United Nations for freaks of all shapes, colors and forms. There were Hippies, Diggers, Bohemians, New Youth, New Left, New Negro, and of course the 'pharmaceutical religion.' It was being preached through LSD and other hallucinogenic drugs; everyone was just trying to get their kicks, get their groove on.

The music in the nation was also changing. Gone were the pop chart favorites despised by the sub-cultured youth. Instead an angry, mind awakening, alternative music was sweeping through the United States. Pat Boone, Frank Sinatra were just too square. They were seen as the 'Establishment.' This is what the establishment wanted you to listen to and buy with the almighty American dollar.

Leading the change in music revolution, you need look no further than the San Francisco music scene, where it was based. The Dead, Janis, Jefferson Airplane, Quicksilver Messenger Service, these cats and chicks knew how to reach the youth of America. Whether it was at the Fillmore, the Fire House, the Avalon Ball Room or even the Drunken Leprechaun; everyone got their kicks from all these talented and upcoming musicians.

Outdoor festivals were becoming a gathering place for all the youth. This also gave the different musicians a chance to play in public and provided great exposure. On stage of course, you would have poets, anti-war organizers preaching peace and love, mimes, and comedy troupes. As far as I was concerned, the world was quite frankly going insane, but what the hell. I was always guaranteed a piece of ass, good weed and kickass wine at these outdoor festivals, and from time to time a great brawl would erupt.

"Make Love Not War", fuck that bullshit! Hell my dad died, so we could all have this freedom that we're accustomed to in the United States. These Hippies and other freaks would degrade what he died for and believed in. It didn't take me long before I was punching someone out at a festival; after I got laid of course. Hippie chicks were good for that. I'll make love to you baby, then I will go to war and beat your old man out of his drugs or whatever else I could use.

I really wanted to get my night time kicks in the summer of '66. However, my eleven P.M. court appointed curfew, no motorcycle, and all my funds going towards my lawyer's fees really put a cramp in my style. Jake, to a certain degree, actually paid attention to either what the judge or perhaps mom had to say. I was limited in my involvement with the Hell Hounds, no more club runs and limited time spent at the Oakland Clubhouse.

Lately the Hell Hounds had been flexing their muscles not only in California, but also across several other states as well. Dick Coltrane was now the President of the San Francisco Chapter. It seems the old President Dave Ballard went on a fishing trip and actually became fish bait.

Von Kruger really wanted the Hell Hounds to challenge for the heroin and speed trafficking trade in North America, not just muscle for hire by certain Mafia organizations. Ballard was playing both the Battaglia, the head Mafia family in San Francisco, and the D 'Angelo family of Sacramento, against each other for his own personal gain with no proceeds going towards the Hell Hound's kitty.

I had by now scored with over twenty women, and I still wear a condom. Ever since my run in with the evil gonorrhea and that damn Q-Tip, the experience will be forever etched in my brain.

I would see Natasha about town from time to time, but unfortunately she was still with David. She was more of a hippie than he was. I was gaining all kinds of sexual experience from the Vigoda sisters as well as a couple of other older women that would let me play. I knew when the time ever came for Natasha and I to ever get it on, I would rock her world in a way David never would, could, or even should.

I've never had feelings towards someone like I have for her. Hell, normally I would just erase her from my memory banks, but I couldn't. I would see her from time to time and get those butterflies fluttering in my gut. I'm positive she had the same feelings, as her face would light up and her cheeks would go red when we made eye contact with each other. One day, she will be mine.

Liz and I never made out again but I could still feel chemistry between the two of us. Lucy and I don't even talk anymore. John Walters is finally out of Juvie Hall and I really do believe he still blames himself for the Blais's death, as he is really hard-core into the drugs.

Speaking of drugs, the new drug of choice sweeping the nation was this LSD, a man-made hallucinogenic almost like, but more intense than, peyote or magical mushrooms. Hippies were doing large doses of LSD, and it seemed they had adopted San Francisco as their homeland. Lots of guys in the Hell Hounds were doing LSD, including Jake and

Jerry. Several of the Dirty Dozen had tried it, but as much as I wanted to, so far I hadn't. I kept hearing that little voice in the back of my head saying, "Don't do anything that will kill your soul." Kind of weird actually because Jake does it, and he's that little voice I keep hearing. So I stuck to my weed and weed bi-products, 'downers' from time to time, and of course booze, but my first drug of choice was women.

I was eventually presented with a Black Belt in Karate from Charlie Adams, but I never did go back and train in the Dojo again; it had left this bad taste in my mouth. It was nothing personal against Charlie. However, the way I lost my title and then wasn't allowed to compete for the USA Championship, or any other sanctioned tournament, soured me about the whole Karate Association.

I was working out at Popeye's on a regular basis and was really starting to show results. I was now over two hundred and fifteen pounds. Work was all right. I saw lots of illegal activities take place on the docks, but I kept my mouth shut to my fellow co-workers. Although I did mention several activities that were of interest to Jake and Jerry. I thought perhaps there could be some sort of financial gain for the three of us.

One day in particular, Jake came by and picked me up after I told him a story about the previous night's work. I had seen several Cadillac's on the docks at around two in the morning. A ship from Taiwan had just arrived and the people from the Caddies walked right up the gang plank to the ship.

Jake took me to the Drunken Leprechaun. Once inside, we were taken to Joseph O'Reilly's private office. Inside were several very heavy set Italians in suits. The one Italian who seemed to be in charge was Sonny Battaglia; he was the New York Mafia's choice to run their criminal enterprise in California. I knew exactly who he was. Anyone involved in any criminal activity knew who Sonny Battaglia was, and you feared a man of his power.

Jake introduced me to Sonny. He was a very cold person, and there was a very dark ominous aura about the man. He had a weathered face and his eyes were like a Great White Shark, very cold and ruthless. As I stood there, Sonny just eyed me real closely up and down. At first it kind of gave me the creeps. Was I being viewed like a cattle buyer? Was Sonny looking for any sign of fear coming from me, a sign perhaps of weakness.

"I understand you work on the docks?"

Jake taught me to treat people with power in the underworld with respect. Do not act tough or cool; be yourself and even be humble. "Yes sir I do, I work steady nights there."

"I also understand you saw some vehicle and human traffic last night?"

"Yes sir, around 02:00, I saw two Cadillac's pull up to a ship that just arrived from Taiwan. They boarded the gang plank and went on to the ship till about 04:30."

"Did you get a good look at these people? If you saw them again, would you recognize them?"

"Yes sir, I would be able to recognize them."

"How old are you, kid?"

"I'm seventeen, sir."

"I have a son, Michael, a couple years older than you. He is in Stanford. Do you go to school?"

"I was suspended for knocking out my Vice Principal. I'm going back in September though, to finish off my education.

"Good for you. I heard you're a good fighter and you seem to be a smart kid. Should things not work out, get your brother to get a hold of me. I could always use some young muscle."

"Thank you sir, I will keep that in mind. Anything else sir?"

"Yeah, do me a favor kid, go grab a hamburger and shake, don't leave the restaurant. I might have something for you." Sonny then passed me a twenty dollar bill and I did as told. I sat out front and ordered a hamburger, fries and a shake.

Before my food arrived, Jake and Joseph O'Reilly came by and sat with me at my booth. I asked Jake, "How did I do?" Jake answered, "You did a real good job. Sonny liked you and he has a job for you."

Damn, does he want me to whack someone? I'm not sure I could do that after seeing the murder at Disney up close and personal, not to mention the killing in the desert.

Jake told me to sit at another booth, one that faced the entrance to the Drunken Leprechaun. Jake said, "Some people are going to come in, and they are going to ask to see Joseph in the back room. We just want to know if these were the same people that you saw on the docks." Jake stressed that I had to be 100% correct. I wondered why?

After about twenty minutes three Italians showed up looking for Joseph, and they headed to the back. Jake came out and asked, "Were they the three?" I said, "No." Ten minutes later, four more Italians came in. There was no doubt in my mind, they were the four from last night. I told Jake my answer. He said, thanks, and for me to go home now. I didn't ask why. I just did as told and left without hesitation.

A couple of days passed and Jake said, "Let's go for a ride." We drove down to San Jose for some fish and chips. As we were sitting on the wharf eating our food Jake told me he had a question, no, make that a proposition for me. "I'm going to ask you something, no pressure, just something to think about. Either way I will be happy with your answer."

"Sonny Battaglia was quite impressed with you, Mitch. Most of the people he has working for him are heat scores to a certain degree and bring heat onto themselves by their lifestyle and stupidity. Sonny would like you to be his spy, shall we say, while you are on nights. You aren't to report back to him, you are to report anything to Joseph O'Reilly or myself. Mitch, you must keep this very hush- hush, no one is to know who you are working for. Joseph will give you directions, you will also be paid very well, and you won't be breaking any laws. I think it is a great way to make fast cash while making some solid criminal contacts."

Without hesitation I said, "Count me in, I will be discreet. Sonny knows that I have to go back to school in September, or I go to jail right?"

"Yeah he knows this Mitch. I'm glad to hear you are in, and also glad to hear that school is a part of your future."

'Now I can finally make some money that doesn't go to lawyers, and I can buy myself another bike. Man, I hate beating the feet to get around." Jake started to laugh.

When I asked, "What was so funny?"

"Something told me you would say that, and now you can go out and buy a new bike. Sonny Battaglia made a few phone calls on your behalf and guess what? You will be getting the insurance check for your stolen bike. I would say probably in two days or so."

I was so happy. Damn this was great news. "Can we go down and see Donnie Terek? He said that he could get me a deal on a bike once I get some cash."

Jake said, "Sure, let's go and see what kind of bikes Donnie has available."

We couldn't arrive at Don's motorcycle shop fast enough, and once we looked around it didn't take me long to find my next bike. It was a 1955 Harley Davidson Panhead FL, painted midnight black with lots of chrome. It was a fair amount bigger in size and power than my old Ironhead, but I knew I could handle the extra weight and power after riding Don's bike when he was injured.

Jake knew I wanted to take the bike home so he paid cash for it. I would just pay him back with the insurance money and from working. That is, after all, what big brothers are for.

I phoned mom and told her I wouldn't be home for supper, but assured her I would be home in time for my curfew.

Don, Jake and I went for a long ride, all the way to Big Sur. It was great bonding time with my brother and his best friend, the man whose life I saved.

Once school was finally let out for the year, the partying really started. Even though I still had my curfew on weekends, and had to work steady nights; I still liked to catch a good bu*zz*. Like any smart soldier, I found a way to get around my curfew for partying purposes; well sort of.

I would get off at eight in the morning and if there happened to be an all-night kick ass party, I would head there right after work. I would get right into the booze and weed, and let me tell you, with no sleep after working all night. It didn't take much before you were hammered. It was a different kind of bu*zz,* and sometimes I wouldn't get any sleep before heading back for another night shift on the docks.

I'm not superman, and like anyone else I needed proper sleep, or I did until I was introduced to Amphetamines. 'Beans, Uppers, Bennies' they looked like an aspirin pill but contained speed, and yes these are the same pills that the Wizard offered me when I was fighting for the California Championship. I actually turned him down, I wanted to win the tourney fair and square, and you know how that turned out; still pissed by the way, enough of that rant.

I would pop the pills and within twenty minutes the hairs on my head felt like they had static electricity. They decreased appetite and increased stamina and sex drive. When mixed with weed and booze, and I mean large amounts of booze could be consumed while on these beans, they gave you advanced stages of euphoria. I now know why injecting speed was becoming so popular and so financially rewarding, as it was quite the rush.

I remember leaving an outdoor festival down by the bay, sitting on top of a cargo crane, and still being able to listen to the music and see the mass of concert goers. It was quite the view being that high up.

The only view I didn't enjoy from the top of a cargo crane was seeing the transport ships full of soldiers, marines or naval personnel, heading west towards the Pacific Ocean and knowing their next stop would be Vietnam. As they would pass under the Golden Gate Bridge, I wondered how many of them would never see home again. The next time some of them would be on American soil, they could be in a flagged, draped casket, just like dad. Now that was a true bu*zz* killer, no matter what drug you were tripping on.

Every day the TV brought footage of the war waging in Vietnam right into our living rooms. That is when the respect for dad and his values became so clear to me. TURN ON the television, TUNE IN to the gallant soldiers fighting for their country, and I wanted to DROP OUT of school to fight in Vietnam and be a proud American. I wonder what Leary would have thought of my statement; in retrospect to what his statement meant? Fuck him, he's just a commie hippie anyways.

The summer seemed to drag on forever and I was actually looking forward to going back to school. Working steady nights had its benefits, but I missed having a normal Monday to Friday routine. I missed playing football for the school, missed all the female students; well maybe not all of them. I missed just being a kid, I guess!

Mom always said to enjoy the teenage years, because when you're an adult, you will have the struggles of the world on your shoulders. You screw up as a teenager from time to time, it is expected, and can be forgiven in most cases. However once you're an adult, the rules to the game changes.

I left my job at the docks one week early to have a little fun before heading back to school. Sonny Battaglia said I did a good job and if I ever decide to choose an alternative way of making a living to come and see him. I'm not sure if I could really handle that lifestyle. I know for sure one of the men in the one

Cadillac who I recognized was later found with cement weights attached to his ankles at the bottom of the San Francisco Bay.

It bothered me a bit I guess, but ever since the two killings earlier in the year, I saw this as a justifiable action, and an alternative means of making a living. Yeah, the value I placed on human life has changed, and not for the better. I found myself more aggressive in any physical confrontation on the streets, but always aware that I'm on probation. I have been fingerprinted and the cops now have a mug shot of me; they know exactly who I am. The fact that I'm also a Strongbow and related to Jake and Jerry; it meant I had more heat on me than most.

Mr. Nash, my beloved Vice Principal, is no longer at my school. He was transferred. The school board made it very clear. There would be no tolerance for any infractions. I would be expelled, not only from my school but from all the schools in the Bay area, and they would immediately let the Select Service Committee know that I was eligible for the draft and to serve my country.

Just to break my balls and heart even more, the school board suspended me from playing football. After last year's antics during the Championship game my school wouldn't even allow me to help coach the boys. I really miss the camaraderie and team bonding.

I couldn't see or hear the chains that were shackled to me by the school board, but I could sure as hell feel them, and they were getting heavier day by day. Damn judge wants a seventy average, or I'm thrown in Juvie Hall. The idea of just going through the motions and getting high before every single class was no longer an option. Not that it stopped me from, shall we say, bribing other students to do my homework for me. Weed, beans, and Jane Cooper's breasts were all used as tools of bribery. Dad always said, "Adapt to all situations" and that is what I did.

I think about the actions or non-actions that really hurt the most was that I wasn't allowed to go to hunt camp. My probation officer forbade me to go. He said they wanted to make a kinder, and gentler human being out of me; killing deer would only bring out the animal in me.

Even though Cole Winters and I tried to use the 'Heritage' angle, I was still denied. Sometimes I think the hippies weren't that far off with their marches and demonstrations against the establishment keeping a person's rights down; sometimes.

# FREEDOM - NOVEMBER 13 1966

Ritchie Havens had this song called 'Freedom' which he performed amazingly at Woodstock. In the song, he sings that he feels like a motherless child. Well I was a fatherless child.

Today was to be the last day of my probation. My freedom had finally arrived, and I could rid myself of these chains. Yeah, we were eleven days from Thanksgiving, but mine came early. The greatest upside of no more probation was no more curfew!

When I would go to parties on the weekend, I knew I had to be home by eleven P.M. or I broke my curfew and would have screwed up my probation. My probation officer would come by and check once every two weeks or so just to make sure I was indeed home. Hell, he would even send a patrol car over to make sure I was home. With all the stress I've put on mom in the last year or so, I didn't want to hurt her anymore than what I had already done.

If I was at a party and had my eye on a girl, and wanted to either get to know her better or have sex with her, I had to have the whole flirt, pick up, foreplay, and sex done in time so I could be home by eleven; now that was pressure.

Even the pressure not to totally beat someone

senseless was hard. Hell, I would go to certain parties, invited or playing the part of a door crasher. The Dirty Dozen were really getting a nasty reputation as people who you don't want to fuck with.

From time to time, someone would call me out to fight. I had to think to myself, would this guy charge me with assault if I kicked the shit right out of him? I never had any fear of losing a fight and was always more than willing to either fight as an individual or as a gang. I just didn't want any new charges while on probation.

After Thanksgiving dinner while Jake and I were having a cigar on the front porch, I asked if he could get me set up with the Wizard. He was the Oakland Hell Hound drug dealer.

Jake smiled and asked, "What are you thinking of moving?"

I said, "Just weed, some oil and hash, maybe some beans, nothing that would get me in too much trouble. There's just so much money to be made, and the cops hate the hippies so much, they will be the heat score, not me. Jake, you have all these hippies coming here from all over the world, and they need to score. There's just so much cash to be made, man, and with me staying away from Lucy Thom, well she was my main source before."

Jake said to come by the clubhouse this weekend,

and he will get me in to see the Wizard.

Before heading over to the clubhouse and talking to the Wizard, I needed a partner I could truly trust, a good business partner with good business sense, and yet the ability to be ruthless if need be. There really was only one choice. Norm Sinker. I would go halves on everything from now on with Norm. He would get the exact price I was paying but we agreed not to step on each other's turf as far as our drug customers went.

We also agreed to charge the same price to all our clients, thus no bidding war or loss in profits. No trying to out duel each other. Even though I had chosen Norm as my partner and trusted him totally, I never told him exactly who I was getting the drugs from. I'm sure he figured it was from someone in the club, but speculation never arrested anyone.

Ricky Thom and John Walter were the only other members of the Dirty Dozen that were selling drugs. Walter was on a downward spiral and couldn't be dependable. His profits went right back into his body, via drug use. Ricky was just plain ruthless and he liked to rip people off; he couldn't see the bigger picture when it came to dealing. He's still that little slut Lucy's brother. It shouldn't make a difference but it did, so no drug deals with Ricky.

After sitting down and discussing prices with the Wizard, I was in shock. He would give the same price as a Hell Hound, which was basically fifty percent cheaper than what I was paying before through Lucy. Fucking cunt must have been ripping me off.

The Wizard was also a very shrewd businessman himself. He had certain rules I had to follow, or I could go somewhere else to get my drugs. One fuck up and I was history, no matter who I was related to.

Rule # 1, no strangers were to be present when the Wizard would drop drugs off, or when I asked about purchasing them.

Rule # 2, no drug talk over any phone no matter how safe I thought the phone was.

Rule # 3, when paying in cash the smallest bill would be a ten dollar bill; twenties and fifties were preferred.

Rule # 4, the Wizard would front me drugs but it would cost me more, an extra ten percent, and a ten percent interest rate per day of non-payment in full.

Rule #5, The biggest rule from the Wizard was courtesy of Jake; no chemicals to be dealt. Jake said if he finds out I am dealing or doing chemicals, he would shoot the Wizard between the eyes, and I'm not worth being shot over.

I shook the Wizards hand and said, "Let's do some business! Norm and I had enough cash for two pounds of weed, and a five-gram vial of hash oil."

By Christmas, I had made over a thousand dollars profit. I always had an ounce of personal weed and usually some oil and hash, not to mention the power and prestige that went along with being a dealer. I still had students on the take doing my homework. Why change things now that I'm off probation?

To cover my tracks as much as possible I continued working part-time at Popeye's on the weekends. I never had to touch my earnings from the gym, and the dealing money also covered my bike insurance, taking dates to the show or dinner or even a concert. Mom had only a single income so there's no way would I hit her up for cash, and it was really cool actually buying everyone in my family Christmas gifts with my own cash.

The only trouble I ever had was with this rich Jewish kid, Hyman Rothstein from Snob Hill. I guess some of his drug customers liked my prices better and I was being a real pain in his ass taking his customers away. He put the word out on the street how he was going to fuck me up real bad; he didn't care how tough my reputation was or who I knew.

I went to Jake for advice and he did a background check on Rothstein. He was some doctor's kid, no real hardcore connections. He had his little street gang including David, yes Natasha's boyfriend David; this might get interesting.

Two days before Christmas I received a phone call from Jake. "Hyman Rothstein is playing billiards in a pool hall named Chicky's." Jake knew the owner of Chicky's and told him to make sure that Rothstein stayed there until we arrived.

He was there with five other guys, so Jake got on the blower. The statement we were about to deliver was going to be very loud, and very clear.

Jake said he would meet me in front of Chicky's. I called Scott Kantonescu and Fraser Dalton and said, "I need to settle some business." Man, with Rothstein being a Jew, too damn bad Herman was out for the count with the flu. He would have jerked off in excitement at the thought of laying a beating on these guys.

Scott and Fraser also had their own Harleys, so we all drove over together. Jake was already there with Fraser's brother Caleb, Big John Derksen, Don Terek and Johnny "Mad Dog" Kantonescu, whom I have not seen since the murder in the desert.

Jake told me in front of everyone else this is my beef; he and his boys are just there to shoot a game of pool. Go in and prove myself to these street punks, let them know you are a person not to be fucked with. The message has to be sent so other street punks won't also become a thorn in my side.

Scott, Fraser and myself walked in first and asked

for a table, all the while scouting the joint out, seeing how many witness there were. Chicky asked if I was a Strongbow. I just smiled and said, "Yeah." He told me right off the bat, "Anything you break, you pay for." "Good enough", was my reply.

I asked for a table right beside Rothstein. As the three of us walked towards our table, I was trying to figure out exactly which person was Rothstein. Well, I knew who David was, so that left only four to choose from. David, I knew, would tip his hand as to who Rothstein was.

David didn't fail me. As soon as he recognized me, he went over to this one individual and whispered something into his ear. I knew it wasn't some sort of Jewish foreplay, although it did bring a smile to Rothstein's face and direct eye contact with me.

Fraser was racking up the balls when Jake and his crew walked in, two in the back door and three through the front door. There was only one other table being used in the pool hall. I guess they spotted the danger signs and knew there could be impending danger. They paid Chicky and abruptly left the pool hall. That just left five Hell Hounds, three Dirty Dozen and Rothstein and his party of five.

Jake told Chicky to go for a walk. Jake didn't come over. He and the other Hell Hounds just racked up the balls and started to shoot pool. What they did though, was they shot pool at the tables closest to both entrances. With the pool hall now empty of witnesses and the Hell Hounds making sure no one else would come in or leave, I walked over with a pool cue to David and his friends.

"David, how are you doing? You seemed to have healed up pretty good from the last time we met." A huge part of me wanted to ask how Natasha was. However, I remember what mom told me after the big football brawl. *"If I truly like her, why embarrass or hurt her?"* Yeah, I didn't want David taking anything out on her.

I could tell that David was nervous. He had this fear, the same exact fear he showed in the ring. "David, I'm looking for a Hyman Rothstein. Word on the street is that he wants to fuck me up real bad. Now, none of your girlfriends here would be Hyman Rothstein, would they?"

I walked towards the person who David first whispered to when we came in. This guy tried to pick up a billiard ball ever so on the sly, but I spotted his actions. "Why the fuck would your parents name you after a female body part?"

Hyman tried to whack me with the billiard ball he was hiding in his right hand. He swung and missed. I countered by nailing him with a left hook, and then I grabbed him by his hair, and drove him face first right into the billiard table.

One of Hyman's friends tried to come at me with a pool cue in his hand, but Fraser interrupted that action and whacked him in back of the head before he succeeded in his mission. He was knocked out cold. Scott looked at the remaining three and asked if they would like to go 'night-night' like their buddy. None of them moved, they just watched in horror at me in a full rage.

I lifted Hyman's bloody face off the table by his hair, "You still want to fuck me up?" I grabbed the eight ball that was on the table and drove it right into Hyman's face. His perfectly aligned white teeth went flying from one billiard pocket to another. Hyman wasn't quite knocked cold, but he was in a world of hurt. I reached inside his pocket and took whatever cash he had on him. I told David to make sure Chicky gets this cash. I'm not sure how much it costs to get blood out of the felt tablecloth. David was scared shitless. He was terrified as he came over to get the cash.

"David, I have a message for your friend here once he comes back to his senses. If I ever hear word that he wants to fuck me up, or plans on any retaliation, the pain I will inflict upon him will be far more evil and deviant than what the Nazis did at the death camps." David didn't answer, he just nodded his head.

I walked over to the other pals of David's. "Any of you three wanna go me right now, one on one?" None of the three even looked me in the eye. "If any of you call the cops, I will fuck you up as well."

I asked for a piece of ID from all of them and wrote down the information. "I know where you all live. I will burn down your houses and kill everyone living inside if the cops are called. David, don't disappoint me. Make sure Chicky gets that cash."

Jake asked if I was finished.

"Yeah. I'm done big brother."

Jake and his Hell Hounds walked over to David and his friends, they walked by each and every one of them ever so slowly, just to let them know they are truly fucking with the wrong person. John Kantonescu barked at one guy and he started to break down and cry; now that was classic.

The eight of us left Chicky's and rode off back to the clubhouse. Jake said I did well, real well. I thanked him and the other Hell Hounds for their support.

Lucky for Hyman and I guess myself to a certain degree, Hyman never did cause trouble again. Never a peep was heard from him. Maybe I should shake down his parents for helping straighten up their delinquent son, lord knows they couldn't.

# SACRED FIRE
# DECEMBER 31, 1966

New Year's Eve, a great excuse to party and hopefully pick up a chick, and even more hopefully get laid. The Oakland Hell Hound chapter was having a big bash with some local musician and his group, his name was Carlos something. His group was all the talk of San Francisco, as they were born from its underbelly. Carlos would always get his drugs from the Wizard and that was the connection.

The mutual deal was that Carlos would perform for a pound of hash and all the booze his band could drink. The parties at the clubhouse were always wild with lots of booze, drugs and by the end of the night, naked chicks wanting to get laid. Let's face it, this was every seventeen-year-old guy's fantasy! I have lived it several times.

The only rule Jake had for me was, as always, no chemicals. As far as the drugs went, pot, hash or oil was acceptable. If I were to dip into chemicals, he would beat me. If anybody in the club were to give me anything hard, he would kill them. Jake always drilled that into my head, "Don't do anything that can kill your soul."

Around ten A.M. I was hooking up with Wizard. He was fronting me a pound of pot for $120. Norm

Sinker my drug partner, was going halves with me. With eight ounces of weed each, we would sell an ounce for $15. We would never make a large profit but when you are seventeen years old, how much do you really need?

Well, you make sure you have your personal stash of dope, enough money for gas, and insurance for my bike. If I wanted to take someone out on a date, I didn't have to hit mom up for money. After all, she was the only bread earner in the house, with Pam in college, and Rachel and I still in High school. How could I hit her up for cash?

Jake was cool with this but he told me to be careful and if I was busted, I was on my own. High Risk, High Reward, I guess you could say.

As expected the Wizard was right on time. Mom and my sisters were shopping for groceries, so it was imperative that he arrived when they had gone out. I guess being the Oakland club's main drug dealer makes you a business man, even if it's illegal business. Like any business man, you don't want to lose customers.

Wizard brought the compressed pound all in one bag. He was told by a lawyer that if you were to bring sixteen, one ounce bags, you would be charge with trafficking. This way all together, it's just possession.

Once he left I separated and weighed all the pot,

and as luck would have it, I even made out with an extra ounce, as the weed weighed heavy. I guess the guys who compressed and weighed the pot were a little high at the time; my gain, sorry Norm! High Risk, High Reward! I did the work and brought it over to his house. There was always the possibility of being busted on the way over.

I would never carry drugs while driving my motorcycle by myself, or make that, large amounts of drugs. Cops hate bikers and we're always a heat score, being continuously pulled over and searched for either drugs or guns. I would take the bus over or get a ride with mom. I told mom, "My bike's misfiring, could I get a ride over to Norm's?"

I hung at Norm's and we smoked a joint, just to make sure our investment was good stuff. My goal for tonight was to make it back to the Oakland clubhouse before midnight. Norm had been there once, but the club really frowned upon anyone under age. Norm was going to his cousin Gail's for a house party. He was to sell her an ounce and if luck would have it, perhaps he could move the rest of his weed to other partiers.

Norm asked me, "Do you want to go the party for a bit? Not only as back up for him, as when you deal people are always trying to rip you off, but also his cousin liked the look of me. She did nothing for me sexually. Well, maybe a six pack would help.

I was ready to turn Norm down, when he said something that caught my attention. "That blonde broad you masturbate over every day, what was her name? Natasha, yeah she will be there at Gail's, they're close friends. Remember?"

Now what kind of business partner would I be to Norm, not covering his back? Of course I will go to Gail's party. Damn Natasha. I have often thought about her right from the very first time I met her. I really fell 'head over heels' for her. Having that cup of coffee with her before I went to the free clinic, she would look at me with those beautiful blue eyes and her mystical smile. Naturally, her boyfriend David would or should be with her tonight. However, I already broke his nose once. He wouldn't be a problem even if he wanted to be. I would just kick his ass once again.

A week ago I laid a beating on his one friend, so hopefully that memory is still fresh in his head. Perhaps a fist drilled into his head will remind him I'm not a person to fuck with. Perhaps even to impress Natasha again, I might just have to do that. When I broke David's nose in the tournament, she shot me the dirtiest look, but she smiled at me later on. She kind of gave me the, "he's an asshole and deserved it" impression. She was also there with mom and my sisters when I finally won the tournament.

Perhaps she really dug what a good fighter and animal I could be. Was it my power, my looks or just wishful thinking on my part? Hopefully, I will find out in a couple of hours. I really found the conversation and body language spoke volumes, that we both had feelings for each other. Only her boyfriend is getting in the way. I feel it, I know it and I believe I will convince her that me being a non-Jew is not the end of the world.

I took a bus home from Norm's and took a long shower, making sure I scrubbed every part of my body and that I smelled good for tonight. I was extra careful not to scrub my penis too hard, as hopefully Natasha will take care of that herself tonight. Now the real test was, what to wear?

I wanted to impress Natasha by wearing my super tight jeans, but if I had to fight, I wouldn't be able to use my legs. So I just put on my normal jeans, a Hell Hounds Oakland T-shirt, my leather jacket and my bikers boots. I stuffed an ounce of weed down my pants, jumped on my bike and headed back to Norm's where the rest of our motley crew, the Dirty Dozen, would hook up.

We were no Hell Hounds, but for a bunch of high school kids, we were all really tough and always backed each other up. We were starting to get a real good reputation in San Francisco, and also Oakland, for being a solid youth gang who took no shit and could really fight, steal and deal.

Gail told Norm he could bring the Dirty Dozen as soon as her parents took off to Vegas for the New Year. I believe Gail also wanted us there to make sure no one acted up, or tried to destroy her parent's house, as her and Norm were cousins. She knew the crew would make sure of this.

Fraser Dalton and Scott Kantonescu rode their Harleys, with a girl on the back of each bike. After we made a liquor store run, I lead the charge on the way to the party.

I had Jane Cooper on the back of my bike. I promised her a ride the last time I fucked her. She was just a fuck friend nothing more, nothing less. I was a bit worried that if Natasha saw her on the back of my bike she would think we were an item. Lucy Thom would have been more of a threat to Natasha, as she still gets jealous of me with other girls. Then again, Natasha's boyfriend David was going to be at this party and Jane has these kick ass "Double D's" which made a great back rest. Jane offered to hide my ounce of weed between those "D's." She said if we were pulled over by the cops, she would take the rap for the weed as long as I paid her fine. That worked for me.

We pulled up around seven o'clock and there was

already a good crowd gathered. All of us had the baffles taken out of our tail pipes so that our bikes were extremely loud. The crowd all turned their heads as if we were Vikings coming to pillage their land and take their women. Well, take one blonde named Natasha, at least for me anyways.

I drove my chopper right up to the house and you could see the windows rattle as we all revved our bikes before shutting them down. Who did I see look out the window? Natasha. She looked at me with that innocent smile of hers. I gave her a wink and an evil grin! Coming to a party that I didn't want to attend, and then having her shoot me a huge smile made it all worthwhile.

Dirty Dozen members even had our own charter, or make that rules to follow.

- Rule # 1: When going to a house or bush party: eye up the competition as more often than not, there would be brawls by the end of a party.

- Rule # 2: Eye up the pussy situation… Enough said

- Rule # 3: Put your booze in a spot that's safe, and of course stash some booze on the side; as we would drink up other people's booze first before breaking into our reserve stash.

- Rule # 4: Have an escape route in case the cops

raided us.

The competition was nothing really tonight, just some rich kids who might act tough but when the bell rang, they would turtle and cry for their mommies.

I had my target and was determined this was the night to make my aggressive move instead of just dreaming about Natasha, either good, bad or wet. Tonight the heavens and stars were aligned for me; I could feel it and I had to go with it. My gut instinct was rarely wrong.

I eventually told Jane "Don't hang off me as I have my eye on someone." She wasn't happy, but she knew she was just there to play with. I, of course, got my ounce of weed off her before blowing her off.

I went into the living room where the snobby rich kids were and most importantly where Natasha and David were. I pulled out my ounce and started to roll up a one handed joint to impress them, sparked it up and passed it around.

I asked David how his nose was. I hope there are no hard feelings towards me for breaking it. I could tell he was very nervous around me, after all, last week I pounded his one friend's face in with a cue ball.

Every time I looked at Natasha, he was getting more nervous and insecure. I was hoping the pot would make him even more paranoid. I also purposely leaned in and gave Natasha a 'super toke' just to get that much closer. When I backed away from her mouth, I gave her the Wang, Dang, Doodle look, that hopefully she would also see by the end of the night, but by then we would both be naked.

The bu*zz* was kicking in and the tunes sounded real groovy. I told David to get us a round of drinks. This was my chance to talk to Natasha and like a scared guy that he was, David did what he was told.

I asked Natasha was she really still that serious about David.

She answered, "I'm not sure." Natasha then asked me, about the girl with the massive tits who was on the back of my bike when we pulled in.

I told her, "She just wanted a ride to the party, nothing more." Just when I thought I can say no wrong, as I had the whole positive groove happening, I asked Natasha, "What did David get you for Xmas?"

She smiled awkwardly and said nothing! I just shrugged my shoulders and asked if David was just plain cheap, or didn't he think that she was worth it?" Yeah slam the guy even more!

Natasha reminded me she was Jewish and so was David. Damn, how could I of forgotten that serious detail? Maybe I was more nervous than I thought being around her, or the weed was kicking in a little harder than what I first expected.

Talk about dead air, and not being able to say anything back. All of a sudden I felt really stoned with cotton mouth. Damn I threw a hand grenade when I wanted to hit a home run. I just thought she liked wearing jewelry. I guess the Star of David on her necklace should have reminded me. Not very good recon on my part.

Natasha could tell I was uncomfortable and said, "No biggie."

The fear in my stomach subsided and the butterflies were dancing once again. Hell, with her being Jewish and knowing my mom is from Germany, it didn't stop her from showing an interest in me; that is a good thing, a real good thing.

Time for plan "A"; time to get David so drunk, he makes a fool of himself or worse. I had John Walter, who at seventeen was already a raging alcoholic, do shots of Mescal with David. To make things even better, John would talk him into eating the worm.

David would want to impress his girlfriend Natasha, prove that he's just as hard a partier as anyone in the Dirty Dozen. David went shot for shot with John. I was actually impressed. However, three times I had to take John aside and remind him that David was to eat the worm, not him. Damn, drunks. You can't rely on them, but thankfully, David ate the worm.

From the first shot till the downing of the worm, it took forty five minutes. I used that time to impress Natasha with my good boy charm, and telling David he should take it easy as there was nothing to prove, all the while moving closer to Natasha.

Damn, I should be a used car salesman instead of just a dope seller. Now for plan "B". I gave Jane a dime bag of pot to come on to David. With all that booze he'd consumed, there was no way David could get a hard-on and have sex with her. Like a drunken dumb ass, he went for her like I knew he would. The key now was to have Natasha catch David coming on to Jane, as Natasha was already getting mad at him for getting so damn drunk and mouthy. Yeah, he turned into a total fucking jerk off.

I told David at one point to back off being a loudmouth goof to Natasha or I would break his fucking jaw. He could barely stand, never mind fight. I remember my dad telling me, sometimes when you hunt, whether you are using a bow and arrow or a rifle, your best weapon is your brain.

My gut told me not to knock him out or even fist fight him, just let Jane go in for the kill, as Natasha was truly a special catch. Natasha was clearly upset seeing David make a play for Jane. It was blatantly obvious what he wanted, and what he wanted was

Jane's "DDs". Natasha went outside with Gail and tears were rolling down her cheek.

I went outside and asked Natasha if she was all right. I gave her a hug and I didn't want to let go, she was so upset and hurt. I was feeling like her protector. I then told Natasha, "When I get upset, I go for a long motorcycle ride and it always clears my head." I then asked if she would like to go for a ride with me.

Without any hesitation she said, "Yes." I told Natasha she can wear the helmet that Jane was wearing; it was in the spare bedroom. "Just grab it and I will wait for you out here," so not draw any attention to us leaving together.

I knew all along that Jane had taken David in the spare bedroom. Natasha opened the bedroom door and saw David, playing with Jane's "DD" puppies of power. Natasha screamed, "WHAT THE FUCK"!

David was in shock as he looked at Natasha, he looked at Jane's breasts, then back to Natasha, and then Jane's bare breasts one more time. Then his eyes rolled back in his head and he puked all over Jane and those "DD" puppies of power.

I knew there might be trouble so I came back inside and raced to the bedroom after hearing Natasha's screams. It took everything in me not piss my pants laughing, seeing Jane's DD's covered in puke, but I looked at Natasha and said two words, and only two words, "Let's split."

Natasha ran outside and was quite upset. I was right behind her. I fired up my bike, looked at her and said, "Jump on back, let's go for a ride." She did just that and away we went, no destination in mind just a ride, an escape for her. It gave me a chance to get close to her, closer than I have ever been before.

We headed for the coast and Natasha held me so tight I thought she might break a rib or two. I felt kind of guilty doing what I did, setting up David for failure. However, no one forced David to drink that much, or to play with Jane's breasts. He did that all by himself.

As luck and my plan would have it, Natasha and I were finally alone, and that is all I ever wanted, just a chance to be alone with Natasha. I didn't have to flex my muscles and not a drop of blood was spilled, just a gallon of puke and some tears. I wonder if dad would have been proud that I used my brain, and not my fists or legs as a weapon.

Natasha and I drove along the coastline, and stopped and looked out at Alcatraz. I shut off the bike and asked was she all right, as she was still whimpering. She leaned over and kissed me on the lips. I swear I could feel this electric charge coming from her lips. They were so soft and full, even more delicious than I imagined. While I was hugging her, I could feel the pounding of her heart and I knew deep down she was still upset about the situation at the house.

I wanted to comfort her like a warm blanket on a cold winter's day and let her know that no one would ever hurt her again as long as she was with me. Her smile and sparkling blue eyes told me I was winning her over. My intuition was usually always right, and she does indeed like me, more than just a casual friend who made her smile. I asked her, "Do you have to be home at a certain time?"

"No," she didn't, and as far as her parents knew, she was sleeping over at Gail's house.

A very intrigued Natasha then asked, "Why?" Her eyes lit up brighter than the North Star I talk to, when she asked me this.

I took a deep breath and a bit of a gamble and asked would she like to go to the party of her life at the Oakland Hell Hounds clubhouse. She seemed nervous and intrigued at the same time. Has she had heard all kinds of horror stories about what happens at these parties?

I assured her these people are a part of my family. My brother Jake was Sergeant at Arms, and my cousin Jerry was club President of the Oakland chapter.

She had seen several of the Hell Hounds with me

at the karate tourney. I told her that Jeannie Terek, the girl who gave her the flower at Agresta's for her sixteenth birthday, would be present as her husband Donnie is also a Hell Hound.

I reassured Natasha she would be welcomed as part of the family. As long as I said she was my steady girlfriend, no one would bother her.

Natasha looked at me, smiled with seductive smile of hers and said, "Really? I have to say I'm your steady girlfriend?"

"Unfortunately, you have to say it. Some of these guys are pretty smart, so you might actually have to play it up a bit, once we are at the clubhouse."

Natasha leaned over and gave me another long kiss. This time, I felt her tongue wanting to play tag. I was more than willing to oblige and played tonsil hockey for what seemed to be an hour. Once we both came up for air, Natasha looked at me and said, "Don't we have a party to go to?"

And with that, I fired up the beast and off we went to the Oakland Clubhouse. As we crossed over the Oakland Bay Bridge, I realized how beautiful the view was. This chick on the back of my bike really had a strange effect on me and I really liked it.

The clubhouse was an old governor's residence that was situated on an acre of land. The club was now fortified, as they put up cement walls with barb wire along the top, and a solid double steel front entrance door. The courtyard was also heavily fortified, as the club had its rivals from other motor cycle clubs. The 'Thunder' were hard core bikers and the Hell Hounds biggest rivals, and the 'Deguellos' were a pure Mexican motorcycle club.

As we drove down Hamilton St. where the clubhouse is located you could hear the music playing. Cop cars were stopping people on both sides of the road as they arrived. The cops stopped us and asked for our ID and also asked if I had been drinking.

Since I only had a couple at Gail's, and it was now 21:00, I was pretty sure I was alright. I'm sure with the French necking we were doing, Natasha sucked all the booze from my mouth anyways. The only thing I worried about was the half bag of pot I had stashed down my underwear. I said, "No."

The cops took down all the info, and this one particular uniform cop yelled to the plain clothes cop, "We have another Strongbow on the streets." The plain clothes cop came over and started questioning me about my relationship to Jake and Jerry. I told the cop, "Go fuck yourself! Unless I am under arrest leave me alone. I have done nothing wrong."

The plain clothes cop told me he believed my bike might have stolen parts on it and he would have to take it to the station and have it ripped apart. He also believed he smelt booze on Natasha, and with her being under age he would charge her, put her in jail, and call her parents to tell them where she was and who she was with.

Natasha grabbed me by the arm. I could tell she was scared, so I unwillingly told the plain clothes cop how I was related to Jake and Jerry.

The plainclothes cop lectured me about how I was young and a life of crime never pays, and the police will now be watching me, basically busting my balls, blah, blah. He then started to lecture Natasha, "Proper young Jewish ladies do not hang around bikers." He said she would soon be turning tricks, stripping or drug running, and she would be found dead in the gutter within five years with a syringe sticking out of her arm.

I'm sure whatever trust I built up with Natasha tonight was now on very shaky grounds, fucking cops. I asked the plainclothes cop what his name was. "Barry Getz," he stated. That is a Jewish name. I wonder if he saw the Star of David on Natasha's necklace and wanted to save her from the heathens.

I started to think it might be a good idea for Natasha to put her necklace on the inside of her shirt. I flashed back to what Jeannie Terek said to me a year or so ago about Natasha being Jewish. "*Some of the boys are true blue Aryans."*

Even though she is with me, booze and especially in large quantities, does strange things to people. Just ask David or Jane's puked filled puppies of power. Natasha agreed to put it on the inside of her sweater.

After the lecture, the cops let us carry on and we drove up to the front gates. There were four guys from the club stopping incoming guests, making sure they were a friend and not a foe. Jake was in charge of security for the night and handpicked his crew. Three were full patch members and one was a prospect.

Big John Derksen was in charge of the main gate for the night. He was truly a big man standing 6'8" and weighing around 340 lbs. He was solid with no fat; his forearms were bigger than my legs. John was from Rhodesia and the rumor was he was a member of the Rhodesian Light Infantry, had killed his commanding officer, and fled to the United States. I saw him with his shirt off one day, and noticed all these nasty scars on him. I asked, "What happened?" He answered with a devilish smile, "The Rhodesian bush is the most dangerous place on earth." He could be very cold with that stare, as if his soul was nowhere to be found.

The second full patch was my karate training coach Caleb Dalton, who was on the 1960 USA Olympic boxing team. He was a true heavyweight and could still knock out an elephant but got into all kinds of trouble with the law. He couldn't decide where he would make more money, in the ring or being a criminal. Either way he still fights a lot, and just like in the ring, his adversary ends up knocked out or worse. His younger brother Fraser is a member of the Dirty Dozen.

The other full patch was my close friend Don Terek. Don had actually served with dad in the Airborne in Vietnam, and was a great soldier. However, he couldn't handle the B.S. of taking orders from some officer who had never even had a nose bleed in his life, never mind having never seen combat action. He too was an "Advisor" in Vietnam until the army gave him a section eight.

Don always talked very fondly of dad and said, "He was a great soldier to serve with." Don being so close to dad was also like a big brother to me. He said himself, "Your dad always talked about his family." Donnie had this brother's-in-arms debt to my dad's memory to look out for me and my family. Dad assured Don he would do the same, if he didn't make it home from Vietnam.

The prospect was an Albanian named Johnny "Mad Dog" Kantonescu, who was just plain psychotic. He was big into body building, and was the first guy I ever heard of who injected steroids. I knew that they were used on horses to build muscle, but why the hell would a human want to look like an animal, and in his case, act like one? His younger brother Scott was a Dirty Dozen member, who I've been close friends with since grade nine. I must say ever since the killing at Disney, John just looks different to me.

To get into the Hell Hounds club, you must first be a prospect for 88 days, which is not as easy as it sounds Should you pass that test, then you become a striker for 8 months and 8 days. Hell Hounds, the first letter in each word is the # 8 in the alphabet, and the founder of the club Eric Von Kruder, was big into this numeric stuff I guess. If you passed and were recommended for a full patch, the executive committee would approve or deny you. Being a prospect meant you were basically a nigger for the patches; you didn't ask why, you just did. This usually involved some minor criminal activity. The club had to make sure you weren't a cop trying to infiltrate the club.

Once you get accepted to striker status, it gets real serious. You have to prove you're solid for the club, and the rumor is you have to be willing to kill someone for the club. Not all are tested but several have been, and if you deny the kill order the odds are you would be killed yourself.

Tonight was one of the biggest bashes of the year, all prospects and strikers had to stay sober and do security all night. This would be a perfect night for the enemies of the Hell Hounds to hit the clubhouse with everyone drunk and not able to defend it with a clear head.

As I pulled up to the front gates, Natasha was once again hugging me tight, and I could tell she was breathing a little harder once she saw the four Horseman of the Apocalypse standing at the front gates. I was little afraid she would hyperventilate, pass out and fall off the bike.

Once I introduced her to the boys and they smiled at her, I could feel her relax. Although with her chest breathing that hard, I actually kind of liked it. I still can't figure if she was a large "B" or a small "C," as she was breathing heavy into my back, but hopefully I would find out soon enough.

The boys asked me who she was I said, "My girlfriend." Derksen asked, "Steady?" We both answered at the same time, "YES." Natasha thanked me for pre-warning her as to what the only correct answer should be.

I parked my bike and walked hand in hand with Natasha to find Jake and my cousin Jerry. I wanted to show off the girl I had been infatuated with for the last couple years.

The whole compound was like a circus atmosphere. There were freaks, strippers, Playboy bunnies, famous rock musicians as well as movie and television stars, all there for the same reason, to kick it down and ring the New Year in with one hell of a kick ass bang.

One of the first celebrities we ran into was Pearl. She had this bottle of Southern Comfort in her hand and was already catching a glow. She came up and gave me this great big hug and kiss, and asked me, "Who is this pretty young lady?"

I introduced her as my girlfriend [man, I was starting to like that sound] and Pearl told her what a fine young man I was, and what a cute couple we made; talk about getting brownie points. Natasha was blown away meeting her and had an ear to ear smile talking to Pearl. She said she had a gig at Kezar Pavilion in Golden Gate Park, but would be back once her gig was over.

Before Pearl left, she gave Natasha this big, long hug and told her that if I don't behave myself to let her know, and she will slap me silly.

I stopped and saw one of the patches, "Spider," and asked did he know where my brother was. He told me, "Jake is in the main house shooting pool." Spider also asked me if I wanted to do some peyote or magic mushrooms.

I looked at Natasha and smiled back at him, "No thanks man, I want to remember tonight." As far as I was concerned, peyote and magic mushrooms were natural, so they didn't or shouldn't fall into the chemical classification that my brother would kill me for.

Damn, for eighteen months now, I wanted to be with this girl. Why ruin the night getting so wasted. First impressions are important and only come once, and last time I did some 'Shrooms' I got really sick to my stomach. Natasha had already seen one boyfriend, or ex-boyfriend, puke tonight. She didn't need to see another.

We headed straight for the games room, and there was my brother playing pool with Heather Summers, Miss March, 1965. I guess Liz must be working at the hospital tonight, and true to Jake form, he was showing Heather proper form on how to shoot pool.

Once Jake saw us, he shot me this big brother smile and gave Natasha a real good looking over. He asked, "Who is the kitten? Is she the one responsible for you having all those crusty Kleenex under your bed?"

I went redder than the snooker balls on the table. Jake went over and gave Natasha a big hug and welcomed her to the party. He told her that if she needed anything, just let him know, and if little brother gets out of line, he'd be more than willing to smack me back in line.

I told Jake about the plainclothes cop hassling us. He asked if it was Getz. I said, "Yes."

"Fucking Jew", snarled Jake; Natasha cringed but knew not to say anything.

Jake ordered one of the prospects to get us all a beer and I started to roll up a joint. Jake toasted, "To good times, new friends and lovers," and the four of us clanged our beers together. I sparked up the joint and passed it around.

The games room was so cool. It had two large billiard tables, six pinball machines, dart boards and a real kick ass bar with all kinds of weird paintings on the wall, including the Hell Hound symbol. There was also a shrine with pictures of fallen members on it.

After we finished our beer, Jake suggested I show Natasha around the rest of the compound, as it was all set up with a medieval theme.

He told me there was a fortune teller who was blowing people's minds. I could tell by Natasha's facial reaction that was where we should head next.

I asked him where Jerry was. He stated, "Upstairs with Von Kruder discussing business. Let them be." Jake said he would let him know I was here asking for him. Jake also let me know that Carlos was coming on at eleven o'clock and if Pearl wasn't too fucked up, she would also jam with him.

So off to the fortune teller we went. Once we were outside, I asked Natasha, "Well, what did you think of Jake?"

She said that Jake looked more native than me, and my mom looked too young to have Jake.

I told her, "We have the same father, but different mothers. Jake and Pam are true blood brother and sister. Their mom died while giving birth to Pam. My dad was in the army, stationed in England. Three years later, at the end of the war, he met mine and Rachel's mom in Germany."

She asked me ever so sheepishly, "What happened to your father?"

I told her he was killed in Vietnam in 1963, and that he was a member of Special Forces who died when his chopper was shot down.

Those sparkling blue eyes now looked at me with sadness. I could tell this really upset her. She gave me a hug and said, "Sorry."

At first I wasn't sure how my next statement would go over with Natasha, as she was into the whole "Peace Movement." Well, she would either hear or feel my sentiments sooner or later. So I told her, "My father was a proud Sioux warrior, a career soldier who died in battle, a risk he knew all too well, so there is nothing to be sorry for."

I then asked her about her family.

Natasha told me she has one brother, Doug. He is eighteen. Their parents separated and divorced three years ago. Her real dad is a dentist in New York City. Her mom remarried a jeweler named Barry, or as I call him, Barney Rubble. Thus the reason for all her rings and chains; that thumb ring did something for me, I must say.

I was dying to find out, "Did Barney Rubble ever say anything after the first time he saw me talking to you?

"Barney said you were trouble, a real rebel without a cause, and nice Jewish girls stay away from rebels, and I should do just that."

I started to laugh, "So what do you think now?" Natasha just smiled and leaned in kissed me some more. I wondered what Barney would say now.

They had this fortune teller set up in a tent with candles flickering and incense burning for a mystic setting. Madame Bujold was her name. I'm not sure whether it was the beer or the joint we just smoked, but I had this weird feeling when we walked in the tent; it kind of creeped me out. Even that hair on the back of my neck that I ask my barber never to cut was standing up by itself.

Madame Bujold had one dead eye and one wandering eye. She also had this mole on the side of her face. Hollywood couldn't have typecast a better person. Natasha said she wanted to go first, and all the power to her.

Madame Bujold took hold of Natasha's hands and put them over the crystal ball, all the while not touching the ball itself. Madame Bujold closed her eyes and started to chant. She told Natasha she was going to tell her what the future held for her, all the while gliding her hands over Natasha's hands. After a couple minutes, she opened her eyes and said to Natasha that she is confused girl right now; she is innocent and pure but wants to take a walk on the dark side. That the person who will be her soul mate in life is someone that she already knows, but that at this point it is still a mystery to her who it is, and when she finally figures that out, it will be too late."

She continued by saying, "This time next year, you will have your heart divided into two. Although both will remain pure, one half of your heart will be broken. You may be far away from here, but your thoughts will never be far from your soul mate, no matter the distance."

Natasha looked so confused and worried, and I

could tell she was replaying in her head everything Madame Bujold said, but it still made no sense to her. Natasha looked at me and said, "Come on chicken, your turn."

The hairs on the back of my neck were still up but I couldn't show Natasha that this old woman was scaring me. She has seen me knock people out cold, fight and play football through tremendous pain; what kind of a tough guy would I be?

Madame Bujold did the same routine with the hands. This time the chanting took over ten minutes. With her body almost having seizures and shaking, her hands became very clammy until finally Madame Bujold opened her dead eye first and just stared right through me. She then opened up her good eye. This was starting to freak me out and as I went to talk she said, "SILENCE."

Madame Bujold took a deep breath and told me, "You also know who your true soul mate is, but you will spend most of your life trying to search for her after you push her away. You will take a journey to the dark side and will stay there, never to return to the light. You will face many tragedies and will cause even more. You will travel a great distance trying to set your soul free, but this will create an even more tortured soul.

She finished with, "All you have to do is to look to

the light for guidance and forgiveness, but your anger and hatred will never let you see this."

Fuck me and pass another beer over before I shoot this bitch. Man, my bu*zz* was gone now. Talk about a downer. Natasha just stared at me, stunned. I said to Natasha, "Let's get out of here." All of a sudden Madame Bujold's words were suffocating me and I needed air, had to breathe.

Fucking rubbish, this old hag doesn't know shit. "Voodoo Garbage" I said out loud.

I grabbed Natasha by the hand, exited Madame Bujold's tent and walked quickly towards where the musicians' stage was set up. Natasha told me to slow down a bit as she couldn't walk that fast. She told me, "Don't let the words of that madwoman ruin the night." I stopped and thought for a minute, caught my breath and realized Natasha was right.

I asked, "Did she scare you with what was said about me?"

She smiled and said, "It would take a lot more than a few hocus pocus words from some old witch to scare me away from you."

Wow. What a statement from Natasha. That made me feel so good inside and I could start to breathe normally again. I snickered and agreed with Natasha. Fuck, what were we all freaked out over? They were just rambling words from a madwoman.

Man, I really needed to smoke a joint and get mellow. Natasha and I found this secluded spot, and I rolled up a joint for both of us and sparked it up. After a few tokes, I could feel my shoulders starting to drop and the ramblings of that madwoman Madame Bujold were just a fleeting.

I heard someone yell "Mitchell." It was Jeannie Terek. She was ear to ear with this smile as she approached us. She looked at Natasha. "I recognize this beautiful young lady. I'm glad you took my advice, Mitchell."

As embarrassed as I was, Jeannie was just telling the truth. Jeannie gave Natasha a hug, welcomed her and commented on what a groovy looking couple we made. Jeannie helped us to finish off the rest of the joint, and then headed off to spend some time with Don. "We will all hook up shortly and hang together." As Jeannie walked away she repeated once again, "Good for you, Mitchell."

Natasha looked at me with one eyebrow raised and a goofy look on her stoned face, "And what advice would that be, Mitchell?"

I was embarrassed and yet I have waited so long to be with Natasha. This may be the one and only chance I have to tell her how I really feel about her. Who knows, maybe she's turned off with the events of night so far. I didn't want to scare her off even more thinking I'm some obsessed stalker.

"I want an answer M-I-t-c-h-e-l-l, or no more kisses for you tonight."

Well, I guess I'm forced to tell her how I feel. I took a deep breath and prayed my mouth and thoughts were in tune with each other. "Tash, ever since the first time I saw you, I've had this crush on you. I think you're the most beautiful woman in the world. Jeannie has been like a big sister to me, so after she met you and gave you the flowers for your birthday, she agreed how beautiful you are and told me I should pursue you."

Natasha's eyes were now starting to well up with tears. She came and gave me a hug and real long kiss. "I have always had a groovy thing for you too, Mitch. Between David, Barney and my mom, I was really confused. Well, I'm not so confused now."

With me being stoned I was a bit confused myself by Natasha's statement, but her leaning into me and kissing me affirmed that I had managed to send the correct message to her. I said to Natasha, "Let's go to over to where Carlos and his band are starting to warm up."

On the way over, I noticed the Wizard and walked over and introduced him to Natasha. He asked me if I would like to try this hash with opium in it.

Natasha passed but told me to go ahead as she could tell I was still a bit freaked out, and needed a chance to mellow out. The hash was harsh and made me cough, but the bu*zz* was instant, and just what the doctor ordered. I thanked the Wizard, and off we went to get our seats.

Just before we sat down, Carsta and Eva Vigoda approached us with this silly stoned look on their faces, giggling like two school girls. Yeah, they were high for sure; their eyes and mile-wide smile confirmed this. I looked at both sisters, smiled back and just shook my head.

They were both strippers for the club and were dressed as if they were on stage ready to perform. Sluts, God love them! They just looked at Natasha and laughed. Eva then grabbed me by the crotch and asked if I would like to bite her apple in the Garden of Eden.

Somewhat shocked I asked, "What the hell are you on?" They said they both dropped a hit of LSD a couple hours ago, and were really flying high. They couldn't get that goofy smile off their faces.

Eva asked who my girl was. I told her, "My girlfriend, Natasha." Once again they just looked at each other and started to laugh. They were fucked and that was a fact!

I could tell that Natasha was very uncomfortable

around these girls. Perhaps what Getz had told her was sinking in. I actually had slept with both of these girls in the past. I wonder why they call it sleeping with someone. There was no sleeping involved, just hard core sucking and fucking.

I also hoped and prayed that as high as the Vigoda girls were, they wouldn't spill the beans to Natasha about us getting it on. They were club girls and took care of the boys' needs. The boys keep them high and they drop their pants and stripped for the drugs. I guess their souls were dead. I told them that the Wizard had some groovy hash and they should go see him before it was all toked up. They both started to laugh and skipped away singing, "We're off to see the Wizard."

Natasha looked at me and squinted up her eyes. Before she said anything I said, "They are pretty fucked up." Natasha just smiled.

Perhaps my stone-induced paranoia was kicking in. I wondered if Natasha could tell something had happened between the three of us. Really, that was before her, so what could she really say? I'm not even sure if I should ever tell her what really went on with the Vigoda sisters.

I had brought a sleeping bag with me and I spread it on the grass for the two us to watch the show. About fifty feet behind the stage, there was a huge fire pit that was fully engulfed in flames seemed to dance to the music. With the stars and the full moon aligned above, it was a cosmic trip in itself.

Carlo's started off with 'Jingo', a rather catchy tune. As we were sitting there, the joints were being passed around and I was really catching a bu*zz*. The next song was 'Soul Sacrifice'. By this time I was wasted and the fire had me in an extremely hallucinogenic deep trance that I couldn't escape. I actually saw visions of what the fortune teller Madame Bujold was talking about. I broke out in a cold sweat and my mouth was so freaking dry. I tried quenching my thirst with a cold beer; no such luck. I don't think my heart could beat any faster, it felt as though it was going to jump right out of my chest. The more intense the song, the more intense my vision and the fire and flames became.

I remember my father telling me that he would have visions. Jake would tell me that the old man was doing too much peyote, which my dad would do on the reservation when he needed to clear his head and look for direction. He called this the 'SACRED FIRE', as he would see the visions though the flames, just as I was doing now.

I saw the deer from hunt camp laughing at me, the prairie dog having my blood smeared over him, the mountain lion now was back pacing, with fangs the size of swords. I suddenly felt myself back on the reservation in '63, and my grandfather, the Shaman, telling me of his vision when I was first born. I can hear his and Jake's voice warning me not to poison my soul.

I couldn't break away from the trance that the dancing flames provided, and the story it was telling me. Whether I liked it or not, I was on board for the trip and there was no way of getting out of it; there was no escape pod or parachute to wear. My head and my soul told me the vision was showing my future with death's shadow following me wherever I went and family members crying.

I felt the pain of my dad's death all over again. My grandfather Kohler's death at the hands of my dad, I felt his pain, his last breath. Every person who was close to me, I seemed to feel their pain and agony. I saw the deer from hunt camp laughing at me and the prairie dog having my blood smeared over him, the mountain lion now was back pacing with fangs the size of swords but this time he kills grandpa as I'm too distracted on my own self-pitytrip to save him.

I saw myself as a warrior in a foreign land, but failing in my quest. I then saw my dad taking away my Sioux warrior status, saying I failed him and every single Strongbow family member for generation upon generation and I won't see the Spirit World or those

Strongbow family members who have died before me after all. My soul has now been cast into the flames of hell.

The song and the vision seemed to go on forever, until Natasha leaned over and gave me a kiss. This action seemed to break the cursed vision. Fuck me, it was over. Hell, this girl truly had a mystical power! I always felt from the first time I met her, I wanted to protect her from any harm, and yet she was the one who was protecting me. I looked into those deep blue eyes of hers and realized she was my soul mate, and I would never let her go. Madame Bujold was wrong. But I couldn't tell Natasha about the vision or the fear it brought me.

I'm now going to be given a second chance to change, and try and figure out what it was all about. The one thing I knew for sure was I'm not doing anymore dope tonight. We are high enough, but a couple more drinks wouldn't hurt.

The next song was called, '*As the years go passing by*'. I just embraced Natasha throughout the song and really dug the cool vibe that was coming from her.

About ten minutes before midnight, Jake, Heather, Don and Jeannie set up a spot beside us, and all was well in my world. I felt protected by seeing big brother Jake. He smiled at me and I knew he not only dug Natasha as well, but also accepted her, which really meant a lot to me. I finally saw Jerry, as he jumped on stage, and did the countdown to the New Year. Three, Two, One, Happy New Year!

What a night so far. I leaned in and kissed Natasha to usher in the New Year. It lasted for at least 10 minutes until Jake tapped me on the shoulder and told me to come up for air. I gave him a hug and he asked me, "Are you happy?"

I think the ear to ear grin told everything. I hugged Heather, Jeannie, and also Donnie. Yep, no doubts about it, my world was indeed perfect and I was so looking forward to 1967 and all the challenges it would bring. I know deep down I have found my soul mate, and all things looked groovy.

Jerry invited us up to his office on the second floor in the main clubhouse. He wasn't so receptive towards Natasha at first. He almost interrogated her which made us both uncomfortable. However, this was because there was a rat/snitch or a cop working inside the club, as too many drug deals or scores had resulted in club members being busted.

He didn't get to be club president by being gracious. You have to be street smart and a crude business man. Basically, you are the CEO of a company with a 44 magnum in your back pocket and one finger on the trigger, ready to waste the competition or your employees if need be.

Jerry asked Natasha for her full name. When she answered, "Natasha Konstantinov", Jerry asked if she was Russian. He didn't ask about the Jew part, but I think he knew. If she was with anyone else that might have been a problem.

I told Jerry she was a student and that my mom was her teacher for the past two years, and I told him where she lived. Natasha also said she worked part time at Goldberg's, her step-dad's pawn and jewelry shop.

Jerry said he knew who her stepfather Barry was, as he would pawn hot items for the club from time to time. So yeah, he knew the whole Jew thing for sure now. Eventually, he walked over and gave her a hug and told her to keep me in line and if I got out of line, he would take care of me.

When we left Jerry's office she asked me why some of the club members had this 8 ball symbol on their club vests.

I told her, "I don't know."

What it really meant was they had killed for the club and commanded more respect from the other club members. Jerry, Jake and Don had the 8 ball crest. There were still some things I just couldn't tell her.

For the rest of the night we just tripped around the

compound and watched people get more and more wasted and fucked up. That in itself was a show. Eventually we ran back into Pearl, but she was right out of it and could barely speak, which was sad to see.

I didn't smoke any more dope, but the beer buzz was starting to happen. I still hoped to get laid, and I was at the point where if I drank any more booze that might not happen. First impressions are sometimes lasting ones, so the decision had to be made; kick it down or try to get me some loving. Damn. What's a fellow to do?

I finally realized that I should just let nature take its course and continue to kick it down. Should I happen to get me some that would be the perfect ending to a perfect night with my perfect woman.

Around 04:00, Natasha said she was really tired and needed to crash. Where could she sleep?

I told her, "We both could share my sleeping bag and sleep under the stars, or you could go in it yourself, and I can sleep on the ground beside you to make sure no one would hassle you." This was her call. Mom raised me with values and forcing someone to have sex wasn't an option.

I had the sleeping bag all set up for her, when Natasha looked at me and said I could join her if I promised to behave myself.

I told her I would try but couldn't promise, with a devilish grin and seductive wink.

We both got into the sleeping bag fully clothed. I still wasn't sure if I was going to get any, but this was as good of an opportunity as ever. I started to bite her neck while feeling her breasts through her shirt. She didn't stop me and with her nipples getting erect, I knew she didn't want me to stop.

Eventually I made my way under her bra and felt the warm, soft flesh of her breasts. C cup for sure! The more I played with them, the faster her tongue was moving. With her letting me get to second base and the booze giving me liquid courage, I started to rub the outside of her crotch. I could feel the heat and moisture coming from her, and she still didn't tell me to stop. I was so damn hard now as she was also rubbing the outside of my crotch and I thought I might blow my load right in my pants.

I think I might score was the song playing in my head when I threw all caution to the wind and started to unzip her pants. Suddenly the hand that was rubbing me stopped and grabbed my hand that was trying to find its way to her pussy.

Natasha said I wouldn't like what I would find. All of a sudden my beer buzz was back and I was totally confused. "Aunt Flow" had paid a visit, she said. I was still totally damn confused. She smiled looked at me and said, "My monthly friend dropped by for a visit." Now I got it, and yes, that's all she had to say.

We started to neck once again while I put her hand back on my crotch, and with my other hand pulled out my dick and put her hand on it. She just smiled and starting stroking it. She put my other hand back up under her shirt so I could start to once again feel those beautiful "C" cups of hers.

The excitement and anticipation of being with Natasha brought me to quite a quick climax as I shot my load, and what a monster load it was. I seemed to cum for five minutes straight, all the while Natasha didn't miss a beat, stroking me off. Being so close together in the sleeping bag, I shot all over her pants as well. As I was blowing my load, it took everything in me not to pass out. I could feel my eyes roll back in my head as I was cumming; damn that felt good. I couldn't speak afterwards, just hugged her ever so tight until we both passed out.

We both woke up the next morning to sound of over fifty motorcycles starting up. It was a rude awakening. But there was nothing rude about the first person I saw. Natasha. Damn, it wasn't a nice dream, this was reality. What a night, what a perfect night, and what a perfect way to start the morning.

My cock was rock hard and ready to go again, but by now Jake was standing over me saying the club was going on a "Poker Run" to San Jose and just take our time and leave when we wanted. There was some grub in the main clubhouse and he would give me a shout in a day or two.

With that, I tucked my dick back in my pants and we grabbed some grub. We tried to wipe the cum stains from our jeans the best we could and then we smoked a joint to clear our heads of the hangover.

When we were ready to leave Natasha jumped on the back of my bike and I drove her home. She told me to let her off at least a block before her house, as her mom and Barney Rubble are kind of anal towards bikers, especially if that biker was yours truly.

Even though Barney fences hot items for them, I did what Natasha asked and dropped her off a block before her house. I shut off the bike and asked if she had a good time last night.

She said, "This was the wildest night of my life and I never felt so alive." I took a bold move and asked her if we were now an item.

She responded back, "Would you like to be an item?" "Yes" I answered, "And you, would you like us to be an item?" She responded with a "Yes" too.

My heart felt so strong and full of life after her response. Natasha said that for the next while, when I phone her house to get one of my sisters to ask for her. Eventually, she will tell her mom and Barney about me; as she was sure David will warn them anyways if he hasn't already.

I asked her, "What do we do about David?" I suggested, "I could drop him off the Golden Gate Bridge or take him to the desert and bury him." She laughed and I think she sort of knew that I would and could.

She assured me that she would break it off with him today or tomorrow. I told her, as my nostrils flared, that if he hits her or threatens her, I will fucking kill him, and if he wants to meet me and go at it I'm more than willing to accommodate him.

She smiled and her eyes got big. She really dug me being a tough guy. Natasha assured me that because their families are good friends, no harm would come to her.

I nodded my head OK, reached around and pulled her into me, and gave her the most amazing kiss I have ever given, un-brushed teeth and all; must be love.

I didn't want to let her go but knew I had to. I told her, "I had the most amazing night. I really enjoyed being with you," and thanked her for taking a chance and going with me. I kissed her one more time, fired up my bike, winked at her, revved my engine and squealed out of there. I headed home with a smile on my face and some cum stains still on my jeans.

Made in the USA
Middletown, DE
13 February 2016